EQUILI BRIUM

L.K. REID

Cover Design by Opulent Swag and Designs
Editing by Maggie Kern at Ms. K Edits
Formatting by Pretty in Ink Creations

For dreamers.

AUTHOR'S NOTE

I like to think that Equilibrium isn't as dark as Ricochet was, but it still is a Dark Romance, and if themes such as PTSD, violence, cheating and mentions of substance abuse as well as mentions of child abuse are something that triggers you, then this might not be the book for you.

It might not be too dark for me, but it might be dark for you, and I am urging you to proceed with caution.

I would also like to mention that this isn't a Hades and Persephone retelling. While the main male character does call the FMC "Persephone" on a couple of occasions, it is simply a term of endearment, connected to the fact that he is coming from a motorcycle club called "Sons of Hades".

One extremely important thing—please try to avoid reading or posting spoilers. Once you read it, you'll understand why I'm saying this. Just like the first book, this one ends on a cliffhanger, which means it doesn't have HEA at the moment.

I do not recommend this book to readers below eighteen.

"*Not yet corpses, still we rot.*"
Rise Against, *Dirt and Roses*

PLAYLIST

Music is such an important part of my creative
process, and I can honestly tell you that each of
these songs represents this story in one way or
another.
But one song that marked my journey with this
book is *In the Dark* by Solence.

You can listen to the full playlist on Spotify.

The Way - Zack Hemsey
Paralyzed - NF
Sugar - Sleep Token
My Understandings - Of Mice & Men
Twisted - MISSIO
The In-Between - In This Moment
TheseWallsHaveTeeth - KAMAARA
I Don't Belong Here - I Prevail
Six Feet (with Mike's Dead) - Call Me Karizma,
Mike's Dead
Tamashi - Sixthells, YTD
My Body Is A Cage - Peter Gabriel
Erase The Pain - Palisades
Why Am I Like This - The Word Alive
Lost Within - Fivefold
let go of your love - Thousand Below
Love The Way You Lie - A Skylit Drive
Parachute - Flight Paths
Ghost of You - Outline in Color

Her Eyes - Fame on Fire
Carry the Weight - We Came As Romans
Careless Whisper - Seether
Blessed With A Curse - Bring Me The Horizon
Crucify Me (feat. Lights) - Bring Me The Horizon,
Lights
Call Out My Name - Seraphim
Every Time You Leave - I Prevail, Delaney Jane
You & Me - Memphis May Fire
Vendetta - UNSECRET, Krigare
Wasting Love (2015 Remaster) - Iron Maiden
Nightmares - Palaye Royale
Empire (Let Them Sing) - Bring Me The Horizon
Craving - Charon
Love and War - Fleurie
Warning from My Demons - Slaves
Dark Side - Blind Channel
Ever Dream (Live at Wacken, 2013) - Nightwish
Silence of Reality - Serhat Durmus
Una Mattina - Ludovico Einaudi
Heaven Or Hell - Digital Daggers
The Night We Met - Lord Huron
In The Dark - Solence
Winterblood (The Sequel) - Emil Bulls
Sympathy - Too Close To Touch
All I Feel Is You - The Broken View

ONE

Ophelia

HIS DARK EYES twinkled under the light; happiness evident in them. That tousled black hair I loved so much fell over his forehead, and I had a sudden urge to hug him and never let him go. Our lives were unpredictable, dangerous, and I wanted to cherish every moment I had with him. I wanted to engrave it into my memory, because God knew, we didn't have enough of these.

"How much do you love me?" Kieran asked, as he continued tickling me. I thrashed on the bed, my laughter echoing through the room. "Tell me!" He laughed with me, tossing the sheets from the bed, and diving in for another attack.

"Nooo!" I yelled, trying to push him off me, but he just squeezed harder, leaving a kiss between my breasts. "Kieran! I can't… Stop it."

But I didn't want him to stop.

If I could, I would have hidden him a long time ago, so that nothing could ever harm him. Not his father, not mine, and definitely not all the terrible things lurking in the dark of the night, waiting to attack.

"Tell me and I'll stop." He kissed the corner of my lips, leaving me desperate for more. The cheeky bastard knew what he was doing, and he loved torturing me like this.

I wanted this moment to last forever. He and I, hidden from the world, cocooned in his apartment where nothing and nobody could touch us. The monsters in my head were quiet tonight, but I wasn't surprised. They were always quiet when he was around. I knew he would always be the light I could reach for.

I would kill anyone, everyone, if it meant saving him. Because Kieran was mine. Today, tomorrow, in fifty years, he would always be mine. My savior, my light in the dark, my happiness.

And I was his.

"Tell me, birdy." He blew a raspberry on my stomach, eliciting another round of laughter from me. "How much do you love me?"

His smile matched mine as he crawled over my body, settling between my legs. He was already hard, pressing, pulling a moan from me. *I wanted, no, I needed him. I always would.*

"Kieran," I protested as he stopped circling his hips. "Please."

"Only good girls get to come tonight, and you've been a very bad girl."

"But what if I like being bad?" I taunted him. With a smirk on his face, he bit into my collarbone, the pain mixing with pleasure, with need, sending a thousand tiny shock waves through my body.

"I like it when you're bad." He replaced his teeth with his tongue, licking the spot he bit into. "But you still didn't answer my question."

"I love you, Kieran." I touched his face, feeling the stubble he refused to shave.

"How much, Phee?" he asked again. "How much do you love me?"

"More than anything. More than my life."

His eyes darkened and the smile he wore disappeared, replaced with a sneer. His hold on my body became punishing, his fingers digging into my sides.

3

Before I could protest, he leaned down, his lips a feather touch over mine.

"Then why did you kill me?"

A startled gasp left my body as my eyes connected with the white ceiling, right above the bed I was lying in. That blissful moment people often talked about once they woke up was not something that happened to me. My body felt heavy and the memories of what happened kept slamming into me. The shirt I wore rubbed against the burned skin on my shoulder, right where Kieran branded me like fucking cattle.

They tried to fuck me up, but the game we were playing wasn't the one they were ever going to win.

I lifted my right arm, staring at the bruised finger I could barely move. His malicious eyes reappeared in front of me, the satisfaction he felt from hurting me, it was all there. Kieran's anger was almost palpable in that suffocating room back in their house, and I knew that no matter what we did from that point onward, there was no going back for the two of us. Whatever we had before, it broke the moment Kieran decided to break my sister.

Then why wasn't I happier with this situation? Why wasn't I elated at the prospect of him being gone? I did my job; I fulfilled my duty. I avenged the one that couldn't avenge herself, and yet my heart felt hollow as I tried to erase the memory of his face and the pain more than skin deep.

The dream was a bitter reminder of what we once were. It reminded me of two people that had dreams bigger than the world that was trying to suffocate them. I thought he was the one. I thought he was going to be the perfect partner in this fucked-up simulation we called life.

4

My heart, my soul, my body, and my pain, they all used to belong to him. But this fairy tale was never going to end happily ever after. This story was never going to end with the two of us together, riding into the sunset. The white picket fence and beautiful family was a dream, and it was never going to be a reality.

I used to laugh at the stars in Ava's eyes and her dreams of a better future with someone she loved, when actually, I wanted the same thing. I just wanted it with the wrong people.

Love was supposed to be enough, right? It was supposed to break all barriers and conquer even the scariest lands, but it wasn't. The only thing we got from this so-called love was pain, suffering and eternal madness. If love was enough, it would've saved us both; but it didn't.

It just threw us into an endless pit of despair until neither one of us could cling to anything but revenge. If this was love, I never wanted to feel it again. If this toxic, suffocating feeling came from loving somebody, I didn't want it anywhere near me. I always thought that loving somebody would set you free, but the only thing our love did for me was cage me.

I pulled myself up and stared around the room I was in. Why did people try to cage me? First it was my family, then Kieran, and now Storm was repeating the same story, kidnapping me when I didn't want to go with him. They all expected me to comply with what they wanted from me, but none of them ever asked me what I wanted.

I looked at my left arm, the bandages coated with my blood from the cut slicing through the snake tattoo. For as long as I could remember, this tattoo was a reminder of my love for Kieran, and now it was destroyed. I guess it was only fitting for it to end up like this.

We were born in violence, and we ended up in violence.

Now that I thought about everything we went through, I wanted to kick myself in the ass. I was such a fool. Such a daydreaming fool that I couldn't see what was right in front of me. All of them, all these men in my life, they were all using me.

I thought I meant something to them, but they all just wanted to get something from me.

Storm knocked the shit out of me in front of that church, and now he was nowhere to be found. I didn't have to be a genius to realize that he also wanted something from me.

I wasn't going to fool myself and think that this had anything to do with that day four years ago when I first met him. Even in my darkest moments, I thought that he was the most beautiful man I had ever seen. I didn't believe in love at first sight, but Ava used to talk about soulmates and somewhere along the way, I started believing in them as well.

And that day, it felt as if my soul recognized his.

It felt as if whatever happened, if only I had him, everything was going to be okay. In that moment, just for a brief second, I forgot who I was and what was happening around me.

Back in the church, when I first saw him, when I realized that he was the one we were meeting, it felt as if somebody doused me with a bucket of cold water. I almost forgot the reason for my being there, and every single person in that hall ceased to exist. The feeling of his lips on mine, the way he looked at me as if he could really see me, it all came back.

But none of that could erase the fact that he knocked me out and brought me here—wherever here was.

I looked down and realized that I was no longer in the same clothes I was in back in that horrible place. The shirt I wore was three sizes too big, with an Iron Maiden logo on the front. The black material pooled around my hips as I sat up, trying to remember everything that had happened. Cillian's murderous glare penetrated through my head, but no matter how much it hurt, I had to do it.

Kieran had to die.

But was it your place to act like the judge? It was supposed to be Maya's.

I shook my head as my subconscious glared at me. It was my place, no one else's. He messed with my family, with my people, and I was the only one that could judge him.

Keep telling yourself that. Maybe one day you'll believe it.

"Stop it!" I gripped the sides of my head, struggling to erase the thoughts that were flowing through my mind. I couldn't shake off this weird feeling coursing through my body, as if what I did wasn't supposed to happen. But he would've done the same.

Hell, he almost did the same, and for what? For a crime I never committed. I wasn't the sunshine and flowers type of person. I wasn't somebody you could talk to about the latest fashion because my knowledge about the latest Gucci collection was most definitely limited, unless they started producing weapons.

But I was loyal, and that was one thing I was proud of.

We could've avoided all this bloodshed if they only had talked to me. If they only had listened to what I had to say, we wouldn't be here.

My old clothes were nowhere to be found, and neither were my weapons. Even the knife I snatched when we left the church wasn't anywhere near me. Storm was meticulous, I'd give him that. I wondered if this was just another holding cell, or was he going to try and pretend that he really wanted to have me here?

God, I needed a shower as soon as possible.

I inspected my hand, well, the functional one without a broken finger, and there were dark spots all around my fingers, and underneath my nails. I was okay with blood, but now it just sent a wave of nausea through my body, and I felt dirty. Whoever cleaned me up did one hell of a job, but it wasn't enough to remove all the filth from my hands.

I pushed the blanket to the side and stood up. A wave of dizziness hit me like a freight train, and I fell back on the bed with a weak harrumph.

"Fucking shit."

The last few weeks took a toll on my body, but the adrenaline surging through my veins had apparently been enough to keep me standing before. Not anymore, obviously. I just wanted to sleep for a week straight with no interruptions. The world could be on fire right now, and I wouldn't be able to move a muscle. I had put my body through literal hell.

While my plan with the Nightingales wasn't exactly flawless, it had worked. It had brought me where I wanted to be and given me the opportunity to do what needed to be done. Difference was, this situation right now wasn't part of my plan. Storm wasn't part of any of my plans.

He was supposed to be a distant memory and someone I never wanted to think about. Now he was here, consuming my thoughts, and taking my ass with him when all I wanted to do was find

Maya. At least they didn't drop me in a cell with iron bars.

I could see clothes strewn over the chair in the corner of the room, and I just knew that this wasn't some random room they decided to throw me into. No, somebody lived here. The same jacket Storm and his guys wore mocked me from across the room. The three-headed beast with its mouth open was painted in the middle of it, but I couldn't make up the words surrounding it.

Biting my lip, I pulled myself up, slower this time, and when the dizziness didn't kick in again, I took a small, hesitant step toward the corner where the clothes were. One step and then another one, until I felt confident enough that I wasn't going to end up face-first on the floor. Nothing said the world's worst assassin like the passed out one.

The closer I got to the table and the jacket, the stronger the smell of leather became, with an underlying current of oak and spice. I ran my hand over the smooth surface, tracing the words embedded above Cerberus as well as below.

Tempus Fugit.
Memento Mori.

My Latin was rusty, but even I knew what it meant. I remember seeing it on his jacket years ago, but I never really gave it too much thought. Time is indeed short; I just still didn't grasp the concept that I might die as well. *Sons of Hades* was splashed above the insignia. The bold letters should've sent fear crawling down my spine, but they did nothing.

I wasn't afraid of these people. The worst thing they could do was kill me, and death wasn't something I feared. At least not anymore.

The pants that were neatly folded definitely belonged to a guy, unless there was a girl who wore the size fifteen boots standing next to the chair. But why would they put me in a room that was obviously in use?

There were no pictures on any of the desks. Fuck pictures, there wasn't even a mirror. I would still like to meet a person that didn't have a mirror in their room. Even I had a mirror in my apartment back in New York, but this one, nothing. Nada.

The walls were bare, and just like that room the Nightingales held me in, this one didn't have plants either. I mean, come on, at least have a cactus.

I had a couple of them, and as long as I didn't have to water them, we were all good. They were also kinda cute, I guess.

I eyed the door, and while I wanted to get the fuck out of here, I also wanted to explore. I had no idea what was behind that door, and I wasn't exactly known for warm welcome committees. The last one wanted me dead, and if this one was anything like that, I might have to pretend that I'm dead until they left me alone.

That's what they told us to do with bears, and no matter what, humans weren't that far off from animals. Predators and prey, it was just up to us to choose which one we wanted to be.

My legs were bare, and if I were going to go out, I needed to get some pants. I tied the shirt I had on me, at my hip, trying to avoid using my right hand any more than necessary. No one ever told you that a broken finger could fuck up your entire arm. With every new movement, the pain sliced through my arm like an electric shock. Swollen and purple, standing in the unnatural position, it didn't look well. Maybe I should try to straighten it myself?

And risk passing out from the pain? Not the smartest idea.

10

Okay, it wasn't the smartest idea, but considering how I got here, I doubted they would want to take me to the doctor. Unfortunately, I really didn't have the luxury of losing my consciousness now, and instead of trying to put the bone in my finger back in its place, I cradled my hand against my chest as I continued studying the room.

The wardrobe in the other corner of the room caught my attention, and I just hoped that it would have something I could use as a weapon. These people were more or less in the same business as me and my family, and if I could at least find a knife, I would be happy. I was a good fighter, one of the best Syndicate ever had, but I was still much smaller than these mammoths, and taking into consideration how weak I've been feeling, a fistfight wasn't something I could win right now.

I walked to it and opened the wooden door, seeing an array of t-shirts folded, separated by colors, and I snickered to myself. Somebody had a little OCD, and I just wanted to know which guy it was. I couldn't see anything else but t-shirts, pants, and boots on the bottom, along with some sneakers. But mommy didn't raise a quitter, and if I could even get an ashtray, it would be enough to knock at least one of them out.

I crouched down and pulled black, military boots from their place. These were going to be heavy on me, but I couldn't be barefoot out there. Red basketball shorts were the next item I took, pulling them on me. If this were a different situation, I would've laughed at myself and the way I looked right now, but this pickle of a situation wasn't something I could joke about. I bit my lower lip and tightened the strings on the shorts.

It wasn't ideal, but it would do.

I knocked on the wood at the backside of the wardrobe, hoping it would contain some sort of a hidden compartment, but nothing was there, just a low thud when my fist connected with the wooden surface, and something akin to disappointment. Goddammit, I was really hoping I would get something, because the first time I saw Storm after I got out of here, I was going to kick him in his balls.

The backside of my head still throbbed from his little knockout exercise.

I absentmindedly rubbed at the spot where a lump was slowly forming, hoping I would be strong enough to face whatever it was behind these doors. Storm's intentions were far from honorable, I was sure of it, and Maya didn't have enough time for me to keep hiding in this room.

There were things I needed to do—people to save and other people to piss off.

As soon as I stood up, the door opened and the instinct to fight arose in me. I spread my legs and bent my knees, ready for whoever it was behind the door, but the person I saw wasn't somebody I feared.

"Atlas?"

The blond giant stood there, scanning the room, before his eyes landed on me. Blue and purple colors marred his chiseled jaw, and he had a cut on his right eyebrow, no doubt gifts from that asshole I shared the blood with.

Is this his room?

He stepped inside, carrying a tray with three covered plates and a glass of what looked like orange juice. I didn't even have to smell the food for my stomach to growl. The three brothers fed me, but it wasn't exactly enough to give me the strength I needed.

12

"What are you doing here?" I asked. Hungry or not, I was also pissed off. "No, wait." I put my hand up, "Scratch that. What the fuck am I doing here?"

"Ah." He placed the tray on the dresser before turning back to me. "I can see you're a little bit pissed."

"No, Atlas. A little bit pissed would be me being sarcastic, maybe I'd use a few curse words, but that's about it. I am fucking livid!"

"Maybe you should sit down. Eat something."

"Atlas!" I roared. "You fucking owe me. I saved your life back there. I need to know what the fuck I am doing here. Either Storm or one of your other guys knocked me out, which wasn't the smartest decision, I might add. So, why the fuck am I here?"

"Shit." He looked at me, then at the door before deciding to close it and sit on the bed. "Look, love, I really don't know what to tell you. Prez wanted you here, and—"

"Do I look like I give a fuck what your prez wants?" I walked from the wardrobe to the front side of the bed and stood in front of him. "You had a deal with the Albanians, didn't you?"

He flinched at the mention as if I slapped him, and I knew I was onto something. "Didn't you, Atlas?"

"Maybe you should discuss this with him."

"Well, darling," I crouched, placing my hand on his knee, "I don't fucking see him trying to explain anything to me. I have shit I need to do, and the last thing I want is to get entangled with yet another crime family. So, you can either answer my questions, or you can tell me how to get the fuck out of here. It's your choice."

"Ophelia, Ophelia." In a blink of an eye, he gripped my hand where I placed it on his knee. "Didn't your mommy tell you the story of Cupid and Psyche?"

"My mommy was too busy getting high to be bothered with Greek mythology." I tried pulling my hand back, but his grip only increased, becoming painful. "Let me go."

"But I can't do that, love." The mischievous smile spread across his face. "You see, if I do that, I am pretty sure you'll either try to run away or knock me out, and we can't have any of those happening. I like my balls attached to my body, and if Storm finds out I lost you, they would end up being cooked for dogs."

We both knew I would run away given the first opportunity, so I tried another tactic.

"I don't care about that, Atlas." I tried pulling my hand again. "You're hurting me," I cried. "Why is everybody hurting me?"

But my whiny little attempt didn't work on this one. Unlike Tristan and the rest of the Nightingales, Atlas saw right through me.

"Cut the crap, princess. We both know that I won't fall for that, just like we both know that you could kill me, right here, right now, if you wanted to. But you don't."

"Fuck off," I spit out. "You don't know me. None of you do."

"Maybe." He shrugged. "But I do know that you are one curious cat, and you want to know why he wants you here."

"You won't have to wait for Storm to see your balls cooked for dogs," I gritted through my teeth. "I'll cut them off myself. Let. Me. Go."

The uncertainty I usually saw in other people's eyes was nowhere to be seen in his. Blue orbs just

14

kept twinkling under the light of the room, but the hold never loosened.

"Listen, Ophelia." He pulled me up, setting me on the bed next to him. "We can do this the easy way, or we can do this the hard way. Easy way means you'd be free to leave this room with me and walk through the clubhouse. Hard way? Well, that involves chains and you confined to this room. Now, be a good girl for once in your life and eat the food I brought you. There are eggs, sausages, orange juice, and some bread. It isn't the Ritz, but it is tasty."

"All of you are just so full of yourself." I huffed. "Every single member of your gender always thinks that they can control me, make me do what they want me to do. You're no different, you and your president."

"Careful, little one." He released my hands and stood up, walking to the tray. "Your claws are showing, and we didn't even do anything to you."

"You call this nothing?" *I wonder what they considered to be something.* "You practically kidnapped me."

"Semantics." He lifted the lid off of one of the plates and my stomach grumbled at the mouth-watering scent spreading through the room. "You're hungry, and I promise this isn't poisoned or spiked with anything that would knock you out again. I'll show you around after you're done, but please, for the love of everything, don't try anything stupid, Ophelia. I am rather fond of all my body parts, and if something happened, I might as well cut them off myself, rather than wait for Storm to get his hands on me."

"Why is he so adamant about keeping me here?" I stood up, walking to the food. I could pout,

I could shout, fight and demand, but goddammit, I needed to eat.

"I don't know, love, and I really don't want to know. But I guess he'll explain everything later." He grabbed a piece of bacon off the plate and smirked at what must have been a murderous expression on my face. No one fucking touches my food. "Now eat, before I eat it all."

I swear to God, he was so going to lose his balls.

TWO

Ophelia

ATLAS WATCHED ME the entire time I ate, with that annoying smirk plastered on his face. In a way, he reminded me of Cillian. Okay, he reminded me of young Cillian before the world tried to eat us alive. There was something mischievous hiding behind his eyes, but there was also a darkness we were all familiar with. His blond hair was tied in a bun, and while he looked like a friendly, good-looking neighbor, I knew he was capable of destruction.

We all were.

I didn't realize it before, but as I ate my food, silence cascaded over us, and the weird semblance of peace enveloped my body. When was the last time I ate without a threat hanging in the air? I was always weary of people, because even a friend could quickly turn into a foe. There was something in our genetic codes, engraved so deep within, that needed to betray, to hurt, to destroy. Some of us fought it and we tried to become better people.

Others, like Atlas, Storm, Kieran, *me*, we embraced the darkness and ran with it. Each of us knew what we were capable of, and we never bothered hiding it. At least I knew I didn't. What you see was what you got, and I wouldn't be going around, pretending I was somebody else. Cute, soft girls, with flowers in their hair and sunshine in their eyes… yeah, that wasn't me. I tasted of war, of bloodshed, of violence so painful that sometimes I wondered if this were all I would ever be.

This broken vessel made for destruction. It kept me up at night when no one was there to keep the demons at bay. It kept me wondering if maybe I deserved everything life threw at me. I was pathetic, I know, but every time the mask fell off, I felt raw, powerless. I knew what I did. I still remembered every terrible deed I did in the name of loyalty, in the name of family, and when I did them, I felt proud. I felt powerful because I thought I was doing something good.

I thought I was making them proud.

"Are you finished?" Atlas asked impatiently as I played with the last piece of bacon on the plate. No, I wasn't finished, because I didn't want to stop this peacefulness we were in. He wasn't my friend, but some fucked-up part of me wanted him to be.

I saw how all these guys behaved back in the church. They protected each other; they would die for each other. It was something I haven't seen before. During the years I'd spent with the Syndicate, it was obvious that each of us were on our own. Missions we went on were always done in pairs, not because we needed the other person, but because we knew one of us was going to die.

It was like modern Rome, and we were the gladiators. One of us always died, and my father always rewarded the one that came back. No, wait, let me rephrase that whole sentence. Everybody else went in pairs, but he always sent me alone. But there was no reward for me to reap. My only reward was the gracious gift of him keeping me alive, or that's what I thought.

The truth was, he couldn't kill me. Not wouldn't but couldn't, because we both knew that the person he would send after me would end up dead and he would be the next one on my list.

"Ophelia?"

"No, I'm not done."

"It seems like you are." He smirked, "Or are you planning on running around the room with that piece of bacon?"

"Fuck off, Atlas," I gritted through my teeth. I didn't have to tell him that my knees still wobbled, and that my head pounded. I hated showing any kind of weakness, even more so when I was in the lair of the enemy, in their territory.

I was too weak to fight, I was too weak to run, and if they wanted to, they could kill me in a blink of an eye. I couldn't even find the strength to fight with him verbally, and that wasn't me.

"No need to get feisty, sweetheart. I was only asking." He stood up and walked toward the window. "You know, I never actually thought that I would see you again."

"What do you mean?"

"I mean," he turned to me, "you were more like a ghost that haunted Storm's life. Hell, you haunted all of us, even the ones that never saw you. He never got your name that day, but he spent the last four years searching for you."

Lies. They were all lies carefully packed to sway me. They were sweet nothings that were supposed to make me feel better, because people like us, we loved to play games and lies were just one of them. It would've been easy for them to break me physically. They could beat me, they could torture me, but they knew that if they didn't break through the wall I erected around my soul, they would never get what they wanted.

I still didn't know what it was, but I was going to find out.

"I don't wanna hear it, Atlas." I shoved the last remaining piece of bacon in my mouth. His words irked me because while I knew they weren't true, I wanted them to be. Why wouldn't I? Even monsters needed somebody to share their burden with, and I thought Storm would be the one for me.

"I'm just saying—"

"No," I interrupted. "I. Don't. Wanna. Hear. It."

I thought he was going to argue with me, try to persuade me that Storm cared about me, but he kept quiet instead. When I looked at him, he was already staring at me as if he were trying to figure something out.

"What happened to you, Ophelia?"

His words felt like a spear through my chest. The things that happened to me... they weren't the fairy tales girls so often dreamed of. They were the nightmares you never wanted to think of. I didn't want to think about it. The pain, regrets, suffering, betrayal—the list was far too long for me to even start.

"Life happened." I looked at him. "And it kept happening, kicking me from all sides."

"Sweethe—"

"Save it."

I stood up and walked toward him. In my weakened state, Atlas's energy felt like he could eradicate me if he wanted to. But something told me that he didn't. Something told me that whatever they were planning, they needed me intact.

"Why am I here, Atlas?"

"I can't tell you that." He grimaced. "I'm not

the one with all the answers. I know you're angry, I would be too, but you are safe here."

"I am not safe anywhere." I snickered. "I will never be safe."

He stared at me for a minute too long, as if he wanted to say something. His promises of safety were stories for little kids who didn't know better. I did. No matter where I went, no matter what I did, I would never be safe. I didn't exactly make a lot of friends in the last couple of years, and the amount of people that didn't want to see me dead could be counted on one hand.

For the first time, I felt all alone. There was nobody out there who would want to see me, who would want to feel my touch. There was not one person who craved my touch, my warmth, my love. And I had it.

I know what people thought about me. This armor of mine, it was both good and bad. It was both protection and damnation, but I didn't know how to get rid of it. I feared that once I did, everything bad that was waiting for me would come rushing in, and the sanity I clung to would disappear.

"Come on." He started walking toward the door. "I wanna show you something."

Or he wanted to kill you.

I glared at my inner self because she was a real untrusting bitch sometimes. Okay, she was a real bitch right now.

"Where are we going?"

I was still in basketball shorts and an oversized shirt. No bra in place, no weapons—I was practically bare.

"You'll see." He opened the door and strolled into the hallway leaving me behind.

The urge to mock his *you'll see* rode me hard,

but I had to be an adult about this. He fed me, okay, he also threatened me for about five minutes, but I was unharmed. What could possibly go wrong?

Wait, don't answer that. Everything could go wrong, but maybe I should start trusting people. Maybe, and this is one ginormous maybe, they weren't that bad. Right?

* * *

WRONG. I WAS so fucking wrong, because not only did he bring me where I didn't want to be, he made me see things I also didn't want to see. I didn't know if it was intentional or not, but I couldn't exactly hate him for it.

Throughout the years, motorcycle clubs have been frowned upon by our families. They called them lowlifes, outcasts, dirty underdogs, you name it. My father hated them with a passion, and I never really understood why.

He often said they were disorganized, impulsive, and dangerous. Maybe I would've believed him if I didn't hear stories myself. MCs were not just outlaws riding motorcycles and causing unnecessary mayhem. They were outlaws, that was true, but unlike our families, they weren't hiding under the carefully crafted masks. They embraced who they were with no regrets.

Atlas waited for me when I got out of the room, and I couldn't miss the small smirk playing on his mouth. I was curious, alright? Besides, I couldn't exactly stay in that room. He told me I could roam around if I played nicely, and what a better way to see the place I was being held at then to accept his invitation.

The hallway was dimly lit, and while it wasn't the Ritz-Carlton, it felt like... it felt like home. Some

23

houses were always so cold, some places lacked soul, like my childhood home. But this one, at least what I've seen of it so far, it felt vibrant. The warmth hugged me, touched my skin, played with my hair, and evoked something in my soul. There were pictures on the walls, and as we passed next to them, I couldn't help but stare.

Smiling faces greeted me. Children and adults stood around bikes and all of them seemed so comfortable with each other. Now that I think about it, all the pictures my family ever took looked staged. None of our smiles were genuine, not like these people.

Some pictures were touched by the hand of time, faded in places, but beautiful, nonetheless. Some had years scribbled in the corner, spanning from 1971 to 2003.

I itched to touch them, to feel them, to take this beautiful energy they were giving this place. I wanted to feel warm, to bask in its beauty. I have never felt like this and it choked me. It choked me because I never had it. Even before they threw me into this sick world, my family lacked warmth and understanding.

I was afraid of my father before I even knew that he could kill a person with his bare hands. My mother was not exactly mother of the year, and Maya and I were often left to our own devices. I didn't know where these thoughts came from, but I started wondering how would it feel to have a functional family? A family that loved you no matter what and supported your choices.

Atlas kept quiet as I perused the pictures, going from one to the other, drinking in the happiness that was evident on them.

"Are these members of the club?" I asked him with a trembling voice.

"They were. Some of those are more than twenty years old."

"They look so..." I trailed off.

"Happy?"

He wasn't teasing me when he asked. A serious expression flickered over his face, and another piece of the puzzle unraveled right in front of my eyes. They were a family. Not by blood but by honor. The substance that connected me with mine was just that, a substance. A red, trickling liquid that didn't really mean anything if there was no respect.

But them, these people in these pictures, they obviously loved each other. Children wore dirty overalls, adults were in all kinds of clothing, but they didn't seem to care—wild hair, wild eyes, and palpable happiness.

"That picture." He pointed toward the one with five different guys, all dressed similarly to what Atlas wore now—leather jacket, dark pants and military boots. "That's when they had just founded the club. The Santa Monica chapter became the main chapter after they opened multiple other locations on the West Coast."

The five men he was pointing at looked thrilled. Their proud smiles felt eternal, and I could feel it in my bones. These people were proud to be part of this world. Unlike me, they wanted to be here. They wanted to be part of this family. They belonged here.

I never belonged with mine.

I cleared my throat and turned to him, trying to stop the burning in my eyes and the heavy pressure on my chest. "What did you want to show me?"

Just like in the room, he studied me for a second before he turned around and walked away without a word being said. I felt like I was under the microscope, and I was usually the one dissecting people, not the other way around.

I stared at his retreating form, unable to move from the spot. How fucked up was it that merely seeing happy faces on these pictures burned my chest? God, I was pathetic.

"Come on, Ophelia!" he yelled. "We don't have an entire day, and I have shit I need to do."

A retort was on the top of my tongue, but I bit it down and strolled toward him. He was nice so far, even if I was technically kidnapped. Funny thing was, I didn't even think about trying to find the nearest exit or the way to get out of here.

Fuck, was I developing fucking Stockholm Syndrome? *You weren't here long enough to develop Stockholm Syndrome, you idiot.*

"There's someone I want you to meet, and I hope you can play nice," Atlas said as soon as I reached him. "She isn't like you and I hope you won't hurt her."

Oh great. He was going to ship me off to some sweetheart, and I was going to become stabby. Look, I had nothing against girls who led normal lives and weren't involved with the violent side of this business, but every single time I would talk with them, it would end up either with a disgusted look on their faces or with me wanting to bash their head on the nearest wall.

We just didn't fit well together, and I stopped trying to be something I wasn't.

Yeah, I killed people. Fucking deal with it.

"If you're gonna drop me with some sunflower, don't bother. She's gonna run away screaming."

The fucker started laughing while I was obviously scowling at him. Did he really think that

26

it was a smart idea to irk me now?

"Something funny, Atlas?"

"No, no." He feigned innocence. "Nothing at all."

"Good, because I want to talk to Storm."

The migraine I woke up with earlier seemed to be taking a hold of my entire head, and I knew I was going to need to sit soon. Getting one too many concussions was catching up with me, and that whole shitshow in the church wasn't exactly a walk in the park. Not to mention the lovely gift Storm gave me with that whole knockout shit.

"He's, uh." I glared at him as he tried to find the words. "He's kinda busy right now."

Atlas was obviously uncomfortable talking about Storm and I wanted to know why.

"Busy doing what exactly?" I propped my hands on my hips and scowled at him. He refused to look at my face and instead started staring at the ceiling, his mouth moving as he muttered something.

"Atlas!" I roared. "So help me, God—"

"I can't fucking tell you, Ophelia!"

His chest rose and fell with each breath he took, and I knew I was hitting a nerve with these questions.

"Why not?" I stood right in front of him. "What could be so important that he couldn't even get his ass here to meet me?"

"Ophelia." He almost moaned. "I can't."

"You can't or you—" And then it dawned on me. That motherfucking son of a bitch.

"He's getting his dick sucked somewhere, isn't he?" Atlas flinched as if I physically assaulted him and it was all the confirmation I needed. My heart squeezed painfully in my chest, and even though I knew I had no right, that icky, green monster

27

hugged me from behind, reminding me why I refused to even think about the opposite gender in this way.

With those two forsaken words, Storm had managed to revive the part of me that slept for almost four years. And I believed him. I almost believed that the possessive way he looked at me meant something. Some part of me wanted to believe in it, because I wanted to cling to the possibility of happiness.

"Oh no." Atlas cringed. "You're getting crazy eyes."

"I'm not getting crazy eyes."

"Yes, you fucking are. Those are I-am-going-to-cut-off-his-balls eyes."

"I don't have crazy eyes!" I yelled. "And I don't give a shit what he's doing."

Uh-huh, keep lying to yourself.

"Argh." I took a step back. "You know what? I don't need him because you are going to tell me what I'm doing here. And don't even try to get out of it."

"Listen, sweetheart—"

"Don't you fucking 'sweetheart' me, asshat." I pointed a finger at him. "You wanted to show me something, then let's go. But after that, you and your merry band of leather-loving fuckers are going to tell me everything." He grimaced again. "And I mean, every single thing."

"Leather-loving fuckers?"

"Well, you're definitely not wearing plaid."

Instead of glaring at me or yelling, Atlas almost howled, bending at his knees. His shoulders shook as he laughed, while I stood gawking at him, impatient to get this over with.

"I swear—"

"Oh. My. God." He started laughing again.

28

"You are my favorite right now."

"Shut up."

He straightened up, still fucking laughing, and something pulled at me, seeing him like this. When was the last time somebody laughed like this with me? He placed one hand around my shoulders, steering me further down the hallway.

"You fucking crack me up, sweetheart. Leather-loving fuckers." He snickered again. "That makes me think of some BDSM shit."

Great, just fucking great. Now my head was filled with images of Storm in leather pants and a whip in his hand. I wasn't even into whips, for God's sake.

"Just." I took a deep breath. "Shut up and lead the way."

"Wait 'til I tell the guys about it. Oh God, Felix is going to love it."

"Who's Felix?"

I was curious. Sue me. I didn't really think he would tell me, but as words rolled off his tongue, I realized that maybe he was telling the truth. I wasn't a prisoner unless I made myself one.

"Felix is one of our enforcers."

"One of them." I craned my neck to look at him as we took a right turn in the hallway. "So, there's more than one?"

"Mhm." He steered left.

"Who is the second one?"

"I am," he answered proudly.

"You're an enforcer?"

"What?" He looked down at me. "Why do I hear doubt in your voice?"

"Because, well," I stammered. "You don't look—"

"I don't look like an enforcer?"

"Well, no." Not that I knew how they usually

looked, but the stories I've heard, enforcers were scary fuckers. They even made me look like Tinkerbell.

"Don't worry, babe," he winked, "some of us have pretty faces."

I rolled my eyes so hard I could almost see the back of my skull. The ego on him.

It baffled me though. How could he live with himself if he did the dirty work for the club? The Syndicate loved me when I had to do their dirty little deeds. When there was a person that needed to be killed, a man that had to be tortured, I was their go-to person for those things. But as soon as the stage lights turned off and I returned to Croyford, they expected me to hide who I was. They expected me to be somebody else—a happy, calm, and collected person.

A tame little girl that when they said jump, I would ask, how high? And I played along.

I tried to be all of that, even if it ate me alive. I tried to be what they wanted me to be because I didn't know better.

It was terrifying trying to fit into the world that wanted nothing more than to chew you up and spit you out. You gave it your all, yet it was never enough.

I was never enough.

It was sad standing in front of the mirror and hating what was staring back at me—empty eyes, empty smiles and an empty soul without a real purpose. I practiced emotions and proper social interactions because I didn't have them. I pushed them away from the fear of breaking apart. And they made me this way. They pulled it all out of me—the darkest parts of me, the deranged and sick pieces of my soul brought to the surfaces—and then they regretted it.

30

I saw it in my father's eyes. He was proud, but he was also terrified. He made a monster, but then he didn't know what to do with it.

Siberian Gulag.

Camps in China.

Fifteen days in the Rub' al Khalil desert in Saudi Arabia.

I did it all. I survived it all because he made me do it. It was all part of my training, he said. All part of this fucked-up plan he had for me.

Did Atlas feel like a monster as well?

"I can see the wheels in your head turning, and no Ophelia, I don't always enjoy my job. You know something about it, don't you?" Yeah, I did. "But we did what nobody else wanted to do. We are the faces that haunt other people in the dark, and we are the ones they are afraid of. But these people here, these people I am going to introduce you to, they're my family. They helped me in more ways than one, and I would rather give my life protecting them in any way that I can, than waste it on something else."

"But what if you waste your life protecting those that don't deserve it?" I asked quietly, knowing full well that we weren't talking about him.

"Then maybe it's the wrong family."

Was it? The way he said it resonated with me, and for some inexplicable reason, I felt better knowing that I wasn't with the Syndicate anymore.

"Now, put a smile on your face." I grimaced instead, which made him laugh in return. "Oh God, you crack me up, sweetheart. But listen, I meant what I said. You are safe here, and while I can't talk about the reason why you're here, I can promise you that no one will touch you."

Famous last words, Atlas.

31

THREE

Ophelia

ATLAS KEPT HIS hand slouched around my shoulders the entire time, and even when we came to the staircase, he didn't let go. I wasn't too fond of meeting new people, because more often than not, those I allowed inside my walls either ended up dead or they betrayed me. I know, I had issues — major fucking issues — but years and years of being stomped on, fucked over, tortured, and betrayed would do that to a person.

We walked in silence, and for one brief moment, I allowed myself to dream about the future where I could have a real friend and a family, even if we weren't connected by blood. The images flickered inside my mind, showing me the future I would probably never have, but I still wanted it. I wanted to wake up in a bed that was my own, and it didn't really matter if I was alone or with somebody else. I just wanted to be free of these chains I kept dragging since that day in my house. I was a prisoner of my own mind and a prisoner of the world I didn't want to be a part of anymore.

The voices traveled through the air, and I immediately stiffened knowing what was about to come. I wasn't a fan of crowds, and by the sounds of it, there were more than two people talking from the room adjacent to the stairs. Atlas gripped my shoulder as if he feared I would bolt, and I had to admit, he wouldn't be too far off.

My flight instincts were at an all-time high, and I blamed it all on the exhaustion rendering my body useless. With each new step we took, my gut coiled tighter, and I suddenly just wanted to be back in the room, far away from the rest of the world.

Faster than I could even think to move away from Atlas's hold, we were at the bottom of the staircase, both of us looking toward the entryway to another room.

"Now remember," Atlas broke the silence around us, "play nice."

My tongue was tied up as sweat beaded on my forehead. I would usually come up with some smartass remark, but not today.

Today, I was apparently shy Ophelia, who didn't like people. Not that I liked them on any other day either.

"You're awfully quiet right now. Are you sure you aren't planning to kill us all and escape with our heads in your bag?"

"I swear to God, Atlas." I pinched his side, earning a yelp from him. "Can you just shut up?"

He did shut up, but not before he pinched my side as well, earning a murderous glare from me.

"Was that really necessary?"

"It did stop your mini panic attack there."

Motherfucker.

He was right. I was close to a panic attack, just because I was about to meet a bunch of people. Who the fuck was I, and what did I do with the previous Ophelia? I used to go face-to-face with

33

men three times bigger than I was, and a small meet-up was rendering me speechless. Did I hit my head too hard?

Atlas didn't wait for me to gather my wits, but instead, he pushed me through the entryway, into another larger room, and right in front of at least ten pairs of eyes. Men and women stopped talking as soon as I stumbled in, and if the energy in that hallway resembled warmth, this one here was arctic cold.

The walls were painted black and red, but the natural light that came from the ceiling high windows basked the space in natural light, giving it an open feeling. A long bar with a mahogany top was located opposite the windows, their club's insignia painted right behind. That three-headed beast I saw on Storm's jacket, and now jackets of multiple other guys, stared at me. All three of them had their jaws open, ready to attack, and I couldn't miss the bullet holes decorating that same wall.

Huh, maybe not everything was peace and quiet around here. For a second there, I got worried that I stumbled across some hippie community and not a motorcycle club.

Nobody said a word as Atlas placed his hand on my back, urging me forward to one of the tables, rounded by chairs. None of the patrons of this bar seemed dangerous enough, but their impassive faces were worse than their fists would be. When people refused to show you their emotions, that's when they were the most dangerous.

I could feel all their eyes on my back as we sat down, with Atlas opposite of me. I wasn't sure if they were all curious, or if they wanted me dead. It wasn't a secret that motorcycle clubs hated my family. The silent war they waged against them seemed to be never-ending, and I knew that many

34

of these people lost their loved ones to one of my own.

Were they even mine anymore?

I guess that some habits die hard, and even though I wasn't part of that world anymore, it was tough shaking it off. Loyalty was everything to me, and mine for the Syndicate used to be so deeply engraved in me that I sometimes wondered if I would ever be free of its hold.

I looked around, meeting the eyes of a couple of them, and the last thing I expected to see was a little kid hiding behind a tall man that stood next to the bar. It was a boy, not older than five, and the pain I haven't felt in a long time sliced through my chest, opening it wide.

Ava's kid would've been four by now.

The man patted the kids head, not even paying attention to me, but I was already lost in the land of what-ifs, missed chances, and broken dreams.

"Ophelia?"

I swiveled toward Atlas, trying to burn the memories, trying to shove them back into the little box inside my head, so that they couldn't torture me today. I already had enough on my plate.

"Is this what you wanted to show me?"

"Not exactly."

"Then why are we here?"

"I told you, there are people I want you to meet."

"I see a lot of people here, Atlas." I grinned. "But none of them seem like they want to meet me. Tell me, did they already hear about *Baba Yaga* and the monstrosities I've committed?"

"I can assure you, sweetheart, you're not the only monster here."

I wasn't?

"That guy there." He pointed behind my back,

at the mountain of a guy sitting with a cute girl on his lap. "That's Butcher."

"Butcher?"

"Oh yeah. You don't wanna know how he got that name."

No, I definitely didn't want to know. His nickname spoke volumes.

"That girl." He looked to his right, nodding at the stunning chick in tight leather jeans and a crop top with the club's insignia. "That's Widow."

"As in, her husband died?"

"No, smartass." He laughed. "As in, Black Widow."

"Let me guess, Marvel fans? Is there Thor and Captain America hiding somewhere around here?"

"That mouth." He kept laughing. "Guys are going to love you. Storm is gonna get in trouble trying to keep you away from them."

"Why, are they going to try to kill me? Because let me tell you something, I can hold my own even against a bunch of bikers."

"I know you can. I saw you fight, and some of these guys here did too."

Now that he mentioned it, I remember seeing the two guys standing next to the door back in the church.

"What I'm trying to say," he leaned back in the chair, "is that they'll try to snatch you away from Storm."

"I don't belong to Storm." That almost came out as a growl. "Why do you men always have this uncanny need to look at us like objects?"

"Hey." He grimaced. "I didn't mean it in that way."

"Well whichever way you meant it, I am not here to be snatched, or fought over. As a matter of fact, I don't even wanna be here."

36

"Retract your claws, panther. You're here because Storm wants you to be here, and you will stay here, because out there," he looked toward the windows, "it just isn't safe for you."

I started laughing because he seemed genuinely concerned about me. Didn't he know that for the last six years, no place was safe for me? I wasn't even safe from myself.

"I see it now."

"You see what?" He turned to me with his eyebrows drawn together. "Ophelia?"

"You're a mother hen. I can already see you mothering the other guys. Big, bad enforcer is a mother hen." I almost fell off my chair as the next bout of laughter ran through my body.

"You're such an idiot. You know that?" He looked serious, but I could see his lips slowly pulling up into a smile.

When I looked around, I noticed everybody staring at us. The thing about peace, at least for me, is that it never lasts long enough. There's always something, someone, that triggers the parts of me that threatened to ruin me completely.

My eyes zeroed in on a guy in the far end of the room, with midnight black hair and eyes of the same color. It felt like seeing a ghost, and even though I knew it wasn't him, my mind refused to cooperate.

And there I go again.

Pain in my chest. As if on instinct, I raised my hand, clutching the shirt at my chest. Now's not the time for a panic attack, Ophelia. Now's definitely not the time.

Breathe in, breathe the fuck out, and let it go. Just let it go. Shove it down.

Inhale and exhale. Open that fucked-up little box you have stored in your mind and shove it there. Kieran, emotions, forget it.

In and out.

The buzzing in my ears quieted down, and when I saw Atlas kneeling in front of me, I realized I must have dropped to the floor at some point. His lips were moving, but I couldn't hear a word he said.

And I didn't see him. It wasn't the blue eyes staring at me. I saw him.

I saw the pain in the dark eyes, just before I stabbed him. The moment when he realized I wasn't going to forgive him. When he realized that I knew.

I knew everything.

"Why did you kill me, birdy?"

No, no, no.

Kieran was in front of me. His eyes haunted, his face bloodied. The stab wound on his chest, blood seeping down his torso.

"I thought you loved me."

He looked sad. He was so sad, and I did it. I pushed us to the darkness. This was all my fault, all my fucking fault. He reached for me, the blood on his hands crimson red.

I looked down at mine and it was the same.

His blood, the blood of everyone I'd killed. Men, women, children; their blood was on my hands.

I condemned them. I did this. I was the disease fucking up this entire world. Oh God.

"No, no, no." I started shaking my head. "Stay away from me! You're dead. I saw you die. I killed you."

"Ophelia."

"No." I closed my eyes. "You're not real. None of you are real."

I started pushing backward until I hit the wall,

38

and then hugged my knees.

"You're not fucking real!"

Kieran crawled to me, trying to touch my face, but I ducked down and without too much thinking, I punched him in the face. He fell back, holding his nose, and when he removed his hand, I realized what I'd done.

It wasn't Kieran, it was Atlas with blood trickling out of his nose.

"Oh my God."

"What the fuck, Ophelia?" he yelled.

"I'm sorry, Atlas." I came closer to him. "I don't know... I just, I didn't see you. It was... It was—"

"Well, whatever the fuck it was, you almost broke my nose."

The bystanders kept their distance from us, their stances hostile. I mean, I would be hostile as well if somebody punched my enforcer without being provoked.

Fucking shit.

It was happening again. I was seeing them again, but most of all, I was seeing Kieran. First the dream and now this.

"I really am sorry. I didn't mean to hit you. I didn't see you."

And I was sorry. He didn't deserve to be punched in the face, but it wasn't him I saw, but fucking ghosts of my past.

Atlas grumbled some more, but after a minute or so, he pulled himself up, wiping away the blood on his chin. It was still trickling out of his nose, but it could've been worse.

"Come on." He extended a hand to me. "Up you go. It's fine, I'll survive."

For the first time in my life, I felt bad for somebody.

I took his hand and stood up, still feeling shaky from the ordeal just a few minutes ago. I needed water, or a nap. Preferably both.

"I really don't know what—" I started when a new voice cut me off. A voice I knew from before. A voice belonging to the person I thought was dead.

"What the fuck are you doing here?"

Nathan, Ava's Nathan, stood at the entrance to the room, the murderous glare on his face directed at me. I thought they killed him.

"Nathan?"

Was I seeing things again? No, no I wasn't, because I wasn't the only one looking at him. Atlas had a confused look on his face, and the guys that seemed ready to fight before now looked terrified.

Well, good to know that I didn't go completely crazy. Just slightly.

Nathan crossed the room in a blink of an eye, and before I could move away from him, he had me pinned to the wall, his elbow pressing at my throat.

"I asked you a question, bitch." He sneered at me. "What the fuck are you doing here?"

He was pressing at my larynx and no matter how much I tried, I couldn't talk. My air supply was getting cut off, and the crazed look in his eyes wasn't the same one I used to see when I looked at him before.

Before everything went to shit.

"Nat-Nathan," I managed to choke out.

"That's not my fucking name anymore." He lowered his head, leveling with mine. "You and your family made sure of it."

I had no idea what he was talking about, but I wasn't going to stand here and choke to death because another asshole thought I did something.

40

They really needed to get their sources sorted out.

"What was that that they used to call you." He smirked. "Birdy? Isn't that right? You came here to die, birdy?"

The tattooed X below his left eye was new, as was the scar going through his right eyebrow. What the fuck happened to him?

The hair he used to keep short, was now longer on the top, and if it wasn't for the murderous look on his face directed at me, I would've said that he looked hot.

He increased the pressure on my neck, and I knew if he continued like this, I would faint.

"What is going on here?" It was the voice that felt like a caress on my skin, the voice that whispered sweet nothings in my ear four years ago. It felt both like salvation and damnation.

"Creed!"

I couldn't see him. I couldn't see anything but Nathan's face and the black dots dancing around.

Creed? Who's Creed?

"What the fuck are you doing?"

He was closer now, so, so close, but I was losing it. Nathan's face was darkening, the whooshing sound in my ears, and my lungs burning.

"I am killing this bitch."

"Are you now?"

He sounded calm, collected. He sounded dangerous, and I had a feeling this was about to go unbelievably bad.

"She killed the only person I loved," Nathan continued, and I held on. I wanted to tell him that it wasn't me, but at the same time, I was too tired, trying to prove to people I wasn't what they made me out to be in their heads.

I was just so fucking tired, and the only thing

I wanted was to find my sister and fuck away from this world. But I was wrong.

I would never be able to get away from this insanity. I would never be free no matter how hard I tried.

"Did she now?"

Storm and I, we were cut from the same cloth, and while Nathan kept pressing at my air supply, I managed to open my eyes to see the sinister look on Storm's face as he came behind him. Faster than you could say sex, a knife was placed on Nathan's throat and Storm pulled him off me.

I fell to the ground, coughing as Nathan started shouting at him.

"What the fuck man?"

I couldn't lift my head, and I didn't even try to. Somebody's hands landed on my shoulders, and the blond locks of Atlas's hair fell over my face. Jesus, what was it with people trying to strangle me all the time?

Not that I didn't deserve it most of the time, but if you wanted to kill me, at least you should have a good enough reason.

"What the fuck, Creed?" Storm started. "That woman you were just trying to kill is mine. And you know what I do to people that try to take away what's mine."

"Storm," I croaked. He would kill him; I knew he would. But Storm didn't know the history we had.

I was pretty sure Creed was fed the same lies as the Nightingales. That I killed Ava, that I destroyed their little ray of sunshine. He didn't know and I couldn't blame him.

"Storm," I started again, trying to make my voice sound stronger, but to no avail. It hurt like a bitch, and I fucking needed some water.

42

"No, Ophelia," Atlas spoke instead. "Let him be. Creed shouldn't have done this."

But he didn't know. He didn't fucking know, and I wouldn't let him die for this.

"Storm, please." I lifted my head, and as if something broke through to him, Storm pushed him away. Nathan, or well, Creed looked pissed, but he knew better than to provoke him now.

"I didn't kill her, Nathan. I found her there, but I didn't kill her. I'm going to find who it was, but it wasn't me. I loved her more than I love myself."

He kept glancing between me and Storm, but before I could utter another word, he rushed outside, leaving everything I had to say unspoken.

"Fuck." Storm dropped on his knees in front of me, the glistening skin of his naked chest right in front of my face. Man, my ovaries just about wanted to explode seeing him partially dressed. But then I remembered where he was and what he was doing, and all the dirty little thoughts I had about him and his body flew out the window, leaving the empty feeling behind. He wasn't here to save me or to help me fix things. He was just another person that thought locking me up would be the way to go.

"Let's get you out of here."

I couldn't even protest as he picked me up like a rag doll and carried me upstairs to the same room I woke up in.

"Whose room is this?" I asked as we entered. Those green eyes flickered over my face as the smirk descended on his lips.

"Mine."

And the way he said it, I had a feeling he was talking about more than just the room.

FOUR

Storm

I WASN'T A happy person.

I wasn't sad either, but I wasn't happy. I was simply... nothing. Numbness, darkness, those I was familiar with.

The absence of emotions made me strong. It was what helped me escape that hell all those years ago. This emptiness in my head, the cold flowing through my veins, it shaped me into the person I was today.

When love and warmth are taken away from you, stolen and never given back, you quickly learn to hide everything you feel.

And with time, even what you used to feel gets drowned in the infinite darkness you were slowly getting enveloped in. My heart wouldn't have gotten me out of the hell they threw me into — my head did that.

But something changed four years ago. It changed when the bluest pair of eyes met mine, and an unfamiliar feeling arose in my chest.

Possessiveness.

I wanted her to look at me and only me. I wanted to hold her, hide her, have her all to myself.

That connection I felt, for the longest time I thought I'd imagined it. It wasn't possible to feel like that for a person I'd just met.

It wasn't love. It was as far away from love as it could get, or well, at least what I thought love was. No, this was understanding. The haunted look in her eyes, I saw it every day in the mirror. I felt it with each breath I took. This burden you carry. The burden of everything they did to you and everything you did to other people. Even when you don't feel remorse, the pieces of your soul still get chipped away with every bloody trail you leave behind.

And I've left plenty of them. She did too.

But I didn't know that the girl I met back then could be my damnation. I didn't know that I would need to betray her before I even had her.

She didn't know that the hope she had on that day would be useless, because the situation I would throw us into years later, wasn't going to be a pretty one. When I made the deal, I only got her name.

Ophelia Aster.

A daughter of a man who didn't just deserve to die. Oh no. Nikolai Aster deserved to be burned alive for everything he'd done. I didn't know her name, but the girl I met was Persephone for me. She was my queen, my salvation. My desire and need.

And I fucked up before we could even start.

When I saw her in that church, when I realized who she was, my heart almost jumped out of my chest. And then I realized who she was with when she never showed up even though she promised she would. Maybe if she did, we could've avoided all of this. Maybe I wouldn't end up fucking this thing up before it even began.

I'd been looking for her, going back to that place every single year, but she was never there. I sometimes thought that she was a ghost, a figment of my imagination. Just something my mind and my heart wanted but could never get.

But she was real. She was fucking real, and she was standing in front of me — a living and breathing person. The only problem was, I didn't know if I wanted to strangle her or if I wanted to hug her and never let her go.

I was pissed off, and I wanted to hide. I wanted to leave her be and take out my frustrations on somebody else. Somebody that wasn't her. But the girl that tried sucking my dick earlier couldn't even get me hard because I couldn't see anything but her.

Ophelia in that church.

Ophelia with Kieran.

The way he looked at her and the way she looked at me.

The first time I saw her.

The first time I kissed her.

It was like an avalanche of memories, and I pushed the girl away, leaving her with her mouth agape.

And Creed. For fuck's sake.

Seeing him like that. Holding her, choking her, I wanted to kill him. I wanted to kill one of my men and I wouldn't even care, because nobody touched her.

No one but me.

No matter what, she was the one I wanted.

She was my queen, and the demons swirling in the pits of her soul, they were calling to me. There was darkness inside of her. The type of darkness I'd never felt in anybody else. It called to me. It was a siren's song for my soul, and for the first time, I wanted to have somebody next to me.

I thought it was impossible. Maybe it was

madness, but I was already a madman. A deranged man, and she was the same.

Her insanity, her depravity, her bloodlust, they were mine to hold, mine to cherish.

"Why am I here, Storm?"

My name on her lips was the sweetest melody.

She was beaten up, she looked skinny, and I wanted to go back there to kill all three of them for what they did to her. I didn't know the story behind it all, but I was going to find out. She killed Kieran, just like they instructed her to.

I was hired to help her; I was hired to destroy her. I just didn't know it was *her* at the time.

She had looked like a fallen angel, standing in the ashes of those that wronged her. I knew with everything I had in me—she was perfect for this life.

If only I could make her stay.

I almost hated myself for knocking her out, but it had to be done. She was getting away, and God knew when the next time would be that I actually saw her.

Then there was the promise I'd made.

I didn't feel remorse when I'd made the deal. I didn't, because I didn't know that the same Ophelia Aster is the girl holding the keys to my soul.

Just when I thought I had it all, life decided to knock me on my ass.

"Storm?" she asked again, a frown marring her face.

Those lips were made for kissing, and right now I wanted nothing more than to do that, but we had to talk. I had to know what the story behind her involvement with the Albanians was. I had to know why she killed Kieran.

People talked, and what I managed to gather was that they were engaged once. Four years ago, to be precise. The same time I met her, and the same time Ophelia Aster disappeared from the face of the earth.

"Where have you been?" I asked her instead. I needed her answers more than she needed mine, and I needed time.

Time to figure out how to get us out of this shit. Time to figure out how to get everything I wanted, because I wasn't giving up on her.

She smirked and sat on the bed, my shirt on her looking ten sizes bigger. A weird satisfaction flew through me. An ownership. I wondered how she'd look with her own cut on, riding on my bike, her thighs squeezing mine.

"I think I deserve an explanation first," she started. "You practically kidnapped me and dropped me here. Then I get Nathan, or well, Creed strangling me in the middle of your club."

"That's true." I smiled. "But you still didn't answer my question. Where have you been all of these years?"

"Around. Here and there, everywhere, I guess."

She was as infuriating as she was beautiful. There was a bruise on the right side of her face, and a cut that still seemed to be healing.

"Who did that to you?" I tried being calm, tried asking it with a mellow voice, but the fury was brewing beneath my skin. My blood was boiling because I almost knew the answer.

"None of your business." She frowned.

"I beg to differ. Everything that has anything to do with you is my business." *Keep fucking calm.*

She scooted backward, putting distance between us. "I didn't know I was your pet, Storm. Thank you so much for locking me up here when there are more important things I need to do."

48

"Which things?" I sat at the edge of the bed, letting her have her space. I didn't know what happened to her, but the darkness I saw back then, it wasn't hiding anymore. It was there on the surface of her skin.

A time bomb waiting to explode.

"As I said, none of your business."

God, this wasn't going how I imagined. I would burn heaven and earth to get to her. I would raise hell if somebody hurt her. But right now, everything about her screamed to stay away. She wasn't ready for me. She wasn't ready to acknowledge this thing between the two of us, and I could wait. I would've waited until my last breath if it meant she would get back to me.

"Why didn't you show up?" Her eyes flashed with something familiar. Pain. It was pain showing in her eyes. "You know, at the spot we agreed on. I waited for you. I went back every single year, but you were never there. I even thought that you were a product of my imagination at one point. So, tell me, why?"

She kept quiet, her eyes looking everywhere but at me. What the fuck happened to her?

"Ophelia—"

"They kept me away." She took a deep breath before continuing. "They chained me to a wall because they thought I did something I would never do." She looked at me this time, but her mind was somewhere else. "They thought I killed her, when all I did was try and revive her."

"Killed who?"

"Ava." She hugged her knees. "They thought I killed Ava, their sister. And there was so much blood, Storm. And I tried. I fucking tried to help her, but they didn't let me. They thought I did it."

"Fuck." *They chained her?* "When did this

49

happen?"

"That night before we were supposed to meet. I was going to come. I was going to leave that life behind me, but they didn't let me. So, I ran away. I ran as fast as I could."

"Jesus, fuck." I dragged a hand over my face. "Then why the fuck did you go back?"

"I didn't exactly go back." She smirked. "They kidnapped me, but they didn't know I had a deal with the Albanians. They wanted Kieran dead, and so did I."

She started looking angry, and I didn't know if I wanted to hug her or slap some sense into her.

"Did they do all this?" The middle finger on her right hand was swollen, purple and blue and I didn't need a doctor to know that it was broken. I didn't want to know what other scrapes and bruises marred her body. If I did, what little I had left of my sanity would walk out that door, and I would end up killing them all.

"They did, but I let them."

"What the fuck, Ophelia?"

"Do you wanna know why I let them do this?" That haunted look on her face was there again, insanity dancing in those eyes. "Do you wanna know why I let them torture me?"

I did and I didn't, because whatever it was made her hurt herself.

"I could've killed Kieran from afar. I was trained by my father, I know how to use not only knives, but all sorts of guns. I didn't do that. I wanted them to suffer. I knew looking at me would be reliving that night all over again. I wanted them to drown in their sorrow. They deserved nothing less for what they'd done to me. Them and my brother."

I've been clenching my teeth so hard I was

surprised none of them broke yet.

"I wanted them to suffer just how I suffered. My family, their family, they all betrayed me. I worked for the Syndicate. I bled for the Syndicate, and my father, the leader of that same organization, he never even looked for me. After everything they did to me, he never tried to help me. I was sleeping on the streets when the Albanians found me. They knew who I was, and they offered me shelter. They gave me clothes, they gave me food, and they gave me purpose again."

"But—"

"I'm not finished, Storm," she whispered. "That day I met you, it was the best day of my life. Ava found out she was pregnant, and I thought we would finally be able to run away from our families. But I was so fucking wrong, and weeks later I realized that fairy tales don't exist. At least they don't exist for people like me. They are pretty little lies mothers tell their daughters. We grow up with these expectations that things would get better. That the sun will shine again, but it doesn't. My life was always a thunderstorm. The kind you can never run away from. So, I accepted the Albanians like they were my own family, but I wanted to get out. Kieran's death was supposed to be my way out."

She slowed down, tracing the gauze on her arm.

"And I didn't wanna do it. I didn't wanna do it because I didn't want to bring them more pain. He cheated on me, ripped my heart out, yet he didn't deserve to die. But I was wrong." She again looked at me. "He raped my sister." *For fuck's sake.* "The same sister I've been looking for for years. So now you know why I did it. Why I allowed myself to work for a family that had no morals and didn't care about anything but themselves. Because they were the only light. They were my sun when I wanted nothing more but to die."

"I didn't... Fuck, I didn't know."

"I know you didn't know, but you need to let me go. I need to find Maya."

She wanted to run away, when I wanted nothing more than to see her running to me. This whole story was giving me a fucking headache, and the idea of dismembering their bodies was more and more appealing with each word she said.

"Will you let me go?" she asked with a hopeful look in her eyes. She thought I was better than them, but I wasn't.

I was worse. I was so much worse, because I wanted her to myself even if she didn't want me. Even if she wanted to get away, I wanted her here. Even if it meant that she'd hate me, I couldn't let her go. I just found her; I couldn't fucking let her disappear again. And I knew she would.

"No, Ophelia," I answered. "I won't let you go."

"You're a fucking asshole!" she screamed, like a banshee, throwing a pillow at my face

"Calm down," I gritted through my teeth. "I won't let you go, but I will help you find her."

"You are worse than they were."

She was angry, furious. Good, so was I. But no matter how furious she was, she wasn't going to go anywhere.

"Oh, you have no idea, Persephone."

"That's not my fucking name," she screamed, and something inside of me broke down. The dam opened, and before I could think about what I was doing, I climbed on top of her, holding her hands down, sliding between her legs.

Now, this is better.

She quieted down, small huffs coming out of her. Her eyes narrowed, her chest rising and falling rhythmically. I lowered my head, my lips a whisper away from hers.

Her sweet vanilla scent drove me crazy. I looked up and saw the blood darkening the white gauze on her arm, but she didn't make a sound.

"You need to understand one thing, baby." I dipped my head toward her neck, my eyes zeroing on the red splatter of blood. "I am never letting you go. So, you can hate me, love me, chill me and thrill me, but you are never getting away from me. You're mine, Ophelia. Mine to hold, mine to own, and no man or woman will ever take you away from me."

FIVE

Storm

EMBEDDED INTO MY soul. That's where she buried herself.

She trembled beneath my body, biting her lower lip, and I wanted it to be my teeth biting down on that sweetness. Her chest rose, grazing her breasts against my chest, and I wanted to do nothing more but to claim her here and now. But she wasn't ready for me.

Trepidation sunk deep into my skin, waiting for her to say something. I was angry at her, but my need for her overrode all the other feelings, and my dick twitched against my leg at the mere thought of her belonging to me. I lowered my hips to hers, pinning her fully. At the first contact of her body against mine, a groan escaped from my chest, almost leaving me breathless.

Ophelia gazed up at me, her ocean blue eyes wide from desire, lips parted and waiting. I dipped my head toward her neck, nibbling at the soft skin, licking from the column all the way to her ear.

"S-Storm," she stuttered, her breathing increasing with each passing second. The way she said my name sent a jolt of desire directly to my balls, and I ached to hear more. I was a starving man, and she was the meal I'd been waiting for my entire life. She was calm to the storm brewing inside my chest, and one taste was enough to know that I would never be satisfied until she fully belonged to me.

I released her hands, my own slipping into her hair, as I started leaving kisses along her jaw, seeking her lips. She lifted her ass, and faster than a lightning, wrapped her legs around my waist, bringing me down with her.

My shirt looked heavenly on her, and I wasn't sure what I wanted more — her in my clothes or her completely naked.

Her plump lips parted, but I wasn't going to give her what she wanted, even if it pained me to deprive both of us that pleasure. It was obvious to me that Ophelia loved to run away from the things that were chasing her, and I didn't want her to use us for that. I wanted her to come to me, to seek me because she wanted me just like I wanted her, but those shadows in her eyes were still dancing their tango, and this wasn't the way.

I didn't want us to start this way.

There were too many lies surrounding us, and until I dealt with the impending disaster, I was going to keep us both separated, at least physically.

Pulling one of my hands from her hair, I grasped her hip, kneading the soft flesh that got exposed in the middle of our little play. As if afraid of what I was going to do, she touched my face, her tiny hand grazing my cheek, then my lower lip. I bit on her thumb playfully, earning a soft glare from her, but she didn't retreat.

She kept her hand there, letting me devour her in the way I knew how. The day I met her, it felt as if the missing piece of the puzzle fell into its place, and I've been missing her ever since. That kiss we shared sizzled my skin, leaving the scorch marks all over the place, and I wanted more.

But I wanted more than the physical connection. I wanted her to feel me skin deep, just like I did her. I wanted to bury myself inside her soul, to hold her, to cherish her, to keep the darkness at bay, because she kept mine.

"Storm." Her lower lip trembled, her eyes filled with unshed tears, and the anger and the violence I felt just a minute ago vanished from my skin, leaving the need to protect her and to soothe her wounds.

There was nothing sexual in the way she looked at me now, but she still clung to me as if she too, couldn't let go. The wall she had when I saw her back in the church dissipated, leaving behind a girl I wanted to see. Ophelia had so many broken pieces, that not even the years of healing would be able to put them all back together.

I knew because I was the same.

We were both products of this fucked-up world. A product of people that didn't care enough about the kids they were supposed to protect. They were the ones that made us this way, and then they abandoned us, as if we meant nothing to them.

Everybody knew stories about Ophelia Aster, the bloodthirsty assassin made in the Syndicate. Everybody knew the stories of slaughtered children, destroyed families, and grown men shaking in fear from the mere mention of her name. But nobody knew about this girl, lying beneath my body, shaking because she was still human.

She bled, she loved, and she was betrayed.

I was so fucking angry at her for never showing up that I didn't even stop to think about the reasons of why she didn't. That cut on her cheek made me see red, but now wasn't the time for me to go into a rage. She obviously needed somebody, some sort of comfort, even if she would never admit it.

The first tear escaped from her eye, leaving a wet trail on her cheek, but she didn't notice it. She kept staring at me, as if she were memorizing my face again, just like that day on the cliff.

"*Agape*," I whispered to her, unable to stop myself. One thing I learned from my deadbeat mother was that Greek word for love. On the days she was sober, she would call me her *agape*, her love. It was too bad it never lasted long.

I nuzzled my face against her cheek, the same one that hosted that violent cut. I pressed my lips against the marred skin and another tremor shook through her.

I held her tight, tighter than before. I've missed her my whole life not even knowing that I did.

"Shh," I soothed her, stroking her hair, and leaving tiny little kisses on her cheek, on her chin, the corner of her mouth, her nose. "It's going to be okay."

People often failed to see the real person hiding behind the mask, and the one she wore, it was almost merged with her skin. I had a feeling that she didn't know when to take it off anymore.

I started moving back, but her arms clamped around my neck, pulling me back again. She nestled her head in the crook of my neck, while her whole body shook with silent sobs. Ophelia held on to me with all her strength, and something cracked inside my chest.

This strong, powerful woman was breaking right in front of my eyes, and I didn't know what to do. I wasn't known for my affection, but she made me want to be better.

I pulled her up with me, cradling her head with my hand. She almost felt like a child in my arms, so tiny, so fragile. I knew what she was capable of, but in this moment, she was raw, she was showing me everything that was wrong. She didn't have to talk for me to understand that the glass she's been filling in, finally gotten too full, and everything she held inside had to spill.

For a moment I thought that Creed attacking her might have triggered something, but she defended him. I would've killed him then and there if it wasn't for her voice calling me, rendering me still. She defended him and I knew that there was more to the story than I was aware of.

I stood up with her still in my arms and walked toward the adjacent bathroom. She stiffened with every new step I took, and I wasn't sure if she was afraid I was going to drop her, or if she simply didn't want to let go. Turning on the light, I closed the door behind us and stopped in front of the shower located in the corner of the bathroom.

"Baby," I rasped. Her state of distress was unraveling me, and I hated seeing her like this. I hated it because there was nothing I could do. She squeezed me harder, a whimper escaping her lips.

"Phee," I started again. "I need to remove your clothes, Sunshine. Can you stand?"

She shook her head, but she wasn't the only one wanting to hold on for as long as possible. I didn't want to let her go, but I knew that a fresh shower could do miracles even in situations like these.

"Ophelia, please." My voice almost cracked. "Let's wash you up and then we can talk some more."

As if sensing that I wouldn't let go even if she

wasn't clinging to me like a spider monkey, she slid down, wobbling on her feet. I kept my hands on her waist, searching her eyes for signs of distress, but she seemed cold, emotionless, and if it wasn't for the wet trail over her cheeks, I would think that I'd imagined the last ten minutes.

I took the hem of her shirt, and like an obedient child, she lifted her arms, letting me remove it. Desire stirred in my groin, but now wasn't the time to be aroused by the sight of her round breasts and tiny waist. She was too skinny, but the muscles on her flat stomach were still visible.

Motionless, she just stood there staring at my chest, refusing to meet my eyes. I would've missed it if I hadn't been too busy staring at her form, but an angry red mark, a red burn mark, stood below her collarbone, a stark contrast to her pale skin. My hand skimmed around the skin, and the hissing sound that erupted from her chest almost drove me to my knees.

The snake wrapped around the dagger was forever etched into her skin, and I wanted to destroy the whole world for the pain they caused her. They fucking branded her like cattle.

"Did they do this?" I didn't have to elaborate who they were, because we both knew who I was talking about. "Ophelia?"

"Yes," she rasped. "Kieran did it."

My molars ground so hard, I was afraid I was going to break them.

Instead of waiting for me, she dropped the basketball shorts to the floor, followed by the lacy underwear she had on when I brought her here. Zoe was bringing her new clothes, but when I brought her here, I didn't want to remove all her clothes. I wanted her to feel safe, but I failed.

59

With every new breath she took, her breasts lifted higher, begging for my attention. I wanted to touch her, to hold her. I wanted to leave my mark on her, to replace all the horrors she went through before me. But it would all have to wait.

I lifted my hand with my palm up, waiting for her to take a first step. I wasn't going to force her into anything she didn't want to do. She was here physically, but I knew that haunted look in her eyes. Her mind and her soul were in the middle of a never-ending war. Sometimes you win a battle, but the war keeps going.

Hesitantly, almost shyly, she placed her tiny hand in mine, giving me a squeeze as if to reassure me when she was the one that needed it more than I did. I led her toward the shower and turned on the water, waiting for it to warm up before I hauled her over the stepped edge. I kicked off my boots and stepped inside right behind her. The space felt small with both of us inside, but I needed to do this for her.

I wanted to show her that there were good things out there. That darkness wouldn't always win, and that there was something better waiting for her, whenever she was ready.

I kept my clothes on, not trusting either one of us not to take this to a different level when we weren't ready to take that step. Her hair darkened under the spray of water, her eyes closing, lips parting, and she never looked more beautiful than she did now. Girls had thrown themselves at me my whole life, but none of them held me captive like she did. My heart didn't threaten to burst at the mere sight of them, and their tears didn't gut me as if somebody just stabbed me.

I traced my thumb across her shoulders, down her arms, all the way to her hand, entwining mine with hers. I caught myself humming "Little Angel" by Charon, but it seemed to calm her. She pulled me closer to her, letting the water wash over both of us. Her naked chest pressed against mine drove me crazy.

My dick was painfully pressing against the zipper of my pants, and as if she knew, she slid closer, palming the aching length through the fabric.

I threw my head back, unable to silence the groan that erupted from my chest. I was unraveling right in front of her eyes, and this plan of mine wasn't working exactly how I imagined. She was quickly taking control of the situation, and all it took was one little touch.

"No, Ophelia." I shook my head, trying to clear the fog that enveloped my brain. "Not today."

Her long lashes created a half-moon shadow on her cheeks as she blinked innocently at me, pouting at the same time. She was going to be the death of me.

And my dick, apparently.

He wasn't too happy. I was denying him what he wanted, but there would be plenty of time to do all the other things we wanted to do. This, now, it was about her.

I spun her around, making her face the wall, but I wasn't ready for the onslaught of emotions at the sight of her back. Red marks marred her perfect skin, some older, some newer, but all of them held a tremor of violence, a promise of depravity and the damnation that seeped into her soul.

With a trembling hand, I traced one of them, earning a hissing sound from Ophelia, but she didn't move away. These scars, these violent, vicious scars, they were the proof of everything she went through, and she still stood tall. She still fought against the current, even when it wanted to wash her away. To destroy her, to eliminate her.

My throat constricted from the words left unsaid, but whatever I uttered now wouldn't be enough to erase the pain she went through. So, I took my shampoo from the small shelf perched in the corner of the shower and poured it on her scalp. She shivered underneath my touch, but she moved backward, coming closer to my body, as if she too needed this connection more than she needed to run away.

I massaged the shampoo into her scalp, untangling her hair in the process, and letting her rest against my chest. I moved toward her shoulders, kneading the muscles there, earning a small groan from her. The delicate arms adorned with tattoos I wanted to know the meaning of were next, and I took my time spreading the shampoo over her skin. I reached the white gauze that was now completely wet, and slowly unwrapped it from her arm, letting it fall at our feet.

Sharp, red lines stood against her skin, splitting the tattoo of the snake in half. I avoided the reddened area, trying to calm my racing heart. I should've called the doctor when I brought her back here, instead of just dropping her in my room. As soon as we finished with this shower, I was going to have Atlas ring Doctor Shiloh, to have a look at her. Her finger looked terrible, and I didn't want to know what other injuries she might have endured during her times with the Nightingales.

"Turn around," I instructed, my voice unrecognizable. I lathered my hands with the shower gel this time while she turned around, and the sight in front of me almost knocked me off my feet.

Her eyes shone bright, as the tears cascaded

down her face mixed with the pouring water from above us. The need to soothe her rode me hard, but first I wanted to finish this.

I placed my hand between her breasts, feeling the steady heartbeats beneath my palm. I dragged my hand up, over her shoulders, over her breasts, and all the way down to her navel. I kneeled in front of her, lifting one of her legs, lathering it in soap, then the other one, repeating the same action. The small X above the tattoo on her thigh caught my attention, and I wondered how many marks did they leave on her body?

How many invisible scars was she truly hiding?

I washed her thighs, dragging my hand over her sex when another thought struck me.

"Did they hurt you?" I looked up, searching her eyes. She must have known what I meant because she shook her head, and the small sense of relief washed over my body, allowing me to breathe.

I stood up and pushed her underneath the spray of water, washing away the soap all over her body—from her hair, her shoulders, and her perky little breasts. I held her close, only allowing the water to wash away the sins of yesterday.

As soon as the last remnants of soap went away with the water, I turned the shower off, stepping outside and holding my hand for her. She took a tentative step, then another one until she grasped my hand, joining me outside of the shower.

I took the white towel off the rack and started drying off her skin with slow strokes, careful not to touch any of the injured areas. I felt her eyes on me the whole time, but I resumed my ministrations without a hitch. Her hair was plastered against her back, and I turned her around, lifting it into the towel and wrapping it around her head. I saw Zoe doing this once or twice and I assumed that she would appreciate it as well.

We stepped outside of the bathroom, with her in my arms, once again clinging to my neck. Her naked body should've made me needy, but the only thing I wanted to do right now after seeing all the marks on her skin was to hold her. I placed her gently on the bed, followed by the protest from her lips, and the wide blue eyes searching for mine.

"I can't exactly sleep in wet clothes."

I pulled the shirt off my body, followed by my pants and my underwear. Her eyes widened at the sight in front of her, and it made something inside my chest flutter with pride. She liked what she saw. She liked it a lot.

I walked toward the dresser opposite of the bed and pulled out a fresh pair of underwear. She didn't move an inch from where I put her, and as soon as I started walking back toward her, with my underwear on, she moved back, all the way to the headboard.

"Easy there." I sat next to her and pulled her into my lap. "You're still hurt."

"I hate this," she mumbled. "I hate being weak."

I frowned at her words, but I understood. I would hate feeling weak as well, even if there was nothing wrong with it.

"Sometimes our bodies need to take a break, Ophelia. This isn't you being weak, this is you being strong for way too long."

She didn't reply, but instead she wrapped herself around me, nestling as if this wasn't the first time for her to be in my bed, in my arms. I should've felt cold after that shower, but my skin sizzled from her nearness, from her body.

This was what I was looking for all these years. This was what I'd been missing, what always should've been with me. She didn't seem to want to talk, and I was fine with it.

I was fine with holding her for as long as she would allow me. Even if it were just for a minute, I would be happy — for now.

She wanted to find her sister, and I was going to help her, but not before she finally started healing. Not before she finally started talking to me and accepting this thing between us. All these years I thought I imagined the connection I shared with her. All these years I thought that my mind came up with this idea of her until I saw her in that church.

This thing between us, it was a living, breathing thing, and I wasn't going to let go. Time was all I had these days, and if she needed years to understand that she was never going to be without me, so be it, I could wait.

I would've waited centuries for her to come to me.

"I'm so tired," she mumbled against my skin. "But I just woke up."

"Then let's sleep."

I moved my body lower until my back hit the mattress, taking her with me. The comforter was hunched underneath my legs, and I kicked it higher until I could reach it with my hand. With one, I held her close to me, holding her neck and threading my fingers through her wet hair, and with the other one, I pulled the comforter over our bodies, shutting the outside world completely from us.

Gradually, she relaxed against my hold, her body going slack from exhaustion. I hummed again, creating my own version of a lullaby for her.

It seemed to relax her even further, and the next thing I knew, her eyes fluttered closed and her breathing slowed down.

My own body seemed to take note from her and decided to shut down. I was wired to stay up for days on end, but all I needed now was to hold her close and sleep with her.

No one was going to take her away from me. That I could promise.

SIX

Ophelia

I FELT RIDICULOUS today.

I was not exactly known for my happy, frilly feelings or breaking apart like I did last night, but there I was, twenty-four years in my ass, and I bawled like a little baby on the chest of a man that technically kidnapped me. I couldn't shake off the memories of him washing my hair, my body, taking care of me when all I wanted to do was to crumble into a pathetic ball and disappear.

That's it, I was most definitely losing my mind. There was no other explanation for the fuckery that had happened last night.

Or maybe you don't want to admit that his soft side calmed you down.

Oh, fuck off. No, I wasn't going to admit that his soft touch and the way he looked at me unraveled the part of my soul I kept hidden inside. He fucking touched me like he cared for me, and when he washed my hair, when he touched my skin in such a slow manner, I almost crumbled to my feet.

I cried for the seventeen-year-old Ophelia that was thrown into this vicious world, and I cried for twenty-four-year-old Ophelia that never knew how it felt to have somebody really care for her. I was pathetic, wasn't I? I was tired. That's it.

I was tired and that's why I dropped all my defenses last night. That's why I sought him, why I needed him to keep the darkness at bay. That was why his touch meant much more than I wanted it to.

Oh, who was I kidding? I wanted him with me last night. Ever since I woke up yesterday, ever since Atlas brought me outside to see the rest of the club, the only person I wanted to see was Storm. I thought about the butterflies in one's stomach Ava mentioned so many times, and this thing inside of me, those weren't butterflies. No, it felt like a stampede of elephants running through me whenever I thought about him.

He wanted answers I couldn't give him right now. I was still too angry, too wound up to even start that conversation. If he wanted to pretend like he didn't know that I came back here to search for him, then so be it. But stampede or not, I wasn't going to fall for his antics this time. No, there were more important things I had to focus on, and Storm couldn't be one of them.

My mind was already split between what I needed to do and what I wanted to do. Mixing him with all the other things I had to think about wasn't good.

This morning I woke up all alone, naked, with my hair still wet from yesterday. He fucking left me alone when I had so many questions. I wanted to climb him like a tree, and I wanted to kick him in his balls, not necessarily in that order. He was good at distracting me from what really mattered right now, and I hated it.

My anger was one thing I could always count

on, and with him so close to me, I couldn't think straight. I wanted to give in. I wanted to remember who I was before they completely obliterated my soul. I missed the girl I used to be. I missed that feeling he had evoked in me when I had met him for the first time.

Even heartbroken and betrayed, he had managed to make me forget about everything else that was waiting for me. He was doing the same thing right now.

Atlas was the one who found me in the room this morning as I sulked around like a hormonal teenager, trying to dress for the day. One look at my face and he shut his mouth like I begged him to yesterday. He didn't say a word even after he took me down for breakfast.

Apparently, it was Sunday today—not that it really mattered to me—but the club had weekly barbeques scheduled for all members. So here I was, in the backyard of the notorious motorcycle club, waiting for my hot dogs to be cooked. The sun pissed me off today with its bright rays and stubborn need to burn me alive. People were pissing me off. The smell of the barbeque was pissing me off... Everything was fucking pissing me off.

Look, I grew up in a sunny place, but this level of humidity was completely new for me, and I didn't really like it. Maybe on a regular day when I didn't feel like I wanted to strangle one particular biker I could enjoy the sunny weather, but not today.

Chairs, tables, several barbeque sets, all of it was brought outside by younger-looking guys who Atlas called prospects. They all wore their jackets— no, wait—their cuts as Atlas called it after he nearly choked on his sandwich with my whole "jackets"

70

tirade. People still avoided me, even after I was introduced to an older couple that could pass for my grandparents, and two other young couples. None of them leered at me, none of them attacked me, but I could feel the nervous energy surrounding them whenever they ended up standing near me.

I was instructed to sit down and wait for my food to be brought to me. I felt like a petulant child, being punished for something. Not that I didn't have to be punished for many things I did, but... You get my point.

"Oh. My. God," sounded right behind me, and before I could even turn around, a petite girl, with fiery red hair, sat on the chair on the other side of the table. Her eyes were wide, cheeks flushed, and she looked more like a pixie than a real human being.

"I can't believe this."

"Uh…" I was starting to get confused. "What's—"

"You're Ophelia, right?"

"Riiight," I drawled. I still had no idea who she was, nor what she wanted, but she couldn't be much younger than me.

I honestly hated unnecessary attention. Large groups of people irked me, and even during high school, I was happier sitting alone rather than with a big group.

Her elbows hit the table, followed by the staring spree directed at me. She looked elated, blue eyes sparkling under the afternoon sun. And while I looked like somebody killed my puppy, she looked like somebody bought her one. I squirmed in my seat, looking around, trying to locate Atlas or even Storm, just to avoid sitting here with her.

Her carefree demeanor reminded me of one

person I hadn't wanted to lose, and it bugged me how easy it was for memories to resurface out of nowhere. Ava would wear the same expression, the happy one. The carefree one.

She never had to worry about the type of weapon she was supposed to carry because she wasn't part of this vicious cycle, unlike the rest of us.

"Who are you?" I finally asked when I couldn't take her staring anymore.

"I'm Zoe-Amelia, but you can call me Zoe, or ZoZo. It's nice to meet you."

Her hand was suddenly right in front of my face, waiting for me to shake it. I reluctantly extended my own, grasping her smaller one. And trust me, my hands were already tiny in comparison with some of the other girls.

What did I tell you? A pixie.

"It's, uh, nice to meet you too, ZoZo." I felt like an idiot saying it, but she beamed as if I just gifted her with a golden retriever.

"I can't believe it's really you." She all but had stars in her eyes, but I had no idea why. Did she mix me up with somebody else? People usually had a completely different reaction to meeting me. Of course, it also mainly happened with them on the receiving end of my knife or my gun, but this was completely out of the ordinary.

"It's definitely me." I frowned.

"If you keep stabbing at the table with that fork, we might have to buy a new one."

"I'm sorry, what?" I was confused with what she said. Who the fuck was this girl?

"The fork, honey." She pointed at my hand. "Are you trying to redecorate or what?"

I looked at my hand, and she was right. There were already marks on the wooden table from where I scratched it. At this point, I'd start killing people without knowing it.

"I was just lost in thought," I answered, refusing to look at her.

"That was some thinking alright."

She kept smiling the whole time, while I just wanted to get away from here. People were whispering around us, staring at me as if I were a wild animal in a cage. I guess that in a way, I was. Angry Ophelia was never a good thing for the rest of the folks that would find themselves in close proximity, and Storm was literally causing havoc in my head with his I-am-here-but-not-really-here bullshit.

My mood was so sour that Atlas didn't even try to joke or to threaten me today. I swear to God, I had to get out of this funk and start thinking about ways to escape.

"Hey, earth to Ophelia." She clicked her fingers right in front of my face.

"Dude, seriously?" I shook my head. "Why are you here?"

"Because you seemed lonely, and I wanted to meet you for as long as I could remember." She shrugged as if it was normal wanting to meet me. She was making it sound as if I was some sort of celebrity around here.

"I don't understand."

She leaned back into her chair, placing her legs on the table. Wow, manners are not to be found around here, apparently. My mother would have a coronary if she ever saw her sitting like this. Not that I was the embodiment of ladylike behavior, but Zoe, or ZoZo, would legitimately give her a heart attack.

Dammit. I liked it.

73

She had this pure energy around her, and it pulled me closer, even if I didn't want to talk to anybody here. I didn't notice it before, but she had a large bag with her with the same insignia as the club.

Noticing me looking at it, she smirked, flashing another one of her brilliant smiles.

"I could get you the same one, if you want."

I didn't want one, but I liked that she was so comfortable being here.

"I'm sorry, but—"

"You're forgiven."

"What?" This chick was fucking confusing.

"You were about to apologize for something, and I'm forgiving you."

And here I thought I was the crazy one.

"You're going to love it here. On Sundays, we do these cookouts, and the guys are doing the whole drive through Santa Monica on their bikes later in the evening. And then there's the training." She kept going and going. Didn't she need to take in some air or something? "There's a big-ass gym in the basement. You're gonna love it. Do you spar? I love sparring. You'll kick my ass, but I think we could be a good fit. What are you doing tomorrow? Maybe I can pass by after work. I'm working at the restaurant owned by the club, just one street lower. Oh, oh, I know. You should come for some pancakes. I know it isn't anything super special, but those are delicious, I'm telling you."

Jesus fucking Christ, Mary, Joseph, Holy Ghost, all the demons, I need fucking help. She was going a hundred miles in a minute.

Mute.

I needed a mute button for her.

"Zoe." I stopped her just as she started talking about her work week. I didn't need her damn schedule. "Could you slow down, please?"

"Oh, of course." Crimson colored her cheeks. "I'm sorry. I must look extremely crazy to you." You think. "But we don't get too many female fighters, you know. And you, well." She shrugged. "You are ruthless. You don't care who or what, you just go for the jugular. I admire that. You're loyal but you're also brutal."

That's one way to put it, I guess.

Funny thing was, I didn't want her here, but I also didn't mind her company. For all the rambling that just came out of her mouth, she was cute. Maybe it was because she reminded me of Ava, or maybe I was lonelier than I initially thought.

I observed her for a minute, and she didn't seem to mind. That carefree smile slowly pulled one of my own, and before I knew it, I was laughing at the ridiculous situation I found myself in. Here I was, on the precipice of my life, and instead of trying to find a way to get out of here, I was sitting in the backyard of the club that could quite literally destroy me, laughing with a girl I just met.

"I like you, Zoe."

"I know. I'm awesome." She chuckled, and I howled again, almost plastering myself on the table.

"Where have you been all my life?"

"Here, in Santa Monica. Chilling, definitely not killing because Indigo, who's my brother by the way, would have a coronary. Making pancakes, babysitting rowdy bikers. You know, the usual."

Motherfucker, I couldn't stop laughing. My chest constricted painfully, my shoulders shook, but I couldn't stop. And it felt fucking good.

I couldn't remember the last time I laughed this hard, and it was a magnificent feeling. Being buried underneath the tragedy, underneath the darkness I allowed myself to sink into, I forgot what it felt like to act like a regular girl, with regular friends, who could make me laugh like this.

"So, Indigo is your brother?" I asked her.

"Don't remind me. At this point, I will never get a chance to find a boyfriend or get married. My brother has scared every single guy in a five-mile radius, and he isn't done."

"Which one is he?" I looked around, noticing people staring at us. Some of them looked curious, some of them weary and some smiled at the sight of the two of us. This whole scene sounded like a bad joke.

An assassin and a waitress walked into the bar... No, okay. I sucked at jokes.

"That one." She pointed toward a guy that stood with Atlas, who kept throwing cautionary glances toward us. Ah, the brother bear. I could feel his protective streak even from this side of the backyard, and I was positive that Zoe wasn't joking about it. "He seems scary, but he's actually quite cuddly." Her eyes widened as soon as the words left her mouth. "Oh God, please don't tell him I told you that. Knowing him, he would end up finding different ways to torture me, or worse."

"Don't worry, dude. I got you." I winked at her. "But, if he is so protective, why is he allowing you to hang around here?"

This would be the last place I would expect her to be with a brother like that.

"Ah, it must be weird for you, seeing us all here, behaving like what my brother and the rest of the club are doing is the normal thing."

"Well," I muttered. "Yeah."

"See that couple over there." She pointed toward the older couple I met earlier, sitting at one of the benches, surrounded with kids. "That's

Michael and his old lady, Cassandra."

"Old lady?" At this point, I was going to need a dictionary. There was no way to remember all these terms they were throwing around without mixing them all up. Old lady, cuts, colors, back door, I would need to start taking notes at this point.

"I keep forgetting you're an outsider." She laughed. "An old lady is like a wife, but we like to think that it's even more sacred than marriage. You could have many wives, but only one of them would ever be your old lady."

"And can girls have an old man?"

She almost fell off her chair with another bout of laughter. I swear, I wasn't usually a comedian, but I legitimately didn't know anything about motorcycle clubs. It felt as if everything they ever thought of me was pure bullshit, and I was only now seeing the true face of them.

"No," she choked out. "We don't get to have an old man, at least there's no term for it."

"Why can't we create a new term? If they can call us old, we sure as hell should be able to do the same."

"Ophelia, you're a bloody genius." She cackled. "I can't wait to tell Storm all about this newfound information you got."

At the mention of Storm, my whole body stiffened, and the anger that was momentarily forgotten, resurfaced again, making me violent. Goddammit, why couldn't he just stay in the bed this morning so that we could talk like adults?

But no, he had to fucking disappear, and I didn't see him yet. It was almost five in the afternoon, and he was yet to show his face.

"Oh boy, I know that face."

"There's no face, Zoe."

"Uh, yes there is. That face there means, I am going to kill him."

I groaned because she was right. I really did want to kill him. The list of reasons was getting longer and longer, and if he continued behaving like this, I was going to need a longer paper and more pens to write them all down.

Zoe leaned on the table, getting closer to me.

"Look," she whispered. "These guys, they're tough. But they're also good. When we lost our homes back in Las Vegas, they made sure that all of us had a new place to sleep, that every single child had enough money to go to school. They might not show it in a proper way, but they care. They really do."

"I still want to strangle him," I growled.

"I get it. It's not the same situation, but I want to kill my brother at least three times in a day, and that's if I'm lucky. The point is, they suck at showing emotions. They think that everyone needs to adhere to what they say, and sometimes they forget to communicate things properly."

She had a point, and wasn't that how I behaved as well? I tried to push people away while trying to save them. I never told Ava the full truth of what was happening because I had been trying to protect her, but now that I was in a very similar situation, I hated it.

Atlas mentioned that it wasn't safe for me out there, and it bugged me that I didn't know what exactly he meant by that. I knew there were people that wanted to see me dead, but something in the way he spoke about it made me rethink everything I ever knew.

Was there something going on out there I wasn't aware of?

"Just give him some time," she advised. "He's

been looking for you all these years. He never gave up, and at one point, I honestly thought he was going to go crazy."

I hated the fluttering in my chest, but I also loved hearing this.

I was always self-sufficient, never needing anybody else. Even after the disaster with Kieran, I managed to survive it. Maybe it was the tragedy that struck shortly after, but I survived. I just had a feeling that I wouldn't survive Storm.

How could I when my whole body sang when he was near me?

"I was supposed to meet him," I whispered. "But I was detained."

It was hard talking about the time I would rather forget, but something about her made me want to open up and talk about things. I'm sure that there was a therapist somewhere nodding his head.

I always knew that there was something profoundly wrong with me, I just never had time to really think about it. Maybe if I managed to get out of this life one day, I would even pay a visit to one of them. Not that I could tell them about the techniques they taught me about back in Siberia, or the slaughter I inflicted upon that family in Belgrade, but I could mask it up.

"I'm sorry, Ophelia." She surprised me with her words. "I'm sorry about everything that has happened to you."

"You don't even know—"

"No, I don't know about everything, but I know enough. I know that you had been thrown into this world of violence when you were still just a child."

"I was seventeen," I gritted out.

"As I said," she smiled, "you were still just a child. I can't even imagine the horrors you witnessed, or the ones you did. But something tells me that you aren't as bad as you think you are."

"I-I." I had no words.

"Broken things can get fixed, darling. Just remember that."

Broken.

Was that how I saw myself? Was I really broken?

I liked to think that I was strong, powerful, but sitting here with her, and finally talking made me realize that there was more to me than just the assassin side. Maybe after I get Maya out, I would be able to finally live in peace, if such a thing really existed.

"Thank you," I croaked. "I don't even know you, but you made me feel better."

"Oh, boo. You're welcome. I think you deserve to have a friend, and I would like to volunteer."

Did I need another friend? What if I failed her as well?

Shadows followed me everywhere I went, and I didn't want to taint her with the darkness seeping from my soul.

"And before you try to give me some bullshit excuse about violence, or some sappy story about you being a threat to me, I am going to stop you." Was she reading my mind? "I grew up surrounded by it. Just because I didn't follow in the same footsteps you did, doesn't mean that I can't hold my own. I can fight. I can defend myself, and whatever you're thinking right there, you need to stop. I'm a big girl that can take care of herself."

Well then.

"I have a bad track record of keeping the people around me alive." And I did.

How many people I cared about had already died? First Ava, then the guys I befriended while I was staying with the Albanians. I killed Kieran, Maya was God knows where, and the last thing I wanted was to throw Zoe under the bus just because she hung around me.

"I don't wanna hear it, Phee. We are going to be friends, and that's final."

"For such a small thing, you sure are scary."

The angry scowl on her face only made me laugh, even though I was pretty sure that she expected quite the opposite. I had no doubt that she could fight. If her brother was one of the Sons of Hades, he probably made sure that she would be able to defend herself. It still didn't sit well with me, but I was going to try.

"Okay," I agreed.

"Okay?"

"Yeah." I laughed at the elated smile that spread across her face. "We can definitely be friends."

"Gods, I feel like I just ran a marathon, trying to get you to agree to this. I was about to whip out my puppy face and beg you for it."

"Puppy face?" I asked with a scowl.

"Oh. My. God." What the fuck did I do now? "You don't know about the puppy face?"

"In case you haven't noticed, I only have one face and that's the I-am-about-to-murder-you face."

"We are so going to practice right now. I don't care. You're going to learn how to make a puppy face."

"But... I—"

"Nope," she interrupted. "She doesn't know about the puppy face," she murmured to herself and then looked back at me. "How did you survive this long?"

"Erm, knives?"

That sent her into another fit of laughter, and for some inexplicable reason, I followed along.

SEVEN

Ophelia

I SPENT THE rest of the day with Zoe, listening to stories about her childhood, and the little shenanigans Indigo and she would get into while growing up with the club. Turns out that their family used to be a part of it for more than thirty years, and both of them are basically a legacy. It surprised me how easy the conversation with her was.

There was no judgment, no prejudice about who I was and what I did. I didn't elaborate on all the things I did, and she didn't ask either. I didn't even realize how much I missed talking with somebody who was my age and who understood this world better than some random person on the street.

Her smiles were genuine, her words truthful, and during the time I spent with her, I almost forgot about everything else. I would usually be angry about losing focus of what I had to do, but today it was a welcome reprieve from the usual fuckery swimming in my head. My past didn't rear its ugly head, and for the first time in forever, my future didn't seem so bleak.

I was right when I saw those pictures. All these people were one big family here, and even if they didn't like every single person, they protected each other. They cared for each other, and I yearned for it. I wanted to be accepted somewhere. I wanted to belong. Wasn't it messed up that the one place I thought I might be, would be the place I was warned about my entire life?

Atlas disappeared an hour after Zoe sat with me, along with Indigo and a couple of other guys. She noticed me looking for them and explained that they had some sort of a meeting. That deep-rooted ache for Storm only seemed to expand as the day went by, but I didn't want to think about it.

At least I didn't have any other episodes like the one yesterday. I tried not to think about Kieran either, or the devastation on Cillian's face. I thought I would be happier now that the deed was done, but I felt... nothing. One big nothing.

Zoe kept me preoccupied, introducing me to other people, their families, small children, but even she could see that the easy-going persona I was trying to portray was nothing but an illusion. I was good at those. I was good at putting on a mask when I needed it, and today was the day for those.

These people weren't guilty of putting me here. They also didn't deserve my wrath or my scowling face when they welcomed me with open arms and warm smiles. Nobody mentioned my history, even though I could sense that all of them knew who I was.

And I was grateful for it.

Even if it were just for one day, I could pretend that everything I did in the past was nothing more than a nightmare I couldn't escape from. I could pretend I was a regular girl, at a regular barbeque, meeting new people. Hell, I went as far as to talk with some of them.

The older couple Zoe pointed at before was part of the club almost since the very beginning. He used to be an enforcer in the early days, and some of the stories he shared were too good to pass up.

The sun was slowly settling down, and everybody seemed to trickle inside. I was confused by the sudden change until Zoe came back to me, explaining what was happening.

"They're getting ready for the ride."

"The ride?" And then I remembered what she said during one of her cute rambling speeches. They went for a ride through Santa Monica.

"Is everybody going?"

"Yeah, most of the people are. Some have their own bikes, some are gonna catch a ride with one of the guys."

My usual response would be to retreat to my room, but for some reason my mind drifted to Storm. Suddenly, I wanted to be a part of it. I wanted to feel that cool air on my cheeks, to hold on to him as we rode into the sunset. But he was nowhere to be found.

"He's inside, with the other guys." The girl was a mind reader.

I got up and crossed the backyard, entering the mostly empty house. I rounded the corner, straight to the area where the bar was located, and there he was.

My breath hitched at the sight of his broad shoulders and the tattoos that span across his body. I had tried memorizing each curve, each muscle and the ink that decorated his body when he stripped down last night. He was sitting down in one of the chairs, surrounded by a few other guys, with Atlas and Indigo on each side.

What I fucking hated though was a girl that approached him from behind, placing her hands over his chest. My ears started buzzing, and I hated feeling like this. I hated the painful spear that went through my chest, or the jealousy that burned in my veins. I never wanted to feel like I did when I found Kieran with Cynthia, and while Storm didn't seem to pay attention to the girl, he also didn't push her away.

Somebody called my name, but I was already in the middle of the room, marching toward them. Atlas saw me first, and whatever he saw on my face made him jump up toward Storm—no, toward the girl that placed her hands on him. Storm lifted his head, saw me and as if the realization dawned on him, he moved himself up, shielding the girl from me.

Atlas pulled her back, right behind him, but I wasn't seeing him anymore. I was seeing her hands on Storm, and I wanted her gone. I would remember this moment later on as something that I shouldn't have done, but right now, all my insecurities coiled within and they exploded. They wanted to see her bleed, because I wasn't going to go through the same shit as I did with Kieran.

"Ophelia." Storm stopped right in front of me, placing his hands on my shoulders. "Stop it."

"Get your hands off of me, Storm." I was furious. Furious because he allowed her to place her hands on him when only a few hours ago, he spent the night in bed with me. Was this how this story would go?

He would whisper sweet nothings to me, and every time I turned my back, some other girl would touch what was mine.

I was possessive, sue me. Red, hot pangs of jealousy sent a surge of adrenaline through my body, and I didn't need my knives or a gun to kill her on the spot. What pissed me off even more was the knowing smirk on his face. The motherfucker knew why I was behaving like this.

"Are you jealous, Sunshine?"

"Fuck off, Storm."

Somewhere around us an "oh, shit" sounded, but my sole focus was on getting to her. I didn't even realize what was happening, but I was suddenly airborne, clutching onto his shoulders as he started walking toward the staircase.

That little, jealous bitch inside of me started dancing around, because here, in his arms, this was my happy place. He was taking me away from the person I wanted to strangle, but I suddenly didn't mind.

My skin buzzed from anticipation, from excitement. I spent the whole day thinking about him, about what had happened last night, and now that we were here, I almost started singing.

And if that made me psychotic, so fucking be it. Normal was overrated, and if he could silence the buzzing in my ears and keep the ghosts at bay, I would take it.

I would take this sweet oblivion over the misery I started slipping into.

He didn't say a word as he carried me upstairs, and I could feel the anger rolling off of him like a tidal wave. It could've suffocated me, but it didn't. It didn't because I knew why he was angry. I was the reason, but I was also the cure.

This possessive alpha male wanted me, and fuck me, but I wanted him as well.

I couldn't tell him that. I couldn't tell him that my skin buzzed with energy every time he was near.

I couldn't tell him that his touch did what not

88

even Kieran's had. It made me feel alive. It made me feel like I belonged somewhere, and I never belonged. I was an outcast, always on the side. Even when they wanted to include me, they couldn't, because the fear was always stronger than their good intentions.

So, they stopped trying.

My father.

My mother.

Both of them pretended I wasn't there. I was screaming, I was drowning, but they didn't care. My mother was too concerned about her drugs, and my father... well, he made a monster he couldn't live with.

So, I accepted it. I moved on. But the way Storm made me feel, it was something I never felt.

It felt like home, and it was terrifying.

It was terrifying because it was raw. This connection, this attraction I felt for him, I wanted to hit him, run away, but I also wanted to stay. And I couldn't stay.

I couldn't give my heart to another man. There were too many scars there, and I feared that the next one would be the one to send me to an early grave.

But my body, I could give him that. I could give him every piece of me, and he could call me his, but he could never own what was inside. I didn't want it. I didn't want history repeating itself. They always found a way to betray me.

So, this is what we had. The physical connection he could get out of me, but nothing less, nothing more.

"You're quiet," he said, pulling me back from my thoughts.

I dared to lift my hand and trace the path from his temple to his lips. He was such a beautiful man.

The way his eyes sparkled every time he looked at me, the way his lips pulled into a smile when he was around me, it did something to me.

But whatever I touched got destroyed. Lives, love, the only thing I was good at was death. And I didn't want to destroy him.

"Just thinking." Just thinking how this man could've been perfect for me, but not now. Maybe if my demons weren't singing fucking Hallelujah in my ear. Maybe if I wasn't falling apart because everything was catching up with me.

Wishful thinking, that's what I'd been doing.

Just another fairy tale I was creating in my mind. Another "what if", but it would never become reality. My reality was a bitter bitch, and perfect things never happened to me. I was alone in this world, and no matter how much I wanted to trust him, I couldn't.

He opened the door with his elbow, pushing through, with me still in his arms.

I wanted to run again. I wanted to hide from him, because when those green orbs looked at me, I had a feeling that he could see right inside my soul. And it was dark there. It was where all the fucked-up things I ever did hid away from the rest of the world. It was where my darkest secrets resided and where they boiled until I couldn't control them anymore. Like I couldn't control my mind now. It was where the ghosts waited in the darkest corners for the perfect moment to strike.

And he couldn't know. He couldn't love a monster. Even if he could handle it, he couldn't know because love is a weakness. Relying on another person was a weakness. Emotions, all of them, they were the tool of destruction. I couldn't let him in.

I wouldn't let him in.

"Come back, Ophelia." I looked at him, and those inquisitive eyes bore into me, and I tried to lock it up. I had to lock it up, because he stripped me bare every time he looked at me.

I had to find a way to make it stop.

"I'm here," I said. "I'm not going anywhere."

"No, you definitely aren't." He stopped in the middle of the room, and I shook my legs, the boots dropping on the ground with a heavy thud. "You will never go anywhere, and if you pull the same shit you just pulled there, your ass will be so red, you won't be able to sit for a week."

"Don't tease me with a good time." I smirked at him, but the way he kept looking at me told me that he wasn't joking. Didn't he know that I loved pain?

I reveled in it because it was the only constant thing in my life.

Pain.

Grief.

Despair.

Three friends that followed me wherever I went.

The ticking in his jaw intensified, and in the next moment, he had me pressed against the wall, my chest against his, our lips mere inches from each other.

"You are a demon, Ophelia." He bit my jaw, and I closed my eyes as the tiny little ripples traveled down my spine, all the way to my lower stomach. "A beautiful demon. A goddess, and I want to consume you. I want to keep you here forever."

A brief kiss, and I crossed my ankles on his back, squeezing his waist. More, I needed so much more.

"If I touch your pussy, will you be wet for

me?" Oh God. "Or will I have to kiss every inch of you, fuck you with my tongue, so that you will be able to take me in."

This man wasn't wasting any time.

I opened my eyes, looking directly into his, and this insane need intensified. I wanted him to own me. I wanted to be his, and maybe for tonight, just for one night, I could pretend.

I was good at pretending. I was good at playing games, and this was just another one of them.

I put my legs down, and he caged me between his arms, the muscles rippling under the strain he was holding himself in with. Tattoos of various colors traveled across each of them, peeking beneath the shirt he wore. I wanted to lick every single one of them, trace them and see where they ended up. I shimmied out of the sweatpants, I had put on earlier, the material pooling at my legs, and stepped out, waiting to see what he would do next.

His eyes traveled from my head to my chest, over my stomach, stopping at my thighs. He placed his forehead on mine, eyes closed, breathing faster than before, swallowing hard. I felt the same.

I felt the burning need inside, and I wanted him to take me. I needed to feel him inside. Tonight, I would allow myself to feel.

Tonight, I would allow him to see me, the real me. The one no one else had seen for years. Tonight, I wouldn't be paralyzed. And maybe, just maybe, we could do this again.

This game, where he got to see me, and I could be me.

Then I could go back to pretending. I could go back to yet another day and live through it. Just exist.

"Storm," I begged, my voice tiny. "Please.

Please touch me."

Please make me forget. Make me forget everything. Just tonight. Just for one night, I want to be free. I want to feel like me. I want to feel normal.

Just a girl and a guy she likes. Just a girl getting what she wants without any consequences. I was tired of pretending. Tired of being strong. I wanted to break. Just for one night, I wanted him to take it all away. I wanted to feel good. Elated, fulfilled.

"I-I just," I stuttered. "I want to feel good. I want to feel good even if it's only for one night. Please, make me feel good."

His nostrils expanded as he took a hold of my head, his nose touching mine. The smell of alcohol, our sweat, and the intoxicating scent of leather was pulling me under. It was all Storm.

"This isn't only for tonight." He kissed my forehead, lingering there for a second. "This is for forever."

My heart almost jumped out of my chest. If only that were possible. If only he could have me forever. If only I could hold him forever, two of us, like this. A perfect picture. But I was betrayed once before by the person that promised me his forever. Who's to say that Storm wouldn't do the same?

I wanted to hold on to him, to his words, to cling to his touch, but I couldn't. I didn't trust him. He knew how to pack those pretty little words and call me his, but the moment I wasn't looking, some other girl had her hands all over him. Call me childish or insecure, but I wasn't going to go through the same pain again.

I didn't want to correct him, but the filthy claws of reality were slowly scratching against my skin. I shook them off and welcomed back the illusion we were creating.

One tiny little lie, one night, and then I could get away and forget about him.

He took the shirt I wore, lifting it up over my chest, and I lifted my arms, letting him undress me. Letting him take care of me. I was strong, but I wanted to fall apart.

I wanted to have somebody there waiting for me. Someone to catch me. Someone to save me from myself, even if I didn't want to believe that it was possible.

I was already dripping, my pussy clenching involuntarily. I needed to feel him inside.

"Naked," I said as soon as he dropped my shirt. "Now, Storm."

He smiled, the sweet smile I didn't deserve, but I could pretend that I did. He took a hold of the hem of his shirt and pulled it over his head, exposing his chest to me. The tattoo of a skull glared at me, taking over his whole torso. Little piercing buds on his nipples were gleaming under the light, and before he could do anything else, I lowered my head, flicking my tongue over the left one.

"Fuck," he groaned, fisting my hair. I pulled the cold metal between my teeth, feeling the rumble in his chest. A heady feeling of power came over me, and I repeated the same over the right one.

Like a blur of events, his pants were on the floor, and he was kneeling in front of me, spreading my legs. My back hit the wall with a thud, and as he latched onto my bare pussy, I entangled my hands in his hair, pulling at the dark strands.

"Holy shit!" I screamed when he latched onto my clit and lifted my legs onto his shoulders. The little hum came from him as he feasted on me was heaven sent. My legs started shaking as he moved from my clit to my opening, and before I could gather my wits, a finger entered me, and then a second one, while his tongue circled around that bundle of nerves.

"Storm!" I shook on top of him, afraid I would fall. "Storm, I can't... Oh my fucking God! I'm going to—" A third finger joined the other two, stretching me, pain and pleasure mixing in one. "Holy fucking shit!"

He fucked me with his fingers, latching onto my clit with his mouth, holding me with his other hand.

"I can't," I started shaking my head. "Fuck, fuck, fuck, holy mother of Jesus!"

It was like an avalanche, spreading from my lower tummy, going higher and higher, until the dam broke down, almost knocking me to the floor. I felt like I was floating in the air.

The sweetest oblivion, the escape, nothing else was on my mind. I could see nothing, feel nothing but him between my legs.

He didn't give me time to recover before he stood up, lifting me at the same time. His lips connected with mine, the taste of me mixed with the heady scent of him. I was drowning, falling, and I didn't want to stop.

I didn't want him to stop.

He took a step back, stroking his dick, and when I dropped my eyes, the piercings on his nipples weren't the only ones catching light and making my heart beat faster.

Holy fuck.

His dick was beautiful, if there ever was such a thing. The two studs on its head, the reverse Prince Albert, made me swallow harder. He smirked seeing where my eyes went and came closer.

"Did it hurt?" I asked him as he kept his

ministrations, the sweat gathering on his forehead.

"A little bit, but it was worth it." I bet it fucking was. "Are you ready, Persephone?"

I was fucking born ready. But I didn't manage to tell him that, because he picked me up like I weighed nothing, and entered me swiftly, knocking the breath out of me.

I was full. So fucking full. His dick kept stretching me even as he stood still.

"Holy motherfucking..." I had no words. No words, but as he started moving, my eyes rolled to the back of my head. As he hit that little spot inside that made me quiver, I held on to his shoulders.

What started slow, quickly turned into an animalistic fucking, the only sounds in the room the slapping of our skin together, and the grunts and moans from us.

"You feel so good," he muttered in my neck as he held close, while pounding into me. "So fucking good, I never want this to stop."

I couldn't speak, I could only feel.

Him.

Me.

Us.

My back was going to be purple tomorrow from the force with which he was driving into me, but I didn't fucking care. This felt like everything I ever wanted.

This crazy man, this was what made me feel free.

He pinched my clit with one hand, while the other one sneaked behind my neck, into my hair. The painful pull of his hand and I showed my neck to him. He bit in, kissed, tasted me, and repeated it on the other side.

Sucking, kissing, all the while he kept pounding into me with relentless pace. And it increased, and it went higher, and fucking higher, until I couldn't feel anything else but him.

He was everywhere.

Inside, on my skin, in my head. He kept invading my thoughts. His eyes caught mine speaking what words failed to say. I couldn't look away, couldn't shake off the burning desire mixing with mine.

I was lost to him, never wanting to be found. As he started pushing faster, going harder, I started falling.

Down.

Down.

Down.

My pussy clenched against him and a scream tore out of my mouth. He groaned, his teeth latching onto my shoulder.

Pain and pleasure.

More, and more and more. Higher, better.

I didn't know where he started and where I ended. I couldn't breathe. My heart was racing in my chest, and as he pulled back, his dick still inside of me, he hugged me to him, and started walking toward the bed.

With every move he made, it sent little rivulets of pleasure through my body. My climax extended with his movements.

He sat down, holding me to him and moved to the pillows. I felt tired, so fucking tired, but instead of moving away, I snuggled closer. His cum was leaking out of me. My hair looked like a destroyed birds' nest, but I didn't give a fuck.

This feeling of happiness, or whatever this was, I didn't want it to end. Tonight, tomorrow, fifty years from now, I wanted him to hold me like this. But as fast as it came, this sated, calm feeling started evaporating and I realized what I'd done.

What we'd done.

This wasn't supposed to happen. I was supposed to steer clear of him, not jump his bones at the first opportunity that presented itself. Jesus, fuck, I was a mess. My heart was still in pieces from the last person I thought I loved, and Storm could destroy me inside and out.

Loving him would devastate me, and I couldn't let that happen.

EIGHT

I FELT IT the moment it happened—the stiffening of her body, the shallow breathing, as if she was preparing herself for the words I knew would pierce straight through my chest. I couldn't regret what we just did, even though I knew it was a mistake as soon as we both started cooling down. She was nowhere near ready for what I wanted from her, and I didn't want to have her for only one night.

Ophelia was a woman you wanted to love forever. Kieran let her go, but I wasn't going to make the same mistake.

I wasn't lying when I said that I was never going to let her go. I just had to make her see what was right in front of her. I had to make her believe that there was something more outside of this fucked-up world. And if that meant waiting for years for her to come around, then so be it.

"Don't say it," I started in a gravelly voice. Whatever she was going to say would hurt more than anything else I endured so far. This woman could bring me to my knees, and I wasn't ashamed to admit that. I was too old to play games of tug-of-war with her, and if we were going to do this, we were going to take it slow.

"S-Storm."

"No, I don't wanna hear it. Just… don't. Please," I whispered. I could handle just about everything, but if she said that this was a mistake… No, just no.

The rumble of the motorcycles could be heard from outside, and I knew it could help her to see we weren't keeping her completely shackled. I wanted her to be my equal, but she also had to earn that place.

"Come on." I moved her to the side, hissing as my dick slipped out from her heat. I was still semi-hard, and if it were up to me, we wouldn't be leaving this room. But she wasn't fucking ready for everything I wanted to do to her. I was too rough right now, and with a flickering gaze, I tried looking for new bruises forming on her.

There were already red marks on her hips, from where I held her. I loved seeing my marks on her, but not when her skin was already marred by scars and bruises from somebody that never really deserved her.

But do you?

Maybe I didn't. Maybe I would never deserve her, but that didn't mean I would stop trying. I just hated the look on her face, filled with regrets, filled with anxiety from what we just did. I fucking hated that she looked at me as if I were a stranger, even though I virtually was one.

I hated that we lost years we could've spent together. Years where she could've been treated how she really deserved to be treated. And it still fucking infuriated me that she never came back to me. She must have known who I was, and even if she didn't, this was Ophelia we were talking about.

She saw our insignia; she could've found me.

"Why did you never come back?" I asked just before she could get off the bed. The fire and passion that was burning through her just five minutes ago was now completely gone, replaced with the look of indifference. Her shoulders stiffened, her lower lip trembled, and I wasn't sure if she wanted to cry or if she wanted to scream.

Maybe both?

"I don't wanna talk about it."

I was getting irritated with this cold demeanor she was throwing my way every single time she wanted to avoid the subject at hand.

I almost growled at her. "Well is there anything you do want to talk about?"

"As a matter of fact, there is." She was getting angry. Her right eyebrow arched, her back straightened, and as she got up to stand in front of me, in all her naked glory, I almost forgot what we were talking about. "I need you to let me go. I need to get out of here, Storm."

"Not a chance," I gritted. "You're staying right here, where I can see you."

"You're unbelievable." She scoffed and marched past me. But I wasn't going to let this end up this way. She had to talk to me. I had to know what was happening behind those blue eyes.

I grabbed her arm just before she could enter the bathroom, turning her back to me. Her defiant eyes stared into mine, and I wanted to strangle her and kiss her at the same time. This woman was going to be the death of me, and if I were being completely honest, I wouldn't mind dying if she was by my side.

"I told you already." I smiled, grazing her lower lip with my thumb. "I am never letting you go. And if you don't wanna talk right now, fine, don't talk, but you are staying right here."

"You can't keep me here like some kind of animal!" she thundered. "I don't wanna be here!"

Her voice echoed around the room, and this is exactly what I wanted to have. I would take her anger every day over the cold indifference she was throwing my way. I would rather burn in her agony, than bask in her frosty lack of interest.

My eyes landed again on the mark on her shoulder where he burned her. I almost wanted to carve that patch of skin, just so that I wouldn't have to look at it anymore. That snake was taunting me, and it was haunting her. Did she still love him?

I could try to make her see what we could have, but I couldn't compete against a ghost, and that's exactly what Kieran was.

He was a ghost lingering in the air around us, and no matter how hard I tried, she had to be the one that was going to come to me, not the other way around. I wanted her more than anything else, but I wasn't going to have her if she wasn't willing to give me her body and her soul. This relationship wasn't going to host three people, and I'd be damned if I allowed myself to sink down to the bottom and share her with the ghost of a man that did nothing but hurt her.

"You know what, Ophelia?" I almost wanted to snicker at the narrowing of her eyes and the flat line her lips were forming. "You can scream as much as you want to."

"Bu—"

"You can fucking shout, and pout and be unhappy." I leaned down, inches from her lips when her breathing hitched, her chest pressed against mine. "I couldn't care less. If you want to cry over him, go ahead and cry. But don't for a second think that you are ever getting away from me."

Her eyes widened, roaming over my face. God, what I wouldn't give just to have her look at me like I was her entire world.

"I will help you find your sister, and after that..." I trailed off.

"After that, what?"

My chest tightened at the mere thought, but she had to know that I wasn't the enemy here. "After that, you can do whatever the fuck you want."

I let her go, turning toward the wardrobe.

"Storm—"

"This conversation is over, Ophelia. Go and take a shower. I will bring the clothes inside for you."

I could hear her footsteps behind me. Her presence felt both like fire and balm right now, and I didn't know if I wanted to stay in this room with her or just disappear. I understood she needed time, but God, it hurt like a bitch, pining over her like a fool.

I stiffened when she splayed her arm over my lower back, tracing the invisible line toward my neck. My whole body was strung tight from the mere proximity of her, and her touch evoked something I didn't want to think about, but I also didn't want to stop her.

There was a softness in that touch, a small caress, exploration, and it would've been so easy to walk away from her if it wasn't for this crazy connection we had. I knew she felt it. I wasn't imagining things, but I also knew she was scared. She wasn't scared of me or who I was, but I had a feeling that the organ she protected inside her chest, got broken way too many times for her to let me in.

Another step forward, and her second hand joined the first, going over the muscles on my trapezius, over my deltoids and back to my neck. I wanted to turn around and touch her as well, but the way she explored my body made me stop. She trickled the hair at the back of my neck, sending shivers all over my body.

She pressed her forehead between my shoulder blades and wrapped her arms around my waist. This wasn't what I expected from her, especially after that screaming match, but I wasn't going to complain.

Baby fucking steps, and all that shit. I had to earn her trust before she could relax with me, but I couldn't do that until I fixed the mess I threw us into. It ate at me, at my soul, and I just hoped she would be willing to listen once I told her what I had to do.

But having her here with me was more important than Las Vegas. It was more important than the entire world.

I placed my hands over hers, right above my navel, waiting for her to say something. But sometimes words weren't needed to understand what the other person was feeling. Words weren't something I have mastered over the years, and more often than not, I could come across as a complete and utter asshole, even toward those I cherished the most.

She flattened herself against my back, and it was as if she wrapped us in a bubble, where only she and I existed. Where nothing from the outside world could reach us, and where everything we ever wanted was just here. In this bubble, she wasn't the daughter of a man who didn't deserve to live, and I wasn't a liar who was going to break her heart.

"Sunshine," I murmured, turning my head to the side, trying to catch her eyes. "We really need to go. They're waiting for us."

"Just a moment." She sighed. "Please, just let me have this moment."

So I did. I would let her have as many moments as she wanted, as long as she let me have them with her. As long as she finally recognized that what was happening between the two of us wasn't something she could avoid.

* * *

IF LOOKS COULD kill, I would be a dead man right now. As soon as we got out of the house, Indigo intercepted us, and without a word, stormed back toward his bike, turning his back on me. The scowl on his face would be enough to even send Grinch packing, but right now I couldn't be bothered.

The sun was already setting down, casting red and orange hues, mixed with the dark blue of the sky, over the horizon. My brothers, by far more than blood, openly stared at the two of us as we walked toward my bike, while the rest of the entourage tried to be a little bit more discreet about it.

Atlas was smirking from behind Indigo, amused by the aggravated look on our vice president's face. We should've been at the beach by now, but I didn't have to answer to any of them what I was doing.

The moment Ophelia and myself shared earlier passed as soon as it came, and before I could even turn around, she locked herself inside the bathroom, leaving me in the middle of the room with more questions than answers. She was fighting this, whatever this was between us.

I loathed the distance she was trying to put between us. Even now, as we walked toward the line, she decided to walk as far away as possible from me, not even sparing me a glance. I've tried catching her eye multiple times since she emerged from the shower, but avoidance was obviously her best friend right now, and the girl I held against that wall, while my dick slid in and out of her warm heat, was nowhere to be found.

If she was trying to rile me up, this was the perfect way to do it. Or well, at least I thought so.

I approached my Harley Davidson, sliding my hand over the cool black metal, as she decided to fuck this day even further and walked away from me. Instead of taking the seat behind me, Ophelia sauntered toward Atlas, and slid behind him, as if I wasn't standing there.

My enforcer, one of my best friends, looked like he wanted to flee while I seethed, looking at where she placed her hands. She hugged him around the waist, leaning against him, completely ignoring the fact that I was five minutes from blowing a gasket.

"Storm." Indigo interrupted me before I could saunter toward her, haul her ass up and place her on my bike. "We need to go."

Fucking fuck.

I clenched and unclenched my hands, trying to calm my racing heart and the buzzing in my ears. I wanted to show her the freedom you could feel while riding on the bike, and I wanted her hands on me, not on Atlas.

The man in question looked between me and Indigo with an apologetic look on his face. While the sane part of me knew that nothing was going on between the two of them, the other part, the animalistic part that recognized her as mine, wanted to tear him off his bike and take her back to the house, just so I could show her who she truly belonged to.

But I wasn't going to make a scene. Our lives were already filled with violence and adding more on top wasn't going to solve the problem. She wanted to play this game? Fine, we could play the game.

"Meredith!" I called out to one of the girls that usually worked at the bar. She was already seated behind Carlos, one of our prospects, but if Ophelia wanted to fuck with my head in this way, I was going to fuck with hers.

Meredith was a friend, one of the first I made when I came to the club, and while nothing ever happened between us, my little spitfire who wanted to drive me crazy, didn't know that.

Meredith looked at me over Carlos's shoulder as if I grew two heads. Maybe I did. Maybe I was playing with fire, but two could play this childish game.

"You're riding on my bike today," I said louder than necessary, but enough for everyone to hear. The murmur of voices echoed around us, and I knew that each and every one of them knew who Ophelia was. There were rarely any secrets between us, and my crusade to find her all of these years was not exactly a quiet one.

My good friend got off of the bike and walked toward me, scowling the whole time. By the end of this day, I would have two women angry at me, but I didn't give a fuck right now. It was either this or resorting to violent urges I had coursing through my veins, and I chose the lesser evil.

"Are you trying to get me killed, Storm?"

Meredith gritted through her teeth as soon as she stepped in front of me. "I like my head just where it is. On my shoulders."

I looked at her and then back to where Ophelia sat, and grinned like a fool at the disdain on her face. She didn't like this? Well, neither did I, but there was nothing we could do about it right now.

"Just play along, Mer." I smiled at her. "And trust me, your head will stay where it is."

"Easy for you to say. I don't have a dick Ophelia Aster is crazy about, and I don't want to have her plotting my untimely demise just because you guys don't know how to act like two rational adults."

"Mer." I inched closer to her. "Not now. I need you to get on my bike and smile while you're at it."

"Honey, listen." She placed her hand on my arm, and Ophelia scowled harder, gripping the leather jacket Atlas wore. "I love you like a brother, but I don't want to get between the two of you. She seems like a cool chick, and the last thing I want to have is her knife against my throat one of these mornings. I'll ride with you but fix this shit."

Easier fucking said than done.

I tried to ignore the burning heat at the back of my neck as I straddled my bike, waiting for Mer to climb on behind me. She hugged my middle, trying to keep as much distance as possible between her front and my back, but even if she did press herself against me, it wouldn't matter when the only woman I wanted to have here decided to ride with somebody else.

I turned on the ignition, ignoring the burning in my gut, letting the vibrations of the bike calm my racing heart. It never got old, this feeling of freedom. Even after almost twenty years, I still felt like that fourteen-year-old kid that got to sit on a bike for the first time.

I could hear the rest of the bikes turning on, sending an angry growl into the air, announcing our presence. The Sons of Hades were a force to be reckoned with, and I felt proud, knowing that they were mine.

My family, my people, I just had to show Ophelia everything she could gain by staying here.

We took off down the street, heading for the main road, passing the houses that were quietly nestled close to our club. They all knew what went on there, but they steered clear from us, and we tried to protect them in the best way that we could. We were all aware that they feared us, but I wasn't going to try and change who we were just to appease other people.

We were unapologetically the hell they never wanted to step into, and I was fine with keeping us separate from the rest of them.

Meredith gripped my waist tighter as we sped down the highway, heading toward the beach for the bonfire. For a moment, I allowed myself to forget about the dirty past and the shaky future. The wind hit me from all the sides, caressing my skin, playing with my hair, and I reveled in the feeling.

This wasn't something you could buy or fake. You either loved this life or you detested it, there was no middle ground. Maybe it was because I didn't know better — what with being brought up in an environment far harsher than the one I was living in now — but I wouldn't change it.

I would rather have this freedom, than the lie coating my life. They were all going to pay for the shit they threw us into.

Every single one of them.

110

NINE

Ophelia

I MADE A lot of mistakes in the twenty-four years of my life. Major, fucked-up mistakes that I couldn't get back from. But as soon as my butt touched the seat of Atlas's bike, I knew this might be the biggest one.

Listen, I needed some distance between us. What happened in his room... the sex, the mini shouting match, the need to touch him and show him I wasn't who they all thought I was, it was becoming too much. He was in everything–every single touch, every thought, every action. He was slowly consuming my soul, and I didn't like it.

I didn't want it, especially right now.

I didn't want another person that could betray me, forget about me, and get on with his life as if I never even existed. Maybe I was a fool, but I wanted someone who could see me, the real me, and I still had no idea why he brought me here.

Atlas kept blabbering about my safety, and Storm refused to let me go out of here. In the last two days since they brought me here, I have felt more confused than ever in my life. And no matter the attraction between us, the chemistry, I still had to deal with the annoying buzzing in my ears, and the demons that haunted me for most of my life.

The sickness I was born with still lived inside of me. I had no idea what he wanted to do with me, but I didn't want to stay around to figure it out. I didn't want to, because I knew that once he showed me everything he had to offer, I would want to stay, and that couldn't happen.

There were kids here, families, people that depended on Storm, and my touch could only destroy things, not enjoy them. I wasn't worthy of these people, even if they were as violent as my own family. But they looked after each other, I could see that during the barbeque today. They felt relaxed, they talked about things other than the next mission and who had more assassinations under their belts.

They loved each other, and it was the kind of love I had never felt. The unconditional love that came from years and years of trust and living with each other. I wanted to believe that I could fit in here. I almost did when I talked to Zoe today, but one look at Storm, one slip of my mind, and it could all go to waste.

If my father found out where I was, he would be here in a second, uncaring for these people. I couldn't put them in harm's way.

I already took enough innocent lives, and I wouldn't be able to live with myself if they ended up on that list. This wasn't just another job in which I could turn off all my emotions and go through it as if nothing bothered me. Even as they drove, following Storm, they kept joking around, trying to outrun each other, trying to talk as they drove.

And Storm... Goddammit.

If I were four years younger, I would've embraced him and never let him go, because what

I saw in him was what I wanted to have in my life. I wasn't fooled by this calm demeanor they were portraying around me. I knew if there was a problem, they wouldn't stop until the threat was extinguished.

But I guess that was what kept me from trying to run away.

Battered and bruised, I knew I would still try to run to him. I would try to forget about the world just to get lost in those green eyes. And I couldn't.

Not anymore.

I was so lost in my thoughts that I didn't even realize we were driving closer to the ocean now. The saltiness in the air brought a different kind of peace to me, and I remembered all those years Ava and I spent on the beach in Croyford Bay. All those broken memories. Two unsuspecting kids, two fools that didn't know better.

If I had known what would happen a few years from then, I would've tried to get us out of there. I would've tried to be a better friend, a better sister, before it was too late.

The whole entourage started turning right, toward the parking area right next to the empty beach. Well, calling it parking is stretching it a bit, but I guess that it would do. The rumble of bikes that came with us all the way from the club quieted down as everyone turned their engines off, waiting for Storm to get up.

They behaved like a well-oiled machine, with every one of them knowing what they had to do. Some started unloading their bags from the bikes, carrying them toward the beach. Others brought drinks, taking them to the cooler somebody brought.

How in the fuck did they fit a cooler on a bike?

"I think it's time to get off, Ophelia," Atlas

started as I stared at the people around us. "I really don't want to lose any part of my body, and if Storm keeps scowling at me like he is right now, he is either going to pop a vein or kill me."

I looked to my left, right where Storm stood, ignoring everybody else. The girl that rode with him was nowhere to be found, and I hated the small sense of relief that coursed through my body at the notion. I hated seeing him with her, but I couldn't exactly kill every single girl he was with.

My own insecurities needed to fuck off right now.

Besides, he wasn't mine. He was never going to be mine.

It didn't matter what I wanted because I would never get it. It didn't matter that my heart broke every single time I looked at him, because I knew that he was the one. He was the fairy tale I so often dreamed about, but I was the nightmare.

I was a dark and vicious thing that could only destroy. So, no. I couldn't have him, even if all I ever wanted to do was to have him hold me and never let me go. Maybe it was the shock of what had happened with Kieran, but I knew better.

This crazy desire for him, it started long before the church. It started when I first laid my eyes on him. In a matter of minutes, he managed to erase Kieran from my mind and all the fucked-up shit that was going on in my life. If the world were ending, he would be the person I would want to spend my last moments with.

But my life wasn't a fairy tale, and the faster I got out of this funk I found myself in, the better it would be. This wasn't my family. These weren't my people.

This wasn't what destiny had planned for me.

I was determined to remove him from my

mind, because in a matter of two days, he managed to seep inside my bones. He was already nestled deep beneath my skin, and I just couldn't take another heartbreak.

So, what better way to avoid it than to pretend that you didn't have a heart at all.

I just had to go back to who I used to be. To the arctic cold that lulled me to sleep every night. To the loneliness that consumed more than my body. It consumed my soul. And I liked it that way. When you have nobody to depend on, you never get disappointed.

I marched toward the shore, ignoring Storm, ignoring Atlas calling my name. I ignored the curious faces and judging eyes. They could think whatever they wanted to. I was surprised nobody tried to stop me, since everyone seemed to obey everything Storm said, but they let me pass, parting like the Red Sea in front of Moses.

I had no idea how long we drove, but we were nowhere near the city. With the endless ocean in front of me, and the misery behind me, I sat my ass down on the sand and stared at the darkness in front. I needed a plan, and I needed it fast.

My body was unfortunately nowhere near ready for that, and I knew I had to heal before I could do anything else. As much as it pained me, Maya would have to wait a little bit longer. The condition I was in right now wouldn't help us. I wouldn't be able to get her back this way, and I had a feeling that I would need much more than my sheer will to get her back.

Wherever they sold her wasn't pretty. I heard enough stories about human trafficking, about sex slaves, to know that she wasn't just chilling somewhere in Los Cabos, waiting for me to come to her. I dreaded seeing her because she was a reminder of yet another failure of mine.

It was such a funny notion, but every single person I tried to save either died or lived a life filled with regrets. In the last four years, I couldn't allow myself to think about anything more but the next mission, the next target, the next person the Albanians wanted to see dead. And it helped, in a way.

At least I wasn't living with the constant reminder of everything I fucked up. But now, sitting here, surrounded with silence, I had to think. I hated being alone with my thoughts, and I guess that's why I allowed myself to fall in bed with Storm.

I loathed it. Every single time I allowed myself to think about everything I'd lost, the ghosts of my past decided to visit. And I didn't want to see them. I didn't want to see the faces of people I killed.

"Is this seat taken?"

I turned around only to see Nathan standing next to me. His face was a perfect mask of disinterest, but his anger could still be seen in his eyes. He didn't want to talk to me, which means that somebody else made him come here.

"Don't look for Storm," he interrupted before I could locate. "He didn't ask me to come here. I came of my own volition."

"Let me guess." I smirked. "This time you will try to drown me before anybody else can come to help me.

"We both know that you could kill me three times before any of these guys would be able to even blink." He sat down without waiting for my confirmation. "Besides, drowning you in shallow water is not exactly creative. I like to see at least a little bit of blood."

I looked at him and the serious expression on

117

his face, and couldn't help but laugh. The Nathan I remembered was an easy-going guy with stars in his eyes every time he looked at Ava. He didn't have a chip on his shoulder. Yeah, he severed some heads, killed some people, but I would like to meet a person in this industry that didn't do that.

But he used to look happy. Not so much anymore.

The scowl seemed to be permanently etched on his face now, and a part of me missed the time when we all had a better life. It wasn't perfect but it was better. In the middle of the madness that took place after Ava's death, I completely forgot about him, and I shouldn't have.

I should've found him, tried to explain what happened, because he needed closure just like I did.

"I hated you longer than I knew you, Ophelia." I almost flinched at his words. "I was coming home that night when three guys we worked with jumped in front of me. I thought it was just a silly test, that your father wanted to see if we were prepared for any situation, but I didn't expect them to try to kill me."

I couldn't even look at him. This was all my fault. My inability to take them away from there.

"When I realized that they weren't messing around, it was almost too late, but I managed to escape." He took a sip of a beer he brought with him and silently extended the second bottle to me. I didn't know what to do with my hands, so I took it, hoping it would calm down the nerves rocking through me. "I tried to call you, you know?" He opened the beer bottle with a bottle opener attached with his keys. "I tried to call Ava, but neither one of you responded."

The same pain I lived with on a daily basis was etched into his face. It hid deeper than you would

118

expect, and it wasn't always visible unless you knew where to look.

"I couldn't stay in Croyford Bay, knowing that they wanted me dead. I just didn't know why." I knew why. He messed up the carefully curated plan my father and Logan created. His only crime was love, but they wouldn't have been happy until they saw him dead.

"So, I ran. I packed whatever I could and ran away from Croyford Bay, thinking that you would be able to take care of Ava and our child." His voice broke on the last word, and my eyes misted at the emotion in his voice. "But then I heard she was dead." He cleared his throat, turning to me. "And you were the one that killed her."

"Nathan—"

"But now Storm tells me that isn't the truth, and I don't know what to think."

"I don't... I don't know what to tell you."

"How about the truth? She trusted you. She thought you could help us, and you—"

"I know what I did, Nathan. You don't have to rub the salt into the wound that won't heal. I didn't kill her, but I failed her."

"I don't know if I can trust you on that."

I understood he was skeptical over the whole thing—hell, I would be too—but I was getting tired of this fucking circle we were going around, where people always assumed the worst of me. Yeah, I know. I wasn't the best person. But fucking sue me. I did what I had to, to survive, to see the next day and to protect those I loved. Would I change the way I did some things? Maybe. But I wouldn't apologize for who I was and who I still am.

My own mind was already working against me, and I didn't need the constant reminders from the people around me of things I used to do.

You mean, the things you will do again?

Yes, the fucking things I would do again, and again, and again, until I got to my final goal. I wasn't the sweetheart in this story. I was the villain in all of their eyes, but I guess that it always felt better blaming another person than looking into the mirror.

I knew it because I hated looking in the mirror. I hated seeing the shell staring at me, and I hated remembering the bloody trails I left everywhere I went.

"Nothing I say now will change your mind," I murmured, finally realizing that I was fighting a battle I couldn't win. "Just like everyone else, you think the worst of me, and that's fine. But where were you, Nathan?" I looked at him. "Why weren't you there with her when she was killed? Why didn't you try to find a way to get you guys out of there, if you were so smart to get away?"

"No, that's not —"

"It must be so easy, sitting there, judging me, when you know that I wasn't the one that stabbed her in her stomach." He flinched at the picture I was painting. "Where the fuck were you when somebody decided to end her life and frame me for something I didn't do? Huh?"

"I was —"

"You weren't there!" I screamed. "But just like every other person in my life, you have the guts to blame me for something I didn't do. Well, Nathan, I couldn't save her. Drown me because I wasn't enough to save her from that life."

"Ophelia... I didn't —"

"I knew she was in danger the moment she told me she was involved with you. Did you think about that? Did you think about the shit you were pulling her into just by getting involved with her?"

120

"I-I didn't —"

"You didn't think!" I turned toward him completely. "You didn't think about the consequences, but you men never do, do you? You just take and take and take until there's nothing left of us. Until the only thing left behind is a shell, or in Ava's case, a body. Why didn't you save her, Nathan? You're blaming me, but you are as guilty as I am."

If he thought I was going to sit here and listen to him babble, listen to him trying to guilt me for her death, when he was as guilty as I was, he had another think coming. Man, every single time I thought that his gender couldn't disappoint me more, they proved me wrong.

I understood grief. I lived with it every single day, but I wasn't a weak little girl they could just throw around anymore. No, the Ophelia my father, my brother, all these men knew, she wasn't here anymore. The fucked-up shit I went through — holding Ava's guts on the floor, holding knives against the throats of kids that could've turned into adults that would try to kill me... I just wasn't a little girl anymore.

"I am sorry for what happened, Nathan, and I would change it if I could. But I can't, and neither can you. The only thing I can do is to find out who killed her and why, but that's all. I won't allow you to guilt trip me anymore." I stood up, brushing the sand off my pants. "And that shit back in the house..." I leaned down. "Next time you even think about touching me like that, it won't be Storm with his hands around your neck. It'll be my knife or my gun, and I won't let go. Trust me on that."

His eyes widened, stricken with guilt, with fear and anger, but he didn't answer back. Why would he when even after everything he knew, he still thought I was at fault?

"I don't want you here."

"And I don't wanna be here, you fucking idiot." I took another sip, angry at him and angry at myself. "I was brought here against my will. Did you really think I wanted to come here and play house with you guys when my sister is God knows where, probably being tortured and beaten?"

"Maya?"

"Ah, so you remember somebody else?"

"I do, but I—"

"You didn't think she was missing?" I chuckled. "Figures. You all thought that we had this beautiful life, filled with riches and love. You knew my father, Nathan. He wasn't a loving person. Hell, I'm surprised he didn't already come here to take my ass back home."

"You think he'll come here?"

"I don't know." I shrugged. "But I don't wanna be here when that happens. And the further away I am from here, the better it is for all of you. You don't want to have Nikolai Aster on your ass."

I threw the beer bottle to the ground, right next to him, and started walking away. I was fucking tired of this bullshit. I needed to find Storm and I needed to be gone from here. All these things were messing with my emotions. First Storm, now Nathan, or wait, they called him Creed now. Seeing these people enjoying life when I never had any of it was a recipe for disaster. All these things, all these people, they were threatening to shatter the carefully curated walls I'd built throughout the years.

"Ophelia," he called out after me. I turned around to see him get up and start walking toward me. He scowled, then flattened his expression before looking at me again. "Just don't fuck up

Storm."

"I'm not the one fucking up anything, darling. He wanted me here, now he'll have to see how I deal with shit I don't wanna have thrown my way."

I turned around when he grabbed my arm, pulling me back.

"He laid a claim on you."

"He what?" I swiveled so fast, I was about to have whiplash.

"He laid a claim on you which means that none of the other guys can even look at you. Don't fuck this up." With that, he let go of me, leaving me standing in the middle of the beach while everyone else started gathering around the bonfire.

He fucking laid a claim on me? What was this, the fifteenth century? Since when do we lay claims on people as if they were cattle? I already got branded by one motherfucker, now Storm wanted to hold me here as if I was Rapunzel in a tower.

I tried locating him in the sea of people, and when my eyes landed on the broad shoulders in the leather jacket and the dark hair messed by the wind, I knew where I needed to go.

TEN

Storm

WHEN I WAS a little kid, I wanted to be a Superman. I thought flying would be the best feeling ever, being free like a bird, and if I could be strong like him, nothing and nobody could ever hurt me. I learned the hard way that I could never be free, at least not after everything they did to me. The sickness they possessed spread across my skin, day after day, night after night, until the only thing left was a body.

My cage.

A vast space. No feelings, no pain, no love, and no sorrow. I shut it all down. Endless nights I'd spent crying, begging for someone to save me. Days that felt like years, with their hands on me, touching me, taking away pieces of my sanity. I would've closed my eyes, but they wanted me to watch.

They wanted me to see what my presence did to them. When I stroked their dicks, when I touched their cheeks, when they broke me piece by piece. They wanted me to see it all, to feel their insanity.

I thought that monsters had claws, sharp teeth, and red eyes that glowed in the dark, but I was wrong. Monsters lived inside of us. They didn't hide under the bed or in your closet. No, they resided in our chests, and they spread their tentacles throughout our bodies, like vine leaves, but you could never cut them down.

You can't kill poison with another poison.

I tried. I tried to kill it. I tried to run. I tried to fix what they broke, but I was too late. When my cries stopped, when my eyes adjusted to seeing the horrors every day, for years, that was when I knew that nobody would save me.

No one cared.

My chest felt so heavy, I sometimes thought it would cave in on itself, but it didn't. I was left to live this life, reliving it all each and every day. They didn't break my body, but they broke my mind. Behind the closed lids, I could still see their sinister smiles. I could still smell the cologne they wore.

I could still feel their hands on my shoulders, on my back. Like ghosts they still haunt me to this day, and I don't know how to escape them.

Or at least I didn't.

The day I met Ophelia, that was the first day they weren't screaming in my ear. When she touched me, instead of caving in, my chest expanded, my heart beat faster. I didn't feel filthy.

I didn't feel like an animal they made me out to be.

I learned how to survive, but I never learned how to live. At least not fully. I learned how to defend myself. I learned how to kill, how to torture. How to look a man in the eyes and kill him in cold blood.

But this, this feeling she evoked in me, this was foreign.

Alien.

I didn't know what to do with it; I just knew I

had to have her. And maybe, just maybe, the demons I saw in her eyes, maybe they would quiet with me. Maybe they would learn to coexist, and I could finally rest.

Maybe she could too. Her father was the cruelest man I have ever had a chance to meet. He was the Devil in disguise.

He could make you feel like you could trust him. He would make you drop your guard, and when you least expected it, he would strike. She grew up with him. She was trained by him. Those shadows, she wasn't born with them.

The things I've heard about her, she wasn't always like that. None of us were.

This fucked-up life made us who we were. Maybe it was destiny, maybe it was written in the stars for us, but whatever it was, neither one of us was born like this.

I wanted everything from her. Happiness, sadness, rage, pain, I wanted it all. I wanted to hold her close, so close that she would never want to leave.

But I also had to tell her the truth, and before I did that, I had to find out how to get out of the mess I got us all into.

From the corner of my eye, I could see Atlas heading my way, staring at the same spot I was looking at. The spot where Ophelia sat with Creed, talking with him more than she talked with me.

"Are you going to tell her?"

Wasn't that the million-dollar question nowadays? Was I going to tell her how much I fucked up? I was, I just didn't know how to broach the subject. I still had to call a doctor to look at her wounds, not to mention the fact that she seemed to be shaken more than I would've expected.

"Storm?"

"I will. Just not…" I paused. "Not right now, okay? I don't want to give her one more reason to leave."

"And you think lying to her is the way to build this relationship, or whatever this is?"

I looked at him, hating what he said, because he was right. This wasn't how I wanted to start with Ophelia, but it was the only way for now. Her fight-or-flight instincts were on an all-time high right now, and I had the feeling that even the smallest of things could set her off and make her run away.

The need to protect her right now, to keep her close to me, rode me hard, and I wasn't going to fight it. I would give her space, if that's what she wanted to have right now, but I wasn't letting her go. She wanted to save her sister? Okay, I could help. Hell, I would repeat my whole childhood if she were going to stay.

"You are fucking whipped, aren't you?" Atlas started again, and as much as I loved the guy, right now I didn't want to listen to him. "You can't stop staring at her."

"Get to the point, Atlas."

"I already did, you just chose to ignore me and stare at her. Listen," he placed his hand on my shoulder. "I remember you behaving like a lunatic while you were trying to find her, and if it's possible, I would like to avoid the same shit from happening again. She is wounded, fucked up, and if you really want this to become something that could last for years, you need to find those balls—"

"Hey," I interrupted, but the bastard just started chuckling.

"My point is, you can't expect her to trust us if you don't trust her."

Was that the problem? Did I not trust her?

I trusted that she wouldn't attack innocent people here just to get away, but I had to admit it — I didn't trust her not to do something reckless just to do what she thinks she needs to do. I have never met a person with a bigger savior complex than her. First that friend of hers she was with four years ago, now her sister. Who was going to be next?

And for all her fucked-up shit, I had a feeling that the last person she ever thought about was herself.

"Uh-oh," Atlas started when my eyes zeroed in on a very angry looking Ophelia, marching toward us. My first fucking thought should've been to run away because the murderous look she wore... No, I didn't want to be on the receiving end of that, even though I was absolutely going to be.

Atlas all but ran away from me, leaving me alone with her.

Her nostrils flared as she stopped in front of me, while the wind played with her hair, messing it up even more than it already was. Angry eyes connected with mine, while I was rooted in the spot, waiting for her to speak first. That scar on her cheek was messing with my head and raising my blood pressure. I had to stop myself from touching her right now.

Her body language told me that that was the last thing she wanted.

"Can we talk?" she asked through gritted teeth, crossing her arms on her chest. The leather jacket she took from me was four sizes too big, but goddammit, it looked good on her.

"Go ahead." I was still fucking pissed off about the little stunt she pulled back at the clubhouse. Riding on Atlas's bike, ignoring me after that shit in my room... No, I wasn't okay with that. She infuriated me, made me want to run to her

128

and run away from her. I both hated and reveled in the fact that she had the power to bring me to my knees. Those ocean eyes could be my undoing, and I didn't mind being here for the ride.

She narrowed her eyes, tracing her eyes over my jaw, stopping at my lips. Her own parted as if she remembered something, and as her teeth bit into her lower lip, I wanted us to be anywhere else but here. Back in my room, back in the clubhouse, just away from all these people and the curious stares they were throwing our way. Her eyebrows furrowed, creating a little V in the middle, and I wasn't sure if she hated what she was seeing, or if she too remembered what we did just a few hours ago.

Did she remember the way she melted in my arms, when the masks finally fell off and I could see what was beneath the tough exterior she wanted to portray to the rest of the world? It was insane how connected I felt toward her, and it went beyond the physical attraction and what her body could do to mine.

No, this was the carnal need, as if something inside of me said "mine." I never really stood a chance against her and the way her mere presence calmed down the tempest inside my chest. Right now, I wanted to inhale her unique scent mixed with my shampoo. I wanted to wrap my hands around her wild hair and bring her to me until our bodies collided and not one single inch separated us. I wanted a lot of things I couldn't have, but she was the one thing I wouldn't mind dying for.

Her trance and the way she looked me over finished faster than I was ready, and that dreamy look she sported mere seconds ago got replaced by a sneer and torment in her eyes. Retribution, revenge, it was written all over her pale skin, etched into the pores, and right now I was going to be the recipient of her wrath.

"Why the fuck am I here, Storm?"

"Because we usually come here after every single barbeque?" I couldn't help myself but rile her even more. Everything was better than the look of indifference she sent my way when she came out of the shower today.

I would take her anger over that cold look, every day. She wanted to hide? Fine, I could understand that. But I didn't want her to hide from me. I didn't want her to think that she had to be anything else than what she already was. Whoever made her believe that she had to put a mask on her face, they were wrong.

She was strong, but she was also vulnerable. Contrary to popular belief, she fucking cared about people. Maybe not all, but not everyone deserved to have someone like her to care about them. She was desperate to find her sister, but she wasn't in shape to get to that right now.

"You are fucking infuriating." She almost stomped her foot like a child. "The most egoistical, self-righteous, asshole."

Oh, I loved this game. The one where she pretended she didn't care about me, that she hated me and wanted to see me gone. I didn't need years to understand that she guarded her heart behind stone walls because she didn't want to get hurt. In retrospect, I was the same, but I wanted to give this a chance. I knew we could be amazing together.

"That hit to your head must have messed something up, Sunshine, because none of these nicknames are very creative." It was as if something in me wanted to see her angry. I wanted her to lash out, to scream at the situation. I also wanted her to see that she could have a little piece of heaven here.

That the club accepted even the outcasts, and it didn't matter what she could and couldn't do.

The weak hit to my shoulder came out of nowhere, but as she swayed on her feet, I regretted bringing her out when she was in no condition to be outside right now. I had no idea what the extent of her injuries was, or if there was something wrong internally, but I wanted her to experience this.

Children running along the shoreline. Bikers that were no longer in active service, looking over youngsters and everything they were doing. Young couples kissing, hugging; music playing and the rumble of our motorcycles. I wanted her to get accustomed to this because I could see her here.

She thought she was darkness, but she was light. She was sunshine. I know what I saw four years ago. It was an unhinged passion, the kind that could swallow you whole or lift you up, and I wanted to get lost in her world. She had issues, I would've been a fool not to see them, but she also had so much light.

But now, it was as if they extinguished that life that made her who she was. I wished I could reverse time and bring her with me on that same day. I didn't know that the life would fuck all of her plans, rip away everything she ever dreamed of. That kind of heartache, that pain, it never goes away easily. It turns you into a person you never wanted to be, and before you know it, you start shielding yourself from the people in your life, because you're too scared to get hurt again.

She was scared, even though she didn't want to be.

There are different kinds of fear we go through, but this one, the fear of getting attached to someone because you're terrified of losing them is the one that paralyzes your whole body and mind, stopping you from living the life you could have. Even though she was no longer wearing the shackles her father put on her, she was living inside her head. She was putting herself into a virtual prison, where everybody else came before her.

How could anyone think that this girl felt nothing at all?

How could they fail her this much? I was more than curious about what had happened between her and Kieran. There was something she wasn't telling me, apart from the whole fiasco about Ava's death. I felt for her, but I didn't know Ava enough to grieve the life that was taken too early.

She pressed the palms of her hands to her eyes, groaning out loud, and no doubt contemplating all the ways to murder me and get away from here.

"Storm—"

"Yes?" I wasn't going to give her what she wanted, no matter how much she begged. She thought she could handle everything by herself, but there were people out there that wanted her dead. They wanted her gone, and I'd be damned if I allowed them to put a finger on her pretty head.

She finally opened her eyes, gazing at me with a remorseful expression. "You need to let me go."

"Never."

"Fucking hell," she cursed and started walking back and forth, throwing cautionary glances my way. "Why are you so fucking difficult?"

"Pot meet kettle."

"I don't wanna be here!" she yelled. "I don't wanna be surrounded by everything I never had, Storm. I-I just…" she trailed off.

"You just what?"

She kept quiet for a moment, her eyes down turned, staring at her boots. It was funny how you could only really see the person once they were cracking, once their masks were getting thrown to the ground, and everything they were trying to hide was finally coming to the surface. The hell I went through taught me that the best way to survive in this world, is to create a mask you would wear in front of everybody else.

But we often forget to remove that mask even when nobody else is around us, and instead of trying to breathe, to feel, at least for a few minutes, we shove it all down until the only thing we are familiar with is the poisonous mask we have created. I know I forgot how it feels to be vulnerable, to let other people see what was hiding behind the mask. And now, she did too.

I didn't bring her here to fix her. People couldn't fix people, but we could help each other to at least try and face the things we were hiding from. I was tired of all the nightmares that were haunting me to this day. I was tired of their sick, twisted faces, soulless eyes and the stench of sweat that clung to those rooms they kept me in. We all had our demons, and I just hoped that ours could tango together.

Maybe I was wrong, but maybe I wasn't. She could've run away by now. It wasn't as if she couldn't figure out a way to get away from here, but some part of her wanted to stay. You could only be strong for so long before your mind shattered around you. Sometimes you couldn't run away from everything haunting you, and I had a feeling she was at that point right now.

Her words didn't have the same bite like they did in the church. Her eyes didn't glow with the promise of revenge like they did with Kieran, and even if she didn't need me and she wanted to lie to herself, I fucking needed her.

133

It was like watching a car crash happening right in front of your eyes. In slow motion, painful, but before I could say another word, before I could ask her what she wanted, Ophelia collapsed to the ground, hugging her knees to her chest. A curtain of hair hid her face from me, but the visible tremors shaking rushing through her body sent my heart into overdrive.

"Dammit, Sunshine." I stepped behind her, hiding her from the rest of the people too oblivious to see what was happening on this side. "What's happening with you?"

I wasn't sure if she didn't want to answer me, or just couldn't, but I knew we couldn't stay here. She was in no shape to ride on my bike with me, and as if summoned by my thoughts, Atlas rushed to us. I could see that he wasn't sure what was going on, but I didn't have time to explain.

"I need to use Jax's Range Rover." I pinned him down with a stare, and he didn't bother asking questions.

I sat down on the warm sand and pulled her with me, making it seem as if we were just sitting over here. She didn't stop shaking even as my arms wrapped around her body, taking a hold of one of her own. If anything, the tremors increased with each passing second, and I loathed this helpless feeling. I loathed the fact that I didn't know what to do with her.

"Hey, hey," I whispered into her hair, trying to soothe her. Even with the scent of my shampoo woven into her hair, she still managed to somehow make her own scent. She was a stubborn girl who never gave up on those that needed her. "It's okay, Ophelia. It's gonna be okay, Sunshine."

The first sob broke free of her, and it was like an avalanche of emotions pushing out of her. Her

134

body shook in my arms, but as she grabbed my hand, squeezed it as hard as she could, I knew that being here for her would have to be enough for now.

ELEVEN

Ophelia

THE COLD HANDS of memories I've tried to forget, enveloped my body until I couldn't think. I couldn't breathe. Their claws dug into my chest, opening the wounds I thought had healed a long time ago, but I was wrong. Memories were wicked little things, capable of causing havoc when you least expected it.

They loved to sneak upon you, sending your whole body into a frenzy, torturing you until you couldn't handle it anymore. The melodic laughter of a child sounded somewhere behind us, and I wasn't here anymore. I was back in Yantai, in China.

The smell of wet soil, fresh air, and the dark street were all around me. And the child; the child stood in front of me, smiling, innocent, not yet knowing what a real demon looked like. He watched me as I took the life from his mother, as the last breath left her body.

And then another memory slammed into me; *the smell of ashes, of burned meat and sand rising all around me. The pleading eyes of the Saudi man as I stood there, unapologetic, unwavering, even when his wife screamed at me with tears streaming down her face. I stood there unflinching even when his teenage daughter ran in front of him with the dark veil falling off her head.*

"Rahma!" she screamed at me, begging, pleading, but none of it could stop me. She couldn't stop me even when I raised my gun, pointing it at her father's head. She wasn't able to stop me because the bullet I'd released lodged itself into her forehead, and the thud of her body on the warm ground echoed around us, mixed with the screams of her mother.

And I killed the rest of them.

But the eyes… The honey brown eyes of a girl haunted me to this day.

"Sunshine," Storm murmured in my hair, gripping my kneecaps with his hands. I felt the wind in my hair, the sand beneath my hands, his raspy voice on my skin, but I couldn't snap out of the wicked place my mind took me to.

I heard people talking around us; the laughter, the happiness, the sense of belonging—home. It felt like home, but it wasn't mine. It would never be mine. I didn't deserve it. The innocent people I've killed in the name of the Syndicate were the ones haunting me from the afterlife, and they should. They should condemn me to the deepest pits of hell.

How did I allow them to turn me into this? This monstrous being that shoved everything into a box just so that I couldn't feel.

"It's gonna be okay, baby." Warm lips pressed against my clammy skin, right below my ear, and the involuntary shudder that ran through my body was enough to send my blood pumping again. And instead of running like I should've, I leaned back, welcoming the strong body holding me when I couldn't hold myself.

The air didn't smell like blood and tears anymore, but like leather and cinnamon, and it was all Storm. I wondered if he would want me here if he knew that I tasted more of war and pain than dreams and sun-filled fields. I wondered if he knew that the body he held committed such atrocities, that even a thousand years of bathing in holy water wouldn't be able to cleanse the sins I've committed.

I looked down at the tattooed hands that kept their slow perusal of my legs. He started at my calves, massaging his way up, all the way to my knees and my thighs. And even though it should've felt erotic, the only feeling I got was peace. He made me feel at peace, and I both hated and loved that he could bring it to me.

"Are you feeling better?" His warm breath washed over my cheek. The question asked was a mere whisper, traveling with the wind, and I wanted to soak in the raspy quality that felt like walnuts mixed with honey. Need pooled between my thighs, making me move closer to him.

I didn't know how to communicate with words. I was never taught, and the role models I had were better in issuing orders or being completely checked out, than with the open affection and soft strokes on the hair every child wanted to feel from their parents.

I only knew how to use my body in both combat and sex. His legs stiffened around us, and the muscles on his thighs visibly jumped against the dark denim he was clad in. With the mind of their own, my hands moved from the sand, taking a hold of his thighs, leaving marks in its wake.

Lifting my head, I was met with the tempest brewing inside his eyes, but I knew he wasn't going to make a move. He refused to play by my rules, and my little exploration of his inner thighs ended as he gripped my hands, halting every single movement. His lips pulled into a crooked smile, as he leaned down, placing a kiss on my temple.

It should've been nothing, but it felt like everything I ever wanted. The sweetness I craved even though I fought so hard to show the world I could do everything by myself. Would it be so bad losing myself in him and forgetting about all the bad things I went through?

But as soon as that thought came to mind, Maya's tortured face replaced it, and I knew I couldn't stay. Why did everything feel like it could only happen in a different lifetime?

I tried moving away from him as my breathing slowed down, but the hands that massaged my legs just a minute ago, pulled me back into his body, locking me in place. I should've struggled against his hold, but I was too tired of lying to myself. Too tired of fighting this battle alone, and I let him hold me, even if it was just for a moment.

I wasn't sure if he could sense how indecisive I really was, and I hated thinking about the consequences of this push-and-pull shit that was happening between us. It's been only what, two days, and I've already managed to fuck him, push him away, pull him back in and probably mess with his mind. This Storm didn't seem like the Storm everybody was talking about.

This man didn't seem like a vicious hunter that was usually hired by other families to track, maim, and kill. This Storm cared for me, and if I could allow myself to accept that, I knew I would be happier.

But I couldn't.

I promised myself that the fairy tales I was trying to create in my head were nothing but a little girl's dream that could never come true. It wasn't like I expected a knight on a white horse, or someone to save me. But when I was younger, when all of this started, I dreamed of a future where violence, pain, betrayal, and blood were not present. I dreamed of a future where I could hold somebody's hand without fear of them dying on me just because somebody from my family decided to do so.

Me being here, hanging with these people, leaving my stench on them, this was a recipe for a disaster. I might have avoided my father for the last four years, but I had a feeling that this leash he was keeping me on was getting shorter, and sooner or later he was going to come for me. I just had to get to Maya before that happened.

I wasn't going to go back to the life he wanted for me. I was done being his puppet, his obedient little daughter or how he liked to call me, the Little Dragon. And I also wasn't going to put this whole club in danger.

I just had to figure out how to get away from Storm. This pull he had on me was becoming scary. This need to stay with him, to let him hold me, to let him soothe the wounds I didn't even know were still there, that was going to be our undoing. And he felt it too. He felt the same things I did. I just didn't want to acknowledge it. If I did, it would become true, and as long as I could lie to him and myself, I could keep trying to get away.

The last time I gave my heart to somebody, he shattered it into a million pieces, leaving a broken puppet behind. Who's to say that Storm wouldn't do the same thing? Men had a penchant for destruction, and the object was always my sanity and my heart. I was already hanging by the thread and giving my everything to him would be a mistake.

He wouldn't understand. He couldn't. Whatever was haunting Storm was not the same as what was haunting me. The shadows in his eyes were not created by him, but by other people. I knew what the self-loathing looked like even when you wanted to pretend with the pretty little mask on your face. I saw self-loathing in the mirror daily, seeping through the pores of my skin, leaving scars on the pale surface. Mine came from the things I did when maybe I didn't have to.

His wasn't anywhere close to that. There were monsters in this world, monsters that wanted to taint your soul and take your heart. I was one of them and I knew; I knew what a tortured soul felt like.

The way he caressed my skin in the shower, careful not to touch me anywhere I might not have wanted him to, even though I wouldn't mind, it told me everything I needed to know. Only people who knew what it felt like to be touched without their permission knew how to help when the masks fell off.

And it seemed like he knew. I didn't know how. I maybe didn't even want to know, because the pain he must have gone through was more than I could handle right now. There were only so many people I could help in this lifetime, and unlike before, my sister was my priority now.

I knew what a heavy burden it was, even though Maya was older than me. Although it broke my heart, Storm had to come second right now.

I couldn't handle another broken heart, and saving Maya was a safer option than letting myself fall for him.

I shivered under his hold as the night slowly cascaded upon us, decorating the sky with the bright stars I used to love looking at. The chilly breeze from the ocean tickled the bare skin on my arms, and an involuntary shiver ran through my body, leaving an uncomfortable feeling at the bottom of my spine. For somebody that was technically Russian, I sure hated the cold. I would probably take boiling heat any day over the freezing cold that seeped into your bones until it started hurting.

"Are you cold?" the mountain behind me asked, and even though I stopped shaking and mumbling to myself, he didn't move away. When he pulled me back into his body, I felt protected, as if nothing and nobody could take me away from here. I just knew it was wrong.

It was just another lie my brain was trying to create. Another unattainable dream I would never reach.

"A little bit," I whispered. I hated feeling weak, and right now, after everything I went through, right now I was falling apart. My body refused to cooperate with me, my mind even less. Great, Ophelia Aster succumbed to the humane side of herself. I guess I wasn't a little Satan after all.

"Do you wanna get out of here?"

I almost wanted to laugh because the conversation between the two of us felt strained, and considering I had his dick inside of me today, it shouldn't have. He kept shielding me from the rest of the people, but I could see Atlas lurking on the right side of us, keeping an eye on both the members that were gathered around the bonfire as well as the two of us.

Indigo, the dark-haired menace Zoe pointed to before — I had no idea how the two of them were even related — slowly walked to Atlas, and would you fucking look at that. He was checking him out.

His eyes lingered on Atlas's ass for a second too long, before he finally moved toward his shoulders and lastly his face. As if sensing my stare at him, his eyes flickered to me, narrowed and angry, as if I caught him doing something he shouldn't have. I personally didn't give a flying fuck who screwed who and who loved who. The Syndicate was very vocal about same-sex relationships and getting caught in one meant expulsion or death.

I just never got it. It wasn't as if somebody's sexual preference was going to rub off on you.

However, Indigo looked like he wanted to strangle me and throw my body over the bridge. It was obvious that whatever was going on there, he tried to hide it.

"What are you looking at?"

As soon as he asked, I looked toward the ocean, ignoring the burning stare Indigo was throwing my way. I wasn't sure if their club was okay with the LGBTQ community, and I wasn't going to throw anybody under the bus, even though it seemed as if Indigo didn't want me here.

Hell, I didn't want me here, but Storm couldn't take a hint.

"Nothing," I murmured, burying my face in his neck.

Even though I wanted to run, my body worked against me and all it wanted was to be enveloped in Storm's heat. These fleeting moments were the ones I was going to cherish forever, because once he figured out the hidden truths and poisonous lies underneath my skin, he was never going to hold me like this again.

I felt like a stage-five clinger, but I didn't give a shit right now. Blood and war could wait for one day.

The feathery touch of his hand against my cheek and the curious stare on his face, it was as if he was seeing me for the first time. A shiver ran through his body as my lips connected with the soft skin at the bottom of his neck. My tongue darted out, licking the spot from the little indent to his Adam's apple. My taste buds exploded with the salty flavor of his skin, mixed with spicy remnants of his cologne.

"Sunsh—"

"Let's get out of here." I lifted my head, looking into his eyes. I brushed my thumb over the scar running through his eyebrow, remembering what he told me about his father. I guess we both had fucked-up stories to tell.

The intensity of his stare on my face sent a heat pooling between my thighs, but whatever happened between us today couldn't happen again. I saw the hurt written all over his face when I all but ran away from him once I'd realized what I'd done.

Sex was a powerful weapon, but it wasn't one I wanted to wield against him.

If I started making a list of pros and cons for Storm, the list of pros would be much bigger than the latter, and that bothered me. I think that a part of me knew I could get lost in the thunderous green eyes if I wanted to, and that scared the living shit out of me.

He's been back in my life for less than a week and he was already causing havoc that I didn't want right now. The time was wrong, the life we lived was wrong, and I didn't even want to go into the list of reasons why we shouldn't be together.

No, why we couldn't be together.

"Ophelia," he murmured as his head lowered down to mine, pressing a soft kiss on my forehead. I fucking hated this kind of affection because I didn't know what to do with it. I understood that he had monsters of his own; the monsters he probably fought daily just like I did, but the way he behaved with me, it made me feel cherished.

Precious.

I didn't have butterflies in my stomach when he looked at me. No. Whoever described it as butterflies had never felt this way, because this was more like a stampede of wild horses running through and causing turmoil. Love made me weak once before, and I would be a fool if I didn't learn from my past mistakes.

But he isn't Kieran.

No, no he isn't. He could be much, much worse. What I had with Kieran was familiarity, mild obsession, the knowledge that somebody else was in this mess with me, but Kieran's presence never pulled at me like Storm's did. I realized a long time ago that it wasn't my heart that was hurt when he slept with Cynthia, it was my ego. It was the knowledge that he dared to betray me after everything we went through, but he didn't break my heart with that.

He broke my heart when he raped my sister.

But Storm… He had a power to obliterate me if I allowed myself to dream again. He could crush me like a bug, and I wasn't sure if I had enough trust in me left to let him in. Ava told me once that she felt the pull to Nathan even before he spoke to her. That there was something raw and animalistic in the way his soul called to hers.

Sometimes I wished I were more like her, and less like me. I wished I were the kind of a person that could allow happiness, love and all those mushy, touchy feelings to consume my whole being, because living like this, living with all these regrets was slowly killing my soul.

Storm was going to be just another regret,

regardless of the choice I'd make.

The soft tap on my temple pulled me back to reality, to the concerned-looking Storm and the murmurs around us. "Where did you go, Sunshine?"

"Nowhere," I replied. "Everywhere."

I had a tendency to get lost in my head. To overthink things I had no power over. I learned a long time ago that fighting my mind took more strength from me than fighting men five sizes bigger than me. Physical exhaustion could be dealt with, you could heal, but the mental one… it took me years to learn the signs of my little attacks. I had to figure out the little tells of when the memories would become too much.

I used to have a better grasp on reality, but the whole ordeal with Kieran, remembering all the things we went through, seeing Storm again and realizing I'd lost everything I could have… my mind just shut down. When was the last time I actually slowed down? Sometimes I had a feeling that all I did for the past six years was to fight, survive, fight again, run away, and try to see the light of another day.

Was this how I wanted to live my life?

Atlas broke our little bubble when he walked over to us with an amused look on his face, but concern in his eyes. "Storm," he started. "I have the car ready."

The behemoth behind me kept his hands on my shoulders, not even sparing a glance at Atlas.

"Are you going to be okay riding on my Harley or do you want us to take the Range Rover?" I don't think that anybody ever spoke to me in such a calm way like he did. Even when I was a kid, my mother was too busy snorting whatever she could get her hands on. The way he shielded me from the rest of the world, even though I didn't shield myself. My father wasn't the one to show any kind of affection, which only got worse once they threw me into their world. Theo was a hateful little shit, who enjoyed fucking up my mood, and bullying Maya and me.

Kieran tried, but I was too far gone to even pay attention, and after a year or so, he stopped trying.

But not Storm. I've been nothing but a bitch since I saw him in the church, and what did he do? He kept pushing for more—more affection, more touching, more, more, more. And for somebody that hated any form of affection, I was soaking in what he was showing me.

Soft little touches on my skin, the way he looked at me, the way he cared even though I tried pushing him away, it meant that maybe there was someone out here that wanted to see me happy. It was just too bad I couldn't accept any of it.

"I'm good with the Harley." I always wanted to have a bike of my own, but the timing was never perfect. The confines of the car right now were not something I was looking forward to, and the way I felt on the way here was something I hadn't felt in a very long time.

Freedom.

And even though it had been Atlas I was driving with and not Storm, even though I had a million thoughts racing through my head, it felt exhilarating. And now, I wanted it to be Storm whose body I would hug to avoid falling off. Whatever he had planned for us, I wouldn't mind if it meant getting away from here.

I was jealous of all these people, and it was fucking wrong. It wasn't their fault I was born into a coldhearted and vicious family filled with serpents and lies. I wanted to run away from them, from the sing-song voices, laughter of the children, smiling faces of adults as they watched them play. It wasn't something I was accustomed to. My family never did any of these things.

Picnics were things from fairy tales, and happiness was just a picture we were trying to paint. Hollow souls in our bodies, broken dreams, and broken promises, that's what I was familiar with. Not to mention that I still wanted to talk to Storm without all these other distractions that were doing my head in.

I still wanted to leave, even more so now, and I needed him to tell me why he brought me here.

You know why, you idiot.

Okay, yes. Maybe I did know why, but I refused to accept it. No one in their right mind would ever think of welcoming me into their fold. My family knew that, the Nightingales knew that, and hell, even the Albanians with all their wicked ways knew that. I was never a part of anything.

Always a lone wolf. Always isolated.

"Are you ready to go?" Three sets of eyes zeroed in on me, but I didn't look at the other two. I sought Storm's eyes, trying to get a good read of him, but he seemed to be apprehensive. I had a feeling it had everything to do with me and my little episode.

"Yeah." I nodded, trying to plaster a smile on my face. It absolutely didn't work, because he all but groaned painfully before getting up and extending his hand to me.

"Come on then." Atlas fucking chuckled next to him, but with one look from the behemoth that was hugging me a moment ago, his mouth formed a thin line with a serious look taking over his face.

"Sorry, man."

I should've been irked because he was trying

to help me. After all, for most of my life I've been alone, independent; I-didn't-need-anybody shit. But I allowed him to pull me up, to place his hand on the small of my back and guide me toward his bike.

I half-heartedly waved at Atlas, who once again sported a grin directed at us. My eyes landed on Indigo who observed us quietly, moving from my face to the place where Storm's hand connected with my back, and I honestly had no idea what his problem was.

I mean, I wasn't a fairy godmother, but I liked to think that I had some qualities that didn't involve only murder and mayhem. If people hated me, it was mostly because I did something to them, and I definitely didn't do anything to Indigo. He didn't even know me, and if the sneer on his face was any indication, he already didn't like me. Standing so close to Atlas, I could see the differences between the two.

Where Atlas was light, with his blond hair, smiling face, and tall, lean body, Indigo was dark — blue-black hair, dark piercing eyes, and an amount of tattoos that rivaled Storm's. I had a feeling he could throw me around like a ragdoll, considering that his biceps were the size of my head.

But the funniest thing of them all, was the way he naturally gravitated toward Atlas. I wasn't sure if he even noticed it. I hadn't seen Atlas reacting to him in any way, but where there's smoke, there's also fire, and something tells me that these two would be good together.

What with that whole opposites attract bullshit.

Wait, scratch that. Opposites obviously weren't the best fit every single time because look what has happened to Kieran and me. No, nope on a rope.

Oh, what the fuck. It wasn't like I could stay here and watch how the little secret glances Indigo was throwing at Atlas would unfold. I had to stay focused and think about a way to get away from here. Maybe heal first and try not to kill Storm.

And not in that particular order.

I cleared my head from the thoughts that started taking place and focused on where we were going. As soon as we got to the sleek Harley Davidson coated in black, Storm took a helmet he definitely wasn't wearing earlier and turned to me.

"Na-uh." I shook my head. "I won't be wearing that."

I wasn't wearing one when we came here, and I didn't want to wear one now.

"Ophelia—"

"Nobody else wore them," I argued. Did I sound like a petulant child? Most probably, yes. But I honestly didn't want to wear one, and he couldn't force me.

Storm closed his eyes, pinching the bridge of his nose with his thumb and forefinger. The groan that erupted from his mouth would've been funny if it wasn't for the scathing look he sent my way. I placed my hands on my hips, wincing from the pain that erupted from my right hand. He looked at my swollen finger than at my face.

"The doctor will be here tomorrow to have a look at that finger."

"I'm fine."

"This is not up for discussion. I'm not sure if it's broken or dislocated, but it doesn't look good. When did it happen?" I really, and I mean really, hated this caring side of him.

"A couple of days ago," I murmured. "Just before we came to the church."

Standing this close to him, I could see the tiny yellow freckles around his irises, and I realized that his eyes weren't as completely green as I initially thought they were. It wasn't like I had enough time four years ago to think about the color of his eyes, but now I did.

"That's not good, Sunshine." His finger trailed over my right arm as he took a step closer. "I really am sorry."

"It's not your fault." I shrugged. "You have nothing to apologize for."

"Hmm," he grunted as he lifted the helmet again. "Ophelia," he started again, his voice barely above a whisper and it did something to my insides. The pleading look in his eyes almost broke me down, but I seriously didn't want to wear that fucking thing. "Humor me. Please?"

Those three words shouldn't have meant anything, but they did. He wasn't ordering me around. He wasn't telling me what to do, even though it seemed that way at first. I had to shut my inner bitch up and put on big girl pants. If he was concerned about my safety and wanted me to wear it, why was I being a bitch about it?

Because you hate being told what to do.

Oh, shut the fuck up. Okay, yes, I did hate it when people, especially men, told me what to do, but it wasn't like he was asking me to commit a murder. Though, I would probably agree to that much faster than to the bloody helmet he was holding.

"Fine," I huffed after a minute too long, taking the shiny thing from his hands. His cheek twitched and I knew, I just fucking knew he was moments from smiling, and I wanted to see it. He almost never smiled, and for some inexplicable reason, I really wanted to see it directed at me.

151

When was the last time somebody genuinely smiled at me?

Ava, maybe? So when his lips pulled apart, revealing the line of bright white teeth, softly crooked to the side, I almost combusted on the spot. He needed to get a permit for carrying that thing because *holy fucking shit.* My mouth was agape, staring at the little dimple that showed on his right cheek.

Of course, he had a dimple. Of-fucking-course.

This would've been much easier if he had a tiny dick, shitty personality and I don't know, a beer gut maybe. Not that there was anything wrong with that, but he just had to have it all.

"Are you still with me, babe?"

No, I was on my way to fucking Neverland to meet Peter Pan. I swear to God, Tinkerbell or some shit sprayed that fairy dust on me, because I never went quiet like this. Never, ever, especially not when a guy smiled at me.

Was my life really that fucked up that even the smallest smile from somebody I kind of liked made my brain all mushy?

Let's not answer that question.

"Y-Yeah," I stuttered, and I wanted to fucking facepalm myself. I went head-to-head with men way bigger than me. I probably killed more people than I could count, but one tiny smile, and I'd gone stupid.

I was enveloped in that scent that was all Storm. Dude could bottle it up and sell it. Women all around the world would go crazy over it. Cinnamon and leather mixed with the lingering scent of cigarettes.

Or maybe it's only you going crazy over his scent?

I showed middle fingers to my inner bitch as he took a hold of the helmet I still held in my hand

and placed it on my head. I almost wanted to hold my breath—emphasis on almost—because I was getting dizzy from his sheer presence, but I also didn't want to pass out. If swimming in Croyford Bay with Ava and some of our other friends taught me anything, it was that my lungs had the capacity of a little squirrel and holding my breath was not an option.

He pulled the straps lower, caressing my face with his knuckles, still smiling like he won the lottery.

It was illegal being this good looking, and it wasn't fair for the rest of us. How was I supposed to have any coherent thoughts when he looked like that, with his smiling face and the soft way he observed me?

"Now," he murmured, "you always need to make sure that the straps are tight enough. Otherwise, the helmet doesn't have any function." He clicked said straps together beneath my chin while I wordlessly stared at the alien in front of me.

What happened to mayhem, murder, and all the other shit people said about him?

"Now you're all set." That fucking smile stayed on his face throughout the whole thing, and the urge to plant my lips to kiss them came out of nowhere. As if sensing where my thoughts went, he took a step back, creating a distance between us.

The distance I hated.

God, I was messing this whole thing up. Maybe if I could figure out what I really wanted and stop being a whiny bitch, I could figure out the rest of the shit that was no doubt coming.

"Let's go," he called out to me, as he sat on his bike. My limbs felt heavy, but I willed my legs to move toward the beautiful machine he was straddling. There were too many things rushing through my head, but one thing at the time. Right? First, I was going to talk to him. Then, I was gonna get out of here, find Maya and disappear from the face of the earth.

Amazing plan, wasn't it?

Placing a hand on his shoulder, I lifted my right leg and sat down on the comfy leather. When I kept my hands in my lap, waiting for the bike to be turned on, he looked over his shoulder, frowning at me. What did I do now?

With one swift movement, he pulled both of my hands with his own, trapping them at his stomach. My front was pressed to his back, and my lips were inches away from the back of his tattoo-covered neck. Tips of a black wing were peaking there, disappearing underneath his shirt, and I cursed myself for the lack of time I had to trace each of the patterns he had with my fingers, with my tongue.

The bike rumbled between my thighs, sending little shocks of pleasure to my center. I felt the same way when I rode with Atlas, but the close proximity I was in with Storm had a completely different effect on me. His muscles strained as he pressed on the handlebar, slightly leaning forward, taking me with him.

"Hold tight." I could barely hear him over the rumble of the engine, but I pressed my hands against the hard planes of his stomach waiting for us to move. He once again looked over his shoulder, a smug smirk I wanted to smack, painted on his face.

Pretty bastard.

As soon as he moved us away from the makeshift parking lot, I moved one of my hands lower, reaching the hem of his shirt. His head snapped from the road to my hands, and I started laughing, knowing that this wasn't in any of his plans. As soon as my fingers touched the soft skin of his stomach, just above the waist of his pants, he took a sharp breath, looking from the road toward me.

I planted my chin on his shoulder, lifting his shirt higher, and touching more and more of his skin, until both of my hands were plastered against the soft yet hard surface of his abs, stroking, taunting, teasing, until one of his own stopped my ministrations.

His breathing was shallow, and the wild look he sent my way was enough to know that he wanted to be anywhere else but on this bike and on this road. I couldn't just let him smile at me like that, rendering me speechless without a little retribution.

"Babe," he warned. His voice mixed with the wind was almost inaudible, but I was close enough to hear every syllable grunted.

"Just drive, Storm." I smirked. "I'm getting impatient."

TWELVE

Ophelia

I HAVE NEVER been to Santa Monica before. Not that I didn't want to, I just wasn't allowed.

There was one strict rule both the Syndicate and the Outfit had to follow — avoid the West Coast and only go if you really fucking have to. It was well-known that the Syndicate and the Outfit controlled the East Coast, while motorcycle clubs controlled the West Coast. I never had to obviously, otherwise I would've been here years ago, getting lost on the beach, and enjoying the sunset.

As we rode toward the city, I tried soaking in the purple and red colors flickering on the sky. The remnants of the day painted above us. The sun wasn't visible anymore, but the puffy clouds gathered around, throwing different shades all over the place. I was a sucker for sunsets and sunrises.

There was just something magical how the colors played on the pale blue canvas, and I don't know... the sky always somehow represented freedom, and that was one of the things I never had.

My mild obsession started way back in high school, when I would sit on the cliffs watching over the Croyford Bay, imagining I was somewhere else.

Now that I thought about it, I always had a feeling that I wanted to run away from there. But I couldn't really complain. Up until that fateful night when my father shoved the knife in my hands, I didn't have a bad childhood. My parents never hit me, but they never really cared either. I wasn't sure what was worse anymore — the fact that they never cared or that I cared too much.

I used to dream of the family that had those little outings together, picnics on the beach, summer trips around the country. I used to wish for a mother that read me bedtime stories, the one that told me to stay away from people that didn't feel right. But I got none of that.

And I know I never would because that wasn't my destiny. It wasn't like I could complain. I had more than most other people did. I had a roof above my head, food, and clothes. I had Ava and I had security, at least for a little while.

I wondered what Storm's childhood was like. We didn't have enough time to talk about anything, and I wanted to know. I wanted to know what made him tick, what made him angry and happy. Did he like guns more than knives, and what was the meaning of his tattoos?

And all these wants were something I shouldn't wish for. I wasn't here to fall in love. I wasn't here to stay with Storm, as we rode happily into sunset. These silly thoughts of mine were a remnant of a little girl I used to be, and I tried to silence her down every opportunity I had.

This thing we had going on, this was passion and war, all wrapped in one. I couldn't lie and say that I didn't feel anything for him, but dreams were one thing and reality was another. The reality we lived in didn't allow for dreams to manifest.

Ava used to do the whole manifestation thing, and while I believed it worked for her, I didn't think it would work for me. When you're the daughter of an evil incarnate, all good vibes cease to exist and you are nothing but a vessel wondering on the earth.

My face was getting numb from the wind hitting me, and even though it wasn't as cold as the East Coast during this time of the year, I really wished I had worn something thicker. When we had rode to the beach, it was still sunny, warm, and I hadn't felt like my skin was getting attacked by a thousand little bugs that kept hitting us.

My butt started hurting five minutes ago, and while the leather seats were comfy, they weren't comfy enough for the same position for almost an hour. I didn't know this part of the country and I had no idea where he was taking us, but when we descended the busier road, filled with cars on both sides and people walking, smiling and talking, I had a feeling we were going toward the Ferris Wheel I could see in the distance.

As we slowed down, I could hear other noises coming from around us, and I somehow felt at peace. It was quite funny but being surrounded with so many people gave me an opportunity to blend in and observe. It was something they engraved into my head, and no matter what, I still followed it.

You could never be careful enough and knowing where the danger was helped. At least I knew I could run away if I had to, or I could attack, depending on the situation. But as Storm parked on the side of the street, shutting off the engine of the bike, I knew we weren't here to observe anybody, nor were we here to attack.

I slid off first, and if my shaky legs were any indication, I had to get back to the gym. The last couple of months were rough for me, and I had to admit—I wasn't exactly taking good care of my body. Which was stupid because I needed it to survive.

It wasn't like I could jump into another one, like they could in *Altered Carbon*. Look, I might have caught a couple of shows here and there—some in other people's apartments after the targets were taken out and they had cable, or in my apartment, on the nights I went there.

Storm followed shortly after me, and when I started messing around with the straps underneath my chin, unable to unlock them, strong, tattooed hands grabbed mine, taking care of the situation. His shirt was rumpled from where I lifted it up, and I wondered how he didn't feel cold during our ride.

Or maybe he did, but he wanted to feel your hands on him.

Yeah, yeah, whatever. My subconscious was a raging bitch today, appearing out of nowhere and apparently enjoying this whole torture session.

His lips were pressed into a thin line as he focused on the latch that wasn't budging. His lower lip was plumper than the upper one, and underneath the streetlight, the little scar I hadn't seen below was visible just above his lips. My hands itched to touch him, but that was a one-way street toward fucktown, and we didn't need that right now.

The annoying bugger finally clasped open, and he removed the helmet from my head, taking it to the bike. I was about to ask him why he didn't worry about anybody stealing it, since he just draped it over the handlebar, but when I saw the fearful looks people around us were throwing our way, I knew why.

They all knew who he was, or if they didn't, they knew who Sons of Hades were, and that three-headed beast was proudly painted on the side of his bike. I had a feeling that nobody wanted to be on their list, which was good security, I guess.

Maybe I could try to do the same thing with my car, though, knowing my luck, somebody would fuck with it just because of that insignia.

I fluffed my hair that got plastered to my scalp, running my hands through the long strands that needed a haircut. I mean, it wasn't like visits to the hairdresser were on top of my list, but it was easier in this line of work if my hair wasn't as long as it was now.

Besides, having extremely long hair meant that somebody could easily wrap their hands in it and pull, which would be a huge disadvantage in a fight.

But instead of thinking about fighting, my mind took me back to Storm's room and the bathroom where he washed my hair, wrapping his long fingers around wet strands. Fucker was worming his way under my skin, and it both excited and worried me.

"What are we doing here?" I asked once we started walking toward the pier. I mean, unless he planned to drop my body into the ocean, or I don't know, throw me from the Ferris Wheel, I literally had no fucking clue what we were doing here.

Not that I wouldn't appreciate it if he decided to feed me, since my stomach started growling five miles ago. The smell of hot dogs, burgers and that round candy shit—what was it called, cotton candy?—wafted through the air, and the second wave of complaints from my stomach came to the surface.

I glanced at Storm, who was staring at me, then at my stomach, then back to my face.

I shrugged. "I'm hungry."

"We had barbeque today." He laughed. "You didn't eat, or you—"

"I did, but it wasn't enough."

I wasn't going to tell him I basically inhaled three burgers with French fries on the side, while Zoe talked my ear off. I had to pretend I was at least a little bit girly.

As soon as I thought that a snort came out of me, because girly and I didn't mesh together in one sentence. Ava tried for years to make me wear cute flowery dresses, heels, and clothes that were more colorful than what I usually wore. And she failed.

I always envied those girls that could pull those looks, but on the couple of occasions I wore a dress, including my unforgettable engagement announcement night, I felt like a clown. Okay, that comparison was completely wrong. Even clowns wore those tutu dresses from time to time. I looked like a gremlin that couldn't sit with her legs crossed together even if my life depended on it.

Cillian often used to ask, *Can you please act like a girl?* Which always went with the *No* from my side. Besides, who got to say what a girl should act like?

We could be both soft and strong. Light and dark. Moody and happy. Nobody had a right to tell us how we should look, how we should act, and whom we should date. I mean, men went around like free lollipops were being shared, jumping from girl to girl, but when a chick does anything remotely similar; she must be a whore.

They could all fuck off, because there was nothing wrong in acting the way you felt the most comfortable to act.

Storm took a hold of my hand, and my heart started beating frantically against my ribcage as his warm, calloused fingers wrapped around my much tinier ones, pulling me toward one of the stands. Kieran never held my hand because I didn't want him to.

Storm didn't even ask.

My neck itched, and the pent-up energy from the last three days was brewing inside my chest, and the idiot whose back was basically turned to me as he talked to the lady at the counter didn't know he was five seconds from getting his balls smashed. Though, I wasn't sure what pissed me off more—the fact that he held my hand, or the fact that the cute little brunette working behind the counter, taking our order, batted her lashes one too many times at him, biting her lip and smiling at him.

I seriously needed to rein in the green monster that latched itself to me, because Storm wasn't mine. I couldn't even say anything, and it wasn't like he was flirting with her. But my hands itched to wrap around her pretty little neck and strangle the life out of her.

As if sensing my mood turning sour, he turned to me, questioning me with his eyes, but I didn't budge. Admitting I didn't like the way she looked at him would mean admitting I was jealous, and I could already see how that would go. I was already pulling him in all different directions, and I still remembered the pissed look he got when he realized I wasn't going to ride with him.

God, I was a reckless fuck. I had no idea what he was like, but the possessive demeanor he had ever since he came back—yes, I know it was only two days, but it was enough to know that he wouldn't mind smashing somebody's head in—told me he might as well kick Atlas's ass for the way I behaved.

Don't fucking ask me why. I had never really understood the inner workings of the male brain, and I didn't even want to try. I already had enough shit running through my head and trying to understand them would be like taking that physics class all over again—almost impossible.

"What are you frowning at?" Those three little lines that gathered around his eyes became more prominent as his scowl deepened, and I wondered if he got those because he always had a pissed-off look on his face, or because of the sun. I didn't even know how old he was.

"Nothing." I tried to pull my hand back, but this fucking behemoth wouldn't budge. If anything, he pulled me closer, almost plastering me to his side. When I looked to the side, the chick that was taking his order was frowning, and the deep-seated pleasure coated my insides, knowing it was because of me.

Sue me, I was a raging bitch these days, but some animalistic part of me claimed him as mine, and even though I didn't want to stay, I still wanted him to look only at me. Which was fucked up beyond comprehension, but it wasn't like he gave me a choice.

If only he let me go back after the church, we wouldn't be here, standing so close together, with me frowning at the poor lady that probably couldn't help herself after she saw the handsome fucker.

I snuggled against him, soaking in the heat of his body, and holy hell—it was like standing next to the heater. Why was it that guys were almost always more resilient to cold than chicks? I mean, I went through some extreme situations, but you can bet your ass that I never wore those tiny little coats when I visited Russia, because I wanted to keep both of my kidneys.

His eyes were on me, but I refused to look at him. I thought we were going to talk and I would be able to explain to him — again, might I add — why I had to leave. He offered to help me find Maya, but I couldn't ask that from them. Besides, that impending doom called Nikolai Aster was coming closer, I was sure of that, and they shouldn't be in the direct line of his wrath.

Over the years, I noticed the number of Syndicate's soldiers following me around, but every single one of them either lost the track or ended up dead. Daddy dearest was trying to show me that he still held all the pawns in the palm of his hand, and even if I changed my name to Pepito and moved to Mexico, he could still find me.

Okay, Mexico was way too close. Maybe Spain?

"Let's wait over there, Sunshine."

He didn't wait for me to agree or disagree, but instead started pulling me with him, all the way to the tables with benches, right next to a couple with a young kid. I had nothing against kids, as long as they stayed away from me. Hell, I didn't know what to do with kids when I was a kid.

The little girl turned to us from her mother's lap, her two pigtails bouncing on top of her head. Storm ignored the kid, probably not even seeing her, but I did. I noticed all of them because they either reminded me of a kid Ava could've had or the kids whose lives I took by taking them to the Syndicate.

I quickly shook off the path my thoughts were trying to take me to, walking to the other side of the table, when Storm's hand shot out, grasping mine and pulling me to where he was sitting.

"Seriously? It isn't like I could run away." The angry flare of his eyes told me everything I needed to know. He did think I would run away, and it bothered him—a lot.

"Just... Sit here, okay? There are people even here that are not exactly friendly with us, and I would rather keep you close. Just in case."

Just in case? In case somebody starts shooting at us? I've been in worse situations, but at least I had my weapons with me then. Being here like a sitting duck didn't bode well with me, but it wasn't like I could get away from him.

Jumping into the water was out of question, because freezing my tits off was not something I was looking forward to. Not to mention that swimming with clothes on was out of question.

"I really wish I could see what you're thinking about."

"You really don't. Trust me." I would have a heart attack if another person could see inside my head.

Like seriously, *I* didn't wanna be inside my head half of the time. If I had somebody else in there, you could take me straight to the psych ward. Not that I didn't deserve to be sent to one on most of the days, but one is already a crowd. Two would feel like Tomorrowland, minus the drugs.

"Then you'll have to start sharing what you are thinking about, because that scowl on your face seems to be a permanent fixture, and I hate it." Well, shit. Honest much?

"Me scowling and my thoughts are not why I wanted to talk to you, Storm."

"No?" He smirked. "But what if I wanted to talk about it?"

"Well, tough luck buttercup, because we aren't going to be talking about that."

My mood was already fucked up, and the last thing I wanted to do was talk about the shit passing through my head. Maybe I should ask him which one he would like to hear—the thoughts that told me I should just run away from here and fuck it all up, or maybe the one where I really wanted to stay because I wanted to feel something other than this fucking resentment and cold. Or maybe, just maybe, he would like to hear the one where I blamed myself for everything, but that one occurred only on every third day, so we were fine for now.

Yeah, not going to happen.

"Okay," he murmured. "What do you want to talk about?"

"How about the fact that you apparently laid some silly claim on me?" Just thinking about it made my skin bristle, and I swear, if I had powers like Clark Kent, I would set his ass on fire with my laser eyes.

Instead of looking guilty, ashamed, or I don't know, anything, he smiled wide, showing again that dimple in his cheek. He looked proud as he said, "I did."

I was going to strangle him. That's it.

"And?" I wrapped my fingers around the edge of the table, because if it weren't for that, I would be wrapping them around his thick neck.

"And nothing." He shrugged. "I laid a claim on you, and that's it."

"I'm not a cow or a dog for you to lay any kind of claim on me, Storm."

"Babe."

"Don't fucking 'babe me'. And stop calling me that. I'm not your babe. As a matter of fact, I am not

166

your anything."

The slow way in which he moved his head toward me should've scared me, but it didn't. What did however scare me were the words he uttered next.

"You can keep telling yourself that, Sunshine. Hell, if it makes you feel better at night, keep lying to yourself until you're red in the face, but let me just make something clear." He inched closer, wrapping his hand around the back of my neck, pulling our faces closer. His forehead touched mine, while his fingers massaged my scalp and my neck. "You. Are. Mine."

It was futile trying to get away, because as soon as I tried moving back, his lips slammed onto mine, rendering me speechless.

This wasn't a soft kiss that would elicit a sigh from me. No, this one screamed ownership, possession. As his tongue licked the seam of my lips, a gasp erupted from me, allowing him entrance. Not even thinking about it, I wrapped my hands around his neck, holding him as close as humanly possible.

His tongue touched mine, and it was as if all my nerve endings came alive, trying to fight him for dominance. But before I could climb on his lap because I was that fucking desperate apparently, he moved away, leaving me gasping for air.

His eyes flashed with something indescribable before he spoke again. "And I am yours, baby. As simple as that."

"Storm... You can't... We can't..."

"I'm not asking you to marry me, Ophelia. But I am telling you what's happening here, and you can either accept it or not. I'm not a fool, baby." He took my hand, pulling it into his lap. "I don't know everything that has happened to you, but I am here.

167

I was looking for you all these years, and now that you're here, I am not letting you."

He turned to me, swinging one of his legs over the bench, facing me. "Besides, you need to heal."

"I don't—"

"Yes, you do." He ran a finger over the nasty gash on my left arm, focusing on the snake tattoo. Or well, what was left of it. "I know what you're going to say. You want to leave. You want to find your sister."

Okay, when he said it like that, I sounded like a broken record because yes, I was going to repeat the same words.

"But you are in no condition to be out there alone." Tempest in those green eyes connected with mine, and I hated the clenching of my heart when I wanted nothing more but to be indifferent to him, his touch, the way he behaved with me. "And we both know there are people who would want nothing more but to hurt you."

Goddammit, he was right. If I wanted to find Maya, I had to stop being reckless. Theo said she was in Mexico, but it wasn't like I could just waltz in there, expecting to find her in the first few days.

"So, I have a proposition for you."

If I were a dog, my ears would perk up at that. "A proposition?" The last time somebody had a proposition, I ended up engaged to a cheating bastard, with one dead friend and a whole lot of baggage.

"Stay here." The words of refusal were on the tip of my tongue, as he continued, "I'm not saying stay with me in my room, but you need to heal, Sunshine. And I am honestly not gonna let you go out there while you look like this."

"Geez, thanks."

"You know what I mean." He laughed. "You

168

look like the best thing I always wanted to have, but that is not the point here. That finger of yours…" He looked at my right hand. "I want a doctor to look that over. And I have no idea if there's anything wrong in here." He tapped my temple with his forefinger.

Oh, boy. I could give him a list of all the things that were wrong up there, but then we would have to stay here for at least a month while I wrote them all down.

"Okay," I started reluctantly. "And what do you get in return?" I wasn't falling for this Saint Storm bullshit. Everybody wanted something, it just depended on what that something was.

"I want you to stay." Dark lashes fluttered against his cheeks as he avoided my eyes. My heart fucking went into overdrive, because shit. I don't even know why. "And, if you still want to leave after we find Maya, I won't stop you."

Did he just say *we*? He did, didn't he?

Fuck me sideways and six ways to Sunday. Why was I fighting this so much? He was right, it wasn't like he was asking me to marry him. He asked me to stay, to heal, to meet these people. He wanted to help me find Maya. He did everything in the way I wanted it to be done, and even though it's been two days, I couldn't help myself but be grateful for it.

"Thank you," I muttered. "I-I don't know how to…" I trailed off, clearing my throat. "I don't know how to trust people, Storm. They fucked up that part of me, and it'll take me time to heal from that."

His face darkened at the mere mention of them. I didn't have to specify who they were. We both knew.

"But," I started speaking before he could interrupt. "I can try."

Christmas gifts given to kids, that's how his face looked—shining eyes and a wide smile.

"And I want a separate room." The inner bitch glared at me, but if I was going to stay here, I needed some space from him. I needed time to figure out my own shit, and it wasn't going to happen if I had to sleep in the same bed with him. And it wasn't because I didn't trust him; I didn't trust me.

"Done." He agreed way too fast, even though I could tell that he wanted to keep me in his room. Dammit, I wanted it too, but it had to happen this way.

I was too busy staring at him, battling with myself, that I didn't even notice when the same girl walked to our table, placing the food he ordered on top of it.

"Your order is here." Even her voice was sweet, and it irked me even more because I knew I was the complete opposite of her. What if he actually liked somebody like that?

Argh, I hated these thoughts. I was never concerned about Kieran, until he of course fell cock first inside Cunthya's pussy, but that wasn't on me or the way I looked and behaved. However, Storm didn't even spare her a glance as he thanked her, turning his attention to the food.

A wicked little smirk took a hold of my face, directed at the girl that still stood there gaping at him. Noticing me for the first time, she flinched and took a step back, rushing to her counter.

Good.

I wasn't above wringing somebody's little neck if they couldn't take a hint. I don't give a fuck if you were a man or a woman, but if you see that somebody's not interested in you, just back off. Back the fuck off and don't bother poor people.

170

"Are you going to eat or are you going to keep staring at that poor girl?"

He fucking noticed? Of course, he noticed.

I didn't reply, instead taking the burger he kept for me, unwrapping the foil away from it. The heat seared through my hands, but it smelled fucking delicious. I didn't even mind that we were eating another burger when I already had three of them today. It was a favorite food and all that shit.

I never said I was a wholesome adult, right? Some people had breakfast, lunch, and dinner, with those nice food groups properly checked. I ate when I had time, and I didn't give a fuck about food groups. The kitchen was a foreign concept for me, because after that one time I almost burned my apartment down trying to prepare popcorn in the microwave, I just gave up trying.

But burgers, damn. Whoever invented them, I hope they had an amazing life.

I almost moaned with that first bite, all the ingredients meshing together, hitting my taste buds.

"So, in order to keep you happy, I just need to give you food and all of my problems will be solved?" He chuckled.

"Shut up," I said around the burger, but what he didn't see was the little smile that followed. Maybe this wouldn't be so bad.

THIRTEEN

Storm

THIS WORLD WAS filled with both saints and sinners, and we all knew which category I fell into. It wasn't like I had much choice, considering the way my life rolled out. And I never wanted to be anything else but a sinner — at least I was an honest one — but for her, I wanted to be a saint.

A saint that could fuck her like a devil and then kiss those scars that made her who she was now.

Unfortunately, all the fucking and all the kissing would have to stop for the time being, because I refused to start this relationship based on more lies. I just needed more time to fix this whole mess and then I could tell her.

I could tell her about the demons sitting in the corner of my room every time the lights turned off, or the ones that stared at me every time I closed my eyes. I would tell her everything but only if she stayed.

Women were a passing entertainment for me, and while I admired them and the strength they possessed, I never saw myself with one of them for the rest of my life. Until her. Until this wildfire walked toward me from across that street, brave and reckless, looked me in the eye and almost brought me to my knees.

I had a feeling that she thought I was joking when I told her she was going to be my queen, but I wasn't. In that moment, looking at her, feeling as if somebody could finally see me, I just knew—she was going to be mine in one way or another.

So here we were, me staring at her pouty pink lips while she chewed the last pieces of the burger I bought, humming a tune I have never heard before and occasionally flickering her eyes to me. Women like Ophelia rarely came without a shitload of baggage with them, but I was ready to fight. I was born to fight, and even if it took months or years to show her what she could have, I was going to do it.

But you don't have years to show her, you idiot. You have a time limit now.

Fuck. I did have a time limit. But I didn't want to force her to stay with me. I didn't want to be just another person that took away her choice. If she didn't want to stay, I had no idea how I was going to let her go. I never wanted to wake up without her body wrapped around mine and her hair tickling my face. This morning when I finally realized where I was, two things came to my mind.

I didn't have any nightmares last night.

And, she was clinging to me like she didn't want to let go. Even in her sleep she clung to me, and if that didn't tell me that there was something from her side as well, I don't know what would. I just needed more time to figure this shit out.

She needed more time to heal, and not just physically, but mentally. Seeing her battered and bruised, seeing her sad, it made the monster inside of me plot the demise of all those that ever hurt her.

But I knew that she would have my balls for breakfast if I ever thought of treating her like some damsel in distress.

She wasn't one.

"I'm done," she announced with a smile on her face, crumbling the wrapper of the burger in her left hand. As soon as we got back home, I was going to call our doctor to have a look at her. She put on a brave front, but if anyone knew what faking it looked like, it was me. And while she was good at it, she couldn't hide the torment sneaking behind those ocean eyes. No, she couldn't hide it from me, not at all.

"Is there mustard on my face?"

I almost shook my head, lost in the thoughts of everything that was still standing between us. "What?"

"Well, you keep staring at me like there's something on my fucking face." She started wiping around her mouth, her thumb caressing the skin I wanted to touch. "So, is there?"

"No." I chuckled. "No mustard or any other condiments that might have slipped while you inhaled that burger."

"I was hungry, asshole." Her face was serious, but the tone of her voice turned playful, which was something I now heard for the first time. If my calculations were correct, all this time, all these years, she'd been running away from one monster or another, only to land with the third one—the Albanians.

When they approached me and offered a generous sum of money, I couldn't exactly refuse it. All I had to do was help out their girl to execute Kieran Nightingale, heir of Logan Nightingale. After what they did to us in Las Vegas, I almost accepted the offer without even taking the money.

But then she showed up, and everything basically fell into the water.

What I wanted to know was, why she never came to Santa Monica? Why didn't she look for me? After that day on the cliffs, I promised to help her and Ava. She knew who I was, that I was sure of. Then why? I hated that I had more questions than answers, and that never fucking happened. If Indigo and Atlas saw me now, they would be laughing their asses off. For the first time in my life, I had to learn how to be patient.

Because I knew, I just fucking knew that pushing her wouldn't bring anything but more resistance.

Her skin glowed underneath the fairy lights hanging above our heads, while the wind played with her hair. There was something carnal in the way I was feeling, but I wasn't going to question whatever this was.

Our previous president, Trey, who was almost like a father to me, told me something I would never forget. *Once you find the one, boy, never let her go. It doesn't matter what stands in your path, kill them all if you have to, but never let her go.*

I laughed it off at that time, thinking that "the one" didn't exist for me. How could she when all I ever knew in my life was violence and endless nightmares? But then she waltzed into my life, and it was like being doused in heavenly fire when her eyes first connected with mine.

I wanted to give her the whole world because she made mine better. Their whispers weren't surrounding me whenever she was around. I could breathe, I could believe in a better future where not everything was so dark. I always had a label stuck to me. To some, I was a boy that grew up on the wrong side of the tracks. To others, I was the

175

monster their darkest nightmares were filled with.

But when she looked at me, none of those things mattered, because she didn't show fear and she didn't show pity. I just hoped it would stay the same once I told her the truth.

Darkness colliding, worlds ending, the two of us were a hurricane that could level the cities down if we allowed this thing to turn into something ugly. And for all my sins, I wasn't going to allow us to be tragic. Maybe she didn't want this right now, or at least she thought she didn't, but I knew what a broken soul looked like, and hers was on the brink of completely shattering.

"Come on." I stood up, extending my hand to her. As if it was a foreign object, she looked at my upturned palm before she lifted her head and looked at me. I arched an eyebrow waiting for her to do something, anything but the passive stance she was taking.

It was going to be baby steps with her, and hell, it wasn't like I knew how a normal relationship looked like, but people held hands. Right? I saw Zoe doing it with that one boyfriend of hers we all hated, looking giddy with excitement every time he touched her, but not Ophelia.

I had a feeling she would rather chop said limb off then put her hand in mine.

Her eyes closed for a second before her hand slowly descended onto mine. A foreign feeling of satisfaction washed over me, and knowing she was taking the steps in the right direction was the best type of euphoria. I pulled her up as my heart thundered in my chest. She could've refused. She was as stubborn as a mule, but so was I, and whatever she already imagined in her pretty little head wasn't going to work because I wasn't going anywhere.

Our demons could dance together because this kind of connection didn't happen twice. With shaky legs, she finally stood up, coming only to my chin. I loved that she was tall, yet she still felt tiny every time she stood next to my body.

Pulling her closer to me, she stumbled over the bench, shooting daggers with her eyes, but I didn't fucking care. My hands found the nape of her neck and wrapped around the dark strands. I bent my head down, all the way to her ear, loving the hitching of her breath as my own cascaded over the soft skin between her cheek and her ear.

"You took my hand," I whispered. My tongue darted out, licking the shell of her ear and a shudder ran through her. I gripped the back of her neck, kneading the taut muscles, while I nibbled on the soft skin on her chin.

"I did."

"Does that mean you're really giving this a shot?" I needed to hear her words again. Even though I knew that she already agreed to what I dished out, I needed to hear it again.

Her hands found their way over my chest, rubbing against the exposed skin of my throat. "Maybe." She wrapped her tiny hand around my throat, squeezing softly, making my dick jump in my pants. I was going to have a raging hard-on every single day with her around. Both my body and soul knew that she was it for us. Her other hand went into my hair, while her lower body pressed flush against mine, trapping my aching dick between us. "Or maybe not." She chuckled. "Only time will tell."

I was almost desperate to take her to the first darkened corner on this pier and show her what she did to me and who she really belonged to, but she deserved better. Goddammit, she fucking did, but as she rolled her hips against mine, all coherent thoughts left.

Fuck being slow and a gentleman. I was trying to fool myself into thinking I would be able to resist her and take this slowly.

I grabbed her exploring hand and started pulling her with me toward the street we came from. I wanted us to go to the Ferris Wheel, but that shit could wait until tomorrow or any other day. Right now, I needed to taste her.

We rushed through the sea of people that suddenly started piling up, all of them looking at me as if I were crazy, while Ophelia laughed behind me. She knew what she was doing, and the idea of her enjoying herself with me thrilled me.

I fucking reveled in the melodic sound that escaped her every now and then, but when I finally crossed the street with her in tow, moving us into the darkened alley, her laughter died because we both knew what was about to happen.

Moving her in front of me, I slowly pushed her to the wall, gauging her reaction. Her pupils dilated, her breathing increased, and I knew I wasn't the only one that wanted this. I pushed her shoulders until she hit the wall with a thud, her defiant eyes staring right into mine.

"Hello, Persephone," I murmured, my voice echoing in the empty alley. "You were a very bad girl."

My hands took a hold of the hem of her shirt, lifting it up all the way to her breasts. She didn't wear a bra, and I thanked all the gods that would listen for small miracles. The pants she wore were already going to be a menace. Her chest rising and falling, she didn't move an inch as my fingers skimmed over her pebbled nipples.

"Storm," she moaned, but I wasn't ready to let

her get the release she wanted. I moved her shirt all the way to her neck, exposing the creamy skin I wanted to mark. My lips descended on her collarbone, sucking, licking, tasting, and then moved to one nipple, pulling another moan from her mouth.

"S-Storm," she pleaded. "Please."

I moved up, pressing my forehead against hers, pressing my hips against her, seeking the much-needed relief. I kissed the scar on her cheek, and then moved to the other side—her nose, and her pouty lips that begged to be kissed. My teeth bit into her lower lip, pulling it, then soothing it with my tongue. "I got you, baby."

We both needed more, so much more, and as she started writhing beneath my body, I knew we didn't have enough time for everything I wanted to do to her. I unbuttoned her pants, while she fumbled with mine, both pieces of clothing sliding off our legs as we fought for dominance.

The thud on the ground as the pieces of clothing dropped from us merged with the voices traveling from the street, but if she cared that she could be seen here with me, she didn't show it. There was only need written all over her face, and I was a fool thinking I could deny us this.

She stood in front of me with her shirt wrapped around her chest, bare all the way down, and I knew if we had more light in here, I would clearly see the crown of thorns tattooed on her thigh.

"Are you gonna keep standing there staring at me, or are you gonna fuck me?"

A growl tore out of my mouth, and the need to hold her, own her, possess every single inch of her rode me hard. I was pressed against her in the next second, cupping her sex that dripped on my hand.

"What was that?

She bit her lower lip as my middle finger parted her lower lips and rubbed against the puckered nub that begged to be touched. "Oh, God."

"I can't hear you, Sunshine." My teeth found the column of her neck, and the satisfaction of knowing that she was going to wake up tomorrow with my marks all over her body drove me to the heavens. "You want me to fuck you?"

"Y-Yes," she whimpered. "I want to feel you filling me up."

God-fucking-dammit.

I slid my finger up and down, running a tiny circle against her opening as she thrust in my hand. She clenched around me as I slid inside. Velvety heat enveloped my middle finger, but I wanted to taste her before I fucked her.

Dropping down on my knees, I removed my hand from her pussy, instead spreading her legs until I could smell her arousal. I kissed the inside of her thigh, moving higher and higher until she trembled underneath my touch, begging me to press my lips against her hot center.

"St-Sto-, it's too much..." She trailed off. "Please, please, please."

I lapped on her clit in the next second, while her fingers grabbed my hair, pushing my face closer. Her juices dripped down my chin, my fingers digging into her thighs and the sweet oblivion enveloped my body as I drowned in the noises she produced.

Her thighs quivered as I flattened my tongue against her opening and I had a feeling if I wasn't holding her up, she would already be on the floor. My dick was rock hard, begging for attention, begging to be sheathed inside of her heat.

"I-I need…" she moaned.

I pulled back, gazing at her. "What do you need, Ophelia?"

She looked down at me, her cheeks flushed, eyes hooded, and said what I wanted to hear. "You. I need you."

Like a man possessed, I stood up, lifting her and taking her ass in my hands. With her back pressed against the wall, her hands were free to do whatever she wanted and before I could even react, she wrapped them around my dick, aiming him at her opening. My eyes were transfixed on the spot where the crown of my cock touched her and then slowly disappeared as she guided me inside.

I stiffened when the realization hit me. "Wait." I stopped her, trying to pull back. "No condom."

I was a fucking idiot for not thinking about it earlier. Kids weren't in any of my plans right now.

"Didn't stop you before." She grinned, trying to pull me back.

"Dammit, Ophelia." I was almost completely out when she draped her hands around my shoulders, pulling us closer together.

"I'm on birth control." She kissed my jaw. "See here." She lifted her right hand, but I couldn't see anything. "I have a Nexplanon."

"A Nex what?"

"Nexplanon." The little minx laughed. "It's a birth control implant."

A birth control implant? It took me a second to realize what she was telling me. I didn't have to use condoms with her. I could feel her any time, every time. Not that it stopped us today, but I wasn't in the right frame of mind when she showed up with her angry little face.

I didn't wait for her to put me back inside. I slammed all the way to the hilt, and a scream bubbled from her, filling the air around us. Her heat enveloped me, holding me captive. I pulled out and slammed back in with the same ferocious force. Her head fell on my shoulder and I could feel her lips on me before she bit the skin on my neck.

"Jesus, fuck."

I picked up the pace, my own teeth rattling inside my head. Her head went backward, her eyes connecting with mine again. Underneath the dark shadows, I saw the woman that was meant to be mine, if only she allowed it to happen.

"Do you like being fucked like this?" Thrust. "In public." Thrust. "Where every single person can see how undone you can come for me?"

I rolled my hips, holding her legs, my pubic bone hitting her clit with every single thrust. In and out. The alley was filled with my grunts, her moans, sweet nothings whispered into the air. The terms of endearment, I didn't think she even realized she said.

"Baby, yes." Her eyes rolled to the back of her head as I increased the pace, feeling the incoming eruption gathering in my balls.

"Fuck." My lips sought hers. Our tongues battled against each other, fighting for dominance, fighting for release. Her hands enveloped around my neck, holding me in her embrace. I pistoned inside of her wet heat, knowing that the orgasm I was chasing was close. So, so fucking close. "Are you going to come for me Ophelia," I mumbled against her lips, trying to catch my breath. "Are you going to squeeze me like earlier today?"

"God, yes." Her eyes closed, but I wanted to see her as she came undone by me.

I grabbed her throat, wrapping my fingers around the delicate skin, feeling her erratic heartbeat. "Open your eyes, baby." I didn't have to tell her twice before those blue orbs zeroed in on me. The black of her irises almost ate at the pure blue color I liked looking at so much. "That's my girl."

"That's... That's the spot." Beads of sweat coated her forehead, and I knew I looked exactly the same. "Oh, God," she groaned. "Faster. Please, just fucking go faster."

I smirked, knowing she was so close, and I was the only one that could bring her to the finish line. But instead of increasing my pace, I slowed down, pulling almost completely out.

"What the fuck?" Her eyes widened, anger blazing in them.

"Are you gonna stay?"

"Storm," she whimpered as I circled my hips, only keeping the head of my dick inside of her. She tried moving herself closer to me, but I held her in place, soaking in the frustration coming off her.

"Move, goddammit."

"No." I bit on her lower lip. "Not until you promise you'll fucking stay and heal."

"You're not the fucking boss of me."

She tried pushing me away, but I pushed closer, inching my dick deeper into her. It pained me as much as it pained her, but this was the only way; for now.

"Are you sure about that, Sunshine? Because your body tells me otherwise." I pressed one hand against her breast, rubbing the puckered nipple between my fingers. "These tell me that I am the boss of you right now."

"Fuck. Off," she gritted through her teeth, but it wasn't the usual bark she had. "I could leave here and find somebody else to finish what you've started."

The idea of her with anybody else flickered

through my head, and rage unlike anything I have ever felt turned my blood into molten lava. Her body underneath some bastard, her moans belonging to somebody else, her hair wrapped around another's hand, that didn't bode well with any part of me.

My hand wrapped around her neck, squeezing, punishing her for even thinking that.

"I should fucking chain you up in my basement with no relief." Her throat moved underneath my fingers, and the fire clashing with my eyes made me want to do just that. "Just imagine, Ophelia. I could finger, fuck, and lick you every single day, with no release. No fucking end."

"Do it." The little smirk that played on her mouth just increased the need to possess her. "Do it and I will never be yours. I will never belong to you if you cage me like an animal."

I knew that. I knew that as much as she wanted me, she was going to fight this every step of the way, because being with me meant she was losing her freedom.

"Do it, Storm!" she thundered. "You should ask them what I did to those that tried caging me."

Motherfucker... I smiled at that because I saw what she did to those that tried to cage her. She shoved her knife as far as it would go into their chest. I'm sure Kieran would have something to say about it.

I wanted to strangle her, and I wanted to laugh. I had never met anybody who challenged me as she did. I also never met a person that made me want to be this. I wanted to tell her everything, and even my closest friends never knew what was going on inside my head.

"Fuck it," I murmured before I started slamming inside of her, eliciting a satisfying sigh

184

from her. Mouth open, cheeks flushed, noises that drove me wilder, she became undone as her walls clenched around me.

"Touch yourself." I wasn't going to last. "I want you to touch yourself and show me what you like."

Her hand sneaked between us, spreading her lips, grazing my dick as I pumped inside, pulling another groan from me.

"Storm, Storm, Storm..." she chanted as I slammed harder, deeper, chasing my own orgasm.

"Fuuuuck!" The back of her head hit the wall, her eyes closed, as her inner muscles clenched around me, and I was done. With one last slam inside, she started milking my dick. The aftershocks of her own orgasm rushing through her, I almost blacked the fuck out.

My hips continued pushing in and out as my head rested on her shoulder. I was surprised I still hadn't dropped her, because this shit... Fuck. Her fingers trailed through my hair, stirring my cock again, but I didn't want us to stay here. We were already way too loud, and today wasn't the day where I wanted to be arrested for public indecency. It wasn't like the cops would keep us for way too long, but I had better plans for the two of us.

"I have a question," she whispered.

I cleared my throat, trying to find the strength to gather up the words. "Tell me." She smelled like me, she tasted like my everything, and if she asked me to give her my bike right now, I probably would.

"Were you born in Santa Monica?"

I stiffened as soon as the words left her mouth, knowing that even talking about that place brought memories I could never get rid of.

"No." I stood taller, looking at her. "I came

here when I was thirteen years old."

"With your parents?" she asked carefully. Knowing her history, I wasn't surprised that she assumed something was wrong with mine. Well, something was wrong, alright.

"No, I was alone."

She waited for me to elaborate further and I didn't know if I could.

Trust, honesty, ring a bell?

Yes, it did fucking ring a bell, but I didn't want to rehash history with my dick still inside of her. Not that I ever wanted to talk about that part of my life, but in order for us to move forward, I knew I would have to. One day, I would have to.

Taking a deep breath, I told her what almost nobody else knew. A secret I held close to my heart. A secret too filthy to tarnish this world with, but I had to. If I wanted her to trust me, I needed to start trusting her.

"I was born in Winworth." Her eyes clouded because we both knew who did business there. "I was born to a junkie mother and a father with a terrible temper. I was born there, lived there, until they sold me."

"They what?"

I almost wanted to laugh at the incredulous look on her face. If only she knew.

"They sold me, Ophelia. They exchanged me for their next fix and if I ever saw my mother again, she would beg me to send her to hell."

FOURTEEN

Ophelia

HIS WORDS BOUNCED around my head as I tried to comprehend what he was trying to tell me.

They sold me.

My heart clenched painfully for the boy he must have been and for the man he is now.

They sold me.

The way he said those three words, the way his voice trembled as if he hated sharing it with me, as if it pained him even thinking about it, it fucking killed me from the inside. I wanted to cry for the little Storm that wasn't granted the love other kids had. I wanted to cry for both of us and this fucked-up destiny that was made for us. I wasn't sold, not really, because the devil had a claim on my soul long before I even knew what the true evil looked like.

The only difference between the two of us was that I realized who the real monster is when I was a little bit older.

"I met true evil when I was just a child, Sunshine." His fingers played with the strand of hair that fell over my face. "Other kids were terrified of the boogeyman that could crawl out of their wardrobe, but my boogeyman was the one that gave birth to me. They both made sure that I never had any visible bruises, but I can still remember it as clear as a day. The disgusting smell of our apartment, the tiny little pantry they used to lock me in if I dared to eat when they were too high to even care. I remember it all."

I bit down on my lip, trying to suppress the whimper that was threatening to erupt from my chest. He was a proud man, and the last thing I wanted him to think was that I pitied him. Because I didn't. This tall behemoth in front of me was one of the strongest people I knew. I complained about the lack of love, lack of affection, but I had everything I ever wanted to have. What did he have? Two parents that didn't give a shit about him.

Two monsters that sold a child, and for what?

"How old were you?" I asked carefully as he lowered me down on my feet. Now that the adrenaline, the high of having him in me again trailed off, my legs were shaky, barely holding me up. Noticing it, he draped an arm around my waist, holding me up.

"Four."

One word. One fucking word was enough to make me want to hunt them down and claw their eyes out for what they did to him.

"The scar—"

"It was a gift from daddy dearest when I wasn't able to carry four of his beers. He got a little mad."

"Jesus Christ, Storm."

"No, hey." He palmed my face, drawing me closer to him. "I don't want to see that pity on your face."

"It's not a pity. I'm angry." I huffed. "I am so

fucking angry."

How could they do this? Not that my own family ranked higher than that, but I had other people that took care of me. Other people that fed us, clothed us, and made sure we did our homework. Even in her most fucked-up state, my mother never wanted me gone. I just thought that she was never supposed to be a mother. She was never supposed to have three kids in the first place.

But this, this revelation... My hands itched to kill them. My soul wanted to seek revenge for him, even though it was probably the last thing he wanted. He was proud, stubborn, probably as violent as I was, but he was also broken. Knowing that you weren't wanted by those that were supposed to protect you killed your soul in a different way.

There were different types of love, different types of care, and while you could survive a broken heart from a lover, you could never survive a broken heart from your family. I fucking hated Theo with all my soul, but it also ate at my insides for years that the only brother I had only wanted to see me dead or gone.

It ate at me that the mother I so desperately wanted to love would rather snort another line of cocaine than hug me. But I still had them in my life. I at least had moments where my world wasn't pitch black, where the colors invaded and everything was fine for a few moments.

And what did he have? A lifetime of "what-ifs" and fucking assholes for parents.

"And then what happened?"

The soft look he had while he caressed my face was immediately gone, and the mask he wore around other people was firmly put in place, hiding any and all emotions from me.

190

"That's a story for another time."

He bent down, gathering our pants, extending mine to me and starting to put his on. His body language was off, and a part of me hated that I even asked about it. I knew all about the memories that could destroy your whole day, your whole month. The memories that made me want to press the blade to my skin, just so that they would go away.

They made me want to get lost in the sweet oblivion only the white powder could provide, but then I would remember my mother and the faraway look she would always get when drugs hit her system, and I'd stop. I never wanted to be like any of them.

My father wanted me to be like him, and for a little while there, I wanted it to. I wanted him to be proud of me, to look at me as something more than a mere investment. I wanted to feel that love I only saw in movies or read in books. The type of love that Leanor Nightingale showered her kids with.

Speaking of… "Where's Kieran's mother now?"

She might not be my biggest fan and I wasn't hers, but I didn't want her to be harmed in this game of tug-of-war we were all playing. The innocent should be left alone. I knew that now.

"Taken care of." That didn't give me any relief. "Don't worry about her."

He was avoiding my eyes, which only pushed me to ask again.

"Storm?"

He turned abruptly; the angry glare directed at me a complete contrast to the soft look he was giving me just a minute ago. "It's none of your business, Ophelia."

None of my business? Did he really think I was gonna let him use me only for my body? Stupid fucking men. Stupid, stupid, stupid... Though, in this situation I didn't know who was the bigger fool — me for thinking that men would allow me to step into their world and act like I was their equal, or him for thinking that I would be a complacent little girl.

They all thought I was something they could control when I wanted things completely opposite from that. That whole conversation we had earlier, those sweet little bullshit promises, they all fell into the water with just a few words.

How many times did my father utter the same words to me? How many times did Kieran behave like I was beneath him just because I was a girl? How many times would they underestimate me for me to say enough?

Well, this was enough.

"Take me back to the club." My voice was stone cold as I uttered the words. If he wanted to play this game, he wasn't going to win. I was the master in playing games, and I wasn't going to go stupid just because he shoved his dick into my pussy, making me sing Hallelujah. No, that's not how this was going to go.

He wanted me? Then he was going to have to prove that I wasn't just another pussy warming his bed. Words meant nothing if there were no actions to support them. And for me, actions spoke louder than any other bullshit they were spewing my way.

Trust, respect, love, all of those had to be earned. Nothing would fall miraculously in your lap just because you wished for it. Just because you whispered sweet nothings in somebody's ear didn't mean they were yours. No, you had to fight for what you wanted to be yours, and he obviously thought I would just fall on my knees and suck his cock until the end of days.

He wanted to argue, I could see it on his face, but I was too tired to entertain the idea. Before he could even open his mouth, I was walking outside of the alley, heading toward where he parked the bike. I could hear the angry stomps of his feet behind me, but I didn't turn around. If he was going to behave like a world-class asshole, he was going to be seeing only my back and nothing more.

I already had enough assholes in my life trying to dictate what I did and whom I did it with; he wasn't going to be another one, even if it killed me not having him touch me.

My body was too happy to have his hands on me, but my mind and my heart waged a battle I wasn't ready for. He was just a distraction. Yeah, that's what all of this was. A way for me to run away from the fucked-up mess clattering inside my head. I always preferred shutting down the emotions coursing through my veins because they always messed with my mind.

The heart was such a fragile organ, and I would give anything just to get rid of it. Everything would be much easier if I really couldn't feel anything. I tried shutting it all down, putting it into a nice little box, locked and sealed, but it wasn't working right now.

I blamed him.

I took the helmet he left earlier and placed it on my head, fidgeting with the straps that were annoying the fuck out of me earlier. And just like earlier, I couldn't adjust it myself.

"*Suka.*" Fucking shit. My ears buzzed from the pent-up energy and anger I was carrying around. My hands trembled because I knew I wouldn't be able to put it on by myself, and the asshole to which I decided I wasn't going to talk to was going to have to help me. I wanted to throw the fucking thing across the street, but I couldn't draw attention to me.

Not that riding with the president of Sons of Hades wasn't drawing attention already, but you know, small things. My father had ears and eyes everywhere, and as long as I was here, all of them were in danger.

I could feel his presence behind me, an energy zapping between us, but I didn't turn around. I hated admitting it, but his words hurt something inside of me I thought I buried a long time ago. Which also meant I had another weakness I couldn't afford.

Love is a weakness.

Friends are a weakness.

Emotions, both good and bad, were a motherfucking weakness, and this version of myself, this wasn't me. This meek, complacent, quiet, anxious person, this wasn't me.

I felt it before his hand even landed on my shoulder, and as soon as he made contact, I took a step forward, moving away from him. Anger rolled off of him in waves, but I didn't give a fuck about the feelings of somebody that obviously wanted to just trap me.

No, his little plan could go and fuck itself. I wasn't an animal to be caged. I wasn't a damsel in distress to be saved. No, this bitch could save herself.

"Ophe—"

"Don't even think about it." I moved further away, almost stepping onto the street. Cars honked as they passed in front of me, earning a middle finger from me. I wasn't sure if I wanted to shove it up their asses or maybe Storm's.

Maybe he would like it?

A crash and a thunderous, "Motherfuck,"

sounded behind me before the helmet I was still fidgeting with sailed off my head, flying down the street. I stood there, my mouth agape, looking between the spot where it landed and the asshole fuming next to me.

"Did you just—"

His hand wrapped around my arm, pulling me back to where his bike stood.

"What the fuck?"

"Get on the bike, Ophelia."

"No," erupted from me before I could even think about it. Not that I didn't agree, but I didn't exactly want to see the murderous expression on his face. His eye twitched, and the tempest in those green eyes held a promise of retribution if I didn't do what he wanted.

I ripped my arm from him, taking a step back, glaring at him. Two could play this motherfucking game of who-is-angrier, and he was going to lose. Nothing ever pissed me off as much as somebody trying to control me and trying to downplay what I could do and who I was. I didn't have enough middle fingers to show him how I really felt right now.

All those warm and fuzzy feelings he managed to evoke in me were gone, replaced by the bubbling anger that threatened to burn us both to the ground. This is why I avoided any kind of contact with other people.

Sex was just a transaction between two people—dick inside the pussy, both of you get to come, and that's it. But this shit he was trying to plant in my head, he was trying to make me believe, this wouldn't work. At least not for me.

"Get. On. The. Motherfucking. Bike," he gritted through his teeth as I stood there, still as a statue. I wasn't one of his little whores that would do everything, just because he said so.

If he wanted to have a girl that would ask *How high?* every time he said *Jump*, he was in the wrong fucking church. I don't kneel for men. They fucking kneel for me.

I smiled at him, loving the way his chiseled jaw seemed to grind every single time I spoke, and now wasn't any different. "Make me."

That scarred eyebrow lifted, but I didn't have enough time to react, because he was suddenly right in front of me, pressing his nose against mine. Small puffs of breath washed over my lips, and if I lifted my head higher, I would be able to press my lips to his.

But as he pushed me, I started pushing back. My hands found his throat, his unshaven stubble stabbing into my palms. His lashes lowered, shadowing the olive skin, waiting for my next step. I could kill him right now. Kill him and get away from here.

I could be free of him, and these sick feelings twisting my insides, but I couldn't make myself do it. No matter what, he was already deep beneath my skin, hiding in my veins, taking a hold of my heart, and if I allowed him to sink deeper, I would need a fucking priest to exorcise him from my body.

His scent washed over me as I pressed against the tendons on his neck, earning a grunt from his mouth, but other than that, he didn't move. He didn't try to stop me. I could end all of this. I knew where to press, I knew what to do, but I couldn't.

I didn't even notice my lower lip trembling, not until he dragged his thumb over the soft skin.

"Baby," he murmured, and my eyes closed involuntarily, hating the way that tiny little word made me feel. I didn't want him. I didn't, I didn't, I didn't... But as I opened my eyes and looked into his darkened green ones, I knew that as much as I didn't want him, I needed him.

I needed him to calm the monsters that were quiet right now. I needed him to tell me everything was going to be okay. I couldn't wage this war by myself anymore. I didn't want him, but I needed everything he had to offer, even if I hated myself for it.

I was always self-sufficient, but this, this energy crackling between us, this is what I needed to have in my life. And until three days ago, I didn't know how much I missed it. All these years, that part of me laid dormant, quiet, almost dead, and then he waltzed into my life—again—fucking up all my plans.

"Let's go home, Phee." His lips brushed against mine, and the murmur of people around us, the sounds of cars passing by, the memories I hated, they all disappeared, leaving only the two of us in this little bubble he was putting me into. One soft kiss, then another one, and instead of killing him, instead of suffocating the life out of him, I draped my hands around his neck, pulling him closer.

His hand disappeared into my hair, holding my head as his lips devoured mine. Our tongues danced together, but there was no fight for dominance like the last few times. This time he let me lead.

A whimper escaped my mouth as the heat pooled between my thighs, and I started grinding against him, feeling the outline of his hardened dick.

"We need to get going, babe," he mumbled against my lips, slowing down when all I wanted was to continue what we were doing. "We can't do this here, Phee."

197

I knew we couldn't, but all rational thoughts left my body when his lips connected with mine. I never put too much thought into kissing, because it was just a means to an end. Just another choreographed part I knew how to play. But Storm kissing me was like nothing I ever felt before. My blood turned into molten lava every single time, and I remembered that first time his lips captured mine, on top of that cliff, warming me from the inside out regardless of the freezing weather at the time.

Strands of dark hair fell over his forehead, and for a moment there, I lost myself in the forest green eyes that reminded me of summers and meadows covered with dandelions. This feeling terrified me, but it had been so long since the last time I felt even close to this, I wanted to cling to it. Savor it, trap it, because having this meant I was still alive.

I could still feel something other than the perpetual anger and the need for destruction.

"Come on." He grabbed my hand and led me toward the bike, straddling it before he turned and looked at me. "Hop on."

I was dazed, dizzy with lust and need, and a thousand other emotions I couldn't name. I was unraveling and it was all his doing. I wasn't Ophelia the Assassin anymore, well, I wasn't just her. Everything I kept inside bubbled to the surface, and I was terrified it would destroy my world.

You don't need emotions, moy malen'kiy drakon. Papa's words echoed in my head. He always called me his little dragon, and if I was smarter, I would've plunged my knife through his throat a long time ago. He was the one who pushed me to be this robot, and I thought it was fine. I thought this was how the world was supposed to run, how I was supposed to live.

But I was wrong, and maybe, just maybe, I could finally see how things were supposed to work.

FIFTEEN

Storm

THE MOMENT WE came back to the club, half empty with most of the members still at the beach, Ophelia ran inside, never even sparing a glance my way. I would be lying if I said that it didn't hurt, but I let her be.

I saw the hardening of her eyes when I sputtered those fucking words, and as soon as they left my mouth, I knew I fucked up. I treated her like a piece of ass when she was my equal. Women in this industry were always regarded as pawns when they should've been regarded as queens. I saw it one too many times, where men thought they knew better just because we possessed physical strength.

And I behaved like I was one of those mongrels that wouldn't share what was happening just because she was a woman.

Since I fucked up three days ago with her basically running away from me, it had been radio silence. She wouldn't look at me, she wouldn't speak to me, she moved to another room with Atlas's help — who for the first time in our lives was pissed at me — and she wouldn't let me touch her. I knocked on her door a million times by now, but I was always greeted with silence. I was getting angrier and angrier at this whole situation.

A stupid situation if you ask me. Before we left the pier, I thought things had become better. It wasn't an apology, not really, but I tried showing her what she meant to me, rather than telling her. She wouldn't believe me even if I tried explaining how my chest aches every time she wasn't near. And for the last three days, my chest hurt as if someone has shot me with a gun, leaving the bullet inside.

I rubbed at the spot absentmindedly, as our Inner Circle gathered around me, waiting for the meeting to start. I could feel Indigo's eyes on me, but I kept staring at the paper in my hands and the letter addressed to me. I knew the handwriting; I could recognize it anywhere.

How many times did he send me a letter when I was just a kid, trapped inside that hell, calling me his *malen'kaya igrushka*, his little toy? The urge to vomit was right there, and I knew that my usually olive complexion had turned as pale as the wall behind me. Even after all these years, I couldn't run away from everything they did to me. My body didn't belong to them anymore, but it was as if my soul refused to believe that we were finally free.

It had been eighteen years since I managed to escape The Mansion, but the memories stayed no matter how hard I tried to get rid of them. Women, drugs, alcohol, violence, nothing worked. The only thing that did work was revenge, which seemed to grow inch by inch with every passing day. And I held onto it because there was nothing else grounding me or keeping me here.

But now she was here, and the wrath and pain I held onto suddenly wasn't the only thing keeping me going.

"Storm?"

I lifted my head, seeing Felix's worried face on the opposite side of the table. If I didn't know, I would've never guessed that he and Atlas shared the same parents. Where Atlas was blond, all smiles and pale skin, Felix was dark, brooding, quiet. Hell, he could pass as Indigo's brother rather than Atlas's.

This meeting today was something I've been avoiding for days, but I couldn't hide the truth from them any longer. Indigo, Atlas, Felix, and Hunter were my most trusted men. The four guys that accepted the scrawny little kid that was brought here by our previous prez. They took one look at me and decided that I was worthy of their company.

Which is why I hated the worried looks on their faces and the silence surrounding us. They knew me better than anyone else, and I hated hiding things from them, even if it was for their benefit. We were more than friends, more than members of a motorcycle club—we were a family.

And you don't keep secrets from your family.

I straightened up in my chair as they sat down, waiting for me to speak. I didn't know what to say other than, I fucked up. I didn't even know where to begin, because no matter what I said, somebody was going to get hurt. This was like a game of Russian Roulette, but there would be no winners.

The letter crumbled in my fist, burning the skin, urging me to open it now. But it would have to wait until after this meeting, because whatever was inside, I wasn't going to like it. I could feel evil seeping through the paper already. Even now, I could feel the stench of his alcohol-induced breath, and those roaming hands.

"Storm!" I jumped in my chair when Indigo

yelled out my name. My body was here, but my mind was a thousand miles away. His dark eyes drilled into mine, impatience written all over his face. "Are we going to start this today? What the fuck has gotten into you?"

"Nothing," I mumbled, shoving the letter into the front pocket of my pants. I took a deep breath before I started talking again. "I fucked up."

The collective inhale at my declaration was enough to make me even more nervous than I was before.

"No, scratch that." I pushed the chair back and stood up and started pacing from one side to another. "I made such a fucking mess, and none of you knew about it. Except for Atlas."

Three sets of eyes turned to fidgeting Atlas. He told me a million times not to do this. He warned me that Las Vegas wasn't worth it and that we would find another way to get revenge. But I didn't listen.

God, my stubborn ass didn't listen at all, even though he begged me not to sell my soul to the devil.

"What is he talking about?" Indigo asked him, before looking back at me. "What are you talking about?"

You could slice the tension with a knife, and I was the one to blame. Hell, if they wanted to kick my ass for this, I wouldn't stop them. I might encourage them.

"I made a deal with the Devil."

"What ar —"

"I made a deal with Logan Nightingale."

What and *shit*, and several other curses echoed around the room while I refused to meet any of their eyes. We all knew what he did, what his family did to us, and I fucked up. I fucked up

203

because I was blinded by my own revenge, so much that I never even considered what this would mean for my club, my family.

"How could you?" It was Hunter that asked. His usual calm demeanor was cracking. His eye twitched as he glared at me, but I didn't have an answer to that question. I was an idiot. He stood up and walked around the table, stopping right in front of me. "You know what he did to us. You know how we all feel about those motherfuckers."

"I know."

"Then fucking why?" he bellowed, the vein on his forehead popping.

"Hunt." Indigo walked behind him, probably prepared to stop him if he tried to attack me.

"Don't fucking start, Indigo. He," Hunter pointed at me, "fucked up. The plan was to get back at them for what they did to us in Las Vegas. Or did you forget about that?" he asked. "Did you forget how they burned children, women and men in that fucking church?" His hands landed on my chest as he pushed me backward. "Did you forget the devastation we had to go through? The pain, the grief, those screams of families that lost their loved ones?" Another shove, and Felix and Atlas came behind me. "Did you fucking forget about Lilianna, my wife, or my little girls?"

"I didn't forget." But I felt like the biggest shit right now.

"Then why, Storm? Give me one good fucking reason not to knock the teeth out of your skull right now."

But I didn't have a good reason. The one I had wasn't sufficient to agree to lay in bed with the Nightingales. I wasn't sure who was worse— Nikolai Aster or Logan Nightingale. One of them pretended to be a respectable businessman, while the other one steered clear from the general public and preferred to stick to the shadows.

"I wanted to get Las Vegas back," I mumbled, but before any of us could react, Hunter's fist connected with my face, knocking me to the floor.

"You motherfucker!" he screamed as he jumped on me, laying punch after punch. "Piece of shit!" He pressed his knee against my throat, cutting off my air supply. "I should fucking kill you!"

"Hunter! No!" Indigo tried pulling him back, but the adrenaline, the anger, all the other emotions he's been keeping inside, they all tumbled out, and I was the target. I was the breaking point.

Indigo flew into the chair I was sitting in before, while Atlas and Felix tried to separate the two of us. I didn't fight because we all knew I deserved this. How many times did I promise myself I would never do this? How many times did I promise them I would always put the club first along with their wishes and needs?

I fucking promised them we would never stoop so low, because working with Logan or Nikolai was worse than walking through Hell. They could give you everything you ever wanted, but just as fast as you got it, they would take it away, breaking you apart.

They almost broke us when their henchman attacked Las Vegas while the rest of us were distracted with a shipment gone wrong. They tortured, raped, and killed innocent people. There were children that had just learned to walk. There were women that had just started living their lives.

There were parents, memories, and they burned it all to the ground.

By the time we arrived at the church, it was already too late. The only thing that was left were the ashes and pain so grave I thought none of us were going to recover. Logan Nightingale wasn't the one that gave the order, it was Kieran, but I knew they worked together. Even if Kieran hated his father, he used to tell him everything.

"Let go of me!" Hunter screamed as Atlas and Felix held him away from me. My vision blurred and I could taste the blood inside my mouth. I was tempted to let him finish the job. "He shouldn't have done this!"

No, I shouldn't have. I should've talked to them. I should've told them. When the Albanians came to me with the request to help one of their own with the Nightingale heir, the whole club supported it, because it meant that the one who fucked our lives was going to die. But when Logan Nightingale contacted me days after that, I couldn't say no.

You could've, you just didn't want to.

Okay, I could have said no, but at the mention of Las Vegas and Nikolai Aster's head on a plate, all coherent thoughts left me and the only thing I could think of was revenge.

"So, what now? You're his little bitch?" Hunter kept screaming and fighting against Felix and Atlas, while I kept lying on the floor, trying to move my limbs. My face was wet, no doubt from my own blood, and I wasn't sure if the inability to move came from the punches he threw at me or from this heavy feeling deep within my soul.

Indigo stopped next to me, helping me to get up. No matter how much I fucked up, they always had my back. But this time, I wasn't sure if our friendship would be able to survive. Hunter's whole face was red, both from my blood and the anger he was emanating. He resembled a bull, and I was the target.

"Come on." Indigo pulled me up, almost carrying me to the chair. "You look like shit."

"Yours isn't the prettiest face I have seen either, Indigo."

The fucker only smirked, but I could see the anger brewing in the depths of those dark eyes. They were all disappointed in me, and with a mighty big reason. My head was ringing, but I had to tell them everything. I dragged a hand over my face, wincing as it connected with my nose and I knew, I just knew it was broken.

"We might need to call Doc for this," Indigo said.

"Later." I looked at my palm, at the red hue glistening underneath the light. Silence descended on us and the only thing I could hear were Hunter's grunts and the buzzing of the air conditioner. The three-headed beast with our club's motto glared at me from the wall behind Hunter, Atlas and Felix. *Trust, honesty, respect, family*—those four words were the ones we lived by, and I ignored all of them. If they couldn't trust their president, how could I lead them and make everything right?

"Start. Talking," Hunter gritted out. "I'm five minutes from going nuclear on you, Storm, so you better start fucking talking."

And I did. I told them how persistent Logan was. I told them that even though I said no the first two times, when he brought up Las Vegas and Nikolai, I couldn't resist. Logan knew about the deal with the Albanians, and he didn't care if his sons lived or died. He didn't care who got hurt, as long as he got what he wanted. He was the one that gave us his wife. He set up the whole thing.

"Holy shit," Felix mumbled.

I couldn't look at them. Seeing the disappointment on their faces was too much to handle right now. This web of lies I entangled myself into was getting bigger and bigger, and I didn't know how to get out of it. I lied to them. I lied to Ophelia. I lied to the whole club, and for what? A revenge that should've been thought through before I acted on it.

I dove in without a plan, with poor execution never even thinking about the consequences.

"There's more, isn't there?" Indigo asked when the other three kept quiet.

"What did he want in return, Storm?" Hunter asked, sounding calmer than before. "What was the price for Las Vegas?"

This time I looked at them because the price was more than I was willing to pay. But I told them. I told them everything I'd been keeping inside for the last few months. I told them about the whispers in the dark and the impending war the Syndicate wanted to start. I told them that none of us were safe unless we fought.

I told them that the prize Logan asked for was the one he was never going to get, but it was apparently a wrong thing to say, because in the next moment Hunter all but ran across the room with his fists ready and a murderous look on his face.

No one tried to stop him as he lifted me from the chair and threw me across the room. I wanted to keep all of this between us, but Hunter had different ideas. He opened the door leading to the lounge area, and as I tried to get up from the floor, he pulled me by my shirt and pushed me through toward the open area where several members were sitting around the tables.

All of their smiles disappeared as their eyes landed on me and pissed off Hunter hovering over me.

This was going to get extremely messy.

SIXTEEN

Ophelia

AVOIDANCE WAS MY best friend, but after three days of practically hiding from Storm, I was starting to get tired. He tried to talk to me, but every single time I would even hear his voice, I would leave the room, or just lock myself inside my own.

And while it was a pretty fucking amazing room, it didn't have him, and it sucked.

It sucked even more because it felt as if we were never even separated. Two days. It took him two days between us leaving the church and me waking up to bury himself beneath my skin. But he fucked up majorly, and it hurt more than I wanted to admit.

He wanted me here, not the other way around, so he should fucking act like it.

Are you sure he's the only one that wants you here? It seems that you want to be here as well.

Oh, fuck the fuck off. I made a promise, and no matter how he behaved, I refused to go against my promises. I failed to keep up with those so many times in the past, and this time I was going to stick to it. Besides, I still needed to heal. The doctor that came here a day after our little trip to the beach said that the finger wasn't broken, just dislocated.

The wrapped digit still throbbed, and I remembered how much I screamed when he rearranged the bone. So yeah, if I wanted to help Maya, I had to heal.

Keep telling yourself that.

This was really wonderful. I was quite literally talking to myself, and if that wasn't an inclination of how fucked up my mind was, I didn't know what was.

I've been a cranky bitch for the last three days, and as if everybody could sense where my mood was, most of the people steered clear from me. But not Zoe. Oh no.

I had a feeling that I wouldn't be able to escape her even if I wanted to. And right now, with her babbling about the latest customer issue she had, I really wanted to.

"And then she said, *I want my money back*. Can you believe it?"

Truth to be told, I had no idea what she was talking about, but I pretended to listen. "Mhm."

"Unbelievable. And then I told her..." But I wasn't listening at all anymore because the shouting from the inside of the house pulled my attention. Something was going on, and here I was about to think that they actually ran a monastery instead of a motorcycle club. I still had to see some fists flying around and guns being drawn.

We were sitting on the front lawn, surrounded by more men in leather than some BDSM conventions have seen. Each and every one of them had guns strapped to their hips, and they all watched us like hawks, while at the same time keeping an eye on the street.

One of them was Creed, who spent the majority of the time ricocheting between glaring at me and this sad, devastated look that I couldn't quite decipher. But as the shouting from the inside became louder, three of them, including Creed, ran inside, leaving us with a young guy who had *Prospect* on his vest.

"Are you listening to me?" Zoe asked.

"I'm sorry, ZoZo." I stood up. "My mind is literally oatmeal today."

She started laughing instead of glaring, again reminding me of Ava and her carefree demeanor. God, it would be so easy to stay here forever and have all these people in my life. Even though they all knew who I was and what I'd done, nobody behaved like they wanted to kill me.

"Where are you going?" Zoe asked instead.

"Something's going on, I think." I kept looking at the front door, trying to listen to the raised voices. "I'm gonna check it out."

"Oh no, missy." She stood up as well, glaring at me. "Whatever it is, you might want to stay out of it."

Wasn't it beautiful growing up in an environment where you had somebody else to protect you? This was the main difference between Zoe and me. She had people that would do anything for her, and she didn't have to run into the fire. I had to because I had to know what was going on. If there was a shitstorm, I needed to know because I had to protect myself. I didn't have a brother or a club full of wicked bikers who would lay down their life for me.

I envied her. I envied the carefree demeanor with which she strolled through life. I envied the fact that whatever demons she saw during her life didn't diminish the light in her eyes.

"I need to know, Zoe." I came closer to her and squeezed her hand. "I can handle myself in every single situation." Well, I couldn't do relationships, but you know. If you needed me to kick, maim or kill somebody, I could do it.

After a minute or so, she exhaled and rolled her eyes. One of these days, she was going to roll her eyes so far back that she wouldn't be able to bring them back.

Whenever Indigo spoke with her—she rolled her eyes.

Whenever I tried to refuse staying here—she rolled her eyes.

Whenever she saw Felix with one of the girls from the club—she rolled her eyes.

And trust me, all these situations had been happening quite a lot.

"I just don't want you to get hurt, or worse, kicked out."

I started laughing at her choice of words, because between me getting hurt or getting kicked out of the club, she decided that getting kicked out was worse than bleeding. Now that I thought about it, maybe it was. Atlas kept drilling it into my head that there were people out there who wanted to see me dead, so maybe having this protection from the club wasn't the worst thing after all.

But only until I healed enough.

I was almost counting days until the month was over. He would have to let me go, one way or another.

"I promise I won't get hurt." I snickered. "Or kicked out. I just want to see what's happening."

"Fine." She reluctantly let go of my hand. "But we still need to talk about that mopey look you've been sporting for the last three days."

"What mopey look?" My eyes widened at her statement, and the look on her face told me everything. God, I really didn't miss the whole Spanish Inquisition about my relationships, even though they were almost imaginary.

"We will talk later," she said as she plopped down into the chair, taking her phone out. I didn't really know what to say, because that conversation, whenever it happened, was going to start with the topic of Storm, and right now his name left a bitter taste in my mouth.

Maybe I would feel better if I kicked him in his nuts?

I stood there gawking at her, but when one of those perfectly done eyebrows arched on her face, I knew I had to get away. Otherwise, that conversation was about to start now, and I planned on avoiding it for as long as I could.

I speed-walked toward the front door where several members blocked the entrance and tried to shimmy past them. A loud crash filtered through the air, and I walked faster through the hallway separating the two parts of the house. Shouting and what sounded like fighting came from the lounge area, and when I recognized one of those voices as Atlas's, I knew Storm was going to be there as well.

What I didn't expect once I arrived at the room, was Storm on the floor, getting punched by one of the guys I saw around the house. Indigo stood quietly next to the wall, his hands in the pockets of his pants and an indifferent look on his face.

What in the ever-loving fuck was going on?

Atlas and Felix tried blocking the other guy, but they were no match for the gigantic beast that pummeled Storm. And what did the fucker do? Nothing. He fucking did nothing.

His head kept flying from one side to the other, his body limp. Something ugly stirred inside my chest, and even though I was angry at him, I didn't want him to end up in the hospital with a concussion and broken bones.

"Hey, fucker!" I yelled as I stepped inside the room, bracing against the stares of several other bikers that just stood on the side while somebody fucked their president up. The hulk that was pummeling Storm stopped for a moment and looked at me. "What the fuck are you doing?"

"You," he spat out, and I wondered what I did to this sunshine to get such a reception.

"Yeah, me. What are you doing?" I walked toward them, refusing to look at Storm who started mumbling on the floor, finally noticing me there. The hulk kept quiet, looking at me in that I'm-gonna-fuck-you-up way. At this point, I should probably start making a waiting list of all the people that wanted to either kick my ass or see me dead.

Might need to hire a hostess for that. Maybe Zoe could help me?

"Are you deaf?" I propped my hands on my hips, standing a few feet away from him. "Or do you need me to repeat the question?"

Atlas stood behind him, and if looks could kill, I would probably be a dead woman right now. I had no idea what their problem was, or why all the other members just stood on the side while he kicked the shit out of Storm, and I didn't exactly care. If I didn't have to, I didn't want to witness any violence.

My whole life was already filled with it, and right now, my mood wasn't exactly the friendliest one.

"Do you have a death wish, little girl?" If I had a dollar for the number of times one of the meatheads called me a little girl, I could afford the therapy I obviously needed and a house in the Bahamas. "Get out of here. This is not a place for women."

My eye started twitching at the blatant chauvinistic comment and the snickers that sounded around me from the rest of the meatheads that obviously had the same opinion as the idiot in front of me.

"Would you like to repeat that, buttercup? But try using some big words. We're not in kindergarten anymore."

Ooh's and ah's came from all sides, and I must say, I felt just a little bit better. One thing that always pissed me off was men always putting women down, just because we were physically smaller, because we were women, and because they thought we couldn't handle the shit life would throw at us.

Joke's on them because women could handle a lot more than men could even dream of.

He stepped away from Storm and walked slowly toward me, drilling a hole into my forehead with his eyes. From the corner of my eye, I could see Atlas pulling Storm up, and Indigo, fucking Indigo, finally approached them to help. Creed finally appeared and I wondered where he went if I managed to get here before him. Was he taking a piss?

His eyes widened seeing me there, but I focused my attention on the hulk in front of me.

"Ophelia Aster." He rolled my name around his mouth, tasting it, playing with it. "Are you as lethal as they say you are?"

I shrugged. "Maybe." Two more steps and he was right in front of me. I had to crane my neck to look at his face. "Wanna test it?"

He seemed to contemplate it for a moment, reading me, gauging my reaction, but after a tense minute, he grinned.

"I like you." The feeling definitely wasn't mutual. "I just hate where you came from." That feeling was absolutely, one hundred percent mutual.

"Welcome to the club. I don't like it either." There was nothing there to like. Every single thing I ever loved about my birthplace, about my family, they managed to destroy it. So yeah, if these people wanted to judge me because I came from that family, I couldn't stop them. I knew what we did and what this last name I carried around stood for.

I knew about the atrocities my father committed, about the atrocities I committed as well. Even hell wouldn't want us.

Silence stretched around us until Storm finally decided to rejoin the party and start behaving like the president.

"No, wait." He wobbled on his feet, which would've been almost adorable if it wasn't for the fact that he allowed this guy to kick his ass. I wasn't sure which one I wanted to hurt more—Storm for allowing it to happen, when I knew full well that he could defend himself, or this idiot standing in front of me for attacking him in the first place. "Don't touch her."

He wasn't touching me, but it was cute that he suddenly decided to defend me.

"She had nothing to do with this."

The man laughed, but the mischief in his eyes told me he was going to play. He saw something I didn't, and when his hand wrapped around my neck and he turned us to face Storm, I knew exactly what it was.

I didn't know when or how or why, but I was Storm's weakness. That day with Creed, he would've killed him because he attacked me. And now, after that beating, he cared more about me being unharmed than himself.

Storm's eyes blazed with fury as the mountain behind me started inching backward, moving us away from him.

"Don't even fucking think about it, Hunter." Ah, we have a name, ladies and gentlemen. "She has nothing to do with any of this. Leave her out of it."

"That's really cute, Prez, but I think she does. We are in this newfound mess because of her."

Because of me? I didn't do anything.

"And I'm not sure if I want to go to war just because she has a nice pair of tits."

"You guys are assholes," I interrupted.

The hand around my throat tightened, cutting off the air supply. I gasped for air, trying to breathe through my mouth, but it was to no avail. The grip only increased as I started hitting his thighs.

Storm stumbled forward, followed by Atlas, sporting a murderous look on his face, and the last time I saw him looking like this was back in that church, just before I stabbed Kieran.

"Let. Her. Go." Storm enunciated every word. "I won't repeat myself."

Hunter or whatever his fucking name was, laughed, shaking both of us. "Are you going to tell her the truth?"

What truth? I looked at Storm then at a wincing Atlas, but the blank expressions told me nothing.

"You don't wanna do this here, Hunter. Trust me. I know you're pissed off. I understand that, but I will fucking skin you alive if I even see one bruise on her neck."

Black spots danced on the periphery of my vision, and I was getting tired of this cockfight they'd been having. Behaving like children was no way to solve issues, and whatever it was that Storm hid from me, I was going to find out.

But not like this. Not when I was getting choked.

While Hunter was getting distracted by Storm, I inched myself to the side, leaving enough space to hit him where it truly hurts. I fisted my hand and swung back, connecting it with his groin. The grip on my throat immediately loosened, and as he started bending forward, I moved to the side and lifted my knee, connecting it with his chin.

"I didn't ask you to choke me, asshole." I rubbed at my neck. "And you," I turned toward the shocked Storm, "start fucking walking to your room."

"I-I don't," he stammered. "What?"

"Your room, Storm. Now!"

The rest of the bikers that were standing on the side, watching the real-life rendition of *Game of Thrones*, started rushing out of the room, and under a minute it was only Storm, Felix, Atlas, Indigo, Hunter, and me standing in the room, surrounded by shattered furniture.

"Atlas," I called out, with my eyes still on Storm. "Can you bring us the first aid kit?"

"Uh, sure."

If I wanted to have children, I would either adopt some or have my own, but babysitting grown-ass men was not in any of my plans, and if this was how they behaved on a daily basis... No, I didn't even want to think about it.

"And you." I turned toward Hunter, who was still bent down, holding his junk. "The next time you call me a little girl, I am going to cut off your dick. Understood?"

"Mhm," he mumbled.

I was too fucking tired for this shit. Moving myself toward the stairs, I turned toward Storm who was still gawking at me.

"Want me to carry you as well?"

There was blood all over his face and over his neck. The shirt he wore was ripped in multiple places, and his hair had seen better days. If this were a set for a horror movie, he would fit right in.

"I'm coming," he grumbled, following me up the stairs. `

What the fuck were they thinking?

SEVENTEEN

Ophelia

STORM'S ROOM LOOKED like a bomb went off inside. His clothes were strewn all over the place, and I noticed that the shirt I wore the other day laid on the pillow next to his. I arched an eyebrow at him, but he just shrugged and proceeded walking toward the bed.

Anger emanated from him, and I could feel where this conversation was going to go. He was going to admonish me for getting involved, and I'd probably end up smacking him again for saying it. But when the words never came, I realized that he might have gotten hurt more than I initially realized.

His nose stood at an unnatural angle, while the blood continued trickling from his eyebrow. His whole face was going to be black and purple by tomorrow. I should be happy about it, I really, really should, but I hated seeing him hurt. I hated the blood Hunter spilled, and I hated that Storm let him.

"Why did you let him hit you?" I couldn't stop myself from asking. It's been a long time since I felt this way, like my because he was hurt. Somebody I cared about was hurt. I itched to touch him, to remove the blood coating his face, to make sure that nothing was broken. I expected him to brush me off, to once again be an insufferable asshole, but none of it came.

"Storm?" I closed the distance between us, stopping right in front of him, next to the bed. Pale beige walls were a stark contrast to the darkness our world was painted with, and if I didn't know better, I would've never guessed that this was his room. It was too bare, lifeless, and I wasn't sure if it was only the place he slept at or if he actually called it home.

I entwined my fingers through the long strands on top of his head, feeling the blood coating them, feeling the sharp stab of pain through my whole body when he refused to look at me. I pushed his head back, needing to look at him properly, not even caring about the shitty attitude he was throwing my way the other day. This distance between us wasn't as welcome as I thought at first.

I thought staying away from him was going to help me get my thoughts in order, but it didn't. I knew I was running away from whatever this was between us, but I couldn't stop myself from trying to forget the way his hands felt on my skin, or the way my whole body came alive when he kissed me. It was wrong. It was something I didn't want to have ever again, and yet, here I was, trying to care about the man I was supposed to be running away from.

"We had a disagreement," he finally mumbled, still refusing to meet my eyes. I stepped closer, my chest right in front of his eyes, my thighs between his and one of my hands in his hair, while the other one kept a hold of his shoulder. "It's nothing."

"Why did you let him hit you?" I asked again because I had to know. I was curious by nature, and I don't know, somewhere deep inside, I needed to know that he wasn't as self-destructive as I was. I needed to know that whatever haunted him at night wasn't the same thing that haunted me. I tightened my fingers against the silky strands coated with blood when he slowly, gently, almost too carefully, placed his hands on my waist pulling me closer.

My knees hit the side of the bed as he spread his legs wider, and I would've lost my footing if he hadn't been holding me. "I don't know why," he confessed. "We had a disagreement, and he got pissed."

"He got so pissed that he almost tried to rearrange your bone structure?" I was getting fucking pissed, I just didn't know at whom exactly. This whole situation was pissing me off. "That's not okay."

"It's nothing," he stubbornly answered, repeating the same words, but it wasn't enough. I didn't know him well enough to even try to guess what was going through his head, but something was wrong. The man I met four years ago seemed like the kind of man that wouldn't take shit from anybody. Hell, even the Storm from a couple of days ago seemed like he wouldn't take shit from anybody, but this version of him was something I wasn't familiar with.

"Don't give me that crappy answer," I murmured, still petting his hair. "Don't give me bullshit answers just because you don't want to talk to me or because you're mad at me." He tightened his hold on my waist and closed his eyes, as if even looking at me was something he didn't want to do. As if all of this was too much. "Is it me? Is it my presence here?" My voice wobbled. I actually started liking it here. I didn't forget about Maya or what I had to do, but somewhere deep inside, I wanted this. I wanted to be a part of something that didn't want to kill me.

I wanted to have a family.

His eyes flashed open, bewildered, angry, but I wanted to know the truth. If this was just another place where I wasn't wanted, I would leave. As soon as I got better, I would leave. The last thing I wanted was to be a burden, and for some reason, for my entire life, I felt like one. Even if nobody voiced it, there was a part of me that hated asking questions, hated asking for help and hated being taken care of, because I always felt like people didn't really want to do it. That they were doing it out of obligation, or out of fear.

"Sunshine," he croaked. "It isn't you." I didn't believe him. How could I when he refused to tell me anything? "We just had a disagreement over a mission, but it isn't you."

I started pulling back, dropping my hands from his shoulder and from his hair, but he didn't allow me to. He pulled me closer, so close that my breasts were plastered against his chest. Our heartbeats mashed together, and I could feel the little studs from his nipple piercings grazing me. He placed a hand on the back of my neck, grazing the sensitive skin on the sides and pulled me closer to his face.

"Stop this." A whisper or a plea, I wasn't really sure, but he looked like he was in pain. Not the physical one, not from the injuries, but from the fact that I was pulling away. "Don't pull away from me. Don't you ever pull away from me."

His eyes were burning into mine, an eternal hurricane that could swallow me whole. I would let it. I would let it swallow me whole because I wanted this. I wanted him. Somewhere between lying to myself, running away from him, and trying to think about what to do, I realized I wanted this. I wanted to stay here, to be a part of something bigger, something better.

And he cared for me, I could see that. No, I knew that, because I cared about him too. I probably cared about him from the first moment I met him, I was just too consumed by everything else that was going on around us. But I was tired of running.

I was so fucking tired. I was tired of being alone, of being abandoned, of not being wanted. I was tired of blocking him and not even trying to understand what was happening between us. I thought killing Kieran would bring me some peace, but it didn't. I was still as numb as I was years ago. I was still as shattered as before. But in the span of the last couple of days, where I was acting like a spoiled child, getting butthurt over nothing, trying to block whatever was happening between us, it happened.

Unfortunately, even while I avoided him, I couldn't avoid my feelings. I couldn't avoid the fact that every time I touched myself at night, it was with his name on my lips. I couldn't run away from everything in my life. It was a tiring and lonesome task, and I was tired of being alone.

"Storm." I placed my hands on his bloodied cheeks, wiping the blood, trying to see the damage. "I'm not pulling away, I'm just..." I took a deep breath, tilting my head toward the ceiling. "I'm terrified."

"Sunshine—"

"I'm terrified you'll see inside my soul." I looked at him, trying to coax a smile to my face. "I'm terrified you'll see where all the monsters hide, and you'll hate me. You'll hate me because that's what everybody does. They either hate me, or they abandon me."

"No, hey." His bloodied knuckles ran a trail from my cheekbone to my lips, no doubt leaving a red trail behind. "Your monsters don't scare me. You know what scares me?"

I didn't want to know, and yet I did. "What?"

"Not having you with me. Not seeing you, not being able to touch you, to smell you, to kiss you." He turned his head and kissed the inside of my wrist. "Not being able to see this pale skin of yours." He then turned his head to the other side, kissing the other wrist. "Those monsters you're talking about, those petty little demons, they aren't scary, baby. We just need to learn how to live with them, because even the darkness needs someone to love them, to care for them. Even the broken ones deserve to be wanted. We deserve to be happy."

I wasn't a crier because it had been drilled into me never to show any kind of emotion. It was drilled into me just like a lot of other things, but I was done being the prisoner of my own mind. I was done allowing these shackles to control me, to make decisions for me. I was just fucking done.

"I don't think I do, Storm." I felt it when the first tear fell down my cheek. "I don't think I deserve to be happy, because of the things I've done..." I trailed off, choking on my own words. "I did terrible things, okay?"

"We all did," he murmured as he stroked my cheek once again, wiping away the tears. "But that doesn't mean you don't deserve to be happy."

The hand on the nape of my neck pulled me closer, until our foreheads touched, and our breaths mixed, lips inches from each other. "I think you're the best thing that has ever happened to me, Ophelia." I closed my eyes, unable to take any more of the emotions shining from his own. "I think you somehow brought me back to life, even when you weren't here."

"No, I—"

"I was a corpse, Sunshine. I was a walking corpse, just waiting for death to come and pick me up. I had a purpose, and it was to kill, to avenge, to get my revenge, until I saw you. Until you marched toward me like there was nothing else you wanted to do more. Like the only thing you could see was me, and I felt the same. I felt as if I was struck by lightning when you smiled at me, when you called me Hades. I didn't even know I was looking for you until I found you. People are terrified of us because they know what danger is when they see it, yet you..." He laughed. "You just stood there, brave, defiant, and you asked me about my bike. About my fucking bike."

I slowly opened my eyes, mimicking his moves and entwining my hands around his neck.

"It was a hot bike." I snorted.

He started playing with my hair, as he murmured, "It really was." I felt at peace, and I knew it because I knew what real torment felt like.

"I would burn the world for you if they tried to take you away from me. I would destroy them all if it made you happy." He gave a small kiss on the corner of my lips and I felt the flutter of his eyelashes against my cheeks. "Where you go, I go. What you need, I'm gonna get it for you, just talk to me. I need you to talk to me, because this thing isn't a one-way street. This isn't me just trying to keep you here because I don't want you outside. I am trying to protect you from the outside world because I know that they want to hurt you."

"But you can't protect me from everything."

"No," he agreed. "I know I can't, but I have to try. And I know you're not some damsel in distress. I know you could beat half of my guys and get out of the fight without a scratch, but I want to protect you from the things you might not be able to defeat. I want to give you a home, Phee."

My throat started closing off, Everything he said, everything he wanted to do, it was what I wanted. No, it was more than that. It was what I needed. After years and years of trying to be something I wasn't, trying to please the people who wouldn't even blink if I dropped dead, this was what I needed.

I needed to be, what, loved? I guess that's the proper word. I needed to be safe, even if it was for a little while, and he could give that to me. We could give that to each other.

"My father won't rest until he gets me back, Storm." His whole body stiffened at the mere mention of Nikolai Aster, and I knew there was more to the story that I was unaware of. "I don't want you guys to be in danger just because I'm here."

"Hey—"

"Then there's Maya." I was rambling, but if I didn't say all of this now, I never would. "I have to find her. I have to save her even if it's the last thing I ever do. I just feel so guilty for never helping her before, even though I could've. I could've found a way instead of allowing them to treat me like a mindless robot who only fulfilled orders. I could've done something. I could've—"

I couldn't breathe. I could feel my chest

tightening, my throat closing, and I couldn't breathe.

"Oh God." I started wheezing, trying to catch a breath, trying to move away from Storm, from everything. Trying to close the doors in my head, the ones leading to one of my biggest regrets.

"And Ava—"

I couldn't save them. I couldn't save any of them. I condemned them. I condemned all of them to death and pain, and endless torture. I would do the same with the club. I shouldn't stay here. I shouldn't be here. My tainted soul was going to destroy them all. My father was going to destroy them all.

"I-I can't... I can't... Storm." I started clutching at my throat, clawing, ripping, but I still couldn't breathe. He jumped up, reaching for me, pulling my hands back, but he didn't understand, I couldn't breathe. I had to breathe, but I didn't deserve to.

I created so much pain, so much destruction and sorrow, even a thousand years wouldn't be enough to wash away all the sins I committed. And I was going to commit more, I knew that.

"Ophelia." He held both of my hands as the skin on my neck burned. "You need to calm down, baby girl. Come on, breathe with me." But he didn't understand, I couldn't. I just couldn't. "Come on. Inhale through your nose." He inhaled and then exhaled through his mouth. "Exhale through your mouth. Come on, do it with me."

My whole body trembled, my hands shaking as he held them captive. "Ophelia!" he barked. "Breathe with me. I know you can do it." Maybe I could. Maybe... okay.

I inhaled through my nose, feeling the burn in my sinuses, in my throat as the air slowly filled my lungs, and exhaled on a shaky breath.

"That's it." He smiled. "Again, inhale," he repeated the process, "and exhale."

Inhale and exhale.

Inhale.

Exhale.

One and two and three and four times, I repeated the same until my lungs stopped burning and my body stopped trembling. I didn't even realize I was gripping his hands, or that he was slowly petting my head, or the loving look he was giving me—a worried look at the same time. I didn't even realize when we ended up on the floor, with me sitting in front of him, cross-legged. I didn't realize when I removed my shirt, but I did. I was still in my bra and my pants, while Storm sat in front of me, still bloodied, still hurt but helping me.

His thumb brushed over my wrist, sending small shock waves through my body. I didn't think when I launched myself at him, wrapping my legs around his waist and entwining my arms around his shoulders, hiding my face in his neck. Slow, soft strokes started on my back, as he bent his knees and held me even closer.

"Shhh." I could feel his breath on my ear. "I got you. I got you."

"I'm sorry," I mumbled. "I don't know what... I don't know what happened."

"It's okay, Ophelia. You don't ever have to apologize for these things. You had a panic attack, a mild one, but still a panic attack."

"I know."

"You mean—"

"This isn't the first time I had one of those. Sometimes I can't breathe and sometimes I can see their faces. Sometimes I can see Kieran's face, sometimes Ava's. Other times it's the innocent people I've killed in the name of the Syndicate. I keep getting haunted by these memories, and I don't know what to do about them. I just... I don't know what to do."

He kissed the shell of my ear, then my cheek and then he tilted my head up and pressed his lips against mine. It wasn't like our other kisses, where we were both hungry for more than just a kiss. But this one didn't scream sex or possession, no. This one was a careful, feathery kiss I could feel all the way to my toes. This one spoke to my soul, fed my whole being.

He held me, soothing me with his kisses, with his touch, with his mere presence. There was no rush in the way he caressed my body, going from my collarbone, between my breasts to my navel. There was no rush as his lips skimmed over my jaw, over the scar on my cheek, back to my lips.

Unlike all the other times, I could feel it, feel us. This wasn't about physical attraction. This wasn't about me drowning everything else, trying to forget for just a minute. This was about him taking care of me, and me allowing him to do so.

"You look beautiful," he murmured against my lips. "You are the best thing that has ever happened to me."

You are the best thing that happened to me, I wanted to reply, but something stopped me. I just couldn't get the words out. I couldn't tell him how I felt. At least not yet.

His erection was nestled between us, hidden by the denim of his jeans. I swiveled my hips, rubbing myself over him, as a growl tore out of his mouth, when his kisses became hungrier, desperate. His eye was swelling, but he didn't stop kissing me, he didn't stop touching me, and I couldn't stop either.

I ran my hands over his shoulders, feeling the strong muscles, then over his chest, paying more attention to the nipples with the little studs in them, studs I wanted to taste and pull and bite. I wanted him to own me, and I wanted to own him.

Pulling his hair, I pushed his head backward and started kissing his jaw, his neck, leaving small bites and soothing them with my lips shortly after.

"I never forgot you," I mumbled before giving another bite that pulled another hiss from him. We were going slow, so fucking slow, and I loved it even more than the wild sex we had before. I loved the sounds from him, the growls, the moans. I even loved my own even though I couldn't remember when the last time was I had something like this.

Sex was always just a transaction for me, but not with him. Not when he allowed me to explore his body as he tore off his shirt, throwing it to the side. I scowled at the purple bruises that were starting to form on his ribs, and when I ran my fingers over the tender tissue, the hiss of pain from him sent a jab of pain through me.

I really, really fucking hated seeing him hurt.

"I should clean your wounds." I looked up at him, realizing he was already staring at me. "Those could get infected, and I actually like your face."

"You like my face?" He grinned, looking younger than he was. "Really?"

"Shut up."

"I'm just sayi—"

But he didn't manage to finish the sentence when the door slammed open, revealing a grinning Atlas.

"Your favorite nurse... Oh holy shit." That grin disappeared faster than you could say sex as he started looking in the other direction, away from the two of us. The situation would've been comical if it wasn't for the overprotective stance Storm took, shielding my body with his own and glaring at Atlas.

"What the fuck are you doing here, Atlas?"

"I brought you the first aid kit." He slowly lowered the box to the ground, still refusing to look at us. "And I wanted to tell you that I called Doc, and he's going to be here tomorrow to examine Ophelia."

I snickered as he started retreating. "I'm just gonna... Just gonna leave now. Yeah, that's right. Leaving, I'm leaving now. Didn't see anything."

"Atlas?" Storm started.

"Yes."

"You're still standing at the door."

"Right, right." He dragged his hands through his hair. "Just please lock the door in the future. I don't wanna die because I saw something I shouldn't."

"Get out, Atlas!" I started laughing again as Storm roared. "And close the fucking door. Tell everyone I'm not available for the rest of the day."

"But—"

"No buts."

My whole body shook from the force of my laughter, but I couldn't stop. Storm was behaving like a caveman, and I had to admit—I liked it. I liked feeling like there was somebody who wanted to protect me in every way possible, even if I didn't really need it.

Atlas started mumbling something, but between small sounds of displeasure from Storm and my laughter, I couldn't hear it properly. When the door finally closed after him, I howled, letting the laughter take over my body.

"This isn't funny." He groaned. "I didn't want

him to see you naked."

"I wasn't naked." I chuckled. "I have my bra on."

"No! I am the only one that can see your bra, okay? I don't want to have to kill my own enforcer just because he looked at you in your bra."

I saluted, "Yes, boss."

I wanted us to continue what we started, but one look at his face and the wounds inflicted by Hunter, and I knew he needed his rest more than the needed sex. "Come on, big guy. On the bed and let me clean those wounds."

"No," he groaned and buried his face between my boobs. "I'm okay. Nothing's gonna happen if we do it later."

I dragged my hand through his hair and started massaging the scalp, going from the back of his head to the top, moving slowly behind his ears and then his neck.

"We have time for this, but I really need to look at those and clean them up. You're gonna be in the world of pain later. Those puppy eyes don't work on me. Now get your ass up and into the bed. I'm gonna clean these and then we can take a nap. I'm pretty sure you need one."

Hell, I needed one.

"We're gonna talk later, but for now, I wanna have a look at that nasty cut on your eyebrow and put some ice on that eye. I also want to kill Hunter, but—"

"Hey." He laughed. "I let him do this."

"Regardless, I still wanna kill him. Cut off his balls, make an omelet with them, feed him those same balls, you know, the usual."

The look he gave me as I continued ranting about all the ways I wanted to make Hunter suffer should've had me running for the hills, but it didn't. If anything, I knew I really wanted to stay. I wanted to try and live life without being constantly on the run. He mentioned he would help me find Maya, and I wanted to believe him.

No, I did believe him. I believed him when he said he wanted me, and that was all that mattered.

I stood up first, extending my hand to him. "Up, come on." He squinted at me, wincing at the same time.

"You really love being a nurse, don't you?"

"Well," I started as I pulled him up. "I actually wanted to be a veterinarian, but I became a little butcher instead."

He towered over me as he stood up, and as I tilted my head to look at him, I knew I made the right choice staying here, slowly accepting this, because that tender look on his face was enough to confirm what I kind of, almost, mostly, already knew.

Storm really did care about me.

EIGHTEEN

Storm

THE TWO OF us together probably had more issues than Eastern Europe with their politics. But what happened earlier today told me that she wanted to try. She wanted this—me, us. She wanted to stay.

After she cleaned the cut above my eyebrow and cleaned the blood and the other cuts on my face, both of us just collapsed on the bed, taking a much-needed nap. I didn't even realize how tired I was until I put my head on the pillow, with her wrapped around me. The lights inside the room were turned off, and while I didn't know how long we slept, the darkness of the night seeping inside the room through the windows told me it was more than enough. My eyes slowly adjusted to the dark as I greedily took in her sleeping form, her bare shoulders and her hair spilled over my pillow.

I fucking missed her smell, her taste, even her angry little mouth. The last three days were pure torture, because having someone you cared about so close, yet so far, was the worst feeling known to a human mind. I spent so many years searching for her and having her here without really having her with me... Yeah, that wasn't going to work.

Her head was on my chest, and I could feel the small puffs of air as she exhaled, tickling my skin. With one hand on my pec and the other one on my ribs, it looked like she was hugging me. Her legs were entwined with mine, holding me hostage. Her dark hair was soft beneath my palm, as I started playing with it, dragging my hand through the waves she naturally had. Women's hair was not something I often noticed, but I noticed hers.

God, I sounded like a lovesick fool, noticing every little detail about her. The way she narrowed her eyes when something wasn't going how she imagined it. Or the way her eyes shone when she spoke with Zoe, even when she wore that disinterested look on her face. Or how she talked with Atlas as if they knew each other for years and not less than a month.

I noticed all of it.

She thought she was a monster for what she did in the past, but the real monsters were the ones that were supposed to save her. The ones that were supposed to protect her from real evil. I had no idea if she knew about everything her father did, but I was starting to see that while she had his last name, she was nothing like him. You could always feel the true evil when it stood next to you, and she didn't carry it with her.

The kids from the club didn't cower from her, even though they knew what other people called her. I wanted to laugh every single time she tried to shoo them away, but it was never in a malicious way. I had a feeling she never learned how to interact with other people, at least not in a healthy way. She kept mentioning Ava, her best friend, and it seemed that she was the only person in her life that was well, normal.

I could hear the people talking and laughing through the open window, and I could feel the cool breeze of the December night coming through, washing over my skin. I would probably be freezing right now, if it wasn't for the human blanket wrapped around me. Her cute rambling, the tender way with which she pressed the antiseptic wipes against my skin, apologized every time I winced, the way she scolded me for allowing this to happen, it all made me realize how idiotic it was keeping secrets from her.

If there was anything I'd learned in the thirty-three years of my life, it was that you never lie to the people you care about or the people that care about you. The truth is better than a thousand lies, even if it was the painful one. I just wished I had enough courage to tell her everything she needed to know. To tell her what I did, what her father did and was still doing. But she was still recovering, she wasn't even sure if she wanted to stay here, and I needed her to stay.

I didn't want to give her more reasons to get out of here as soon as her body healed. I wanted to give her more reasons to stay, the good ones, not just because there were people out there that wanted to see her dead and she wanted to lay low for a little while. I wanted her to stay for me, for her, for this tight-knit family we had here. I wanted to show her that life wasn't all dark and bad, and it could be good if the right people were with us.

I wanted to be able to touch her like this every single day — to drag my hand over her arm, over her naked back, over the scars and tattoos. The bruises she got from her time with the Nightingales were slowly starting to turn into pale-yellowish ones, but her finger was still swollen, and I noticed she wasn't using that hand as much as her left one. That cut on her cheek was still red but closed.

I wondered how many scars and bruises she hid inside her soul, just so she could keep walking, keep fighting or running. I wondered if anybody ever asked her if she was okay, or if she needed help. There were stories about the fierce and cold Ophelia Aster; stories that made your blood turn into ice, but the person they were describing wasn't the same person as the one lying on top of me.

But I guess we all wore our masks in a different way. Some wore smiley, happy, careless masks, while some were dark, colored with blood and pain, war, and ache. Some masks could be replaced, exchanged for the better ones, or completely removed. But some got stuck to our skin until we forgot what it felt like not to wear one.

I wore my mask of cold indifference every single day, and I was tired of it. I wanted to have it removed, to have my skin breathe. I wanted to bask in the glory of the morning sun as if it were the best thing that could happen to me. I wanted to hold the woman I cared about, to smile at her without thinking about the consequences.

The muffled sound of my phone ringing pulled me back from my thoughts and woke Ophelia up, and destroying that small semblance of peace I had. I couldn't see it anywhere around me nor could I feel it vibrating inside the pocket of my jeans, but when the ringing wouldn't stop, ongoing for minutes on end, I started moving Ophelia away from me, trying to locate the device.

She gripped my ribs tighter, burying her nose into the column of my neck, moaning in her sleep. "Nooo. I don't want to get up."

"Phee—"

"Let it ring." She clung to me. "Go back to sleep."

I wished I could. I wished I could just close my eyes, hold her close and never let go. I wished I could change who I was and the world I was living in. What would it be like to live life without fearing that it could end in any moment? And not only mine, but my brothers-in-arms.

Not even a minute passed before the phone started ringing again, and whoever was trying to reach me was insistent. Softly rolling her off me, I managed to slip out of the bed before Ophelia could latch onto me again. I realized where the sound was coming from. Dropping to my knees, I could see the light shining from underneath the bed, accompanied by an annoying ringing sound. I extended my arm, wincing at the pain ricocheting from the left side of my ribs through my chest, cursing Hunter and his inability to listen to what I had to say.

My hand connected with the cool surface of the phone just as it stopped ringing and when I saw the caller ID, I wished I had never gotten out of the bed.

"Who is it?" Her sleepy voice was muffled by the pillow she had pressed against her face. I wanted to tell her more than anything in the world, but she wouldn't understand. She would think the worst because she was wired that way. Both of us were. We always assumed the worst possible scenario, never even thinking about the logical explanation.

I kept staring at the screen of the phone when the bed shifted, and she pulled herself up. I could feel her eyes on me, but I couldn't look at her. She would know, and right now wasn't the time for the conversation we needed to have.

"Storm?" Goddammit. "Is everything okay?"

No, nothing was okay. Nothing about this whole situation was okay. I knew what I needed to do, but I didn't want to leave her alone. I didn't want to give her time to overthink everything, so I avoided the topic.

"Why didn't you come here when you ran away from Croyford Bay?" It wasn't the most mature question, but the need to know why she chose not to come here was eating me alive. And it was a distraction from the goddamn phone call that fucked up my entire day. Well, fucked it up even more. "You knew who I was." I lifted my head and looked at her. "You knew about our club."

Her whole face hardened. "You didn't want to come, or?"

"Don't fucking bullshit me, Storm." *What*? "I came here. This was the first place I went."

She got off the bed and started walking toward the bathroom. "But you didn't want me here. You turned me away!" Her scream bounced off the walls of the bedroom before she entered the bathroom and slammed the door.

I was still on the floor, staring at the closed door as my mind tried to understand what she just said. She... No, I would've known. I would've known if she had come here. I wouldn't have spent years looking for her if I didn't want her here. What the fuck was she talking about?

I pulled myself up and walked toward the bathroom, trying to open the door but it wouldn't budge. "Ophelia!" I slammed my hand against the wooden surface. "Open up."

"Go away, Storm. Just go away."

"Not until you tell me the truth. I would have known if you ever came here, my guys would've told me."

The door swung open then, revealing an extremely pissed off Ophelia. I would say she looked hot, but I was starting to get pissed as well. If she hadn't come here that would be okay, but there was no need to lie to me.

"Don't give me that crap. I came here. I begged them to see you and they told me you didn't want to see me. They told me you wanted me gone."

"Who?" I yelled. "Who told you that, because I spent the last four years trying to find you, trying to get you back here. I would never do that."

Her beautiful face transformed with a cruel smile, shutting me out, preparing for a blow.

"Then you, my darling, have snakes slithering in your garden, and you don't even know it."

NINETEEN

Ophelia

Four Years Ago

IT LOOKED LIKE paradise, but it was pure hell.

Kieran and me, our families, it was hell. They thought I killed her. They thought I killed Ava. How could they? She was the only good thing I was left with, and they thought I would kill her. They didn't listen to me, and now she was dead.

Was she buried somewhere?

Did they have a funeral for her?

I didn't even know how long they kept me there. My hands were bruised from the chains they left me in. My heart felt hollow from the loss I experienced. Seeing her there, lying on that cold, hard floor, blood everywhere, it was so much fucking blood. And my knife stuck out of her.

Who could've done something like this? Who would want to kill her? She was one of the best people I ever had the chance to meet.

She was my soul sister, my best friend, and to see her like that, her light extinguished... it fucking killed me.

And them. They were supposed to be my friends. They should've believed in me, but I guess that I never really knew them. I could understand anguish, I could understand pain. I could even understand their need to blame somebody, but what I couldn't understand was the fact that they believed it was me.

So when Theo came, when he freed me and told me to run, I did. I ran so fast, so far away and I didn't look back. Maybe with years they would realize that it wasn't me.

Maybe they would realize they made a mistake. Maybe I could forgive them, but right now, I had to be as far away from them as possible. Kieran couldn't even look at me, and if I were being honest, I couldn't look at him either.

The way he threw me aside, like we never meant anything to each other, as if he didn't know how I felt about his sister. But I guess it was easier to just throw me to the wolves than to find the real culprit.

Maybe I should've been thankful for everything because I finally got to see their real faces. Their traitorous faces.

But at what cost? At a cost of two innocent lives. The lives I wanted to save. I wanted her to grow old, be happy. I wanted her to have everything she wanted to have, and I failed. I fucking failed, and I would never be able to forgive myself.

What was the use of all these skills if I couldn't protect those I cared about the most?

So here I was, in Santa Monica, spending the money Theo left me with, because if there was one person that wanted me, it was Storm.

And he could help me, I knew he could.

When I checked the date, it was already two weeks too late for our meeting, and I just hoped he would want to see me. But he had to. If I explained everything that happened, he would understand.

247

The neighborhood I was in didn't look bad. As a matter of fact, there were kids playing on the streets. People were walking around, laughing, talking, living their lives.

I wondered if they ever thought about the cruel world hiding just under their noses?

Or did they choose to be blind in order to preserve their sanity?

I felt eyes on my back, but I guess that was due to the state I was in. My clothes were disheveled, blood stains on more parts of it than not. Changing my clothes was the last thing on my list of priorities when I managed to leave Croyford Bay. Theo was graceful enough to put me into the private jet and send me to the other side of the country.

I didn't have to ask him twice.

Get out, run, and stay alive.

Those three were the priority.

The old man on the pier told me their clubhouse was on this street, but I couldn't see anything that resembled an MC. Maybe I took a wrong turn somewhere?

A mother with two kids was walking toward me. She was eyeing me, cautious, and I guess she should be. I would've been as well if I saw me on the street.

"Excuse me," I started as she came closer. "Is the clubhouse for Sons of Hades here?"

"Oh, dear." She looked around and pulled the kids closer to her. "Are you sure you want to get into that hell?"

Was I? Not really, but what other choice did I have?

"Please, it's really important."

It was my lifeline. Storm was the last option I had. My father cut my credit cards. He wasn't home when I went there, and all my belongings were gone already. Like I never existed.

She looked me over, and after a second too long, she started talking again.

"Just go until you reach the end of the street. Trust me, you can't miss it."

"Thank you." I started walking ahead before she started talking again.

"I really wish you wouldn't go there. That's a hellhole."

Oh, lady, I already crawled out of one. This one would be a walk through the park after everything that happened.

"Thank you, but I really need to talk to somebody there." She seemed genuinely worried for me, and for some reason it brought up feelings I didn't want to have.

My family abandoned me.

They didn't care, and yet this stranger, she cared enough to tell me that I shouldn't go there. If only she knew the monsters I had already met, the monsters I had lived with and the ones I had slayed.

I didn't wait for her response, but hurried up down the street, hoping to everything there was that Storm was there.

And just like she said, at the end of a street a one-story house, much larger than any of the other ones, stood with its windows blackened and the three-headed dog painted in front. I was here. I was finally here.

Maybe this could be a new start. Maybe this would be a good thing.

That connection I felt with Storm, I couldn't stop thinking about it. The familiarity, the way his touch ignited my skin, it was the best kind of feeling. And I wanted to explore it. I wanted to see where all of this could lead.

I took a step forward when a new voice penetrated through an otherwise quiet evening. I stopped immediately as a tall man, not much older than me, stopped in front of me, the menacing glare on his face a telltale sign that this wouldn't be as easy as I hoped it would be.

"What are you doing?" he asked, almost spitting at me. *Well, kind sir, I was here for some dick and possibly trying to survive. What are you doing here*?

"I'm—"

"Cat got your tongue, girly?"

Girly? Seriously?

"No, darling, cat didn't get my tongue."

"Then what are you doing here? Don't you know who this house belongs to?"

No shit, Sherlock, some of us can actually read.

"Well, judging by that insignia over there," I pointed to the three-headed Cerberus, "I'd say it belongs to Sons of Hades."

"Well," he stuttered, "yeah. But what are you doing here?"

"I need to talk to Storm." As soon as I said those words, he started laughing, clutching at his stomach.

"Ay, girly, Storm won't talk to the likes of you. He's a busy man, and I wouldn't want to bother him with some insignificant girl looking for him, just because he didn't call."

Seriously? Who the fuck was this guy?

"Look, whoever you are—"

"Sam," he interrupted. "My name is Sam."

"Yeah, okay, Sam." I took a deep breath. "I really need to talk to him, and trust me, it isn't his dick I'm after. If you could go inside and tell him Ophelia or Persephone is here, I would truly appreciate it."

"She would truly appreciate it," he mumbled

to himself.

"Excuse me?" I was fucking tired and hungry. I had cuts and bruises where it shouldn't be possible to have, and this fucking cretin was pissing me off.

"I mean, I will check with him, but I can't promise you that he would want to see you."

"Fine." *Whatever.* "Can you please go now?"

He still stood there, looking at me as if he could make me disappear on a wish. Tough luck honey, demons couldn't be exorcised that easily.

"Yeah, yeah," he uttered. "I'm going."

I watched his retreating form as he entered the massive house, and I plopped down on the floor. My legs were killing me. The lack of food, water, and the hours of standing up, it all took a toll on my body. Those three idiots almost killed me, and I couldn't wait for the day I would get to see their faces and make them pay for everything they did to me.

But not now.

Now I had to be smarter than that. Now I had to recover and gather my wits. I couldn't keep going like this. No matter what, I didn't want to die. There was so much more I had to do in this life, and even if the last thing I ever had to do was to make those three suffer, then so be it.

They weren't the only ones that lost her. I promised her I would take care of everything, and I failed. I failed her, and I probably failed my sister because now I would never be able to find out where she was.

Being close to my father and Theo, I at least had a small chance of gathering the necessary information, but like this, I had nothing. Not even a single trace.

She was forever lost to me, and I hated this

251

helpless feeling seeping into my bones. I wasn't helpless. I was a fighter, and they made me feel this way.

They took away everything from me, and I was going to get it all back.

"Girly," the idiot called to me, walking alone. Why was he alone? Storm wasn't here?

"Please tell me that he's here."

I just needed a bed and some food. That was all.

"He's here, but…" he hesitated. "He doesn't want to see you."

"What?"

"He doesn't know who you are. Said he doesn't know anyone called Ophelia or Persephone."

"You're fucking lying. Let me in, let me talk to him." I took a few steps toward the house, but he took me from behind, a barrel of a gun placed to my temple.

"Nah, we can't have that. He said he doesn't know you, and I don't want to get my brains splattered on the wall if I let you in. So be a good girly and leave. I'd hate to kill you, but if I have to —"

"Let go of me!"

"Not a chance. If I do, you'll try to make a run for it, and I don't wanna have to clean your body from the entrance."

What in the actual fuck?

"Now go." He pushed me outside of the gates, blocking the entrance. "I really don't want to use this gun, girly."

Just stop with the fucking nickname.

"Boss doesn't wanna see you. Go try somewhere else."

Storm didn't wanna see me. Storm… He… He

left me as well.

I wasn't a saint, but this... this was… No, just no. I did nothing, and now the only person I wanted to see, the only person I thought could help me, didn't want to see me.

And he had to know it was me. Or maybe I imagined that weird connection between us. Maybe it was all in my head.

What was I supposed to do now?

I didn't have money. I didn't have my knives. I had nothing. Fucking nothing. They all left me with nothing.

And Storm, he could go fuck himself. I would get myself out of this mess.

I had to.

TWENTY

Storm

Present

SHE CAME TO ME.

All these years, I thought she didn't give a shit, but she came here, and that motherfucking idiot ruined it. As soon as she said his name, I knew who it was. I fucking knew because that lying son of a bitch managed to get into my good graces. I thought he was truly one of us—abandoned as a child, scraping for leftovers behind the restaurants, in garbage—I fucking thought he knew what it meant to find a family and be loyal to them.

He made a fool out of me. He could've cost me everything I ever wanted to have in my life, and he was going to pay. The phone I held in my hand went flying across the room, smashing against the wall behind the bed. Four years... Four fucking years I'd been looking for her because he turned her away. Because that spineless little shit didn't let me know she was here.

I started pacing the room while Ophelia stood still at the threshold to the bathroom with an emotionless expression on her face. No wonder she didn't want to have anything to do with me when I brought her here. I was surprised she didn't try to fucking kill me the first time she saw me in that church. That idiot manipulated us both, pushed her away from me, pushed her into the embrace of another fucked-up family.

Where was the fucking common sense in people these days? I almost went crazy looking for her, reassuring myself she was real, she was mine, that I didn't make it all up in my messed-up mind just because I wanted to feel better.

"Storm."

"Not right now, Sunshine."

Molten lava ran through my veins. The need to suffocate the life out of him overpowered every other sense, every other emotion. To kill, to destroy, to eradicate from this earth, because he didn't deserve to live after this. Every single person in our club knew I would burn Heaven and Hell just to get to her, and he fucked up.

"You really didn't know I came here?" Her voice was barely a whisper, slicing through me over and over again. I tried calming my breathing, my rage, because she was the last person I would want to hurt, and right now, I wasn't in the right frame of mind. "Storm?" I felt her hand before I heard her voice. Her hand on my shoulder felt like a cold shower over my burning skin, but I still couldn't turn around. "Look at me, Storm."

I couldn't. One of my people betrayed her. One of the people I thought I could trust fucked it up.

"I can't. I-I... I want to fucking kill him."

"Just look at me." Instead of turning me around, she walked around me, stopping right in front. "Hey." Placing her hands on my face, she inched closer until her breasts were plastered against my chest. Her heat seeped into me, her scent enveloped me and for a moment I forgot about the man I was going to kill. There was only her, her scent, her ocean blue eyes I wanted to get lost in and a strange sense of peace fell over us. "I thought you didn't want me."

Goddammit. Sorrow was etched into every pore on her face and her eyes betrayed the emotions she usually tried to hide. Fear, loneliness, sadness, it was all there for me to see.

I placed one hand over hers, still stroking my cheek, and the other one behind her neck, pulling her closer until our foreheads touched. "I thought I made myself clear when I said I wanted you and only you." Our breathing elevated, the electricity charging through the room, and if the world ended right now, I would be a happy man because she was here. After everything, she was here, and she was slowly opening up. "I looked for you everywhere. I almost went insane thinking I made it all up, because you were nowhere to be found. You didn't give me your name, you didn't tell me where you lived, you didn't tell me anything. And I waited, Ophelia. I waited for four years for you to come to me, to find me, to show me that everything that happened on that cliff wasn't just a product of my imagination."

With a trembling lower lip she muttered, "I'm sorry. I wanted to be with you. All those plans, all those dreams we talked about before everything went to shit... I still want them, Storm. I still want to be happy, to ride into the sunset, to see the world. I still want to find a place for myself. A place where I could be truly me, without all this pain and all this sorrow surrounding me. I don't want to be just a boogeyman. I don't want to be just the creature of nightmares."

256

I kissed her forehead. "I know, Sunshine."

"And I wanna be here with you," she continued on a shaky breath. "I want to see where this could lead, but I also need to save my sister. My family... They are fucked up. I mean, I'm fucked up, but my father..." she trailed off. "He sold her. He would've done the same to me if I hadn't become what I am today. And I feel like I am going in circles in my head. To run or not to run, to be happy or to be miserable, and I can't. I just can't." She dropped her hands and walked to the bed, turning her back to me. "I don't think you could ever love a monster, Storm." Her shoulders shook as she slowly turned around facing me again. Shadows danced on her face, and it took everything in me not to walk over and take her in my arms, hold her, tell her that everything would be okay. I wanted to tell her that the only monsters were those that fucked her up, but I also knew how hard it was coming to terms with everything you did. "They couldn't love me." Her voice broke as she collapsed on the bed, putting her head between her hands. "None of them could love. None. And I'm so tired of this life, Storm. I'm so tired of running and hiding, and killing and suffering, and being somebody's puppet." Her voice started rising with every new sentence. "I'm just so fucking tired!"

She was killing me. She was fucking killing me with her words, and she didn't even know it. If I could, I would take away all this pain she felt and mix it with my own. In three steps, I crossed the room and dropped to my haunches in front of her, placing my hands on her knees.

"I don't wanna do this anymore," she whispered. "I don't wanna hurt you, I don't wanna hurt them, but I don't know how to stop. I don't know how to stop being what they made me to be.

257

I don't know how to stop looking for my sister even though I know it will most probably kill me. I don't know how to be with you. I don't know how to give you my heart when they destroyed it years ago."

"Phee. Stop, please."

"I don't know how to be loved, Storm." She lifted her head and looked at me. "I don't even know how to be a human because I've been suppressing every single emotion. For years, the only thing I knew how to do was to be numb. I don't know how to love you, Storm. I don't know how to trust you, and I want to. I want to trust you, I want to be with you. I want to be happy, but I don't know how. One minute I want to stay here, I want to wake up with you, I want to belong, and in the next one, I want to run, I want to hide, I want to be the assassin they made me out to be. Don't you get it?" Her chest heaved, her cheeks wet from tears and when she dropped her hands on top of mine and started tracing the tattoos with her fingers, I started getting afraid.

Afraid that this was a breaking point, that she wouldn't want to stay. I was fucking terrified that the next thing that would come out of her mouth would be her leaving me, and I wasn't sure if I would allow her to do that.

"I'm not good enough. I was never ever good enough. Not for them, not for Ava, not for Kieran and I know I'm not good enough for you. The only thing I'm good at is destruction. The only thing I can bring with me is misery, and I don't want that for you or your people."

"You're not—"

"But I am." She chuckled, the sound broken and colored with pain. "I am destruction, Storm. I am not sunshine as you like to call me. I am not the girl that could observe the world with rose-colored glasses and smile at everything. I killed innocent people—women, children, men that did nothing but try to protect their families, and I did it all for the Syndicate. There are days where I can feel their breath on my neck, their hands on my shoulders and their voices in my ears. There are days where their faces seem so angelic until they turn demonic, screaming at me, blaming me, as they should."

I didn't know what to say, so I did nothing but listen to her. The laughter and hushed voices from the outside seemed so far away, and my only focus was on her. I ran my thumbs over her naked knees, drawing circles and trying to show her I was here for her, even if she didn't want me here.

"I killed them all." She hiccupped. "And I felt nothing when I did it. I didn't feel bad for them, I didn't feel sad, I just felt nothing!"

Remorse was one of the worst feelings a human being could possibly have, and she was drowning in it. I just didn't know how to help her.

"And I miss it, you know?" She turned her head, looking at the window. "I miss the adrenaline from every new mission. I miss being needed, being good at something. It's a fucked-up thing, but I miss holding the knife in my hand and feeling like a god against those that wronged me and my family. And that's wrong." She turned to me. "It's so wrong, but I don't know how to stop feeling like this. I miss being numb, being cold. Something happened to me in that church and now it's as if the dam broke and everything I've tried running away from, finally caught up with me. The doors opened and I'm suffocating. I'm drowning."

I wanted to tell her it was going to be okay. I wanted to tell her that this pain she was drowning in now was a good thing. It meant she was alive, she was breathing, living, and she was finally free of the restraints the Syndicate put on her. I wanted to reassure her, but it wouldn't be enough. I always hated it when people told me everything was going to be okay because none of us knew if it really was going to be okay. I had no idea if this thing could break her or make her stronger.

I didn't know if she could live with it all and not drown under the waves crashing against her, so I did the only thing I could in that moment. I stood up, sat next to her, and pulled her in my lap, hugging her to me. I held her, trying to comfort her in the only way I knew how.

I held her because I wasn't a man of many words. I didn't know how to tell her that whatever she felt right now wasn't going to break her. I dragged my hand over her hair, over her shoulder, her back, as she clung to me like a kid. I wiped away the tears coating her cheeks, dragging my thumb over her bottom lip, soothing her with my touch.

Nobody ever taught me what to do or what to say. My parents didn't give a shit about me and later... Well, later the only thing I was good at was physical touch. I wasn't allowed to feel anything, to express my opinion, to behave like a human being, so just like her, I shoved it all down.

But I was happy she was finally letting it out. I was happy to feel her trembling in my arms because that meant she was healing. It hurt right now, but we couldn't run away from everything we felt. Us humans, we were such peculiar creatures. Some of us could handle it all, while others—the broken ones—couldn't stand feeling anything.

The broken ones taught themselves not to feel, because we knew that even the smallest emotion could destroy the carefully crafted façade around us. Believe it or not, happiness was the toughest emotion for all of us, because we thought we didn't deserve it. So, we tried to avoid it.

We drowned it with alcohol, with drugs, with sex and we hid behind walls higher than the Chinese wall. We don't want to feel. We don't want to see what we'd become, and before you know it, years have passed and we are unrecognizable and far away from the people we wanted to be.

All these words, everything I felt was on the tip of my tongue, but I couldn't tell her that. I couldn't show her everything inside my head, inside my chest, because I didn't want to scare her. I didn't want her to see where my demons were hiding. Knowing her, she would poke them, she would wake them up, she would try to fix what was broken, because that's what she did.

She didn't know it, but she always tried to fix what was broken. With Ava, she tried to take her away from that life, even though it wasn't her place to do so. With her sister, she was trying to save her, but was there anybody that could save Ophelia?

"Listen," I started slowly, trying to find the right words. "I might not know what to say to you right now, because I truly suck at these things." She started laughing at that. "But I know what might help."

As if woken from the trance, she perked up, lifting her head, and looking at me. "What?"

"That idiot, Sam." Anger blazed over her face at the mention of his name. "I know where he is, and I think we should pay him a visit."

If I wasn't feeling the same anger she did or if I was a different man, I might have been terrified of the look on her face. The vengeful look, bloodthirsty and ready to hunt the one that wronged her. But I wasn't a different man. I was me and this thing, this was what I could give her.

I could help her get her revenge.

TWENTY-ONE

Ophelia

A WEIRD KIND of energy buzzed through my veins as I packed my things to move them from the room Atlas found for me to Storm's. Not that there were too many things, but ZoZo went out of her way to bring me clothes and toiletries, and it was more than I had after I left Croyford Bay. But right now, I couldn't give a fuck about the amount of clothes, or even the fact that Storm all but ordered me to move my shit, as he called it, to his room. We were going out and I was going to have fun.

I itched to get my hands on knives, not even caring that they weren't my usual knives. As soon as he mentioned going out, my whole body woke up, switching me from the misery I was pushing myself further into, to feeling alive for the first time in days. I didn't know where all those things came from, but some part of me felt that I could tell him everything. I believed that he needed to know, because I truly didn't know how to do this thing.

I didn't know how to turn off one part of me in order to turn the other one on. I didn't know how to stop running away, but maybe I could try. Maybe it was good that all these feelings started flooding through me. Ava always said that keeping everything to yourself wasn't healthy, and maybe I should take her advice.

But all of that would have to wait. That feeling from when I used to go on missions started coming back. It wasn't hatred, it wasn't just pure adrenaline, it was purpose. I had a purpose again, even if it was a fucked-up one. All these years, I believed that Storm didn't want me. These last couple of days, I couldn't allow myself to fully fall into his embrace because I believed he turned me away when I needed him the most. Sometimes I felt that my life was just one big lie or a nightmare, and any second now I would wake up in an empty room, realizing it was all just that, a nightmare. Unfortunately, no matter how many times I pinched myself, shut my eyes and willed my mind to wake up, it never happened.

This was my life. I could cry and moan about it or I could finally stop blaming other people and take my destiny into my own hands. I was the only one that could create the future I wanted to have, and what I wanted was right here. I could save my sister with Storm's help. I didn't have to do everything by myself. I didn't have to walk through this life all alone, constantly looking over my shoulder. My father constantly talked about us being dragons, but he failed to realize that dragons weren't lonely creatures. They needed partners, they needed family, and I was going to create one.

As I exited the room I'd been staying in for the last few days, I bumped into Atlas, almost falling along with the two bags I carried with me.

"Shit," I muttered, before a strong pair of hands steadied me.

His laughter echoed against the walls of the hallway, and maybe in another lifetime I would be instantly pissed off, but not today. I started laughing with him, dropping the bags at our feet.

"Where's the rush?" His blue eyes twinkled underneath the lights, but what occupied my attention wasn't the carefree smile on his face, but something else.

"Why the fuck did you cut your hair?" His usually long hair that he wore in a high bun was nowhere to be seen. The top part was still longer, but the sides were shaved almost all the way to his skull, and I didn't like it. Okay, I did like it. He still looked awesome with shorter hair, but I also hated it. "Noooo!" I wailed as if it were my hair he cut off. "Now you're no longer one of the girls."

He almost choked from the force of his laughter and I started smiling again. "You're really good for my ego, you know?"

"Your ego is already more than any of us could handle. Somebody needs to knock it down a notch."

"And that somebody needs to be you?"

I shrugged. "It's not like you're keeping me around for my cooking skills. Besides," I bent down, picking up the bags, "someone needs to tell you the truth."

"Which is?"

"Now I can't pull your hair when you're a naughty boy."

"Mhm." He leaned closer. "But I can pull yours."

He was only joking, but I almost instantly pulled back, my mind flooded with memories of Storm, his hands on me, and the way he held me like I was precious. Well, I would've pulled back if that familiar, thunderous voice didn't make Atlas jump three feet away from me.

"You really don't want to live, do you Atlas?"

I turned around to see a scowling Storm heading our way. "Step away from her and stay away."

His legs ate the distance between him and us, and before I could come up with the retort of him not owning me and me being able to do whatever I wanted to do, he was already in front of me, taking the bags from my hands, rendering me speechless with one look. I wondered if his parents named him Storm because they knew he would be a force to be reckoned with, because the way he looked at me right now, possessive, demanding, even loving, it was almost too much to bear.

I couldn't take my eyes off him, even when Atlas started chuckling, still standing a few feet away from us. I couldn't stop staring even as Atlas's form retreated down the hallway and we were left all alone. We were going to one of their clubs tonight, but it was as far away from my mind as it possibly could be. My body buzzed with a different kind of energy, one that could now connect me with Storm.

It was such a silly little thing, but it felt as if he finally woke me up from the slumber I'd placed myself into. I felt alive, and even though all these memories were flooding my mind, even though I didn't know what to do next, I felt alive.

"I don't like him touching you," he gritted when what felt like another stampede turned my stomach upside down.

"So, if I ask Indigo to touch me, it's gonna be —"

"No." His nostrils flared, his eyes narrowed, and I grinned at the jealousy shining through his eyes. "Nobody touches you but me." He dropped the bags and pressed me against the wall, gripping my throat in his hand. "No one," he whispered as his thumb pressed against the pulse point on my neck and his nose descended into my hair. "You're mine."

"But are you mine?" I had to ask. I hated thinking about other women's hands on him, but I had to know. Men had the ability to render us speechless, to demand from us to be faithful and only theirs, when they wouldn't do the same. I had to know that all of this, these crazy feelings, that I wasn't just some kind of an object for him.

"Do you even have to ask, Sunshine?" His other hand lifted my shirt, sneaking inside and landing right on my waist. "I was yours for as long as I can remember."

Something inside my chest fluttered, my heart started beating faster, my breaths coming out shorter, but the need to run away was nowhere to be found. It was as if my heart and my mind finally started working in sync, both knowing where they were supposed to be.

Here, with him, in his arms.

I guess that this was me trying to be better, to accept things. I settled my hands on his shoulders and started kneading the muscles there, drawing out a groan from him.

"Then I guess I can be yours as well. Might have to go over that whole ownership contract to see what it entails, but you know." I chuckled as his eyes shut closed while I continued massaging his shoulders, the back of his neck and his upper arms. "Are there any benefits in this arrangement?"

I slowed my movements when his eyes snapped open, burning with desire. "Don't stop," he pleaded in a husky voice. "That feels so good."

"Don't we need to go?" I licked over his bottom lip and squeezed the back of his neck.

"Continue doing that and you won't be going anywhere but directly to my bed."

That wasn't the worst idea, but I didn't want to miss an opportunity to stab somebody in the eye tonight.

"Come on." I tapped his shoulder. "Stop being a Neanderthal and move your ass. I have an itch to scratch, and no, get that look off your face and those ideas out of your head."

"I didn't say anything." He chuckled.

"You didn't have to. I can see it all over your face."

I bent down to retrieve the bags but he again snatched them from my hands, giving me a pointed look before he turned around and started walking toward his room. Well, our room, I guess. Was now an appropriate time to freak the fuck out because I was about to?

Maybe.

Possibly.

Okay, no, I wasn't going to hyperventilate because he was again moving me into his room. It wasn't like we bought an apartment together. Right? It was just a room.

"Do you always live in the clubhouse or is this just a temporary arrangement?" I called out as I ran after him, trying to calm my racing heart. See, maybe we weren't really living together.

He glanced at me over his shoulder as he rounded the corner toward the part of the hallway where our room was located, answering me with a grunt.

"Is that a yes or a no?"

"Yes."

Okay, we were back to one-word answers, and I thought I was the one with the personality that resembled a walking bipolar disorder. His much-longer legs were eating the ground while I struggled to keep up with him. I wasn't sure if he was pissed off at me or if this was just his general mood when he couldn't get everything he wanted, but I'd be happy to poke the bear a little bit more.

I kind of liked seeing him all riled up and angry. It did something to me. If you told me a few years back that the whole possessive demeanor would almost rock my panties off, I wouldn't believe you.

"So, where is it?" I asked again as we finally reached our room. He opened the door with his elbow, not even sparing me a glance. Unlike before, the room was illuminated now and on top of the rumpled bed was a black, square suitcase, with their insignia on top of it.

"What is this?"

He dropped my bags next to the wardrobe before he turned back to me. "It's for you."

"Me?" See, I could also do one-word sentences. "What's in it?"

I loved gifts, especially when they came in this kind of suitcase. I had an idea what was inside, but since he resorted to the Neanderthal kind of speech, I wanted to pull more out of him. I basically spilled all my beans earlier, but I had to admit—he looked cute pouting like he was now.

"Open it up." I didn't want to seem too eager, but if my assumption was right, I am about to be met with some weapons. Sue me if I wanted to be giddy about it. "Just open it, Ophelia."

"Someone's impatient."

"I'm not impatient. I just... I just want you to like it, okay?"

"So, are you gonna continue sulking like a five-year-old child if I don't like it?"

"I'm not sulking." *Hah, men.*

"Could've fooled me."

He started grunting and muttering about

268

women, and never really understanding us, and him not being a five-year-old child or sulking or pouting, but I tuned him out and focused on the leathery surface of the suitcase. The three-headed beast on the top with their name looked beautiful — scary, but beautiful. I dragged my hand over the cool surface, tingles racing over my hand, my body, and the excitement I hadn't felt in so long, awoke inside of me.

I pressed my fingers against the metal handle on the front and located the zipper on the side. The sound of it being opened ricocheted in the otherwise quiet room, and when I lifted the lid, I bit down on my tongue. I was close to squealing like a high school girl during a Justin Bieber concert.

One side of the compartment held different types of guns, arraying from a Ruger-57 to a Glock 22, all of them in a sleek black color, neatly arranged one next to another. But my eyes drifted to the other side where my true love when it came to weapons stood. A set of throwing knives was tied together in one corner, their dark silver skin shining underneath the light. I picked them up first, feeling their body, their weight in my hand. This was better than Christmas.

I looked down, still holding the throwing knives in my hand, my eyes wandering over the different types of knives and daggers all for my choosing.

"Do you like it?"

"Do I like it?" I looked up at him, dragging my eyes away from one of the best gifts. "I think me saying that I like it would be the understatement of the year. I fucking love it. I just... I lost my knives in the church and this... I have no words, Storm."

A satisfied look passed over his face, quickly replaced by pride and something akin to wonder as

269

I kept looking between the knives and him. I was going to bring the Glock with me, but knives were always my weapon of choice.

Guns always felt impersonal to me. The knowledge that I had to get close in order to use my knives, that I had to look them in the eyes was always thrilling for me. I hated myself for the innocent lives I took over the years, but the other ones, the ones that truly didn't deserve to live, I didn't mind.

I lived for the fact that I was the last thing they would ever see before descending into Hell. Some of them were rapists, some were abusers, some traffickers. Some failed to fulfill their promises, hurting other people in the process, and the assignments where I got to be the executioner, where I got to take away from them just like they took away from other people, were my favorite assignments.

"I know you prefer knives, but," he approached me slowly, "having a gun with you will give me peace of mind, especially with where we're going."

"Where are we going? You said that you knew where Sam was, but you still didn't tell me where that is."

"We own several, um, clubs." He scratched his chin, avoiding my eyes when it dawned on me.

"Strip clubs?"

"Yes. Strip clubs."

Did he think I would be angry because they owned strip clubs?

"Are the girls working there because they want to work there, or?"

"Babe." He looked at me as if I suddenly grew three heads.

"Don't babe me." I gripped the knives. "Are

they or are they not? It's a very simple question."

He sat down, taking one of the daggers with a red handle in his hand, and flicked his thumb over its tip. "They're there because they want to be there. We might be a lot of things, Ophelia, but we would never participate in human trafficking."

The cynical part of me was pulling me toward the distrustful side, but I knew he was telling the truth. After everything I told him, I knew he wouldn't lie to me about something like that. And the somber expression he wore was enough to make me believe in what he was saying.

"Okay," I finally spoke.

"Okay?"

"Yeah." I grinned. "Okay. I trust you and I'm trying to be a bit better about this whole communication thing, so I'm gonna try to stop assuming only the worst things when maybe not everything is so bad."

He seemed to think about it for a moment, nodding at my words, but his eyes were plastered on the suitcase. I was about to ask him if everything was okay when that little switch turned on again, and his whole demeanor changed from somber to an excited one.

"Get dressed." He all but jumped from the bed and started walking toward the bathroom, still holding that dagger. "I'm just gonna take a shower."

I wasn't sure if confusion was the right word for how I felt right now, but as he disappeared behind the closed doors, I didn't want to ponder over the fact that he didn't want to talk to me when there were obviously things that haunted him, just like there were things that haunted me.

There was no use in overthinking this when there were more important things to do, but I was going to make him tell me everything. Just, small steps. Baby steps, whatever the fuck. If I could talk, so could he.

But right now, I needed to find some blood-proof clothes, and I just hoped that ZoZo managed to snag more of those black t-shirts. I didn't have a chance to look over everything she brought, but I wouldn't be surprised if she sneaked in a couple of pink tops just to fuck with me.

I glanced toward the bathroom door again before I walked to the wardrobe where he dropped my bags and hoped that whatever ate at him was going to disappear by the time he came outs. I was too tired for drama tonight.

* * *

MY HOPES FOR a less broody Storm flew out the window, and he kept ignoring me and everybody else as we drove toward the strip club. Atlas kept throwing cautionary glances Storm's way and I knew I wasn't the only one thrown off by his demeanor. One minute, he was okay, the next, he went completely quiet and brooding. I still rode with him, but it felt as if we were thousands of miles away from each other.

He was angry about the whole Sam situation, but this behavior came afterward, after I opened that suitcase and asked him about the strip club. I wasn't going to ponder over the words used or the questions asked, but something was bothering him. His body was stiff beneath my hands and that playful banter we usually had was nowhere to be seen.

He reminded me of me. He reminded me of all the times I refused to even think about the things that were bothering me, when I would shut off

272

everyone that tried to talk to me. I would retreat and try not to think about the shit running through my head, but it was always useless, because what we feared usually lived inside of us, and no matter what, we could rarely ignore it.

What we feared the most were almost always memories of people, of places, of moments lost or the ones ruined. I didn't know enough about him to try to assume what was going on, but I wasn't gonna sit on the side and wait for him to come out of his shell and talk to me.

I squeezed him tighter as we flew through the streets, going toward the busier part of town. Thankfully, I'd zipped the jacket I wore, otherwise the cold December wind would be enough to knock me off the bike and make me go back to the house where it was warm. I really, really fucking hated the cold.

I despised it, and though it wasn't as cold as it used to get in Croyford Bay or in Ventus City, it was still enough to freeze my nipples. I was about to pull back, to try and lift the collar of the jacket higher, when one of his hands landed on top of mine. He entwined his fingers with mine, squeezing them, holding us together against his stomach. I wished I didn't have the helmet on right now so that I could kiss the back of his neck.

Before we departed from the clubhouse, Atlas told me the name of the club and what to expect when we got there. They owned several establishments that dealt in the same kind of, well, entertainment. Some of them were in Santa Monica, the other ones were scattered across the West Coast, handled by the other chapters of Sons of Hades.

The one we were going to right now was called The Renegades, and it definitely wasn't the kind of a place where respectable businessmen spent their time. Though, my father and Logan Nightingale were supposedly respectable businessmen and look what they did for a living.

The Renegades was located close to the Santa Monica airport, and while it didn't take us long to get to our destination, I was ready to just be done with this night. I hated the energy around us and not knowing what was wrong. Fuck it, I loved knowing things about people I cared about, and Storm was definitely one of them.

Neon red lights on top of the building were the first things I saw as we pulled into the parking area, already occupied by several cars as well as motorcycles. The name of the club flashed on and off under the dark sky, and as we slowed down, stopped and turned off the engines, the same energy that buzzed through me earlier started coursing again, elevating my heartbeat, and I automatically reached for the knives nestled underneath my jacket.

I was the first one to get off the bike, followed by Storm who immediately stood behind me, placing his hands on my waist while we waited for the rest of the bikers to join us. Atlas and Creed walked toward us, accompanied by Indigo who as per usual, wore that scowl on his face. I wondered if he ever really smiled.

I wasn't the most cheerful person, but I smiled... Sometimes. Okay, rarely, but I did it from time to time. He seemed like he had a stick permanently shoved up his ass.

Or maybe he needed to have a stick shoved up his ass.

I snorted as the thought entered my mind, my eyes immediately wandering toward Atlas. I really needed to ask him what the deal was with the two

274

of them. Three other guys approached as well, standing close to us, but not as close as Atlas, Creed, and Indigo. I had no idea what their names were, and if I was being completely honest, I didn't really care to find out. I tried remembering as many names as I could, but I usually sucked with those, and there were too many club members for me to remember them all.

Storm had already briefed them about the situation and why we were here, and I just hoped we wouldn't spend too much time going over the logistics or whatever the fuck they wanted to talk about. Everybody waited for Storm to speak first, but the brooding behemoth kept quiet with his eyes solely focused on the entrance of the club. I followed the line of his sight seeing the two blond girls perched on the rails at the stairs leading toward the entrance, surrounded by the smoke from the cigarettes they were smoking.

Both of them wore leather jackets, both of them looked fucking stunning. Kind of badass if I might say.

Like well-trained soldiers, our little entourage started walking at the same time as Storm did, all of us heading toward the entrance. His hands remained on my waist, even as we walked side by side. I didn't want to make a scene right now, but we were going to talk about this shit. I know, I've been doing the same hot-and-cold shit for days now, but I thought we were over that part. So, he was either going to talk, or he was going to get his balls busted. The choice was solely up to him.

I placed my right hand on the other side of his waist, hugging his back, and with a quick glance at me, I could see the small smile playing on his lips, but when I didn't smile back, that familiar frown was back, his eyes narrowed.

275

"What's wrong?"

Did he really ask me what was wrong? I wasn't the one walking around with the permanent death stare.

"Nothing." I shrugged and turned my head, looking at the short hair Atlas now sported. Indigo was right next to him, and for the millionth time, I had no idea why those two weren't together. Over the last couple of days while I was ignoring Storm, I noticed stolen glances, hidden smiles, long wishful stares, and I just wanted them to get it over with.

I was a nosy bitch right now and maybe thinking about their non-relationship was easier than thinking about the beginning of mine. Holy shit, I was in a relationship. That thing with Kieran, I didn't even think about it as a normal relationship anymore, considering how it started, but right now, this whole thing with Storm was a relationship.

Right?

Unless you fuck it all up as per usual.

Listen, I didn't have enough middle fingers to show my inner self how I really felt. I wouldn't fuck it up, not this time. This time, I wanted to work through the things that were bothering me. This time, I wanted to break the circle of suffering my family put me through. And yes, I knew that tomorrow I would probably go back to my old grumpy self, but for now, I had to believe that maybe I could work through all of this.

Storm's hand on my waist squeezed tighter, making me roll my eyes. Who would've known that grown-ass men were just overgrown children? When I didn't look at him, ignoring him just like he had ignored me for the last hour, he squeezed me again, grunting at the same time.

I know, I know, I was the bitch that kept

ignoring him for days on end, but I had a reason. A small reason, but I had a reason, and he knew it. What was it that Ava constantly told me? The secret to every good relationship is communication, and if he wasn't going to communicate, then I didn't know how he expected me to talk to him.

Not that I knew anything about relationships, but wasn't communication the most important part?

"Ophelia," he grumbled. "Don't fucking test me right now."

"Or what?" I kept looking ahead as I dropped my hand from his waist. His annoyance was almost palpable, and even though this whole game we've been playing reminded me more of high school and the whole I-don't-wanna-tell-you-I-like-you thing, I was enjoying it. I guess that's what happens when you miss out on all the normal things in life.

To say that my emotional maturity resembled more to that of a sixteen-year-old teenager than a twenty-four-year-old woman, would be an understatement of the year. I didn't exactly know how to behave around people. I was still surprised ZoZo didn't run away in the opposite direction, but she seemed to like me, and I started liking her as well. When she wasn't talking my ear off, she was cool, I guess. I knew how to maim, kill, threaten, but I didn't know how to have a socially acceptable conversation, nor did I know what regular people did while they were dating, or whatever this was.

Relationship, you idiot. You are in a relationship.

Middle fingers, high up, whatever worked for my inner self.

"Are you seriously not going to look at me?"

"Are you seriously not going to tell me what's bothering you?" See, two could go around in circles, and one of us was going to have to relent. It

277

was just too bad for him that it wasn't going to be me. If he wanted to be a stubborn mule, I was about to show him what it meant to date a Slavic girl. I could hold a grudge for years. Just ask Kieran, he knows the best just how long I could hold one.

I thought he would let me go, drop his hand, and just continue with the whole ignoring part, but instead, he pulled me closer and pressed his lips to my temple. "I don't wanna fight with you." Really? "But there are things I need to work through and there are memories too painful to think about right now. I promise you," he gave me another kiss, "I will tell you everything, but just... Give me some time."

Damn him and his reasoning. My heart clenched at his words, because I knew what it felt like being haunted by memories and not wanting to revisit them if you didn't have to. Hell, I still wanted to run away and close the damn door that opened inside my mind, but I was going to try. I didn't want to feel bad for him when he pissed me off, but his lips felt like a balm on burning skin. I could try denying it until the end of the world, but I loved his touch. I had no idea what to do with all these mushy feelings. I wasn't even going to try to be rational about them. Just roll with it. I was just going to have to roll with it and let it lead me, well, wherever mushy feelings could lead you I guess.

"Promise?" I finally looked up at him. "I am tired of secrets, Storm. My whole life was filled with them. My parents lied, Kieran lied, my brother lied, everyone around me lied, and I am tired of it all. I want the truth, no matter how painful it is. If it's something that's connected to me, I wanna know." I smiled. "And if it's something that's solely yours, I'm gonna wait until you're ready to tell me. But for the love of everything, don't wait too long.

Patience isn't one of my virtues."

"I do." He gave me one more kiss, this time on my forehead. "I promise I will tell you everything."

I was a distrustful person. People in my life had proven that I couldn't really trust all that many people. They lied, they cheated, they fucked up everything we had, but with Storm, I wanted to believe him, but I needed more time to forget about everything else that had happened and to truly start living.

"Okay. I guess I can deal with that."

The smile that took over his face just as we came to the entrance to the club was blinding, and that fluttery feeling in my chest returned because I was the one he was smiling at. I was the reason he was smiling, and although we had a long way to go, I believed that this could be the start of something really good.

"Atlas? Indigo?" The two girls I saw earlier squeaked as soon as we came close to them, each of them entwining their hands around Atlas and Indigo, squeezing them together. I started laughing because I realized who they reminded me of, put together like this.

Have you ever watched *Snow White and The Seven Dwarfs*? Atlas was definitely Happy, while Indigo with no doubt in my mind resembled Grumpy. Even with the two girls attacking them, Atlas was still smiling, even flirting with them, and Indigo looked like he would rather be anywhere but here.

I could feel Storm's eyes on me as I cleared the tears that had gathered on my cheeks and went into another fit of laughter when Indigo jumped on the spot as one of the girls pinched his butt.

"Oh, this is golden," I choked out. "This is better than a movie."

"You're terrible," Storm said, but I could see he was trying not to laugh. "We need to get inside and not waste our time here." Or maybe he could pass for Grumpy? He and Indigo could share the spot.

He started walking up the stairs, pulling me with him, when the taller out of the two girls squeaked again, destroying my eardrums.

"Stormy!" Oh God. I was going to pee myself if this shit continued. "Where have you been?"

I tried not to laugh, I really did, but as my shoulders started shaking, so did Storm's.

"Yeah, Stormy." I looked at him, ignoring the girl behind us. "Where have you been?"

The pinch to my waist was warning enough to know that there would be a retaliation later. I was counting on it.

TWENTY-TWO

Ophelia

I REALLY TRIED to stop laughing. I really, really did, but even after we entered the club and Storm brought me a vodka cranberry, I couldn't stop. Tears were free falling down my cheeks, and my mind replayed their faces as the two girls surrounded them.

"Stormy," I choked out, earning another glare from the man in question. "Oh God, I can't believe they called you Stormy."

That whole encounter was the highlight of my year. It was better than Christmas and New Year combined in one. Their faces were something I would never forget. I might even try to find one of those sketch artists just so that I could have it on paper as well. If I had my phone with me, I would've taken pictures.

"Shut up, Ophelia," Storm grumbled, but when Atlas started laughing, I couldn't stop the new onslaught erupting from me. "Gods." Storm looked to the ceiling, probably trying to pray or something, putting his hands on his hips. He looked pretty hot in the leather jacket and the black shirt underneath fitting him like a second skin. The tattoos on his neck were peeking from the shirt, and I suddenly wanted to lick each and every line, tracing a path toward his lips.

Grumpy, or well, Indigo, stood right next to him, but he wasn't looking at me. Not even surprised, I knew he was looking at Atlas who was still howling next to me, holding a beer bottle.

Trying to move my eyes from Storm, I took in the club for the first time. The neon sign outside was a clear indication that this wasn't a five-star establishment, but I could see why some people liked it.

The area where the poles were located was smack dab in the center, slightly elevated, and it was the first thing you would see once you entered. Of course, if you weren't laughing like an idiot, that would be the first thing you would see. Booth-type seating was arranged all around the circle stage, and patrons, both young and old, were already occupying most of those seats. Most of the guys seated wore vests similar to Storm's. Some of them had the same insignia and I knew they were part of the club, while the other ones either didn't have any kind of insignia or it was a different one.

Two long bars located on each side of the spacious room were filled to the brim, each of them with two bartenders. The smaller bar we were seated at was deeper inside the room, mostly hidden from the eyes of the public, which I didn't mind. At all. Ava used to tell me I was a creepy people watcher, but throughout the years, my "people watching" helped me more than the skills my father tried to instill in me. People were at their most vulnerable when they thought no one was watching.

The guy sitting at the booth closest to the stage, but furthest from the entrance, kept looking from the bar to the entrance, and back to the stage. He wore a suit, a very rumpled suit, and the way he kept gulping down drink after a drink told me that him being here wouldn't sit well with some people.

Some people probably being his wife or husband, if the ring he just took off was any indication.

"What are you looking at?" Atlas asked, taking a sip of the whiskey he previously ordered. He tried following my line of sight, but he couldn't locate where exactly I was staring.

"That piece of shit there." I pointed to the blond guy I was glaring at. "He just removed his wedding ring."

"Oh."

Oh, was the right reaction. After what happened with Kieran, I had a low tolerance for cheaters. If you didn't want to be with somebody, just break it off. Don't fucking drag the relationship that wasn't working just because you weren't man or woman enough to break it off.

I didn't want to dwell on that again tonight. The memories of that day when I found Kieran and Cynthia in our apartment were already burned inside my mind and reliving that moment and thinking about this asshole's spouse wasn't going to fix anything. I couldn't exactly march over there and demand for him to leave the place just because he was married.

Besides, we had more important things to do tonight, and seeing this only elevated my need to spill some blood.

"Where's Creed?" Storm stood on the side, talking in hushed tones with Indigo, carefully scanning the crowd behind us. Atlas was with me, and the other guys were carefully positioned between us and the passage leading to this part of the club. This was my first rodeo with Storm and his guys, and I had no idea how they worked.

On all my missions I'd been alone, sans a couple of times daddy dearest decided that he wanted the new recruits to be killed off or just tried in the field. Most of them returned in body bags or not at all, depending on how many body parts I was able to salvage.

But them, they worked as a team. Although I didn't know what their roles were, or where Creed disappeared to, I knew they worked as a well-oiled machine. All of them seemed to respect Storm and his decisions, which brought me back to my questions from yesterday. Why did Hunter attack Storm and why didn't he defend himself?

If somebody tried to do that to my father or to Logan Nightingale, they would end up dead, thrown in the nearest ditch. So why the fuck did that shitshow happen? I agreed to let him tell me other things when he gets ready for it, but some things, like that shit, he would have to explain to me. And for fuck's sake, somebody had to explain to me the inner workings of the club. I almost got smacked by Atlas two days ago because I called their cuts leather jackets.

Or maybe I would just have to practice patience, like, for the first time in my life. Even as a kid I was an impatient thing, and it drove our nannies crazy. Theo was the one that was never there, older than Maya and me, hanging out with the Nightingale twins. Maya was the quiet one, calm, mentally present.

I was apparently a hell-raiser.

Needless to say, that whole patience shit I needed to practice was almost snapping in two, because I had no idea what our plan was, or what was going on. This usually sent me into a mini panic attack, but I had to trust them, trust Storm. I knew he wouldn't hurt me, and if we were here for that scumbag that fucked up the last four years of my life, I wasn't going to stand on the side. Well, I hoped Storm wouldn't want me to stand on the side.

The music suddenly changed, and a familiar song blasted through the speakers as the lights in the room dimmed down, only the red hue from the bars visible in the dark.

"I love this part," Atlas whispered, excitement evident in his voice. I didn't have to wait too long to see what was the part that he loved, as the red and green lights mixed together shone over the stage. The smoke filtered over the runaway leading to the backside and the dark silhouette stepped up, just as the Fame on Fire's singer started the chorus of "Her Eyes," driving my blood pressure higher.

The crowd went wild as she sauntered toward one of the poles, playing with it, touching it in a sensual yet strong way and looking over the crowd. I glanced at both men and women gathered around the stage as the lights went up, illuminating the dark skin of the goddess on the stage, with her dark hair in messy curls and a body to kill for.

"Jesus."

I was breathless, speechless as she twirled around the pole, keeping us all in a trance.

"That's Thalia." Atlas's voice was both near and far because the way she moved, the way she commanded the stage, the whole crowd, it was magical. I quickly realized that this wasn't your typical strip club. One look at the balconies on both sides and I knew I was wrong.

So fucking wrong.

That whole statement about businessmen not coming here was pure shit, because those balconies seated men and women in various stages of undress. Some of them kissing each other, some fully dressed, and some moving to the rhythm of the music as the lyrics of the devil in the eyes of the person the singer was singing about danced through the pumped-up air.

It was suffocating, it was liberating, and I wanted to stand up and dance. I wanted to be lost to this feeling, this freedom music was bringing, and I knew whose arms I wanted to be in while doing that.

My eyes found Storm, who was already looking at me with a heated gaze. My breathing became shallow, molten lava rushing through my veins and on shaky limbs, I slowly stood up and started walking toward him. The rest of the world disappeared and the only person I could see was him.

I extended my hand, reaching for his, and when he grabbed me, pulling me to him, I felt like I could breathe again. A faster song came on, my heart following the rhythm of the bass and Storm pressed his hand against my heart, just below my breast, killing me with his touch. I did the same, feeling his heartbeat beneath my fingertips, pumping at the same time as mine.

In sync.

Together.

A soft touch on my cheek as he pressed his palm against my skin, a thumb beneath my eye tracing a path all the way to the scar Kieran left, and a tightening in my chest, and my whole body burned with desire stronger than anything else I had ever felt.

He managed to bring this out in me like

nobody else did. I thought what I felt for Kieran was love, but if we continued on this path, I knew I could get lost in Storm and I wouldn't mind. I wouldn't mind feeling like this for the years that were about to come, because the heartache and the sadness were two friends I wouldn't mind parting with.

They taught me how to be strong, how to be resilient, but it was time for me to become more. To become a woman capable of happiness even as the bullets flew around me, and I could find all of it with him. I knew I could.

I shivered as he lowered his head, his breath tickling my ear. "If we didn't have to do what we came here to do, I would take you to the nearest room, bend you over one of the tables and fuck you until your legs gave out." My legs almost gave out, but he moved his hand from my chest to my waist, holding me steady. "I would show you who you truly belong to." Pressing his finger against my bottom lip, he leaned closer, our noses touching, his eyes burning into mine. "I wanna fuck this pouty mouth, Sunshine. I wanna see you on your knees, worshipping me and then I am going to worship you. Lick your whole body, bite you, suck you, mark you. I want you to feel me between your legs while you walk. I want you to think about me even while you talk to other people. I want it all."

"God," I moaned. Coherent thoughts left my mind, and I was leaving it up to him to decide what we were going to do. I didn't want to fight this, fight us. I didn't want to run anymore. "Please." I wasn't above begging, pleading.

"Later." The bastard chuckled, taking a step back, leaving me hot and bothered and I wasn't the only one. His cheeks were flushed, eyes hooded and the bulge in his pants definitely wasn't because he saw another girl prancing around naked. It was for me. "We have a job to do."

I was about to moan some more, when Creed walked into my line of sight, looking smug himself.

"Storm," he called out before looking out over all of us. "He's in the basement, waiting for you."

"Does he know?" my favorite behemoth asked, still looking at me with a small smirk.

"Of course not. He's as oblivious as he can be."

My excited girl parts quieted down when it all registered. We were going to talk to Sam.

Show-fucking-time.

* * *

THE MORE WE walked through the club, the more I realized that this wasn't some kind of a shady strip club where girls were forced to work, and patrons were sleazy bastards with no boundaries. Some of them were just dancers, like that first girl I saw, Thalia. Some were dressed in barely there outfits, and seeing them freely walking around, I wanted to know how it felt.

To be so free and so happy.

Walking behind Storm, who wouldn't let my hand go even as we passed several other bikers who seemed to know him, we slowly came to the stairs leading to what I assumed was the basement. Whenever somebody mentioned a basement to me, I thought about the one Kieran and his brothers held me in, and the familiar anger would start rising again. It wasn't enough for them to lock me up, chain me like an animal when we first found Ava in their house, but they locked me up again when I let them find me.

Stupid fucking men. Their stupidity and naivety cost them more than they could ever imagine.

"Are you okay?" Storm asked as we walked down the stairs and then through the hallway with several doors on each side, heading toward the one on the far end. He seemed concerned, and I wasn't entirely sure if it was because I kept quiet or because I kept fidgeting. Truth be told, I couldn't wait to get this over with. To hold those knives and to feel like I did so many times before when men that didn't deserve to live came to me.

Instead of answering, I nodded, squeezing his hand tighter. This would be the first time for me to do anything like this with a man I cared about. Kieran never wanted to go on missions with me, and it took me a while to figure out why.

No matter how much he loved me, or at least he thought he did, he could never really accept this part of me. The part my father awoke, trained, and sent out into the world. Maybe that's why we could never really work out. Maybe that's why he cheated, why he decided to hurt me through the person I cared about. The two of us were villains created by a set of circumstances our families threw our way.

Two people, lost in the world and we clung to each other because that was all we ever knew. We thought our destinies were written before we could even talk, but I knew now that we could change them. We didn't have to live by the set of rules our families made for us. We didn't have to follow everything they did just to get their approval.

Somewhere between running away from Croyford Bay, working with the Albanians, stabbing Kieran and being here with Storm, I realized that I was nothing but a brainwashed puppet, too scared to live how I wanted to truly live. The more I thought about it, the more I resented my father and my mother.

The more time I spent in the company of people that truly loved each other, the angrier I became. For so long, I thought love was measured in the things we did for other people, yet I couldn't be further from the truth. Actions mattered, but every relationship had two people, not only one, and throughout my entire life I was always the only one willing to bend, willing to do things for the people I cared about.

I tried changing myself, tried being softer, being less volatile, but it wasn't enough because the other side never did the same for me. I tried saving them, tried loving them, even when I hated them, but they would never even lift a finger to help me.

It came to me now that even if I wanted to go back to my father and try to amend the things while I still had time, seeing how Storm behaved with his people, how fathers and mothers in the club acted around their children, made me rethink the whole situation. My father didn't love me. I didn't think that Nikolai Aster knew what love was.

He only wanted me because I was one of the investments he had, just like all those companies, houses, and apartments. The only connection we had was by blood, both the one that coursed through our veins and the one we spilled. He was more of a stranger to me than Atlas was, and that was saying something, considering the amount of time we spent together versus the amount of time I spent with Atlas.

This could be my family.

These guys that crowded us as we stopped in front of the door, protecting Storm and me from each side. These guys that accepted me.

My family was Storm. He was my home, my beginning, and my ending, and I was going to fight for this. I was going to fight myself and everyone who stood in my path, because I wanted this. For the first time in forever, I didn't feel like I wanted to run away. For the first time, I wanted to experience life to its fullest.

To wake up next to my person, to talk to the people that wanted to hear about my day. I didn't want to carry this weight all by myself, and Storm obviously wanted to share it.

"I will enter first," Storm started, and before I could protest, he silenced me with his next words. "And I will leave the door open. I want you to wait, Ophelia." He looked at me pointedly as if he knew I wasn't one to follow the rules. "I need to talk to him first, because he definitely won't want to talk to you."

I loved breaking them, not making them.

"Ophelia?" he repeated when I didn't answer.

"Fine," I huffed after a minute of silence. "But his death is mine, Storm. I don't give a shit about anything else. I want to be the one to kill him."

The overhead lights illuminated his face with shadows dancing in the areas it couldn't reach, and with one small nod, one small acknowledgment to my demand, he opened the door and disappeared inside the room.

The familiar, annoying voice traveled to us, greeting Storm and fueling my rage. I was going to enjoy this.

Their hushed voices were too hard to hear, even with the door still open, and before Atlas, Indigo, or any of the other guys could stop me, I stepped inside, coming face-to-face with Sam and an annoyed looking Storm.

Fuck it, I was always bad at following

directions.

Sam's face quickly lost all its color, resembling the pale white wall behind his back. A square metal table stood in the middle of the room with four chairs around it, but there was nothing else. The color of the floor tiles was darkened in places where the blood couldn't be washed away.

There were no weapons of any kind on the walls, there were no wardrobes, other tables nor chairs and I knew that this was the place where once you walked in, you never walked out.

"Hello, darling," I cooed, ignoring Storm who didn't seem happy to see me here. I was impatient, fucking sue me. "Remember me?"

I slowly walked toward the table, stopping behind Storm who was seated on the chair, and placed my hands on his shoulders staring at the fidgeting Sam on the other side. The sweat collected on his temples, his lower lip trembled, and I fed off the fear rolling around us in waves.

"Gir.. Girly?" Fuckface asked, his voice shaking. I wanted to punch him in the face for that idiotic name. "What are you doing here?"

"Well, wouldn't you know, Sammy. Storm actually wanted to see me. As a matter of fact, he wanted to see me badly, yet he had no idea I was here all those years ago. Why is that? Hmm?"

"I-I didn't." He looked between the two of us. "I didn't know."

"You didn't know that I looked for her, turning heaven and earth just to find her?" Storm thundered. "Don't fucking play those games with me, Sam. You knew better. Every single one of you knew that I looked for her, yet you didn't tell me when she came to the club."

"Prez, you have to believe me." He started shaking. "I didn't... They didn't tell me. They told

293

me she was dangerous. They told me she would betray you."

"They? Who are they?" Storm gripped the edge of the table, his knuckles whitening from the force he was holding it with.

"I don't know!" Sam cried. "But please...
Please, Prez. I didn't know she was yours."

"Awww, touching," I mocked. "Is that why you pressed a gun against my temple and shoved me into the street?"

"It wasn't like that. I just—"

"It was exactly like that." I walked around the table, stopping next to him. He flinched as I touched his hair, keeping his eyes on Storm. He thought he would help him. What a fool. "You fucked up, buttercup." I leaned down, whispering in his ear, "And now you are gonna be so fucked up."

"No!" He jumped from his chair. "I didn't do anything. You are bad!" He turned to me, frantically trying to get as far away from me as possible. "You are evil. You will bring everything bad to this club, to this family!" He was a perfect candidate for a mental institution, and people said I was the crazy one. "They call you *Baba Yaga*! I know, I know everything. How many children did you kill? How many innocent people died at your hands? How many—"

"A lot!" I yelled. "And there will be many more, honey. You think I'm a monster?" I asked him. "You have no idea what a real monster looks like. What real terror feels like, when it crawls over your skin, when they have no emotions other than their own sick, fucked-up minds. I grew up with one."

"You're a monster! You are!" he kept yelling. I was getting a fucking headache.

"Do you know what I like to do to little weaklings like you? I like to carve them up, take their skin off, remove their dicks, all while they're still alive." I smiled and lowered my voice before continuing, "And when you feel like you're dying, like the pain is too much to bear, I like to revive you with a shot of adrenaline, just so that you can feel everything I'm doing to you. Your screams, they're like the sweetest melody. The stench of your fear, it fuels my rage, because what you did back then, that's treason. You fucked your club over. The same one you were trying to protect from me."

"That's a lie!" He looked at me then at Storm. "You wouldn't, Prez. I did this for you!"

I couldn't move my eyes away from the man who almost ruined my life, who kept me away from Storm. I didn't want to because I wanted to see the look on his face when he realized that this was the end. This was the final destination for him.

"Prez?" he pleaded, but Storm kept quiet, observing him with a calculating gaze. "I promise. I would never betray you, but they told me—"

"Who are they?" I knew what a betrayal felt like, and hearing all of this meant that not only did he fuck up with me, but he betrayed Storm. "Who did you sell us to, you piece of shit?"

Storm jumped up as soon as he asked, rounding the table, and going right for him. I stood on the side, watching as it all unfolded. He wouldn't kill him, but he would torture him until he spoke. I wasn't the only one with horror stories attached to my name.

Storm Knoxx was a name you wouldn't want to utter unless you had a death wish. You wouldn't even want to think about it, because the things he did to those that fucked with him were some of the most brutal, brilliant things I had ever heard of.

In the blink of an eye, Storm had Sam pressed against the wall, holding the gun to his temple. I pulled my knives out and placed the throwing ones on the table, holding only the dagger I chose. The blade was sharp as I ran my finger over it, waiting for the next move, for whatever was coming next.

"I-I..." Sam's face was becoming red as his eyes filled with tears. "Please don't hurt me."

I loved it when they begged.

"You have two options." Storm chuckled as I sat on the table. "You can either tell me and Ophelia will kill you without dragging it out further." Not a chance in hell. I wanted him to suffer. "Or, you continue being a piece of shit, and she can make you wish you were never born." Now that, I could get on board with.

See, if this wasn't the true meaning of a relationship, I didn't know what was.

"No, no, not her." He tried getting free from Storm's grip, but Storm wouldn't budge. "Please, I'm begging you. Don't let her touch me." Now he was just being annoying and whiny. "I don't wanna die."

"Too late for that." I laughed. "You made your bed, now you gotta sleep in it."

"Shut up!" he roared, looking at me. "Shut the fuck up!"

I jumped from the table, taking my dagger with me, and walked to Storm. Placing my hand on his shoulder, I could feel the tension coiling beneath his skin, but this wasn't just a guy that betrayed him. This fucker betrayed both of us.

"Storm," I spoke softly, running circles on his back. "I wanna play too."

"No!" Fuckface roared, but I'd had enough of him. With one swift movement, my hand went beneath Storm's arm, and I pressed the tip of the dagger to Sam's throat, drawing out the blood that trickled over the blade. My finger throbbed as I tried to hold the knife, but it was a welcome kind of pain, because I knew he wouldn't be walking out of this room alive.

"Honey," I looked at him, "the adults are talking now, so please, for the love of everything, just keep quiet."

He opened his mouth to say something again, and I pressed the blade further into his skin, eliciting a painful moan from him.

"Atta boy." I smiled. "Just stand there for a second."

I looked at Storm who looked awed and murderous at the same time. God, he looked good enough to eat, and I was going to spend the rest of the night letting him do whatever he wanted to me.

"Storm," I purred. "Can I please play with him now?"

Instead of answering me, he dropped a kiss to my lips and took a step back, leaving me with a dagger to Sam's throat. I beamed, enjoying this side of him.

"Now," I turned to the maggot. "Sammy. What are we going to do with you?"

"I will never tell you anything. Not one thing."

"Maybe." I shrugged. "Not that I really care, darling. I just wanna see you bleed."

Realizing that I wasn't joking, and that I didn't give a fuck about anything else but seeing him down, he grabbed my hand, trying to push me away from him. I was smaller than Storm, physically weaker, but it didn't mean I was incapable of kicking down guys twice my size.

Men always thought that just because they were bigger than us, they could overpower us. What they often forgot about was that for every inch of their size, we possessed speed they didn't have. Before he could push me away from him, I grabbed his dick, squeezing more than necessary. His eyes bulged and the attempt to push me away died down, followed with whimpers resembling those of a small cat.

"Please, please," he kept chanting. "I have kids."

"Do I look like a give a fuck about your reproductive history?" I blinked. Why did people always mention kids and other loved ones? I seriously couldn't give a fuck about the other people they had. If anything, it only put those same people in danger because if there was one thing the Syndicate taught me, it was never to leave other members of the family behind.

Especially not kids. They almost always ended up being a problem a few years down the road, thinking they could avenge the scumbags they considered to be their family, which was a threat we didn't want to deal with.

"You're a heartless bitch, Ophelia Aster!" He spit in my face. "A cold, heartless bitch."

I paused to think about it, cleaning the spit from my face. "I've heard worse names."

"A piece of shit!" He wasn't creative, was he? "You will burn in hell!"

What was it with people constantly giving the *you'll burn in hell* speech? It wasn't like I didn't know that what I did was a big *no bueno* in the eyes of God or whatever deity there was. And if there really was Heaven or Hell, I didn't really give a fuck which one I ended up getting into. This life already prepared me for eternal suffering.

"Yeah, yeah, I know." I pulled him by the collar of his shirt and threw him toward Storm. He pulled him to the table, throwing him right on top.

Sam landed with a huff, moaning, crying out, and begging.

As Storm held his arms down, I became giddy with the possibilities of where to start, what to do, and which part of the skin to remove first. I tore through his shirt, throwing it open, revealing his mostly bare chest. The same insignia Storm had tattooed on his upper arm, stood proudly on Sam's left pec, but he didn't deserve it.

"What do we have here?" I climbed on the table and sat on top of his stomach, immobilizing him. "You don't get to die with this on you." I dragged the tip of the dagger over the edges of the tattoo, staring at the open jaws of the three-headed beast. "I don't think Cerberus would want you to be one of his hosts. What do you think, babe?" I looked at Storm. "Should I start with this one?" I stabbed the tip of the dagger into the center of the tattoo, still looking at him. "He shouldn't have it."

Heat coiled in my stomach as Storm dragged his eyes over my face to my breasts that were threatening to spill over the black t-shirt I wore. I wiggled on top of Sam who continued moaning as I dug the dagger deeper, still waiting for Storm to answer.

"I think it's a fantastic idea, Sunshine."

"Both of you are psychopaths!"

"Aww, poor baby." I leaned down, looking into Sam's eyes. "I honestly prefer creative and all that crap, but, suit yourself."

"Help!" he started screaming. "Somebody help me!"

I pulled the dagger out, but the relief that washed over his face was short-lived when I returned to the edge of the tattoo and started cutting through, lifting the skin up, making the Cerberus come to life as the skin moved with the dagger. His screams pierced my ears, and the pain and fear on his face fed into the darkest parts of me. The parts I missed and at the same time, resented.

The parts I knew I couldn't live without and I was starting to be okay with it. No more hiding, no more running, this is who I am. This is who I was always supposed to be.

I threw the piece of skin to the side, the blood seeping from the open wound on his chest, dripping onto the table. My hands were colored red, a stark contrast on my pale skin.

"Fuck!"

"Are you gonna talk?" Storm asked him again.

"Fuck you!"

I moved to his throat and sliced the skin on the side, letting the capillary blood trickle down. He thrashed beneath me, but between Storm's hold and me sitting on top of him, he wasn't going anywhere.

I loved the blank canvas, ready for me to do what needed to be done. Focusing on the olive skin of his chest, I dug into the pectoral muscle on the other side, slicing a piece of his skin. The screams were music to my ears, and as I moved lower to his abdomen, he tried lifting his head, looking at where I went.

"N-No," he murmured. "Please, anything but that."

Did he think? "Now you just gave me an idea, buttercup."

I slid lower, sat on top of his thighs, and started unbuttoning his jeans. "No!" he wailed as I reached inside, feeling the smooth skin above his dick, not one hair in place. Would you look at that? He actually groomed.

"Don't... I'm begging you!"

"Just tell me who you worked with and she

might stop." Storm laughed above him, taunting him, waiting for an answer. I knew he wanted to know who fucked with the club, but I could see he enjoyed watching this.

"Never!" He was a stubborn mule. "I will never tell you."

Jesus. Tone down the fucking screaming, dude.

"Ophelia." Storm glanced at me, then at Fuckface's flappy dick earning a grin from me. Ah, he wasn't circumcised. I pulled the excess skin, looking between him and Storm, smiling from ear to ear.

"No. No!" I think he was a parrot in his previous life. Dude just kept repeating the same word over and over again.

"Oh yes." I placed the dagger where the head of his dick began and pressed, drawing a circle around, cutting the skin off. Storm winced, Sam screamed, and I laughed as the blood coated his pants.

"Fuuuuuck!"

I pulled at the skin still attached to his dick and dove back in, cutting more until it became nothing more but a wobbly thing in my hand. Sam's breathing was becoming shallow, his eyes started closing, and I knew we were about to lose him.

Pressing against the raw tissue on his dick, I dug my nails deep, earning another painful howl from him.

"He said... He... Oh my God."

"Who said what?" Storm asked as Sam deliriously spoke the words.

"Watch your back, Prez." He looked at him. "The snakes are everywhere."

Snakes? Wait.

"Which snakes?" Storm shook him as he

301

started slipping into an unconscious state. "Which fucking snakes?"

Sam's eyes snapped open, a smile forming on his face. "The Nightingales."

The name felt like poison in my ears. The mere mention drawing out everything they did to me and knowing that this idiot worked with them behind Storm's back left a bitter feeling in my chest.

Before Storm could ask another question, I slammed the dagger into Sam's cheek, digging it all the way to the handle. He started choking, unable to fully open his mouth, and I pulled out the dagger, letting the blood flow freely from his mouth.

"Ophelia!" Storm's voice registered somewhere in the back of my mind, but that God forsaken name kept ringing in my ears, bringing back the memories of all the shit they put me through. "Stop!"

But I couldn't stop.

As Sam opened his mouth, I dug the dagger deep, hitting the back of his throat. He gurgled on the blood that started flowing, and as seconds passed, the thrashing and moaning stopped.

I wished my memories could stop like that.

"You have traitors in the club, Storm." I didn't want to look at him, but if what Sam said was true, we had bigger problems than him not mentioning me to Storm. "And that could be a major fucking problem."

"I know." He nodded.

"I'm sorry for…" I pointed to the mess beneath me. "But he mentioned them, and I—"

"Hey." He placed a hand on my cheek. "It's okay. I get it. At least I know who he'd been working with, now I just need to see how deep this shit went. Alright?"

He moved back, rounded the table, and pulled me off Sam's body. "Let's just go home," he murmured against my hair.

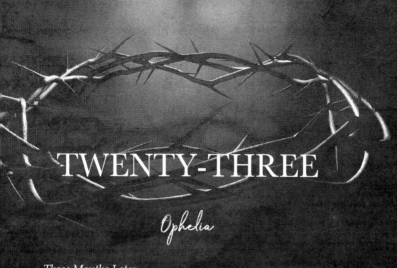

TWENTY-THREE

Ophelia

Three Months Later

"TRUTH OR DARE?" Zoe smiled, looking straight at me.

We were all sitting around the table in the backyard of the clubhouse, with me perched on top of Storm's lap, Atlas on our right side and Creed on the left. Indigo was on the other side of the table, with his arm around the chair Zoe was sitting in. Even Hunter joined us today. Nova, a new bartender who started working a week ago, was on the other side of Indigo, scowling at Creed who kept trying to get her attention.

It's been almost three months since the whole visit to The Renegades and me being at the club, and I had to say—I never expected to feel this at peace. Turns out, Storm had a house not too far away from here, still completely unfurnished but with a direct view of the ocean. A couple of his guys were sent to Mexico, to try and find out as much as possible about Maya's whereabouts, but so far, we hadn't had any luck.

I knew now how foolish it would've been for me to go there blindly, with no real backup and no proper information. The only thing we knew was that she was held by the Carrillo Cartel, one of the largest cartels in the region. If we didn't want to start a war with them, we had to tread carefully, especially since I didn't want to alert my father of what we were planning to do.

He had connections all over the world, and if he sold Maya to one of those mongrels, he most definitely kept in contact with them.

Strong fingers pressed against my waist as Storm's breath tickled my ear. "Sunshine? It's your turn." All eyes were on us. Atlas was smirking, Indigo scowling—no surprise there, right?—and Zoe looked like she needed to pee as she wiggled in her chair.

"Truth," I responded, followed by a bunch of groans from the rest of the guys.

"You are boring," and, "Little coward," sounded around us.

"Shush everyone," Zoe warned. "Hmmm, truth." Storm started kissing behind my ear, my neck, burying his face into my hair.

"You guys are almost disgusting," Nova groaned. "There's a room upstairs with your names on it."

"Shush it, Nova."

"Okay, I know!" Zoe exclaimed. "Kiss, kill or marry."

"The what?" I stared at her like a deer caught in the headlights.

"Kiss, kill or marry. Which of the guys here, excluding Storm—"

"No," the man in question protested.

"Shut up, Stormy." I laughed, earning a soft bite to my shoulder.

"So, as I was saying." Zoe cleared her throat and started again. "Which of the guys around this table would you kill, which one would you kiss, and which one would you marry?"

"Dude, there are four of them here, excluding Storm, and out of those four, only one of them would survive."

A chorus of voices erupted around us, with Creed being the loudest one, because we all knew which part would go to him.

"What are you guys doing?" Felix, Atlas's brother approached us just as Hunter started bickering with Atlas, throwing napkins at him.

"Ophelia is choosing who to marry, who to kill and who to kiss," Zoe responded, her eyes sparkling with interest. Oh-ho-ho, I didn't see that one coming. Little ZoZo liked Felix.

"So, what's the answer?"

Storm sat straighter, tightening his hands around my waist as if to remind me who I really belonged to. Not that I could forget. This whole relationship-y thing was much appreciated by my vagina.

"I would," I looked at Indigo, "kill Indigo." Everybody started laughing at that. "Definitely kiss Felix." Storm kept groaning behind me as I started laughing. "And of course," I placed my hand on top of Atlas's, "I would marry Atlas, my one true soulmate."

"Okay, that's it." Storm stood up, lifting me with him. "No more truths, dares, or whatever the fuck."

"But we were just getting started," Zoe cried out as Felix brought a chair, placing it next to Nova. "Don't take my Ophelia away."

"She's not your Ophelia," he grumbled, keeping me close to him. "She's mine."

Such romance today, mushy feelings, whatever the fuck, but I liked it. He entwined his fingers with mine and started pulling me away from the garden, leaving the chorus of cheers and laughter behind us. I had to ask Zoe about that whole thing with Felix, and I fucking wanted to know what was going on with Atlas and Indigo.

I apparently became a nosy motherfucker when I wasn't busy killing people and drowning in my own grief. Truth to be told, it felt good not worrying whether somebody was going to kill me in my sleep. There was only one thing still bothering me, minus the whole Maya situation.

Since two weeks ago, Storm seemed distant. I didn't want to think about bad things or overthink this whole situation, but he was hiding something — phone calls he didn't want me to hear, meetings with guys I knew nothing about. He was slowly pissing me off. And he didn't wanna talk about it. He didn't want to admit that something was wrong, even though my gut was telling me that there was something extremely wrong.

I was trying to enjoy all these new things — him, Zoe, Atlas, even Indigo started growing on me. More like fungus, but still, he was there. The day after we came back from The Renegades, a doctor paid us a visit, checking Storm's cuts and bruises, and scolding us because I fucked up my finger — again. It was healing, that's what mattered, right?

I knew, however, that if it wasn't for him wrapping my finger and ordering me not to move it more than I needed to, I wouldn't be able to use it at all. I hadn't felt pain ricocheting through my arm as I held the knife and stabbed Sam, but as soon as we came home, it crashed into me like a freight train. I couldn't move my arm, let alone my hand.

My favorite mother hen, Storm, called the poor man at three in the morning, demanding him to come first thing the next day.

I had to give it to him, he was better at this than me, which was why his sudden mood changes and the hot-and-cold demeanor threw me off my feet. He was distant yet caring. Cold, yet demanding. What did I tell you? A walking bipolar disorder.

Surprisingly, I didn't mind the attention he was showering me with, but I had a feeling there was a reason for this mildly obsessive behavior of his, I just didn't know what the cause behind it was. The little touches, kisses, his hands on my body, it didn't matter if we were with other people, or if we were just eating dinner, he had to have his hands on me at all times. Atlas and the rest of the guys behaved like they were walking on eggshells around him, trying to keep their distance from me, never talking about club business when I was there, and it irritated the fuck out of me.

I escaped from one prison; I wasn't going to willingly submit myself to another one.

"Storm," I started as we slowly ascended the stairs, his hand firmly holding mine. "I think we need to talk."

His whole body froze mid-step, the grip on my hand becoming painful. Maybe I worded it a wee bit bad. Okay, I worded that whole sentence really badly, but we did need to talk. I was starting to get whiplash from his behavior, and no matter how hot and bothered he made me feel with this whole caveman-like style, it had to stop.

Next thing you know, he would have me pregnant and barefoot in a kitchen somewhere, making pancakes for breakfast and wearing a checkered apron. I know, I know, pancakes are not the worst thing ever, but I was a health hazard in the kitchen. I couldn't even make popcorn without burning it all down. Trust me, I tried, I failed, and I am never doing it again.

I pulled at his hand, trying to bring his attention to me. "Can we? I am really fucking tired of the silent treatment and not knowing what is going on."

"I already told you what's going on with Maya—"

"This isn't about Maya and that situation." I pulled my hand from his, taking one step up and coming face-to-face with him. "This is about you not talking about anything. This is about me wanting to know about things that matter to you. Jesus, fuck, Storm, I don't even know what the names of your parents were."

His scowl deepened at the mention of the two people that sold him, but he never wanted to talk about it. He never wanted to talk about anything that concerned him. Sam admitted that Logan Nightingale had people in the club, and I wanted to help. I loved taking the time to heal, to get better, to calm my racing mind and stop seeing Kieran and all those people I hurt.

I loved being able to think about things that hurt me and the damage my parents caused, but I was ready to get back into action. My finger healed, my scars pale pink, my mind was sharper than ever, and I wasn't going to sit around waiting for him to come to me, when I could help them.

"They're dead, that's all you need to know about them." He took a step down, avoiding my eyes.

"Storm—"

"I gotta go. I need to talk to Atlas."

"No. You need to come with me to our room and talk to me for fuck's sake. You know almost everything about me, and I think it's only fair for me to know at least something about you." But I knew I was talking to a wall. He'd already shut me off, deciding to keep quiet, to keep me in the dark. "You know what," I smiled, "do whatever the fuck you want to do. Tell me, don't tell me, it's up to you, but I didn't get away from Nikolai Aster just to end up with somebody who couldn't see me for who I really am. And if you wanted to get a domestic girlfriend, or whatever the fuck this is we're doing here, I am not the one.

"Sunshine." He finally looked at me. "It's not—"

"I don't care, Storm. I really fucking don't."

I started walking up when he called out again, "Ophelia. Please."

"You know," I turned around and looked at him, "I know there are things we still didn't talk about. I know there are demons both of us are living with, but I actually thought that this would be different from my relationship with Kieran. He tried to shut me out, he tried to change who I really am, and you are doing the same. You're shutting me out, Storm. Physical affection can only go so far before it isn't enough anymore. I am not your puppet, I am not beneath you, and if you can't see that, then I don't know what I am doing here."

His eyes turned frantic; nerves written all over his beautiful face. "You can't—"

"I'm not going to run, if that's what you were going to say. But I'm also not going to let you turn me into something I don't want to be. Maybe I was right. Maybe none of you are able to love a monster."

I had to get out of here, get away from him. I

didn't lie to him when I said I wasn't going to run, but I couldn't stand here for a minute longer looking at him, knowing he was hurting me like the others before him. The old scars that never truly healed reared their ugly heads again, reminding me of everything my father taught me.

Not to show them my weaknesses, not to show them my fear, and I didn't want Storm to see how badly his behavior was affecting me. I didn't want him to see how badly I wanted this to work, because I finally belonged somewhere. It wasn't just him, it was the whole club. Zoe, Atlas, Indigo, the little kids that always wanted to play, those fucking Sunday barbeques I wanted to loathe but couldn't, because I actually enjoyed doing something normal for a change. I wanted to stay here, but I wasn't going to be a prisoner.

No, I wanted to be free and if he couldn't give it to me, then I guess I would have to find it in another place. Falling into the same trap two times when I knew better now would be the end of me. I couldn't live my life halfway. What you see is what you get with me, and if he wasn't going to trust me enough to tell me about things that were bothering him, then this thing between us wasn't meant to be.

"I'll see you around," I murmured before rushing upstairs, leaving him behind.

The walls in the hallway seemed to close in on me. The memory lane of those who made this club mocking me, telling me I wasn't good enough to stay here. But I was. I was fucking good enough. All these men were the ones that weren't good enough for me. My entire life I searched for love and acceptance in places that weren't able to give me any. I was taught how to be alone, but nobody ever taught me how to deal with a heart that wanted to love. I spent my years trying to convince myself that it was better to be alone.

No one could hurt me if I was alone. No one could shatter me if I didn't allow them to see behind the cold mask I mastered portraying. I spent my life trying to please people that never wanted to see me succeed. How do you live your life not being happy with yourself?

I made myself believe that being an assassin was all that I could be, but those beliefs were lies I covered myself with, hiding from the bitter reality lurking around the corner. And that reality... It told me I wasn't as cold as I wanted to believe. It would be beautiful if we could switch off our emotions, if we could live without grief and without sorrow, but we couldn't.

It wasn't an easy path to take but facing what hurt us was a path toward healing, and I needed it. The problem was, I wanted Storm to be the one I would share that path with, not because I wanted to lean on him, not because I wanted him to fix me, no. I didn't need him to fix me, because I wasn't broken. Chipped, maybe, but not broken. I just wanted to share this life with a person I loved.

Fuck.

I loved him. I was in love with him.

I placed my hand on the wall, the cool surface seeping into my skin. My heart thundered in my ears, the sweat collecting at the nape of my neck and my breathing gradually turned shallow as the reality of what I just thought about settled into my core.

I couldn't love him. No, no it was too soon. Too soon to give myself to someone who didn't appreciate me—again. And what did I know about love? I thought I loved Kieran and that story ended up filled with violence.

But Kieran's betrayal didn't hurt you as much as Storm's lack of communication is hurting you right now.

No! I couldn't love another person, not like this. Not when I wasn't even sure if he wanted me for me, or if he was just mesmerized by the character I played so well. This fucking sucked. This heavy feeling settling in my chest majorly sucked, and I didn't know what to do about it.

I couldn't tell him. I couldn't allow him to have one more piece of me when he wasn't willing to give me even the slightest piece of himself. But I couldn't leave him either.

God, even thinking about leaving him made me want to drop down to my knees and weep. He has already buried himself deep beneath my skin. He was in my veins, my heart, my soul. He was everywhere, he was everything, and he was one demon I didn't want to exorcise. He was the prettiest demon I had, and I wanted to keep him with me until forever ended.

Until the worlds collided and everything else died, but I wanted him with me. The mere thought of not having him in my life sent my heart into a frenzy, while my mind tried to come up with a million different scenarios of a life without him.

It would be a sad, empty life—no love, no happiness, just pure nothingness.

Damn you, Storm. Damn you for making me love you. Damn you for showing me affection. Was I that starved, that fucked up that the smallest signs of affection made me fall for somebody?

No, you were just made for him and he was made for you.

No. No, the stories of people being made for each other was just that, a story. A last resort made up by those that wanted to cling to something because everything else in their life fell apart.

It's okay. It's going to be fucking okay. It had to be. Voices from behind the closed doors I was bent in front of came closer and I knew I couldn't let them see me like this. If any of the members saw me like this, they would tell him, they would call him, and I wasn't ready to look him in the eyes and lie about the extent of my feelings.

Especially when he kept his mouth shut about everything.

I straightened up, taking a deep breath, and shoving the panic rising in my body into that little box where everything I didn't want to deal with slept soundly. This was just another thing I didn't want to have to think about. Not right now.

There were other things far more important than uncertain feelings I was probably imagining. Nope on a rope. I wasn't going to think about them.

What was love anyway?

I strode down the hallway straight to our room before anyone could see me or talk to me. Most of the people here were pleasant enough, but I just wasn't in the mood for small chitchat today. The way he disregarded my need to talk to him made me want to stab something, and nobody deserves to be on the receiving end of my wrath when I was in one of these moods.

As soon as I opened the door, I was welcomed by the cool air coming through the open window. I never thought I would actually say it, but I loved springtime here. Unlike Croyford Bay, I didn't have to look like a panda so that I wouldn't freeze my ass off. The layers, people. I hated the layers of clothes I had to wear to get warmed up.

Whoever didn't experience winter and spring in Croyford Bay, with the snow reaching their shoulders and having to wear three pairs of socks so that their toes wouldn't fall off, they didn't know what a true struggle meant. Here, I could go outside with just a jacket during the day, and I didn't have to worry about losing my kidneys, or my skin getting dry because Mother Nature decided to fuck with us.

I flipped the switch on, illuminating the room. The bags I moved here a month ago were now completely empty, stored beneath the table in the corner of the room. All my clothes were mixed with Storm's in the wardrobe, and it both warmed me and cooled me down. No matter how hard I tried telling myself that we weren't living together, we were. Just because it wasn't a house somewhere in the suburbs, it didn't mean we weren't already sharing this life.

It took me almost a year to let Kieran talk me into having a key to his apartment, yet it took me a few months to let Storm whisk me to his little, dark kingdom. God, I fucking wanted to smack him on the back of his thick head. I walked to the bed, ready to play some music on the phone he bought for me, but I froze instantly when I saw the black envelope with my name neatly written in silver ink.

I knew that handwriting. I knew who used black envelopes and the silver ink on them.

I knew it because I also delivered plenty of those to the people that were close to their doomsday. I knew it because the true boogeyman used it, while I was his puppet, spreading his sickness all over this world.

With a trembling hand, I picked it up and stared at the mockery scribbled on it.

Ekaterina.

One word. One fucking name, my middle name, and it was enough to send me back to that night in Siberia when I found the strength to overcome the things clouding my mind. The scars on my back started itching, as if I were still there, listening to the sound of that fucking whip and my skin splitting open after each hit. His sinister voice, the eyes the same color as mine, the coppery taste of my blood on my tongue, I was still there.

I was once again a nineteen-year-old kid, battling things no one should battle at that age. I absentmindedly reached for the scar on my lower back, remembering the blinding pain, the mockery, the sadness, and grief. The lack of compassion my father showed me, the way he tortured me, trying to bring out the worst in me.

Such a foolish little girl, trying to impress a man who wouldn't care if I lived or died. I gripped my stomach as the nausea rolled around and ran to the bathroom before I could lose the lunch I'd had all over the bed. I dropped to my knees just as the bitter taste entered my mouth, emptying my stomach into the toilet. I closed my eyes, trying to calm my breathing, trying to suppress the heaving, all the while holding that poisonous envelope in my hand.

He found me and now no one here was safe. I had to warn them, I had to get them ready for the misery he could bring with him, trying to get to me. Oh my God, Zoe. I had to warn Zoe. I had to tell her to run as far away from here as possible.

Get to one of the other chapters, get somewhere safe. And all those children... tears gathered in my eyes, threatening to roll down my cheeks, but I couldn't cry. I had to fucking warn them. Put those big girl panties on and do what was right.

But just as I started getting up, moving the strands of hair that fell out of my ponytail, I started heaving again. Gripping the toilet seat with one hand, I clutched my stomach with the other, letting the contents roll over my tongue, joining the rest of it inside the toilet. I flushed once, then twice, then three times, even though nothing but small spurts of water rolled inside.

Small, black dots danced around the periphery of my vision, my whole body weak from the vomiting. Fucking hell, just thinking about it makes me want to puke again.

I moved myself from kneeling in front of the toilet, to my butt, and pulled myself toward the open door to lean on it. Loose strands of hair were plastered against my sweaty skin, my mouth tasted like fucking garbage, but I was suddenly too tired to try and pull myself to the sink. I was too tired to do anything. I was terrified.

And I wasn't terrified for me. This fear making my heart jump inside my chest wasn't because I feared for my life. I feared for the lives of all these people that were in my close vicinity. Nikolai Aster was as ruthless as he was cunning. He wouldn't stop until he got what he wanted, and this envelope in my hand was proof that he was going to come for me. He was going to destroy the world to get his prized possession back.

That's what I had always been, just another object.

I slowly tore it open and pulled out a folded black piece of paper that matched the color of the envelope. Motherfucker.

Glad that Storm wasn't here with me to see this, I unfolded the paper, bracing myself for what was written inside. The first thing I saw was the emblem of my family—a dragon with its wings wide open and blood-red eyes inside the circle of Cyrillic letters my father engraved into my mind.

Family.
Honor.

Respect.
Eternity.

The fucking Aster legacy. Our family tree went as far as the first rulers of Russia, its history painted with the blood of every single person that ever dared to stand up and speak against us. I should be proud of them, but I wasn't. I fucking hated everything we stood for. Every single life we took just so that we could continue spreading our empire, building our legacy.

"*Dorogoy.*" The first word on the letter shook me to my core.

It's time to come home. You've had your fun, playing house, and making them trust you, but it is time to come back and continue your work as part of the Syndicate. You have one day to come to me, and I'll know if you tell them about this letter.

You don't want them to suffer because you were an insolent child, right?

Nikolai Dimitri Aster

No, I didn't want to go there. This was my home; these were my people. I didn't want to be a part of the Syndicate anymore. I wanted to be free. The motherfucker signed it as if it was some kind of an official letter, and not a threat. As if he wasn't trying to destroy my life—again.

One part of me wanted to hide, to run, to get as far away as possible, but I couldn't do that. Not anymore. I had people I cared about. I had a place I wanted to grow old in. I couldn't let him destroy that because he behaved like a spoiled brat who couldn't let go. No, I wasn't going to sit and let him shatter my world into pieces. This time, I was going to fight him.

But I couldn't tell Storm, not yet. I had to come up with a plan first, and I knew who could help me. Creed worked with my father almost as much as I did, and if anyone would know what to do in this situation, it would be him. He could help me. I knew he could.

I crumbled the fucking letter in my hand, willing it to disappear altogether. Pulling myself up, my legs were shaky, my hands clammy, but I took a step to the sink and started washing my face, then rinsing my mouth with mouthwash, hoping it would remove all traces of what had happened mere minutes ago.

My father's claws were slowly coming closer, but this time he wouldn't be the one winning the war. No, this time I was going to use everything he ever taught me, and I was going to fuck him up for everything they did to me.

With a fuzzy head and an exhausted body, I knew I wasn't going to accomplish anything if I went to search for Creed tonight. I could also end up running into Storm and I didn't want to look him in the eye and lie about this. There were way too many lies in my life already, and he was one person I didn't want to lie to.

I closed the bathroom door behind me and walked toward the bed, ready to close my eyes and let myself fall into oblivion. I lifted the mattress, shoving the letter with the envelope as far as it would go, letting it drop down with a thud. Storm wouldn't look beneath the mattress and after I talked to Creed tomorrow, I would talk to him as well. No matter how angry I was, no matter how many issues we had that we needed to work through, this went above and beyond just the two of us. Nikolai Aster was a force to be reckoned with and we needed to protect our people.

Shimmying out of the leggings I wore during the day, I sat on the bed and pulled the covers closer, lifting my legs on the bed. My stomach still recoiled as I thought about what my father could do, and I gulped down the acidic taste that started rising in my mouth.

Tomorrow.

Tomorrow I was going to deal with this shit. For now, I just wanted to sleep. Just to let it all go.

TWENTY-FOUR

Storm

I'VE BEEN SITTING on the edge of the bed, unable to move away from her sleeping form.

She was furious yesterday, and I knew I hurt her when that was the last thing I wanted to do. But I didn't know how to even broach the subject, to start talking to her about what was bothering me. I didn't want to lose her when the truth came out, and I didn't mean just that whole deal with Logan Nightingale, I meant everything. Who I was, what happened, it was going to break her, and I didn't want to see that light vanish from her eyes.

I could see how much she enjoyed being here, talking to Zoe, being surrounded by our members. She seemed relaxed, full of life, far away from the angry woman in that church. She thought I wanted to change her, but I just wanted to help her. I didn't want her to be anything else but herself. I knew what loneliness felt like. I knew what feeling isolated from the rest of the world felt like.

Her father did it to me, and I wanted her to have real relationships with people that were not based on the job or killings. She thought I didn't want her because of what she did, but that was as far away from the truth as it could get.

I was thrown to the fucking wolves as a kid, fed to those bloodthirsty creatures with human features but souls as dark as the deepest pits of hell. Nikolai's friends, associates, they all watched and laughed. To this day, I still remembered the feeling of their eyes on my skin, of his eyes on my back.

Of the way those serpent eyes bore through me. I was powerless, just a kid, and they did it all anyway. I couldn't stop them then, but I could stop them from laying their hands on her.

Maybe she would end up hating me once I told her everything she needed to know. I was going about this all wrong, but it was the only way. This fucked-up situation was the one I never wanted to put myself in. I never expected to meet her, to need her, to want to worship the ground she walked on, but I was happy I did. Whichever deity brought this siren, this goddess to me, I was thankful because she brought me back to life.

And maybe she would want me to die, because her father, after I was done with him, he wouldn't even want to live anymore. I would take everything from him, just how he took everything from me.

My innocence, my peace, my childhood.

She was going to resent me. She was going to leave. She was going to take away everything with her. I was angry, furious even, because destiny chose this for us. It fucked us over. If there was a God, he must have had a good reason to punish us like this. Were we such bad people in our past lives?

Why did some of us deserve this kind of torture, while the other ones lived freely? They lived and killed with no consequences.

They had tortured and destroyed with no regrets.

Parents selling their children to get another fix, just how mine sold me. They sold me to one dragon I never wanted to meet. They sold me to the man who looked like a dream, pretended to be a father. Pretended to be a protector, and when the time was right, he ruined it all.

He just took it all away.

My safety.

My sanity.

My heart was left somewhere in the ruins of my childhood, somewhere within the walls of that house they kept me in. It shattered all over the walls that held mine and the screams of others.

This time when I barged in, I was going to destroy them all. Strip them away from everything they had. I just had to figure out how to save her. And if she wanted to leave, I would just hold her tighter. I would hold her, chain her to me, and even if she hated me, I could never hate her.

I could never hate her, because four years ago wasn't the first time I saw those blue eyes, I just hadn't known it yet. It took me a while to truly realize who Ophelia was and what she did for me, saving me with the simplest touch, a simple hug. And that innocence she possessed once; it couldn't be given back, but at least what was left of her mind would be kept safe. At least she would be alive, and that was all that mattered. Because a world without her wasn't a world worth living.

She stirred in her sleep, those icy eyes landing on me almost instantly.

"Storm," she murmured with a husky voice. What I wouldn't give to stay with her here, to hold her in my arms, kiss those pouty lips, drown myself in her, but I couldn't. This was the only way to fix this mess. This was the only way for her to see what I'd tried to do.

I had to go.

"What are you doing here?" She started pulling herself up, rubbing her eyes. "What time is it?"

"Go back to sleep." I placed a hand over hers, memorizing each and every curve of hers. If this shit went sideways, well, I guess that this would be the last time I got to see her.

"What's going on?" She was more alert now, looking around the room, trying to locate the danger. "Are we under attack? Why are you dressed?"

It was in the moments like these that she showed she cared. I wasn't the only one that felt this insane connection. She felt it too. And no matter how many times she wanted to deny it, she felt it all.

"No, everything is okay, actually."

"Then why are you up?"

I moved the hair that fell into her eyes and smiled at the confused expression on her face.

"We're going on an errand, the boys and I. Creed is going to stay here, Atlas and the rest of the guys will be with me."

"I don't believe you." Her eyes narrowed on me, the inquisitive way she was trying to convey almost making me laugh.

"What, that Creed is going to stay here?"

"Cut the crap, Storm." She moved closer to me. "When an MC goes on a 'run,' it's never for small shit. So tell me, what the fuck is going on?"

Instead of answering her, I pulled her closer, fisting her hair in one hand and angling her head just enough for me to kiss her. Just for a little while, for a few minutes. Just to taste her and remember how it feels.

She moaned beneath my lips, opening wider, pushing back. Her tongue darted out, meshing with mine. She draped her hands around my neck, and before I knew what was happening, she was in my lap, her legs straddling me.

Her ass in my hand, her hair in the other one, she held me, and I held her as we fought for dominance. I wanted to stay. I wanted to stay with her and just be like this. Just the two people under the cloak of the night, coming together.

The kiss became frantic, that familiar need inside my chest rising higher and higher until I couldn't fight it anymore. It was filled with desperation, with anger, with all the things we left unsaid.

I pushed her down to the bed, my body hovering over hers. She started pulling her t-shirt up, exposing her breasts–two biteable globes, begging for my touch. I moved to one breast, my tongue playing with the puckered nub. Her back arched, her pelvis connecting with mine — pushing and pulling.

I was pretty sure I lost a few strands of my hair with the way she gripped my head as I started descending lower, going toward her pussy. I could hear the rumbling of the bikes on the outside, all of them waiting for me, but my focus was on her and the way she writhed beneath me.

I pulled my knife out and her eyes sparkled with renewed interest. I chuckled at the needy expression on her face and bent down to capture her lips once again, gripping her hip in my left hand. I went lower, over her neck, over her collarbone and that fucking scorch mark on her skin, dragging my finger over the destroyed skin.

I sliced through the fabric of her panties on

both sides, throwing the ruined piece to the other side of the room. Her eyes widened with arousal as I started dragging the blade of the knife over her chest to her opening. She shivered underneath my touch, and when I saw an X on her thigh right above the tattoo of a skull with the crown of thorns, I remembered who gave it to her. I knew it was that fucker I wanted to remove from her head.

I looked at her—hooded eyes and sleepy smile—and I took it all in.

"I am going to erase him from your memory." A kiss. "I am going to remove every trace of him from your head, from your body, until the only thing you can see, the only person you can feel, is me. Only me, baby girl."

Her eyes glistened with unshed tears and I knew that whatever was haunting her was still on her mind.

"Would you like me to do that?" I wanted to help her if she would allow me to. "Do you want to forget everything?"

"Yes." Her voice echoed through the room. "I want it all. Make it go away. Please, Storm."

I placed a kiss on her hip bone before moving to the top of her pubic bone. She pushed herself onto my face.

Greedy.

Desperate.

And I would be a liar if I said I didn't love it. The way she needed me, the way she wanted to know more even though I didn't know how to give it to her. I didn't know how to be the man she needed.

"Touch yourself," I ordered. "I want you to show me what you like."

Without a moment of hesitation, she moved her hands down her body, from her collarbone over her chest, from her stomach all the way to her pussy. I spread her legs, and as she pushed inside of herself, her moan reverberated around us.

"Storm."

She started moving her hand, her fingers going in and out. She was squirming in front of my eyes, while I watched, transfixed. I wanted her to have my mark on her, to have a reminder of everything I was to her and to just remember us this way. If I never came back after today, I didn't want her last memory of me to be that fucking fight.

"This is going to hurt, baby. But it will feel so good."

She belonged to me.

Not Kieran, not the Syndicate, but to me. I was a sick fuck, but she was as well. If she wanted to, I would tattoo her name over my chest because she was already tattooed on my soul. Her imprint was already too deep, seeping deeper into my bones with each passing day.

I wanted her to feel what I was feeling. This crazy fucking urge to have her with me. I wanted to take her with me, hide us away and forget about the world.

She was fucking with my head and I was here for the ride.

I just hoped she was ready for everything I was going to give her.

"Please." Her head was thrown back. "Please. I want to feel alive. Please, please, please."

We wanted the same things. She wanted to feel alive, yet the only time I truly felt alive was when I was with her. Even when she looked at me with hatred. Even when she didn't want to be in the same room with me. Even when she was so angry with me, she couldn't stand to look at me. Even when she yelled, and complained, I always wanted her.

I gripped the handle of the knife and held her right leg down. Her smooth skin was going to look perfect with my mark on.

"Are you ready?" Instead of an answer, I got a frantic nod. "Keep touching yourself. And don't come until I tell you to."

"What?" That got her attention. "But, I-I can't."

"You need to let go of that control, baby. Just give it to me." I kissed her thigh. "Trust me on this."

She was silent, processing what I asked of her, and after a few seconds, her fingers started moving again. Slowly at first, then desperately, frantically, seeking the oblivion we both wanted to be lost in.

I pulled myself up, rearranging my aching dick, but this wasn't about me. Tonight was about her.

I pressed the tip of the blade on the skin of her thigh, her eyes following every movement. The movements of her hands increased, and I knew I didn't have too much time.

"Do not come."

"Fuck."

Blood seeped out of the cut I made, pooling onto her skin as I carved an S. Her moans became louder as I continued to the next letter of my name, the satisfaction flowing through me.

"Storm."

"No, not yet."

"Please, Storm," she cried out. "I can't."

Blood dripped down her thigh, and as an O went around followed with an R, she screamed.

"Fuck, fuck, fuck," she stopped her hands. "I can't. I fucking can't. I need to come, baby. I need to fucking come."

"Shhh." I moved onto the next letter and kissed the inner part of her thigh. "I told you not to stop, didn't I?"

"Fuck, you're cruel," she complained but she started pushing in and pulling out, adding a third finger.

Her whole body shook as I finished the M. I dove, licking the blood around the wound, her moans fueling my desire.

"Stoooooorm!"

I pulled her hand out, and with the coppery taste in my mouth, dove, taking her clit into my mouth. I pulled at it with my teeth when she jumped from the bed. I threw the knife to the ground and pushed inside with three of my fingers, feeling her clench around me.

"Please, please, please," she begged. "I can't. I can't hold it anymore. Oh my God." She bit on her lip. "Stooorm! Fuuuck!"

The noises she made, the way she moved against my mouth, wanting more, pushing her pussy in my face, it woke the carnal desire inside of me. I gripped her bloodied thigh, pressing on the wound and bit on her clit, pulling, licking, pushing in with my fingers. I looked up, seeing her eyes roll to the back of her head.

"Come for me, Persephone. Give me everything you have. Come on, baby."

"Motherfucker!" she screamed. "Oh fuuuuuck."

Her walls squeezed my fingers, her whole body shaking while I continued lapping at her clit, extending her orgasm. Her blood coated my hand, and I knew that this was going to hurt once she came down from the high.

"Oh my God." She was breathing hard as I stopped my ministrations, placing my chin on her stomach. I started making circles on her stomach, the blood from my hand leaving marks.

"Did you just mark me?" She sounded angry, but there was a smile dancing on her mouth, and I knew she liked it more than I did. I loved the contrast our skin made—mine filled with tattoos, darkened by the time I spent outside in the sun, and hers milky white, smooth, and untouched.

"I did." I grinned. "And I would do it again, and again, and again."

Something passed over her face. Something I knew very well; she was just too afraid to voice it.

Yearning.

"Come here." I removed my boots and pushed myself onto the bed, pulling her on top of me.

"What about you?" She looked at me with those doe-like eyes.

"I'll survive." I kissed her forehead, holding her tight. "Now go to sleep. You'll be exhausted in the morning."

"I'm still angry at you." Her voice sounded small, hurt and I hated that I was the reason behind that.

"I know, baby, I know," I whispered, looking at the ceiling as she nestled her head in the crook of my neck. "But I promise you, as soon as we come back, we're going to talk, and I'll tell you everything you want to know."

"Everything?" she asked as she lifted her head, looking straight at me. Hope shone through her eyes and I stole another kiss, unable to take my hands off her.

"Everything."

TWENTY-FIVE

Ophelia

DEVOID OF ALL emotions.
   Empty.
   Numb.
   Or at least that's what I wanted people to see. I'd been hiding behind the cold mask of indifference my entire life, even before all of this started. I knew how to bite my tongue and quiet it all down. I knew how to pretend that nothing ever got to me. I was a master at this game of pretense.
   Of masks, and silly games. Of putting a cold façade on my face, when all I wanted to do was scream and scream and fucking scream... But I didn't want to play that game with him. I didn't want to dance at another masquerade ball because I was too scared to confront everything I felt for him. And I was scared. Trust me, I was fucking terrified. It was tough getting rid of all the brainwashing my father did to me.
   It was tough shaking off that constant feeling of distrust, even though my heart and my soul knew they belonged to him. I couldn't continue living my life with the whole I-was-hurt-before shit. I had to shake off all those things, all those

memories, all the crap I dug myself into. I had no idea what happened last night, but something switched. It was as if the light turned on, and I could finally see.

I could finally see him, and I wasn't afraid. I wasn't afraid to love him, to be with him, knowing he was it for me. He was the one I wanted to spend my life with. My anger at him didn't come from a bad place. I understood secrets and holding on to them like your life depended on it.

Mine were nestled close to my heart where no one could see them, but I wanted to share them with him. It took me a month to fall for him, to lose myself in those green eyes, and I couldn't be angry about it. If I didn't want it, it wouldn't have happened.

Seeing him with the members of this club, observing his interactions with both male and female members and the respect they were showing him, it wasn't just out of fear.

It was pure respect based on mutual understanding and everything he did for them. I'd heard rumors of how he ran things.

I'd heard rumors of their past. Something happened in Las Vegas, but nobody wanted to talk about it with me. And I understood that. They still saw me as a stranger, and I knew it took time for all of them to trust me. They were polite, they talked to me, but I could still feel the distance they were keeping because they didn't know me.

I was an Aster after all.

Drakon.

The unholy fire. I wouldn't trust me either if I were them. But I would earn their trust. I would earn my place here, and I would protect them. I didn't want to walk through this life like a shell of a person anymore. I wanted to live. I wanted to love. I wanted to know what it felt like to have a place I could call my own.

And this was it. This was my place.

These people were my people now. I thought I knew what acceptance and love felt like, but it was all a lie wrapped in a perfect little package to keep me in place, to keep me quiet. I thought I loved Kieran, but what I felt for him was nowhere near these newfound feelings for Storm. Kieran was my lifeline, because when they ripped everything I knew away from me, he was the one thing I could cling to. He was the one person who could understand what was going on in my head.

A habit. Kieran was a habit I couldn't shake off, but now as I searched through my heart, there were no traces of that love. What he did to Maya, it was unforgivable, but when that knife went through his chest, when I finally did what I was supposed to do, I didn't feel liberated. I didn't feel happy.

I felt nothing because I wasn't the one who was supposed to avenge anything. It was Maya. She was supposed to be the one holding that knife if she wanted to. She was the one that got to decide whether he lived or died. God, I was so lost in my revenge that I didn't see the flaws in my plan. I was just like my father, only doing what I thought was right and never considering what other people might want to do.

Rage, pain, sorrow, they consumed me. They turned me into the one thing I didn't want to be — just another bloodthirsty Aster. It was time to let those things go, to leave the past behind and look toward the future I could have.

It was time to look forward to this thing with Storm, this intense feeling in my chest.... The way every single nerve ending in my body hummed whenever he was around. When he looked at me, when he touched me, when he kissed me, when he marked me....

I dragged a hand over the fresh cuts he left behind.

Storm.

He carved his name onto my body, and if any of this happened a year ago, I would've been mad. Hell, I wouldn't even had allowed him to do it, but Ophelia from one year ago didn't know what I knew now. She didn't know how to let go, or how to accept the good, life was throwing at her.

I did, and I was letting go.

I left the pieces of myself in places I could never visit again. I left them with people that didn't deserve it, and I could never get them back. But I was going to try.

I was going to pull myself together and stitch those broken pieces. The human body was a remarkable thing, and if anyone could put themselves back together, I could. All of us carried scars that reminded us of difficult times, but we survived, we were still here, and that's what mattered. I survived, and these scars weren't going to define me.

Pain was a familiar thing, but I didn't want it to be the only thing I ever knew. I had to stop making myself believe I was the worst monster on the planet. I had to let it go if I wanted to live and make all those lives that were lost count. Ava wouldn't want me to live like this. She wouldn't want me to live my life filled with regrets. If she were here, she would probably kick my ass for all those pity parties I was throwing for myself.

I turned my head toward Storm's pillow, calming myself with his familiar scent. I had to find Creed and let him know about the letter my father sent me. They had to know that the mole was closer than we thought at first, and whoever placed that letter in our room had direct access to all of us. Which also meant that all the things we talked about could've been sent to my father, and we didn't even know.

I shoved the worry I had for Storm and whatever they were doing today aside and stood up, stretching my legs and back. My thigh was sore from the cuts, but it was a good kind of pain. A reminder that I wasn't alone. Lifting my phone from the nightstand I realized it was later than I expected. The clock showed 12:15 in the afternoon, which meant that I didn't have a lot of time and we had to act fast. I just hoped Storm would be back in the evening and I would be able to come up with some sort of plan with Creed.

He was a freaking enforcer, he had to know the inner workings of the club and what could be done in these situations. I dropped the phone on the bed and walked toward the wardrobe, taking out one of Storm's shirts and putting it on. The fact that his shirts almost reached my knees always made me laugh, especially since I wasn't the smallest girl. I loved that it still smelled like him, that I could somehow feel him with me.

I pulled on a pair of shorts, not bothering with underwear and ran out of the door. The hallways were empty and as soon as I got to the lounge, I spotted Zoe talking with Nova who was behind the bar. Creed was nowhere to be seen, but if anyone knew where I could find him, it would be Zoe.

"Hey," she said as soon as she spotted me. "You slept in?"

"Apparently I did." I smiled, trying to scan the billiard room for any sign of Creed, but he wasn't there. "Have you seen Creed?" I asked her, meeting her eyes. "I just need to ask him something."

She scanned my clothes with a knowing smirk, and I knew I would have to tell her about the previous night.

"Zozo," I started again. "Have you seen him or not? It's kinda important."

"I think he's in the office. You want me to call him for you?"

"Nope. Could you just point me in the direction of the office?"

"Maybe I can help you with something. Is it about Storm?"

My head swiveled back at her and the realization hit me. She probably had more information about this run they went on. If her brother went with Storm, she must have.

"Maybe." I answered. "Do you know where they are right now?"

Were they even alive? I didn't want to call him, not until we got everything ready. I didn't want him to worry about this as well.

"No, not really." She eyed me warily. "But I do know that they only went to Las Vegas. Something about some bird." Shit. "With an N. What was that thing I heard Indigo saying?" She stopped for a moment. "Ah yes, Nightingale. I have no idea why he was mentioning a bird, but, might be some club or something."

It wasn't a fucking club.

It was their death.

What the fuck were you doing Storm? And which Nightingale were you meeting with?

Fuck, fuckity fuck.

See, this was why I hated secrets. He should've told me what was going on. Now I would just spend the whole day worrying about them. I was terrified for him because I knew how much Logan hated all MCs. Storm had kidnapped his wife, had helped me, and God knew what else... I had no idea what Logan's reaction was going to be.

"Are you okay?" she asked, and I realized I'd been mumbling out loud. Dammit, Storm. Today really wasn't a good day to add worrying about you onto the pile of shit I had to deal with.

"Yeah, yeah." I shook my head. "Amazing." I smiled at her, and she took a step back as if she saw a ghost.

"Holy shit. You just smiled. Wait." She took her phone out of the pocket. "Could you do it again, because I wanna take a picture."

"Oh fuck off, Zoe." I pushed the phone away. "Can you show me where to find Creed or not?"

"Fine," she huffed. "If you go through that door," she pointed at the door leading outside of the billiard room, "you will see stairs, leading to the basement—"

"Yeah, I'd been there the other day."

"That's good. Then you must have seen three sets of doors downstairs."

"Yeah, and I went through the first one you see once you're down."

"You've been in the changing room. Office is right next to it. That black door, that's the office."

"Amazing. Thank you, ZoZo."

I started walking backward, slowly turning when she took a hold of my arm, and spun me around, into her embrace.

I didn't know how hugs worked, okay? So when she squeezed the life out of me, her hands clasped around me, I held mine next to my body, not knowing what to do.

"Um." I lifted my hands and tapped her on her back, but she wasn't letting go. "Okay." I tried pulling backward. "It's time for me to go."

"You're so squishy." She breathed into my ear. "And your skin is so soft. What are you using?"

Blood of my enemies.

"Uh, nothing." This was getting awkward. "Zoe, I really need to go."

"Okay, okay." She finally released me. "But don't forget about the barbeque today. Boys should be back by that time."

Yeah, if they survive.

No, stop that. They would survive—both the Nightingales or whatever was going on, and my father. We were going to get through this, and I was going to have a big cheesy hamburger tonight, hug Storm, and finally talk to him about everything.

I squeezed her shoulders and without another word, ran toward the staircase leading to the basement. I hoped Creed would know what to do because I most definitely did not.

TWENTY-SIX

Storm

AS WE CRUISED down the street, I could still feel her taste on my tongue—the coppery scent of her blood, her lips on mine. Last night I owned her moans, her body, and her soul. The sight of my name on her body did something to me.

I always knew that I wasn't one for sharing, but with her, I would go through every fucking person out there if they ever dared to touch her. Heaven and Hell together wouldn't be strong enough to keep me away from her.

And I hoped she wouldn't run, because if she did, I would chase her.

I would chase after her to the edge of the world. I would chase her until she couldn't run anymore, and I would show her everything she'd been missing.

I wasn't a good person. People from my past made sure that I would never grow up to be a sane person, but I was hers.

Fuck all else, I belonged to her. On some insane, chemical level, our atoms merged together. They called to each other and I was answering the call. The only question was, would she?

She thought that four years ago was the first time we met, and to be honest, I did too at first. I didn't know who she was, but when Kieran said her name, her real name, it was as if the light switched on.

I knew those blue eyes. I knew them, because on one of the days when I was falling apart, those blue orbs felt like a salve on the wound. She had pigtails back then. Those sick fucks let her run around the mansion I was kept in, and her five-year-old self found me in the backyard, while I contemplated ways to kill myself.

And she gave me her candy. She told me I looked sad, and that I shouldn't be sad.

She told me the world was such a pretty little place, and I saw myself in her. I saw a five-year-old Storm looking back at me, because I used to think the same. But she helped me. Those ten minutes spent with her were a lifeline I didn't know I needed. She was the reason why I ran away.

Ophelia was the promise I made. Another kid would never go through what I went through. I don't know if it was fate that put her on my path again, and I don't even fucking care. It was something.

The church we left two weeks ago stood in front of us as we cruised down the street, heading toward it. I didn't want to have this meeting. I didn't want to see Logan's face. Whatever happened today was going to set the course for our future. We would either end up going into war or he was going to let it go.

I wanted Las Vegas back. It was the whim I had ever since they stole it from us. And I was going to get it back, the only difference was the way I was going to get it. So, we could do this shit nice and easy or slow and painful. It worked for me no matter which way we took.

Nightingale blood getting spilled wasn't something I shied away from. The privileged, the rich, the ones on the top, they were the plague of our society.

They controlled everything, and behind their closed doors, that was where their masks fell off, where the real monsters were visible. Secrets were forged behind those doors, lives destroyed.

And they didn't care. They never cared about the hungry, homeless, or sick. All they cared about were their assess and nothing else. And all of them had to fall.

All of them would fall as soon as I got my hands on each and every one of their necks. I didn't care if it was life or death. They had to pay for everything they did.

Just as we pulled in front of the church, the built-in phone in my helmet started going off.

"I'm busy—"

"Don't you dare to drop this call, asshole," Creed started from the other side.

"What the fuck, man? I'm about to walk inside."

"Yeah, I know, but since you picked up your ass and left me here with Ophelia, who by the way, could kill me and everybody else here before any of us would be able to even call for help, and never told me if you told her the truth, I decided to give you a little call."

"Creed," I started, as I carefully observed the surrounding area. "Are you sure you aren't a fucking girl?"

"Fuck off."

"I'm just saying." I snickered. "That was one hell of a sentence, so I just wanted to make sure that you're okay."

"Storm, cut the crap. Did you tell her or not?"

My mood was already bad, but with the Spanish Inquisition from his side, it just plummeted further down. Of course, I didn't fucking tell her. What was I supposed to do?

Maybe while my lips were on her pussy, I could lift my head and say, *Oh, by the way, before I forget. I was supposed to give you to Logan Nightingale because he wants you dead. But that was before I knew who you were. Ah, also, your father sold me into a sex trafficking ring full of children when I was seven years old, so he has to die as well. Oh, I'm also planning to kill each and every member of the Council that resides over North America, but I hope you don't have any other family members there. I really hate double funerals.*

Yeah, I didn't think so.

"I didn't tell her—"

"Storm," he growled.

"Creed, don't fucking start with me. I left you there so that you could keep an eye on her and keep our people safe. She's still healing, and we are finally at a good place. I just need more time."

"Dude, she is going to kill you, Atlas and then me, and I don't want to die."

"She wouldn't do that."

"Storm." He took a deep breath. "Ophelia kills traitors. She doesn't give a shit what kind of treachery it was, she kills them. No questions asked. She never asks why or how, or whatever other shit people come up with in order to be spared. No, she simply doesn't give a fuck. You're a traitor, you're dead. That's how her mind works. I've seen her in the field, and I am telling you—she is going to be pissed. Not about the whole story about Logan, but because you didn't tell her. She will feel used."

"Creed—"

"Now, I don't know if your dick has some magical properties or some shit but keep doing that fucking shit. I have had enough fucked-up shit to last me a lifetime. I don't need any more."

"Creed—"

"So yes, I think you should tell her. Tell her the truth, dude. How you ended up helping her, that it wasn't only the Albanians you were working with. Just tell her, okay?"

"Creed—"

"And for fuck's sake, please don't wait too long."

"Creed!" I yelled. "Can you please shut the fuck up?"

"I am just telling you what I know. And I know that I need to hide all the sharp objects in this house on the day you decide to tell her about it. I've seen her kill a man with a pen. A fucking pen, Storm! She stabbed him in the eye and let it water out, and then," he took a deep breath, "she continued pushing the goddamn pen inside his head. So excuse the fuck out of me that I worry about her reaction."

"Why are all of you making her sound like a psychopath?" I didn't fucking get it. "We all did fucked-up shit. We even did worse things, so what's so different."

"No, Storm." He laughed. "I've never seen a person enjoy the smell of the fresh kill more than her."

"Well, I'll deal with it when it's time. Just don't fucking tell her about Logan and Nikolai. I want to keep that shit away from her for as long as possible."

"Storm." I could feel his frustration over the phone. "What if she asks where you went? Huh? She is not some club bunny who will be satisfied with the simple, *oh they just went for a run*, answer. Trust me. I know Ophelia. I knew her way before any of you had a chance to meet her. She is ruthless, she is relentless." He took a pause. "Now that I think about it, she is exactly the same as you. Mark my words, she will feel betrayed."

"Well, I thought that my enforcer would be able to deal with her while I'm out trying to save all of us."

"You are not fucking listening to me, Storm. When she finds out about your involvement with Logan and the deal, about your plan for Nikolai, she will go crazy. Well, I mean crazier than she already is."

"Careful, Creed." I gritted my teeth. "You really don't want to talk about her like that."

"This will end bad, Storm."

"And I'll fucking deal with it!" I roared. "I'll handle Ophelia, but I need you all to stop being paranoid idiots and concentrate. Keep her occupied. I don't know, do the barbeque earlier, whatever you wanna do."

"Okay. Fine. But don't tell me I didn't warn you."

Atlas stopped next to my bike with an impatient look on his face. Yeah, I fucking know. But whenever Creed started PMS-ing that meant somebody had to calm his ass down. And that somebody was usually me.

I nodded at Atlas before he turned his back on me and started walking to the entrance.

"Creed, I have to go. I'll call you later, okay?"

I didn't wait for an answer before I pressed the button on my helmet and dropped the call. This church felt like an imposter in this neighborhood, like something out of a Tim Burton's movie.

It was dark, years and years of storms, sand

and wind etched into its facade, and yet it still stood.

This is where they butchered them all. This is where the blood had been spilled the most. Where the cries of those children were muffled with the blades of their knives. Where mothers begged for mercy, and fathers kept quiet because they knew there was nothing they could do.

They took innocent people. Family members that never even wore our cuts, but they took them anyway. They slaughtered them like animals, letting their blood flow over the floors of this church.

This wasn't a holy place. This was a gate to Hell.

So when I took a deal, when I agreed to help Ophelia as the Albanians asked, when Logan came to me and asked me to bring her to him, I only found it fitting that this church would be the final resting place for the one that gave the order. For the one that sent their soldiers to kill our people.

Kieran Nightingale.

He loved to pretend that he was a knight in a shining armor. He liked to pretend that he was a savior. What a fucking joke.

At least I knew what I was, and I accepted it a long time ago. They always wore these perfect little masks, trying to fit into society. Ophelia didn't.

Ophelia knew who she was, just as I did. Ophelia knew that when the knife was in her hand, she was the most lethal force they ever made. And I've seen the betrayal in her eyes. They left her.

Her own family left her, and when she plunged that knife into Kieran's chest, I wanted to take a picture of it and keep it forever. We still needed to talk about him and her feelings for Kieran, but with that talk I would have to talk about my demons, and I wasn't sure if I was ready yet.

What I did know was that there was so much pain in those ocean eyes, and I knew she loved him. There was a painful history there, and if I had to guess, their families were somehow involved. Her father, his.

Maybe Kieran wasn't a monster. Maybe he was just like us, just made to fit into their little world, his mind twisted, corrupted, pulled to the sides he didn't want.

None of us belonged here. Homes they told us we had, they weren't homes at all. Those were not families. My own sold me, theirs turned them into machines.

I would've felt sorry for him if he hadn't gone against my own. I would've felt bad for what happened two weeks ago, if it wasn't for the fact that his word was the one that doomed my people. Innocent people.

I was positive that Logan knew what happened here, but it wasn't like he cared. I'd observed them over the years. He didn't care about his sons, about his family. The only reason those three men lived for this long was because he needed somebody to take over this sick empire he'd created.

The same way Nikolai did. I only wondered who was going to be Nikolai's heir now that his son was gone, and Ophelia was lost to him. Was he going to look for her now? Would I have to protect her against him as well?

"Are you coming?" Hunter stopped next to my bike, placing a hand on my shoulder. "I don't want to be here longer than necessary."

And I understood why. His wife and two daughters were butchered here. Two little girls that didn't deserve that. Neither did his wife.

And he couldn't save them. He was too late to save them.

Sometimes the demons weren't the ones that tortured us. Sometimes they were the people we failed to save.

"Yeah, I'm coming."

"Let's get this shit over with." He started walking toward Atlas, who stood at the entrance, waiting for the rest of us.

Felix was observing the street, always the one to make sure that we weren't going to be ambushed. That we weren't going to be fucked over.

"Felix?"

"I think I am going to stay here, with the bikes." He didn't turn to look at me but continued staring at the first house after you passed the church. "I don't trust them, so I would rather keep an eye out here. The rest of our guys are waiting for a sign, and someone has to be able to signal it before they slaughter us all here." He looked at me this time. "Again."

We were all haunted by the things that happened here two years ago. Some more than the other ones, but no matter whom we lost, this excruciating pain was always there.

Felix, Atlas, Hunter, Indigo, and many more, they all lost somebody here.

"Felix," I called to him as he started retreating toward his bike. "I appreciate this." He was uncomfortable with words of gratitude. He was uncomfortable with praise.

He and Atlas were brothers, but if I wasn't familiar with the fact, I would've never guessed. I'd never met two people so different.

While Atlas was loud and easy-going, Felix was a complete opposite. In our time together I didn't think that he uttered more than several sentences to me. But he was a loyal soldier—always on the lookout, always thinking about the things that could go wrong.

I guess that when life throws you curveballs, you learn to live on the constant lookout for the next shit to happen.

Leaving him next to the bikes, I walked to Atlas and Indigo who stood side by side in front of the door. The tense lines were visible on their faces and whatever happened today was going to be a precipice for everything that was about to come.

My future with Ophelia.

The future of our club.

Every single thing.

"Alright," I started. "Let's get this shit over with."

TWENTY-SEVEN

Ophelia

I TOOK A step back.

Then two.

And then three until I hit the wall behind my back, sliding down to my knees.

My chest hurt. My fucking head hurt, and the tears I didn't even know I possessed threatened to spill over after what I had heard.

He lied to me. Storm fucking lied to me.

When I came to the door of the office, it was already slightly open, but before I could knock, I could hear my name on Creed's lips. They were discussing me, and worst of all, they were discussing my father. They were discussing Logan.

Was everything Storm ever told me a lie? Just another deceit, perfectly wrapped into a package I was supposed to accept?

I was right. All this time he was feeding me lies, and I almost believed him. I wanted to build a future with him when all he did was use me for his own gains. I fell for a man who didn't really love me back. I fell for a man that was dealing with Logan Nightingale.

I can't. I can't go through this again.

Oh my God, this fucking hurt. This heavy feeling in my chest... I hated it. This feeling of helplessness, this dread spreading through my body.

And to think that I wanted to make this my home. I wanted to wake up to those green eyes. I wanted to have somebody in my life. I wanted to fucking trust him, and he ruined it.

He just did what every single person in my life did. He betrayed me.

He took my heart and smashed it into pieces. He fucked up just like the ones before him.

I couldn't believe that this was happening again. That another person in my life decided to just fuck me over, as if I meant nothing. Or maybe I was just reading too much into this fucked-up connection I had with him.

This insanity connecting us.

What was I thinking? Believing that a man could be trustworthy? That just because he didn't belong to the Syndicate or the Outfit, that he would be different.

Men always wanted something. There was always an ulterior motive to their actions, and I was too blinded, too hopeful this time to see that.

And all that talk about me belonging to him, it was all a fucking lie. Me worrying about him, about Atlas, trying to be calm. Trying to be patient... He was the worst kind of traitor. The kind that managed to steal my heart and make me believe in a fairy tale. Was that meeting four years ago orchestrated as well? Was everything I thought I knew a lie? Again, just a lie.

Fuck, I had to get myself out of here. If Creed found me like this, he would know that I heard their conversation, and he would try to stop me.

No, if I had any doubts about leaving this

place, this just cemented my plan. Get the fuck out and forget about all of them. Forget about Storm, forget about Kieran, my father, Logan, the Albanians. I was going to move to fucking Madagascar if that was what would get me away from them.

But Storm.

Why? Why would he do this? Why do they all fuck with me like this?

Kieran and his brothers were bad, but Storm was much worse. At least with them, I knew why they wanted me dead. At least with them, I wasn't expecting a better outcome. I didn't expect mercy. I didn't expect forgiveness or love.

But with him...

He fucking tricked me. Made me believe in this bullshit he'd been spewing at me. This need he had for me.

I had to give it to him. He was a better actor than I was. He managed to fool me. He even went so far to mark me, to make me think I was really his.

But he was never mine. He was never going to be mine.

Fuck. My chest was caving in on itself. It felt as if my ribs were crushing my heart, my lungs. I couldn't breathe.

I was gasping for air, clutching at my chest. This pain was worse than the day I found Kieran between Cynthia's legs. This pain rendered me speechless. It was cruel making me believe in a lie, in things that would never be possible. A happily ever after.

A guy made for me.

He made me want to stay. He made me think it was worth it when it wasn't.

Having another person in your life was never

worth it. They all proved it to me time and time again. Why was I even trying anymore?

Stupid. I was fucking stupid.

Would I ever stop with these silly thoughts of fairy tales? Even when I told myself that I didn't believe in them. Even when I said they weren't real, deep down, I wanted it.

I wanted it all.

I wanted the love that would consume my whole body. I wanted a wild and crazy love. Relentless and forgiving. Insane and soft. I wanted it all.

Why couldn't I have it? Why was I doomed like this?

Was I not worth it?

The only thing I ever wanted to have was a little bit of understanding, a little bit of light in this infinite darkness I was shrouded in. Even if that light was somebody's dark, I wanted it all.

Why did he have to betray me?

But it didn't matter. None of this mattered. My feelings, my emotions, nothing mattered but finding Maya.

Shut it down, Ophelia. Just shut it down.

I was a master at shutting things down. This shouldn't be any different. I didn't have time to fall apart. At least not now.

I pulled myself up and swiped the tears that spilled over my cheeks. They didn't deserve my tears. These men, they didn't deserve anything. My loyalty, my trust, my pain and my love, they deserved none of it. So I would pull myself together again. I would put all of this behind me and forget their names.

Forget their faces and their fake promises.

I would survive this. This thunderstorm of my

life wasn't stronger than me. Storm wasn't going to destroy me or the little sanity I was clinging to.

I wouldn't allow it.

Come on, Ophelia. Step by step. Get out of here.

And I did. I took a step forward, and another, and another, until I reached the staircase. One moment at a time. I was going to survive this avalanche.

None of the guys were there in the billiard room when I finally reached the first floor, and I was thankful for the silence that greeted me. I didn't want to see any of them.

Did they know? Did Zoe know? Were they all just laughing behind my back? The Great Ophelia Aster on her knees in front of a man that was only using her.

I was embarrassed and I was angry.

I unknowingly played their game of deceit, as if I was a puppet. I didn't play games. I made them. I was the assassin of the Syndicate. I was the force to be reckoned with, and I succumbed to my desires this time. I lost track of what was important and what was in front of my eyes.

Storm didn't want me. He just wanted what was attached to me. My last name, my connections... He didn't fucking want me and my darkness, and that thought sent another wave of searing pain through my body. God, I was going to be sick again.

They say that heartbreak is only a mental thing, but then why did it feel as if my whole body was crashing down? Why did it feel like my heart squeezed painfully with each thought of him?

I was going to make him pay for this. But patience. I needed time to gather my thoughts, to make a plan. I had to prioritize things that were more important right now then my need to rip his heart out and feed it to the dogs.

Trust was the most important thing to me. Trust was more important than love and family together. And he lost it.

When Creed mentioned those two names, those two demons, I knew. I fucking knew they just wanted to use me for who I was. He didn't give a fuck about what was going on behind the closed doors of my mind. He should get an Oscar for his performance.

This was just more proof that nobody could ever want a monster. They would always just be afraid of me, or they'd want to sell me to the highest bidder. That was all there was.

Use me, abuse me, play their little games with me. And I was done.

I was fucking done trying to fit into their worlds. Done trying to play by their rules.

Zoe stood next to the bar, talking to Nova. My God, how foolish I was. Storm must have sent Zoe to try and befriend me, to try and make me fall further for the lie they were concocting. Well, their little plan backfired, because I couldn't wait to see how much they would bleed.

How much they would beg for mercy, while I'd have none.

She turned around, seeing me behind her, and smiled. Another fake thing. Those fucking smiles were as fake as a pair of Balenciaga shoes at the local Walmart. I had to admit, they almost got me. I almost crumbled down and opened up to her.

I almost believed her because she reminded me of Ava. Her lightness, her easy-going personality, she almost got to me. But Storm knew all about my history. He knew about the shit I went through, and what a better way to fuck with somebody's mind but to give them the thing they wanted the most.

Or well, one of the things.

A friend.

Someone to talk to. Someone who didn't want to see you dead.

"Ophelia?" Even her voice grated on my nerves now, the urge to strangle her here and now overtaking my whole body. I closed my right hand into a fist, pain skyrocketing through my body as my nails bit into the skin.

If I didn't, I would kill her. I would bash her head on the table in front of me and I wouldn't even blink an eye.

But I had to pretend everything was okay. If I didn't, if they figured out that something was wrong, I would end up locked down and unable to escape. My foolishness got the best of me, and I thought that just because Creed lost Ava, just because we both failed her, he would understand my need to find Maya and to find a place where I could belong. Stupidity at its best.

What was that thing my father taught me? Never trust them. The only person you have is you. Even a friend could become a foe, and these people, they definitely weren't my friends.

"Are you okay?" She took a few steps, coming closer to me. Didn't she know not to come close to a wounded animal? Didn't she know that tigers attacked even when they showed submission? "You look a little bit pale."

The concern in her voice, the worried look on her face, it was all a lie. Was it Logan or was it my father that hired them? Storm already worked with the Albanians to help me with my task, so I wouldn't be surprised if they sold their souls to them in order to get more money.

My God, didn't they have any morals? I

thought that MCs lived by a set of rules, but I guess that when you weren't one of them, you didn't exactly matter.

I didn't matter.

"Yeah, I'm fine." I tried to brighten my voice up. "Just hungry, I guess."

She seemed skeptical. Nova first looked at me, then at Zoe, putting down the glass she was polishing.

"Well, you're lucky then," Zoe smiled.

I looked at her. "Why's that?"

"Barbeque is going to be moved to an earlier time." She squealed and that urge to strangle her, yeah, that just intensified. "Creed decided that we should just start now, and the boys can join us as soon as they get here. So, get your ass ready because we are starting in less than an hour."

"Got it." What a fucking joke. A barbeque. But maybe this would be my chance to escape. My chance to get the fuck out of here. "I'll be in the room so you can just call me once it's all ready."

"You got it, boo." *Oh God, I'm going to puke.* Fake motherfucking bitch.

"Just call me, would you?"

"Definitely."

Storm, Atlas, Creed, and then her ass—that was the order of the people that were going to die. One by one.

I pushed myself up the stairs, trying not to break down in front of them.

Keep it together, you bitch. You survived worse things than this. What was another betrayal? Just a regular day, right?

I entered the room, shutting the door and locking it behind me. The sheets were stained with my blood. More proof of what we'd done last night. I let him mark my skin when I didn't even know

357

him. Who the fuck was I? I didn't allow myself to do such stupid shit. I never allowed myself to care, never trusted people. What was so special about Storm that I threw that rule into the garbage?

Anger brewed underneath my skin since I'd heard Creed. I felt the pain and loss over something I never really had. It was as if a bomb went off, and I rushed to the bed, throwing the sheets off.

I took them in my hands, and piece by piece, started ripping through the fabric. I wanted to burn them.

I wanted to burn him from my mind.

I threw the pillows to the floor, removing the pillowcases off of them. Rip by rip, piece by piece, just how they ripped me.

All of them.

I wasn't destroying only what Storm and I had done. I ripped the pieces my father destroyed. The small pieces my mother left behind, the love she never gave. The absence of my sister and the betrayal of my brother.

I ripped it all. I pushed it all away from me. Everything I had been keeping in got unleashed. My anger, my pain, I released it into the world with each destroyed piece and I just wanted to scream.

Scream and scream and scream, until my voice went hoarse. Until I couldn't feel this poison inside my veins.

Kieran cheating on me, his brothers accusing me of something I didn't do.

Ava dying.

Her body lying there in the pool of her own blood.
My family never looked for me, never helped me.

They all used me. Every single one of them. I didn't deserve that. I only ever wanted them to accept me. I always put all of them before me. Before my needs, before my sanity.

They took everything from me. Every good piece of me, they tore it apart and built something vicious. I didn't want to be this.

Yet they never asked me what I wanted—not my father, not my mother, not Kieran and definitely not Storm.

I would've helped him with what he needed, but that wasn't what he needed. That wasn't what he wanted, because I was again just a pawn in their sick little games.

Pulling me to one side, then the other one, would this pain ever stop? This madness, this sadness, and anger.

Fuck them.

Fuck them for making me this way. Fuck them for making me think I wasn't enough. Fuck them for screwing with my head. Fuck them for never seeing everything I could've given them.

My chest was rising and falling with every breath I took. I fell on the floor, surrounded by the pieces of fabrics I tried tearing with my hands. I only managed a little bit, but it was enough to destroy it.

It would be a welcome back gift for Storm. A true "fuck you" to his face.

I had to calm myself down. I had to put my mask back on, take a goddamn shower and get ready to get the fuck out of here. I was going to slip out while they were all busy with the barbeque. Get on one of the bikes and drive.

Just drive. At least into town until I could get a car or something. And then I would have to figure out how to cross the border and get to Mexico. The apartment I was using while I worked for the Albanians was still under my name. I could regroup and plan properly.

And after I found Maya, I would come back.

I would come back to burn this place down. To destroy them fully for what they wanted to do to me. I would cleanse their sins in fire, even if that were the last thing I would do in this life. And if they took me down, so be it.

I had nothing else worth living for.

No friends, no lovers and definitely no family.

I was always alone, and alone I would die.

TWENTY-EIGHT

Storm

THESE WALLS HAD seen more tragedy than some of the battlefields in Europe. This church had been a witness to a genocide, and the God that was supposed to protect them all, he hadn't been here.

That deity in the sky, or whatever you believed in, it let innocent children pay for the sins of their fathers. It didn't allow them to live their lives, to be free.

We would never know everything they could've become.

So, we would fight. We would fight for everything we'd lost, and everything that could've been. We'd seek revenge for those that couldn't get it themselves.

All those souls that vanished in one night, all those people they murdered, this was why I made that deal. I fucked up.

I knew I fucked up everything with that, but I was going to fix it. I just hoped we would all get out of this alive.

Logan Nightingale stood at the same spot I was at when Kieran, his brothers, and Ophelia came here the other day. Silver streaks in his hair and lines on his face were a clear sign of his age. It was funny really. He could pass for a regular dad if you looked from the outside, but no one knew monsters better than the ones that actually saw their real side. And I saw his. I saw all of theirs.

I waited my whole life to be where I was right now. To be at the position where I could get revenge for everything they did to me.

Logan Nightingale was just one of them, but I'd let him think that he had the upper hand here. Maybe he did. I was positive that this day would end up in a new war — us against them. But maybe it was about time to move our asses and do this.

My guys were thirsty for their blood. I was thirsty for their blood, and we had many reasons to be. These seemingly perfect CEO's, America's favorite philanthropists, were murderers. Liars. Child traffickers. I didn't even want to think about the array of other things they were involved in.

Don't get me wrong. We weren't saints. There was nothing holy about Sons of Hades, but children, we never touched them. They were a hard limit for all of us.

Yet this monster in front of me didn't care about any of that.

"Did you know that this church was built in nineteen fifty-three?" he asked, turning to me. "It was one of the first things built on this side of Las Vegas."

"Sorry, Logan. I wasn't really interested in the history of the place. It's a building, that's it."

"Oh, but it gets interesting." He was getting on my nerves. "The story goes that there was a witch coven here that got chased away and sent to what is today known as Winworth." My stomach recoiled at the mere mention of my birth town. "Aren't you from there?"

363

"Logan, I didn't know that it was a history lesson today."

His left eye started twitching at my interruption, as Atlas laughed. Was I supposed to be wowed by this knowledge?

"As I was saying," he started again. "A witch coven lived here, and locals believed that they'd been worshipping Lucifer himself. So of course, the Church took it upon themselves to try and eradicate them. Now, this was what, two hundred years after the Salem witch trials, so they had to do it in secret. They liked to make people believe that they were just evicted and left peacefully, but, the Church sent these modern day crusaders who burned the place down during one of their ceremonies away."

Peachy, more bloodshed.

"What is the point of your story, Logan?" I was getting tired of this.

"The point is," he stepped closer, "that this place was built on the blood of people that once lived here, and even the Holy Spirit couldn't cleanse it from its spirits. Tell me," he put a hand on his chin, "how fast did Kieran die? Was it painful? I want to know everything."

What did I tell you? This man cared about no one but himself. His son died here, and he wanted to know this. No sorrow, no pain in his dark eyes, just curiosity and chilling cold.

"Ophelia stabbed him with a knife."

"Did she twist it?" His eyes twinkled. "Did she torture him first? Even after all of her mistakes, I have to admit that she is one hell of an executioner."

"What the fuck?" Indigo mumbled behind me.

"Did he bleed? How much did he bleed?" And I thought my parents were fucked up. "Come,

come." He placed a hand around my shoulders, pulling me toward the altar. "Tell me everything. Paint me the picture. Where did he die?"

What a fucked-up world we lived in.

"I can see some blood stains there." He pointed toward the place where Ophelia indeed stabbed him. "Is that the place?"

"Yeah." I nodded. "That's the place. Listen, Logan—"

"Magnificent. Oh, I have to take pictures of this."

He let go of me and walked to Kieran's final resting place. Sick fuck.

"He was your son." I couldn't help myself. I had no love for that guy, but still, he was his son.

"Ah." He waved me off. "I have the other two. And if those two perish for some reason, I can always make more."

If I hadn't already seen what these people were capable of, I would've been shocked after his admission. Their families, their children, they were mere puppets used for the sick games they played. I had no doubt in my mind that this man was the reason for everything bad that has happened to those three brothers. Maybe even Ophelia.

"Whatever you say, Logan." It wasn't my place anyway. "Can we talk about important things, or are you going to give me another history lesson?"

"Careful, boy—"

"I am not a boy, Logan." I came closer to him, getting in his face. "I am a man. If your sons are allowing you to call them boys, that's their problem, not mine. But you won't call me a boy when we both know I am everything but a boy."

"Okay, okay." He gulped, looking at his guards who swarmed around us.

"Tell your dogs to retreat or you'll need another plastic surgery." I grinned. "Now, Logan."

A minute passed, maybe even two, before he told them to back away. "Step away, guys. Everything is fine."

"See." I took a step back. "That wasn't so hard, was it?"

He straightened his suit and ran a hand through his disheveled hair. Drops of sweat were visible on his forehead, and I guess it was true what people said—these monsters were afraid of us. They were all talk, but no bark, unless there was a whole line of guards separating them from the likes of us.

He could talk, but he couldn't stand up on his own. They were used to hired help. They were used to having other people doing their dirty little deeds for them. I wasn't.

I was the president of our club, but that only meant that I was the first one that would head into a battle, not hide behind the closed doors.

"Where is Ophelia? I thought that you would bring her in. Is she outside?"

"No."

"What do you mean, no?"

"I mean, no, she isn't here. I'm sorry, but I only speak English. If you'd like me to repeat it in any other language, I'm afraid we will have to use a dictionary or something."

"Stop being a cheeky little shit and tell me where that bitch is."

"She's not here." I smirked. "And she's not outside."

"I can fucking see that!" He was getting aggravated. Good.

"I would suggest you tone it down. We can talk like two grown men, can't we?"

"We could talk like two grown men, if you actually accomplished what we agreed on. You and your idiots weren't capable of subduing one girl? A girl!"

"First of all," my voice turned serious, "that 'girl' you're talking about is a woman you're trying to fuck up. That 'girl' could kill a room full of grown-ass men before you could finish your breakfast. Second of all," I lifted my index finger, "I have some questions I'd like to get answered."

"I'm not telling you shit. We're done here. Boys." He turned to his guard.

"Na-uh-uh, not so fast." I pulled my Springfield, our insignia etched into the gun's handle. "Call them off."

"You fucker—"

"Call them off, or your blood will join your son's on this floor. Call your guys off."

His jaw ticked and I could almost hear him gritting his teeth.

"You are not going to get out of this. We had a deal, goddammit."

"And now I'm calling it off." I grinned. "I won't repeat myself again, Logan. Call these baboons off or I swear to God, I will color these walls with your brain."

"You're a motherfu—"

"Call them off!" I roared. I knew that both Atlas and Indigo had their guns up. I could see them from the corner of my eye. But we were outnumbered at the moment, and I had no idea what the situation outside was. Knowing what a slithering snake this asshole was, he probably had sniper rifles aimed on the entrance of the church.

"Lower your weapons," he muttered finally. "What do you want, Storm?"

"I want fucking answers." I came closer to

367

him, taking his arm and leading him toward the altar. I pushed him down, his eyes level with my hips. With my gun still aimed at his head, I crouched down looking into his eyes.

"A little bird told me that Kieran maybe wasn't the one that gave that order."

"I have no idea what you're talking about."

"Oh, you know. You definitely know. Stop playing fucking games with me and tell the truth for once in your life."

"Whatever I tell you, you're just going to kill me."

"Hmm." I shrugged. "Maybe. Maybe not. I've been feeling rather generous lately. Maybe you'll get to live so that you can tell your pal Nikolai that I'm coming for his ass as well."

"Nikolai will eat you alive—"

"No, you idiot. I will eat him and spit him to the ground. I am just worried that my digestive system won't be able to handle such an amount of poison. Now," I pressed the barrel of the gun to his forehead, "who gave the order for the massacre that happened here?"

"Please, Storm." He trembled in front of me. "I am sure we can work something out."

"Can you bring all those people your guys killed back to life?"

"No, but—"

"Then there's nothing we can work out. Nothing at all. The only thing you can do right now is tell me the truth. Who the fuck gave the order?"

"Storm, I can—"

"You can't do shit! And when I am done with you, you will never be able to hurt another family, another child, another woman. Never again, Logan. So I can either kill you now, or you can tell me what I need to know."

"You wouldn't dare," he challenged me.

"You have no idea what I am capable of doing." I pulled the safety off. "I could cut you up into pieces and send you in a box to your wife. How's she doing? I hope we didn't scare her too much."

"You said you would only take her, not scare her. She's driving me crazy. Going for therapy and all that shit."

"Well, if she hadn't tried to bite one of my guys, maybe we wouldn't have."

I looked at Atlas and Indigo, both of them aiming at the two guards the shithole in front of me brought with him.

"Tick fucking tock, Logan. I don't have the whole night. Who gave the order?"

"I did, goddammit!" he confirmed. "I did, and I would do it again. This world needs to be rid of your people. You are the lowlifes that need to be exterminated. Like rats."

"Is that so?"

"It is," he spewed.

"Another thing." I scratched my temple with the gun, the urge to just kill him brewing in my veins. "Were you ever going to let us walk out of here alive, or were we going to die no matter what?"

"What do you think?" He smirked. "You and your kind, you can all burn for all that I care. With you gone, I would've been able to take over the West Coast, and soon enough, I'd be able to destroy Nikolai as well. Ophelia would've been an additional plus. He cared about nothing but his precious little princess. His precious little heir. He trained her himself, made an assassin out of her. No wonder she managed to escape you."

"She didn't escape."

The smug expression on his face slipped as he realized what I was saying.

"She's with you?"

"Oh yes. Alive and well, and in my bed. Both you and Nikolai can go and fuck yourselves, because I am not giving her to you."

"Oh, you poor soul." He laughed. "Ophelia Aster isn't a girl you could ever own. She is wild, reckless, psychotic. She can't be owned because that one, she doesn't have a soul. She doesn't have a conscience. Human emotions are foreign to her. I've seen her kill men, women, children, and she never once showed any semblance of emotions. They were all just a job to her. So that little lie you let yourself believe in, it was just that. A lie. She could never belong to you. She didn't even belong to herself. She belonged to the Syndicate because the only thing she is good at is murder."

"Shut up, Logan."

"Why? Is the truth too hard to swallow? She belongs to the Syndicate. They are the only ones that could handle her crazy ass. And that girl." He laughed. "I would've loved to have a girl like her in my outfit. She is relentless. When she wants you dead, no matter how much you run, you will end up dead. She is like a shark when it smells blood. They trained her well."

"You're lying."

"How do you think she got that nickname? A boogeyman. *Baba Yaga*. She was as cold as Russian snow. A true Russian princess, and you, you are nothing to her. Just a little toy. My son was one of her toys, and as you can see, she killed him."

"She killed him because he fucked up."

"Maybe." He shrugged. "Or maybe not. She also killed my daughter, and they grew up together. They were best friends. What kind of person does that?"

"The kind of a person you made. The kind of a person that never knew anything else but the pain you idiots subjected her to. The kind of a person that never knew anything else but darkness, blood, and depravity. That kind of a person, Logan. I know because I am that person. And your kind," I pressed the barrel deeper, "your kind was the one that made me this way. So, if you're trying to tell me that she's a monster, good. So am I."

"You have no idea what you're talking about, you idiot. She can't be tamed."

"I don't want to tame her." I straightened up, still holding the gun to his forehead. "I want her wild, free of all of you. Free of your world."

"You'll never be able—"

"Goodbye, Logan."

"No, wait—"

"Keep Hell warm for us."

I braced myself for the necessary hit, but the door smashed open, and Felix ran inside.

"We have company!"

"What—" My momentary distraction gave Logan time to move, and as his leg connected with mine, and his hand smacked mine away, the gun went off. I fell to the ground, trying to gather my wits but I could already see him running away. I fucking had him. I had him, right there, right in front of my gun, and I lost him.

"Fuck!"

He was almost on the other side, his guards covering his back. I aimed my gun and shot, the bullet barely grazing his shoulder. But he yelled in pain and started falling forward but they took him by each arm and held him up.

They started firing at us, bullets like a thunderstorm around us.

Several guys dressed in black from head to toe entered the church with semi-automatic rifles in their hands.

"Hide!" I yelled to my guys as I tried running toward the same door Logan just disappeared through. But the guards formed a semi-circle around, shooting at us and I had no other choice but to hide.

I shielded my head and fired at them while I ran behind the altar. Their bullets were getting lodged into the walls of the church, the floor, around our heads. I saw Indigo and Atlas hiding behind the statues of some saints that were left behind, firing back at them, too close to them for my liking.

Felix somehow ran all the way to the altar, hiding behind the pipe organ, covering my ass.

Just a few steps more. A bit longer. The door was just there. But I didn't manage to run there because Atlas beat me to it. It felt like slow motion, his body moving through the air, trying to reach Logan, shooting at the lone guard that was left behind. Indigo yelled after him, and Felix shot again, hitting another guy at the door, but none of it mattered because the next shot didn't end up in the wall.

It ended up inside Atlas.

"No!" I roared as he fell on the ground. A cacophony of voices rang around, the gunshots echoing in my ears, but my eyes were solely focused on Atlas's unmoving body. The last guard slipped through the door, leaving us with a handful of the new ones that were brought in as reinforcements, but as Hunter started shooting, joined by Felix, they fell one by one, until nothing but silence greeted us.

Indigo was already kneeling next to Atlas,

holding his head in his lap. I could see his lips moving but there was no sound.

"Storm!" somebody yelled, and I wanted to answer, I did, but I couldn't move from my spot. "Storm, we need to move him. We need to go."

But I couldn't move. The only thing I could see was the blood spreading over Atlas's chest and a frantic Indigo shaking him.

"Storm!" A hand landed on my back, rocking me back to the present, and when I turned around, Felix was standing there with panic written over his face.

Fuck, fuck, fuck. "Fuck!"

I ran toward Indigo, joined by Hunter and Felix, and tried to assess the damage. "Is he breathing?"

"Barely," Indigo croaked out. "We need to get him to the hospital."

Atlas's eyes were already closed, his lips slowly turning blue, and I knew we couldn't waste time. "Get him up," I ordered. Hunter and Indigo lifted him and started carrying him toward the entrance. "We need to get to the Old Casino." The three of them looked at me—a confused Felix, an angry looking Indigo, and a calm Hunter. "Trust me."

I pulled my phone out and started dialing the old friend that still lived in the area. Atlas had to be okay. He fucking had to.

TWENTY-NINE

Ophelia

I STOOD IN the middle of Storm's room going over the things I would need in order to get out of here. The tears that threatened to spill earlier were dried up now, taken over by the anger coursing through my body.

I wasn't even sure what I was angrier at — Storm and his betrayal or my stupidity and fragile heart that wanted to believe that somebody in this world could actually care about me — not about my father or the skeletons I hid in my closet, but only me.

What was that saying? *Fool me once, shame on you. Fool me twice, well, shame on fucking me.*

Getting out of here would be nearly impossible, but if I managed to sneak out during the barbeque, I could hit the road, regroup somewhere in Vegas, and hopefully get to Chicago by the end of the week.

I could've knocked half of these men on their ass and simply marched out of here, but no. Oh no. Little Ophelia wanted to play house. I lost three months of my time, and for what? Because Little

Ophelia thought that she could be understood, maybe even loved.

There's no such thing as love in the world I lived in. There never was and never would be. Fucking fairy tales dancing around my head were just that, fairy tales. Silly stories I used to hear and wanted to believe in.

Sometimes we hide our hearts from the fear of getting hurt. But apparently, when we finally open them, the same shit happens again. Somebody rips them apart. Shatters them, steals them away.

Well, I wasn't gonna stick around and wait to see what Storm had planned. Like the wholesome adult I was, I was going to run. After all, that was my best quality.

Running away.

And I mean, what would happen even if I stayed?

He would come home and would try to explain what happened and why. And like a good little stupid girl, I would probably fall for his shit.

I would fall for his bullshit because I wanted this.

I wanted him and everything he had. His baggage, his demons, I wanted it all. I wanted to give him my heart. I wanted to show him who I truly was, not this picture everyone painted of me.

I couldn't trust myself around him. He had a power over me no other man ever possessed, and it freaked me the fuck out. Last night while he was carving his name into my flesh, I could feel it in the air.

This madness that connected us. This weird energy flowing between us.

I could feel the fight leaving my body. I could feel my heart expanding in my chest, this fucked-up euphoria coursing through my veins. I could feel my love for him taking over my body.

I was high. High from him, from the way he looked at me. The way his hands glided over my body, leaving scorch marks behind.

I guess I should've congratulated him. He shattered my walls, almost had me fooled. Almost had me trusting him fully.

I wasn't sure if that guy, Sam, really turned me away, or if the situation just worked itself out in Storm's favor.

I guess I would never know, because after today, I never wanted to see him again. They all played a part in this game he was carefully building. What a good laugh they must have had at my expense.

Silly Ophelia Aster, falling for a guy that never wanted to have her. He was more interested in her name than her as a person.

Fuck it.

"Ophelia." The knock on the door pulled me back from my thoughts. "Are you in there?"

And where the fuck else would I be?

I walked to the door and pulled it open, revealing a smiling Zoe. God, I wanted to punch her in the face.

Maybe she had nothing to do with this, maybe she did, but I just needed to punch something. It couldn't be Storm for obvious reasons, so somebody else would have to do. I just hoped that I would be able to get through this evening without any blood on my hands. I had a feeling that these people wouldn't wait for their precious prez to handle me.

And look, I could handle two or three of them, but I couldn't handle a bunch of angry bikers, so yeah.

Temper down.
I am the fucking epitome of Zen.
Love, peace and all that crap.

"Zoe, hi." I grinned at her. If they could play this game, so could I. Just look at me being all friendly and shit. Ava would've been so proud.

When her eyes lit up at my happy demeanor, I could almost see us wearing matching bracelets and *Best Friends Forever* necklaces. Dream on, dreamer. My whole life was filled with pretending and masks, so why not use it now?

"What's up?" I asked her as she stood there, gaping at me. *Well, come on, ZoZo girl, we don't have the whole day. I have places to be, people to kill, a broken heart to mend... the usual things.*

"I-I," she stuttered.

"You…?" Patience wasn't one of my virtues, but fuck if I was going to let myself slip now. No, nope. Zen. Fucking Zen.

Maybe I couldn't kill them, maybe I didn't want to kill them, but I could fool them long enough to get out of this shithole.

"I just came to tell you that Creed and the rest of the guys already did the full setup. We're starting in about fifteen minutes."

"Fabulous." *Did I just fucking say fabulous?* God, my stomach recoiled.

"Yeah, great." She seemed confused. Welcome to the club, girl, and meet the new and improved Ophelia. I was proud of myself. None of them were dead.

Yet.

"So, will you join us?"

"Of course, I will. Give me—" I stopped, trying to locate the clock in the room. "What time is it?"

"It's only six, but you have time. We will be

going the whole night."

"The whole night, huh?" I bet that they would also get super drunk.

"Just give me twenty minutes and I'll be there. In the backyard, right?"

"That's right." God, she had the sweetest voice. I really, really liked her. I liked them all and they fooled me. Why did she have to end up being part of this charade they created?

When she didn't move from the door, I took a step back, looking at her skeptically.

"Is there anything else?"

She seemed to think about whatever she wanted to say for a moment, before opening her mouth.

"It really isn't my place." *Then don't fucking say it.* "But I think that Storm really cares about you."

Oh for fuck's sake, not this, not now. Was today National-Lets-Fuck-With-Ophelia day?

"Yeah, I don't—"

"No, I get it. You don't wanna talk about it, and that's fine. I just wanted to ask you not to give up on him. These guys—" She stopped for a second, taking a big breath. "They've been through a lot. Storm's been through a lot, and I've seen the way he looks at you."

Yeah, I bet that he looks at me like Charlie looked at the Golden Ticket for the Chocolate Factory. "Just, don't give up on him. I know that what they're doing isn't legal." Girl, have you fucking met me? "But they're not bad people. That's all."

"Don't worry. I'll take good care of his heart." Such good care when I put it into a glass box after I rip it out of his chest. "I'll see you downstairs, okay?"

"You got it, babe."

With a smile, she turned around seemingly happy with this whole conversation, and disappeared down the hallway.

Goddammit. What was this weird, fuzzy feeling in my chest?

Nope, Ophelia. You aren't fucking staying.

And I wasn't. I had twenty minutes to get my ass ready, and to head down to the office and try to find a weapon I could take. Storm stored those knives he gave me in the basement, but I had no idea where exactly. I didn't really need to use them during this month. Another fucking mistake, not knowing the environment I was living in.

I walked around the bed straight to the wardrobe and pulled out a hoodie from the top shelf. The asshole wouldn't be needing it.

I on the other hand, I had no idea where I would end up. I needed to get a hold of Cole or even Agon. At this point, I didn't even give a fuck which devil I was going to get entangled with. As long as it wasn't Storm or my father.

But you wanted to talk to your father.

Yes, I fucking did. I wanted to know why he did everything he did, and then I would stab him in the throat for everything he did. However, my personal issues could wait, but Maya couldn't.

She'd already waited too long for me to find her, and staying here, playing house with Storm wasn't helping. I wasn't his equal.

I was his prisoner.

Truth was a stingy bitch, but it had to be said. This turmoil in my chest had to quiet down because there were things more important than my feelings. I just had to remember how to shut down all the emotions and everything that was happening.

Yeah, that's what I had to do. Shut it all down. Numb it.

Those devilish eyes had to become a memory, just another thing I wanted to have but couldn't. You wanna know why? Because I was who I was. I was a murderer, a cold and emotionless assassin. The only place left for me in this world was six feet under.

Love and all this bullshit that I tried making myself believe in had to vanish from my life. I wasn't born for happiness.

Tying the sleeves of the oversized hoodie around my waist, I took one last look around the room, carving it all into my memory — the bed he fucked me in, where he held me, where he whispered sweet nothings, that wall right next to the door where he broke my resolve and took me...

I went willingly, I knew what I was doing.

The pressure in my chest increased, my heart beating rapidly against my ribcage.

This was it. This was where I said goodbye.

Come on, Ophelia. Just part with it. Remember the lies and get out of here.

But my legs wouldn't move. I was gripping the shirt at my chest — Storm's shirt. The white skull painted on it seemed to be mocking me, reminding me of what I represented.

Death and despair.

There was no life in me, there was no light. Wherever I went, darkness followed. Everything I've touched had turned to dust or had become a thing that hurt me the most.

Lies.

Betrayal.

False promises.

Those were the things I was surrounded with. I just couldn't understand why my soul decided to trust him. I just couldn't comprehend why in the ever-loving hell could I ever lower down my guard.

I almost begged him to stay last night.

I didn't want him to leave.

His hands around me felt like paradise. As if somebody gave me a small piece of Heaven, and I wanted to cherish it. I wanted to hold on to it forever, but I was wrong.

No matter what, I was born to walk through this life alone and it was probably for the best. Goddammit, I had to warn them about Nikolai. No matter what, I couldn't leave them blindsided about it. He probably wouldn't do anything once I was gone from here, but they should know.

I lifted the mattress up and pulled the letter daddy dearest left for me. There was a notepad on the nightstand, and I grabbed it along with the pen, and started writing on it.

My father has spies in the club. You need to be careful.

O.

I placed it on top of the bare mattress with the letter he sent me, as well as the phone Storm got for me.

Right, now move your fucking ass out of here.

One leg in front of the other, I slowly crossed the length of the room, all the way to the door.

Deep breaths, Ophelia. Just take it slow.

This pain wouldn't last forever.

It couldn't. I knew that it couldn't, but it didn't feel that way.

As I opened the door, my bravado, my pep talk, my strength and anger all were replaced with a sudden wave of sadness. The heaviness in my chest, my heart was collapsing, and even though I knew there was nothing wrong with me, at least not medically, I knew that after this ordeal was done, I would have to lick my wounds in private.

I would disappear. Go somewhere where no

one knew who I was.

Stalling wasn't going to get me anywhere, and with newfound resolve, I opened the door and stepped into the hallway. There were no other sounds apart from the thump-thump sound of my boots. Well, Storm's boots, but that wasn't the point.

I would have to burn all these clothes once I got a hold of my own. A cleansing of sorts.

New beginnings and all that crap people were constantly spewing about.

Reaching the top of the stairs, I peeked toward the lounge and felt relieved when I saw it completely empty. Maybe I would be able to get out of here without any casualties.

I had to get to the office Creed was in before. I was positive that they had some weapons there, maybe even car keys.

But I had to be fast.

I fast walked to the billiard room, heading to the small hallway and then the staircase leading to the basement area. I kept glancing around, expecting one of them to show up at any time. Or as my luck would have it, Zoe would show up and I would have to knock her out before she could run away and alert the others.

I all but ran down the stairs, jumping over the last two. Plastering myself to the wall, I inched closer to the office door.

Please, please have those doors unlocked, I prayed. I'd never asked for anything, but let those fucking doors be open.

I pressed myself against the door, trying to hear if anyone was inside, but there were no sounds. Well, I guess that there was only one way to find out.

382

I pressed on the doorknob and when the door opened, I let out a relieved breath. At least something was working in my favor. A lone desk stood in the middle of the room with papers scattered everywhere. I walked to it, getting behind it.

Think, Ophelia. Think. Where would they keep the weapons?

I looked around the almost empty room, but there were no safes, only barren walls and their insignia on the left side.

Drawers?

I crouched and opened the bottom drawer, but nothing but papers greeted me. The second one was the same, but when I pulled the third one open, a grin spread across my face.

A Glock .44 laid on top of the papers, along with a lone knife.

Fucking bingo!

I took it into my hand, the familiar weight spreading sparks of joy through my body. I pressed the button on the side of the grip, opening the magazine. I counted the bullets inside the magazine, my face stretching wider with a smile.

Seven bullets.

Double fucking bingo.

I didn't have a holster for either one of these, so I pushed the knife inside my boot, and stood up. I lifted my shirt and pushed the gun into my pants, thankful that these pants were tight enough.

I was ready to get out of there when something else caught my eye.

On top of the stack of papers was a folder with familiar writing on it.

Project X.

Wait. That sounded familiar. Wasn't that... *Shit.*

Kieran asked me about Project X, but I'd never heard of it before. Rage and confusion were clouding my mind. This here was all the proof I needed to know that Storm was truly working either with my father or using me to work against him.

I opened the folder but there was nothing inside. Well, nothing but a lone picture of a familiar house. I've been there before; I just couldn't remember when.

I'd read somewhere that the human mind blocks the memories it doesn't want to remember. Was this one of those situations? I sometimes couldn't remember the faces or the places, but this one felt so familiar.

This wasn't a onetime thing.

The photograph was old, as if it had been taken with one of those old cameras. It had a red facade and bushes in front of it. I couldn't see much, but it didn't look cheap.

Fuck it.

I didn't have time for this shit. Memory lane would have to wait for some other time.

I pushed the photograph to the front pocket of my pants and headed out of the room. None of the bikers had come down and I called that being real fucking lucky this time around. I said it once and I'd say it again—there was no fucking way that I would be able to take out more than one of them.

I quietly walked upstairs, fucking relieved that the coast was still clear.

I knew that the exit doors were in the second hallway, right outside of the billiard room. But so was the exit to the backyard.

I contemplated my options for a hot minute. I couldn't exactly jump through one of the windows in the lounge, so I was going to take my chances. I looked toward the lounge area and seeing that it was still clear, I dashed to the hallway getting closer to the door.

Laughter, loud voices, children, and adults, I could hear them all in the backyard. They seemed happy, content.

Well, good for them.

A bowl on the small table next to the door had one pair of keys inside, and the skull with the small cross on one of the key chains told me it was Creed's. I saw him holding this same set of keys just yesterday and I knew what my transportation was going to be.

I grabbed the keys, but just before I could open the door, a blond boy appeared at the other door, looking at me funnily.

"Who are you?"

Fuck me sideways. I was okay with most of the kids in the club, but only because they knew me now and I knew them. But I have never seen this boy, and I felt lost. I never really knew how to talk to them or how to placate them. Do I talk to them like I would to an adult person, not that I was being extremely successful even in that, or do I talk to them with a baby voice? He was a younger kid, but for the love of everything, I couldn't even guess how old.

"Hey, buddy." *Seriously, Ophelia? Buddy? What's next, you're going to pat him on the head?* "How are you?" *Wanna ask him how's the weather while you're at it?*

"I don't know you. My mom said that I shouldn't talk to strangers."

Smart kid.

"No, you shouldn't."

"I am going to call my mom." God-fucking-dammit. "Mo—"

"No, wait." I stopped him just as he was about to scream from the top of his lungs. These little monsters had very strong voices. He could wake the dead, not to mention Creed.

"Do you want to play a game?" His eyes lit up, and I knew I had him.

"What kind of a game?"

What kind of a game? Fuck me. I had no idea what these kids liked to do nowadays. I could go into a fight with the best of them and end up as a winner, but give me a small kid and I had no fucking idea what to do.

"Um." I started thinking. "Hide and seek." He didn't seem taken by this idea, still wary of me.

"I don't know."

"Tell you what." I smiled at him, or well, I tried. I was pretty sure that it looked closer to a grimace than an actual smile, but what the hell. At this point, I would try anything. "If you go back and hide, I will buy you your favorite toy."

"Really?" His eyes lit up again. God, I am good.

"Yeah, really. But you have to keep quiet about this. I will come there in twenty seconds and if I am unable to find you, you can choose whichever toy you want to have."

Har-fucking-har.

"Even the Batman one."

Eh, what the hell. "Even the Batman one," I agreed. "Now go. But remember, this has to be our little secret."

He nodded but didn't move from his spot. I looked at him expectantly as he started laughing at me.

"You have to start counting, silly."

"Oh, shit, right."

"You said a bad word!" he exclaimed. Oh, kid.

You were surrounded by badass bikers and now you were calling me out because I said shit. Fucking seriously?

"Sorry, darling. That's going to be another one of our secrets. Okay?"

He seemed to think about it for a second, but just nodded again. "Okay."

"Alrighty then. One," I started counting. "Two, three..." Before I could get to four, the little boy turned around and ran outside. Crisis fucking averted.

I opened the door not wasting another second. I couldn't slam the door, no matter how much I wanted to, so I closed it slowly, cringing at the click sound the door produced.

I ran over the front lawn, but my distracted ass didn't see the guard running toward me.

"Fuck!"

"Where the fuck do you think you're going?"

I had no idea who this guy was. Even from the distance, I could see that he was much taller than me, way heavier as well. What the fuck did these people eat for breakfast? His muscles seemed to have muscles, and the scowl on his face told me that I was in more trouble than I wanted to be.

I could see the bikes parked just behind him — my ticket to freedom.

Sorry, honey. This bitch won't get locked up again.

"Prez said that you have to stay inside," he said as he came closer, and I could see that he wasn't much older than me. One of the prospects most probably.

"Your prez can go fuck himself."

"Wha —"

I increased my pace and slammed into him at full force. In any other situation, this would've been a reckless thing to do, but he obviously didn't expect me to continue running. We fell to the ground, his head hitting the pavement.

Ouch. That even hurt me.

He grabbed my hips, trying to throw me off of him, but I couldn't allow him that. With all my strength, I pushed his hands down, feeling the sweat trickling down my back.

Damn, my stamina was shit.

"What the fuck are yo—"

I didn't wait for him to finish the sentence before I slammed my head to his, hitting the bridge of his nose with my forehead.

Sonofabitch.

That fucking hurt. Black spots danced in front of me, but the dude on the ground kept struggling.

Second time must be better. I slammed my head again and this time his eyes shut down.

Ding-ding-ding, bingo again.

I left him lying there, unconscious, but at least he was alive. I usually didn't do it like this, but he was just a minor hiccup in my brilliant plan.

Hah, brilliant my ass.

My head was throbbing, and I could swear that I gave myself a minor concussion as well. Fuck it, if I fell off the bike somewhere on the road it would be better than dying here or at the hands of the Nightingales.

Better yet, I didn't want to end up in my father's clutches again, and if Storm was working with him, that was definitely going to happen.

There were only three bikes parked on this side of the clubhouse, and I hoped that one of them belonged to Creed.

There was a button on his keys, and after pressing it, the beeping sound went off from one of the bikes and I knew that it was most definitely his.

Huh, I didn't even know that they could make keys like this for bikes.

"Ophelia!" I turned around to see Creed exiting from the house, a pissed-off look on his face.

Well, sayonara, bitches. I am getting out of here.

I was just a few steps away from the bike when he called out again.

"Don't you dare get on that bike, Ophelia!"

"Fuck off, Creed!"

I pushed the key in and jumped on. I'd only ridden a motorcycle a couple of times, but I still remembered how to turn it on. Was I going to crash and burn somewhere? Most probably. But I didn't care anymore.

As I turned the key, pushing on the clutch and turning the ignition on, the rumble of the bike spread through my body, leaving the tingling feeling between my legs.

Damn, I should've gotten a bike earlier.

"Ophelia!" I turned around only to see Creed running towards me. "Storm is—"

"I don't fucking care!"

"Don't! Ophelia!"

But I didn't want to listen to him anymore. They had the chance to tell me what the fuck was going on. They had the chance to tell me why exactly I was being holed up here, but they didn't.

Liars. They were all liars.

"Have a nice life, Creed." I grinned at him and flipped him off before I took off.

His voice carried after me, but he didn't try to follow. I knew that I needed to put as much distance as possible between me and them. It wouldn't take them too long to track me down and bring me back.

The difference was, this time they would be taking me back in a body bag, because I wasn't going to come back willingly.

THIRTY

Ophelia

FEAR.

It lives inside our minds, taking over our bodies, preventing us from doing what we really want to do.

And what I wanted more than anything else in this world? I wanted to be fucking free.

Free of these chains my family put on me. Free of everyone's expectations of me. Free of all these men that thought they could control me. Just free.

As I drove through the streets of Santa Monica under the cloak of night, I felt free. As the wind hit my face, my head was clear. For the first time in I didn't even know how long, it was completely empty.

There were no second thoughts, no anxiety haunting me. There was no assignment I had to think about. Storm, Kieran, my father, my sister, they weren't there.

Maybe I would be able to do this, to completely disappear. Maybe after I found Maya, I would be able to just vanish into thin air and try to forget this part of my life. This constant chasing, constant pain, constant bloodshed, and worry.

I could start anew somewhere where nobody knew who I was. Yeah, I could definitely do that.

I didn't notice anyone following me, but I knew that I had to get rid of this bike as soon as possible. I'd been driving for almost four hours and I knew that I wasn't too far away from Las Vegas now.

Tiredness started taking over my body, and my eyes started closing by themselves. I couldn't go to any of the hotels, what with the lack of money and no identification. But there was an abandoned warehouse the Nightingales used to use that was just on the outskirts of town.

If it was still abandoned, I could crash there and then get going in the morning. If I could just get rested for a little, I would be good to go. The trip between here and Chicago was going to be a tough one, but it wasn't as if I could just get on a plane and get my ass there. I had to get my head in the game.

I had to find Maya, get myself out of this mess and disappear.

My mind was already broken enough. I would have to be truly crazy to go back.

But what about Storm?

That asshole could go and die for all that I care. Even if my own heart was breaking at the mere thought of him being hurt, I would have to move forward.

None of them deserved me. None of them deserved to have me.

Those pieces of myself I kept leaving with them, I would never be able to get back. And I regretted that. I fucking regretted trusting the wrong people.

Giving them parts of me, giving them pieces of my soul, when they never gave me anything in return.

God.

This fucking sucked. This tight feeling in my chest, it sucked. I was far better when I pretended that I didn't have any emotions. It was much better when I made myself believe that I had no heart and soul. I could cope better. I could go through days without breaking apart.

But right now, my mind was destroying me. It was pulling back memories I buried so deep. That fucking chest I kept closed for years has opened, and I had no idea how to close it again. I had no fucking clue what to do right now because this suffocating feeling wasn't something I wanted to live with for the rest of my life.

I didn't want to see them. I didn't want to see the faces of all those people I'd hurt. I didn't want to see his face, and the only lithium I had, the only person that could help me and keep them away was the one person that betrayed me.

Again.

How many times would I have to go through this? Was I such a bad person in my previous life that I had to suffer through this one?

For fuck's sake, I was just a child when they threw me into all this. And what was I supposed to do? Run? They would've found me. They would have never stopped until my bones were lying in the backyard of our family house.

So, I did what I had to do. I destroyed those they'd sent me to destroy. Even if it wasn't enough, I was still alive. I was still breathing. But breathing and living were two separate concepts. I knew that now.

I wasn't living. I was a walking, breathing machine, and I was so tired of being a machine.

I was so tired of being alone, being on the run, being bloody and rejected.

Why did people have to reject me? What was

so bad in me that none of those I'd trusted showed me affection? Was there something living inside that kept everyone away? Was I really as poisonous as Kieran said?

This pain, this fucking sadness, I just couldn't, not anymore. I couldn't take it anymore.

The sign on the road showed that I was a couple of miles away from Las Vegas, and if my memory served me correctly, there was an exit sign right about... Bingo.

I turned right, almost ready to crash here and now.

Luckily, Creed kept the reservoir of the bike full, otherwise I wouldn't have been able to go anywhere.

As I exited from the main highway, the road turned narrow. The old industrial zone I'd been to before was filled with familiar buildings, I now just had to find the one I was looking for. I remembered the grey color of the facade, but that was about it. Maybe if I saw it, it would come to me.

It had been years since I last came here, so I wasn't entirely too sure that I would get the right building. Hell, maybe they didn't even own it anymore. With my luck, it would end up being owned by somebody else, with a full alarm and all that shit.

I passed several warehouses and office buildings and was getting to the end of the line when it caught my eye.

Separated from all the others, the warehouse I was looking for stood in the dark, surrounded by trees and debris that weren't there the last time we visited. I revved the engine of the bike and turned toward my destination. There were no lights and half of the windows had broken glass. I guess I was right—it was still abandoned.

I turned off the ignition and climbed off the bike. My legs felt like Jell-O, the time I'd spent on the bike without stopping, catching up with me.

Storm's hoodie was still tied around my waist, and a small pang of longing went through me, wishing that he were here right now. Wishing that what I'd heard today was just another trick my mind was playing on me.

But it wasn't, and in my usual fashion, I didn't know how to cope with this overwhelming feeling in my body. I wished that someone, somewhere had taught me how to cope with emotions. How to deal with happiness, sadness, love... How to live with myself, and not run from it.

Because that's what I'd been doing my whole life. I'd been running from all these things.

Unbeknownst to me, I'd been running from Kieran, from my family, from who I really was, and now I was running from Storm. Maybe I should've stayed, and he could've explained everything to me.

No, no, absolutely not. He betrayed you. Lied to you. Led you to believe that happy endings exist for people like you.

Yes, he betrayed me, and nothing he could ever say would make up for the shattering feeling in my heart. Just when I started trusting him, just when I started believing that maybe I could stay, and he would be the one, he fucked it up.

I walked over to the first window, its glass broken, the shards on the ground. The debris beneath my boots crunched with every step I took, and I tried staying alert, but my body was already shutting down on me.

I just wanted to sleep and to start my life again tomorrow. Get out from the West Coast and forget about the last two months.

I stepped inside the darkened room and saw a lone chair in the corner. Right, there used to be offices here. The Nightingales, just like my father, kept some legal businesses around the country.

I untied the hoodie from my waist and put it on. I needed a shower and something to eat, but it would all have to wait until tomorrow. I wasn't going to move from here. Taking a few steps forward, I collapsed onto the old chair, the particles of dust dancing around me. I guess that no one ever used this warehouse anymore.

I should check the rest of the rooms to make sure that nobody else was here, but tiredness took over, and before I knew it, cocooned in Storm's hoodie, I closed my eyes, letting the darkness take over.

* * *

VOICES WOKE ME up, and the unmistakable sound of footsteps nearby was what had me jumping out of the chair. Someone was inside the warehouse.

I looked around, but the darkness shrouding the warehouse made it impossible to see and the disoriented feeling after the sleep I had made me weary.

Shit, did Storm already manage to find me?

The footsteps came closer, right from the room next to this one. Somebody was whistling and it made all the hairs on my body stand up.

I had to get out of here.

Inching closer to the window I came through; I was ready to jump out when the person I thought I would never see again appeared in front of me.

"No." I started shaking my head. "No, it's impossible. No, no, no. You aren't here."

His black hair seemed even darker, just slightly illuminated by the light from the streetlamp. Those perceptive eyes traveled over the length of my body.

"You're not here. This is just my mind playing tricks on me." I closed my eyes and tightened my hands into fists, the nails biting into my palm. "You're not real. You're not real," I started chanting. But when I opened my eyes, he was still there, just looking at me.

I took a step back, retreating deeper into the room and he followed through, entering, coming after me.

"I fucking killed you!"

He smiled at me. A carefree smile, the one I hadn't seen on his face in ages.

"Hello, birdy."

No, no, no, fucking no! This couldn't be happening. I stabbed him. I saw him bleed.

But you didn't see him die.

No! Fuck that. He died. He must have.

"I've missed you, baby girl."

"Stay away from me!" I screamed at him. "You fucked me over when you were alive, and now you keep coming back to finish the job."

I took another step back and hit something soft. Something that wasn't a wall.

Turning my head, I saw wide shoulders, up and up, and I saw another person that promised to kill me.

"No!" I tried stepping away from him, from Cillian, but he took a hold of my arms, keeping me against him. "No, no, no. Please," I cried out. "None of this is real."

"It feels very real to me," Cillian whispered in my ear.

Frantic, scared, I tried pushing him back, but

he was stronger, taller, and I knew that any of my attempts would be futile.

"Where have you been, birdy?" Kieran asked. The ghost of my past came closer, that soft smile I used to love, playing on his face.

"Kieran—"

"Shhh." He grabbed my neck, pulling my head closer to his. He placed his forehead on mine, closing his eyes.

It wasn't painful, but something in his demeanor pulled at that tormented piece of my soul. He seemed almost... soft. Almost like the Kieran I used to know.

"I've missed you so much."

"K... How?"

He caressed the spot beneath my ear with his thumb, the soft humming coming from him.

"How are you alive?"

"I don't know, birdy. I don't fucking know. I guess that you missed, or maybe you never really wanted to kill me."

"No. No!" I pulled back, the back of my head hitting Cillian's chest. "I killed you. You were supposed to die. You were supposed to—"

A sob tore out of me. The tears I didn't even know I had anymore spilled from my eyes, coating my cheeks.

"I killed you," I cried. "I stabbed you and watched you bleed. I-I-I can't." My legs gave away and I dropped to the ground as Cillian released me from his grip.

"The blade... The knife went through your heart. How—"

"Birdy." He crouched in front of me and tried to touch my face.

"No!" I crawled away from him. "No, don't touch me. I will wake up. I just need to wake up." I closed my eyes, plastering myself to the wall. My head was in my hands, throbbing, painful... Please, please, please, he couldn't be alive. I had to save Maya.

I had to save my sister, and if they were here, it meant only one thing.

My death.

"Please..."

"Birdy. Hey." He caressed my hair, twirling the strands in his hand. "It's gonna be okay. It's all going to be okay."

"No, no it won't. Nothing will ever be okay."

Stupid. I should've made sure that he was dead. I should've checked.

"You're going to kill me, and she... Oh God, Maya—"

Another sob tore out from me and I couldn't see him. Tears kept falling down my cheeks and both he and Cillian were just two blurry shapes in front of me.

"I'm sorry—"

"Birdy." He came closer, spreading his legs on the sides of me. He pulled me away from the wall, my crouched form fitting between his legs. Those arms I thought I would never feel again landed on my back, and a hug followed next.

"It's going to be okay, Phee. I promise you. You are going to be okay."

"It hurts, Kieran." I sobbed into his shirt. "It hurts so much, and I don't know what to do."

"I know, baby. I know, and I'm sorry."

"Why did you have to do it?" I asked. "Why did you have to betray me like that? I loved you more than anything and you destroyed it all. Why, Kieran? I just need to know why."

He kept quiet and the sound of shuffling feet told me that Cillian had left the room.

"Please," I wailed. "Just one thing. If you want to kill me after this, do it, but I need to know. I deserve to know. Why did you have to rape her? Why did you betray me? Why are all of you betraying me? Was I not enough?"

"Oh, Phee—"

"Tell me! I deserve to know the truth."

His hands moved to my head, keeping me a prisoner to his chest.

"I'm begging you, Kieran. I am fucking begging you to tell me the truth. You can kill me if you need to. You can destroy me, but please... I just want to know."

"I'm so sorry, Ophelia. I am so fucking sorry."

I knew he was sorry. I had seen it in his eyes a month ago, just before I plunged my knife into his chest. But it still didn't answer my question.

"I wasn't okay, Phee. It all happened after the whole fiasco with Cynthia." I stiffened at the mention of her name. "And that's just another thing I am sorry for. I made so many mistakes with you. I hurt you so much because I was weak. Because I didn't know how to cope, and then my father came to my apartment."

Logan-fucking-Nightingale.

"Maya was with him. I don't know how or why, but she was there. And he threatened me with Ava, baby. It was either her or Ava, and I couldn't put my baby sister through that."

"Oh my God."

"It doesn't justify my actions, but I just... I couldn't. At that point, I'd already failed you. You were so consumed by darkness that I knew. No matter what, you were already too deep inside this whole shit. And if I couldn't save you, maybe I could save Ava. Now look where that got us."

"Why didn't you call me? Why didn't you tell

me?"

"I tried." I pulled back and looked into his eyes. "I'd tried to tell you so many times. But that look on your face just before you stabbed me, I never wanted to have that. You fucking hated my guts. How could I ask for forgiveness when I did such a monstrous thing? Huh? I knew that the two of us, we were done. What I did to your sister, no, what I was forced to do to your sister, that was something our fathers would've done."

"Kieran—"

"No, listen. I know that what I did was monstrous. I feel sick every single time I think about it, and maybe if I wasn't such a pussy, such an idiot, I would've been able to help us all. Instead, I played right into my father's hands because I was weak. You were right, Phee. I always tried to please him. I always tried to save everybody else, but the thing I did... I fucked everything up."

He was sorry. I could see it in his eyes, he was so fucking sorry. But I wasn't the person he needed to seek forgiveness from. I could never really forgive him, and it wasn't my place to do so.

He had to ask Maya to forgive him.

"Wait, so you aren't here to kill me?"

He laughed at me and moved the hair from my face. "No, baby. I've been waiting for you to get out of there, because there was no way I would be able to infiltrate their clubhouse. I meant what I said in that church. I love you, Ophelia. I think that I never stopped. Even when I thought you killed my sister, I just couldn't shake this feeling." Oh, Kieran. "You will always be here." He placed a hand to his chest. "When I woke up in the hospital after the church incident, the first person I asked for was you. Cillian and Tristan wanted to go after you, but I stopped them. It wasn't your fault, and you did what every single one of us would've done."

"Kieran—"

"We do need to talk, birdy. There are things you don't know and you should."

"What things?" I asked as his lips connected with my temple, then with my cheek. "Kieran?"

"Just let me have this, please."

He skimmed toward my mouth, kissing the corner but it felt wrong. His lips on my skin, his hands on me, it all felt wrong, and I knew why. My heart didn't belong to him anymore. It stayed behind in that fucking clubhouse with a man that didn't deserve to have it. So why should I let him control me with this? Why shouldn't I let myself enjoy this for one last time?

"I need to taste you. I've missed you so much, Phee. So, so much."

"Kieran—"

"No, please. Lie to me. Lie to me, Ophelia and I will believe everything. Just let me have this."

My heart screamed at me, but my mind was made up. I wasn't thinking, I never really do, but I wanted to forget everything about Storm. I didn't want to feel like my heart was about to burst from my chest.

Kieran's eyes were pleading with me, and in that moment, it was like old times—only the two of us, loving each other, holding each other. If I had to use Kieran to rid my body of Storm, I would. I would do anything to forget about those green eyes or the way he felt inside me. I would sell my soul to the devil just so that I wouldn't feel him in my heart.

I pulled him by his neck, meshing our lips together. He moaned into my mouth, and I climbed in his lap, my center connecting with his dick.

THIRTY-ONE

Ophelia

"ARE YOU SURE about this?" Kieran asked as I ground on top of him.

I definitely wasn't sure about this, but it was a welcome distraction from the mess swirling in my head and in my heart. I had to stop thinking about Storm, and if this was the way to do it, well, fuck it.

"Yes," I moaned, kissing his jaw, going lower to his neck. His grip on my hips tightened, reminding me of the times in the past when he became rough. When he was exactly what I wanted.

This attraction I felt toward Storm, it had to go away. I couldn't live like this, with him inside my chest.

"Touch me." I took the hoodie off of me, throwing it somewhere in the room, leaving me in the tank top I wore underneath. "Touch me, Kieran."

He hesitated and I thought he wouldn't do it. The thought itself sent a new wave of panic through my body. If I couldn't forget with Kieran, I wouldn't be able to do it with anybody else.

This man in front of me, this dark-haired, lost

man used to be my everything. My days began and ended with him, and if he couldn't erase the man that haunted me now, no one else would.

"Please, K. I just want to forget. Just for a minute, for a day, I want to be free. Please, set me free."

Something flashed in his eyes and in the next second, I was in the air, my legs wrapped around his waist. The thing that I always loved about him was the strength he possessed. The way he always handled me, it was never soft, but it was what I needed.

Maybe I wasn't made for sweet loving. There was something in my head, some wire that went bad and I didn't know how to enjoy the sweet sides this life could have. There was an irreparable damage inside of me, and I didn't know how to stop the rotting.

It was spreading from my soul to all my organs, and there was no cure.

I never knew how to process everything that was happening around me. I never knew how to process the loss, sadness, anger... love. I never fucking knew how to process love. I could do physical. I could torture, kill, kiss and fuck, but I couldn't tell you that I loved you.

Maybe Kieran knew it and he never pushed me for more. Maybe some part of him always knew, just like some part of me always knew, that we would never last forever.

I liked to think that Ophelia from the parallel universe had it all figured out. Maybe I was just a shadow that was supposed to pick up all the bad things that should've happened to her. A shadow self, a mirror, just an image of a happy person.

If that other Ophelia was truly happy, I didn't mind carrying the burden of this life. I didn't mind being the demon everybody thought I was. Somewhere, in another universe, there was a version of me that knew how to love.

There was a version of me that had a loving family, a normal family. Maybe that version had Kieran or Storm, and she was happy. Just your regular girl.

"Phee." He brushed the hair from my face. "Stay with me. Just, be here."

Be here.

I understood what he was talking about, because Kieran knew better than I did how my mind worked sometimes. Those countless nights when he held me close, when that line between hallucinations and reality became too thin, he knew.

I deserved all of this. All this pain, all this suffering, this damned feeling inside my chest. I deserved to be forgotten and unloved.

I almost choked when the realization hit me.

I was unloved and unwanted. The child that was made into an assassin. The child that no one ever asked about her feelings. They didn't want me.

"Kieran." I choked on the emotions clouding my mind. My throat felt tight, something erupting from inside. Something I hadn't felt in a very long time. "This... It hurts."

"I know, baby. I know." He kissed my forehead as he took me to the table in the other corner of the room. I couldn't see him in the darkness, but I could feel every plane of his face as I touched it with my hand. His beard had started growing, but those eyes shone with all the love directed at me.

So why did I still feel unloved?

"I love you, birdy. I will always love you."

I wanted to tell him that he shouldn't as he

took my tank top off, but I couldn't. I needed to hear this more than he needed to say it, because these words were the fuel that would help me to keep moving.

At least someone loved me. Someone thought that I was worth it. He thought I was worth all the pain, all the blood and tears.

Even if the person I wanted didn't feel the same way, I wanted to at least believe in this tiny, little lie. I loved lies. They had kept me going for so many years. I'd lied to myself that my father cared about me, when in reality he never cared about anything but his own sick little gains. I was just a pawn in this game he played, and God knew what he actually did to Maya.

The cold air of the night hit my skin as Kieran removed my bra, my nipples puckering underneath his gaze.

"You're so beautiful." His head dipped down, taking one nipple into his mouth, then the other one. Swirling his tongue around the pebbled buds, I arched my back, pushing my chest into his face. "I've missed this. I've missed us." But I didn't. I didn't miss him because I was consumed with Storm. I just couldn't tell him that.

The wetness pooled in my core and I started clenching my legs around his waist.

"Are you mine?" he asked me, and I could've lied. I could've told him that I belonged to him and only him, but the name on my right thigh was the one I belonged to, even if it was the one I wanted to forget.

"For tonight." I pulled him to me before he could say anything, kissing him, taking everything he was willing to give me.

He traced the scar on my cheek and moved away momentarily, the weight of what he had done to me visible on his face.

"I am sorry, baby. I was a fool. I was blind, filled with rage and I just needed someone to blame. And you were there. You were the perfect culprit."

But it was too late for apologies, for forgiveness. He should've talked to me instead of attacking me.

"It's okay, K." I took his hand, turning his palm to me. "I forgive you." I kissed his palm. "I forgive you for that. You don't have to carry that guilt with you anymore. I will never be able to forget, but I forgive you."

Closing his eyes, a shuddering breath left his body, and I knew I did the right thing.

"But Kieran, Maya has to forgive you for what you did to her. I can't forgive you for that. It isn't my place, and it isn't my pain. That is one thing I could never forgive you for."

"I know, birdy. Trust me, I know."

I knew that this was our goodbye. He and I weren't meant to be together. There was too much pain, too much history, and staying with Kieran would mean betraying Maya.

I couldn't do that, and somewhere deep inside him, he knew that as well.

"Your pants need to go away, birdy."

"Just don't rip them." I laughed. "This is the only pair I own for now."

"I'll buy you another pair," he growled as he started unbuttoning them. "I'll buy you ten thousand pairs, but this one has to fucking go."

I dreaded the moment he would see what was carved on my thigh, but he had to. My body belonged to him for the night, but my soul stayed in Santa Monica.

"You sound eager."

"I haven't been inside of you for far too long. My dick misses you." A kiss. A touch. A caress on my skin. "I need to be inside you so badly, you've no idea."

"I think I can feel it." I chuckled.

I lifted my butt from the table as he pulled my pants down, discarding them on the floor. He couldn't see the scar in the dark, but as his hand took a hold of my calves, going higher to my thighs, I knew that it was a matter of seconds.

"What is this?" he asked as his hand finally landed on the elevated flesh, the letters there forever marking me. I could see the furrowing of his eyebrows, but I couldn't see his eyes as he crouched lower trying to see what it was.

"It's nothing." I whispered, my voice too weak to say anything else. "Just let it go, K."

But he wasn't letting it go. His fingers traced the pattern there and when his eyes met mine, I knew that he could tell what was carved there.

"Storm."

It wasn't a question; it was a statement said through the gritted teeth. It was the realization that I wasn't his anymore, that another man held my soul in the grip of his hands.

He stood still, the pressure on my thigh increasing but I needed him to let it go. I needed to let go of everything, and I needed this, tonight.

"Please, K. Just let it go."

"How did you two meet?" he asked instead, and whether I liked it or not, I had to tell him the truth. "When?" His eyes met mine, the torment evident in them.

"Four years ago. I was with Ava when I first saw him."

"Dammit, Phee. There are things you don't

know. Things that you should know, and they involve Storm."

Which things?

"That wasn't the first time you met him, baby. You met Storm long before that."

What? How?

"What are you talking about? I'd never even seen him before that day. And before you even think about it, I never cheated. Unlike you," I had to add.

"That's not fair."

"No, you know what wasn't fair?" I pushed his chest. "Finding my boyfriend, no wait, my fiancé, fucking somebody else. That's what wasn't fair. Me meeting Storm, that was nothing compared to what you did."

"Ophelia —"

"No! You have no right, Kieran! You have no idea the hell I went through after your brothers decided that I was guilty. Where were you, Kieran? Where the fuck were you while I was screaming for someone to save me? Where was the man I wanted to marry at that point? You were probably fucking some random slut while the chains in that basement kept cutting off the circulation in my wrists."

"Stop it, Phee." He tried taking a hold of my arms, but I wasn't having it. The memories of everything that happened, seeing him with her, hearing them and their accusations, it was all bubbling up.

Emotions were tricky, and I kept mine hidden for way too long. I guess that it was time for all of it to come out.

My pain.

The betrayal I felt.

Forgiving him wasn't enough, but this

volcanic eruption in my chest had to go out in some way.

"Where were you?" I screamed, my throat burning from exertion.

"Phee—"

"Tell me, goddammit!"

But he didn't tell me. His lips landed on mine, and he gripped my hair, holding me in place, one hand wrapped around my neck, cutting off my air supply.

Vicious.

This was what I needed. Vicious Kieran.

He slammed my body into the wall and kept up with the punishing kisses. This was a battle. It always was a battle with the two of us.

I never wanted to give him the power over me and he never wanted to admit that the two of us were all sorts of wrong for each other.

The man that was meant for me, the man that messed up was probably already looking for me, and Kieran wasn't him.

"Is this what you want, birdy?" He bit my jaw. "Pain?"

"Yes." I bit his neck as soon as he moved slightly back. "I want pain, because if there is pain, everything in here," I pointed to my head, "stops screaming. And I need it to fucking stop."

This was the last time. I kept repeating in my head that this last time had to count.

By letting him do this, I almost forgot the feel of Storm's lips on mine. I almost forgot the feeling of that knife on my thigh and his fingers inside of me.

I wanted to fucking forget the person that was living inside my heart.

His hand tightened around my neck, and with

411

a punishing bite, he kept lowering his head from my collarbone to my chest.

This was going to leave marks, but I didn't care anymore. As long as I didn't feel anything else but what was happening now, I was happy.

As long as I could forget everything else, this was okay.

Bruises, cuts, scrapes, that was my love language. I didn't know how to do it differently.

But you almost did it with Storm. You almost let him see your heart.

Fuck off. Fuck the fuck off right now. He was going to get buried as well, along with all my mistakes and regrets.

He could drown with the rest of them because this body carried more than it could count.

"Fuck me, Kieran. I want you to fuck me like it's the most important thing in your life."

He ripped my panties in half, the fabric falling at my feet. I spread my legs as he cupped my pussy in his hand, the punishing grip for both him and me.

"I am going to fuck you so hard they will hear you screaming my name all the way to Santa Monica."

As Kieran kneeled in front of me, spreading me wide and dragging his nose against my inner thigh, my eyes landed on a figure in the dark.

Cillian.

His rigid stance almost made him look like a ghost. I still wondered why I never noticed him. Maybe his demons would've danced better with mine.

When Kieran's lips started sucking my clit into his mouth, I couldn't move my eyes away from Cillian. I imagined his lips on me while Kieran drove me closer to the brink. I cupped my breasts

412

into my hands and bit my lip. He was breathing harder; I could see his chest rising and falling faster now.

One finger entered me, and I moaned, pulling my bottom lip between my teeth.

Cillian took a step closer, than another one, and another one, until he was standing just behind Kieran.

His blue eyes were hooded, and I knew that he wanted this as much as I did. No matter how fucked up this was, we didn't know any better. We were both cut from the same cloth. We were both fighting the same demons, just on different levels.

Our heads were our cages, but for tonight... For one night, we had to escape.

"Do you want both of us, birdy?" Kieran asked as his fingers continued stroking my inner walls. He was taking it slow, extending my torture. "Do you want Cillian as well?"

"Yes," I answered, without a moment of hesitation.

Cillian didn't waste a second to stand next to me, pulling my hair and lifting my head up.

"You want both of our cocks to fill you up, baby girl?" His voice was raspy, those hooded eyes seeing more than I wanted. "You want to be our little toy?"

"Fuck yes!" I screeched as Kieran hit that spot inside that made my legs quiver. Kieran increased the pressure on my clit, lapping at the juices flowing from me. He relentlessly kept his ministrations, as Cillian gripped my throat, bringing my lips to his.

"I like your lips, Ophelia," he whispered above me. "They taste like the sweetest sin."

I could feel his hardness at my hip, and I gripped him with my right hand. His eyes closed

413

on a groan before he attacked my lips, his tongue seeking entrance into my mouth.

"Oh fuck." I moved away as Kieran increased his pace. "Holy fucking shit."

Cillian squeezed my breast and my eyes started rolling to the back of my head from the intensity I was experiencing.

Kieran between my legs, and Cillian gripping, caressing my body; they were everywhere.

Taking a step back, Cillian removed his shirt, revealing a broad chest and the V-trail I wanted to lick since the last time I saw him. He smirked at me and moved closer, leaving soft kisses on my neck, over my chest and moving his hand between my legs.

Kieran started spreading my juices to my back side, his finger playing with my other opening.

"Shit," I groaned.

"Do you want to come, little birdy?" Cillian asked me, flicking one nipple with his fingers.

"Please." I needed to come. I was clenching around Kieran's fingers, and with each stroke Cillian set upon me, I was getting closer and closer.

"Should we let her come, Brother?" Cillian asked Kieran. "Or should we make her wait?"

"I'm not sure." I could hear the amusement in Kieran's voice. "Were you a good girl?"

Cillian squeezed my clit, and I slammed my head into the wall, my legs almost giving out on me.

A finger entered me from the backside, and I almost jumped from where I'd been standing when Kieran started moving in my pussy, while at the same time pulling his other finger out.

I clenched around him. I was almost there.

Almost.

Almost...

What the fuck?

They both stepped away, leaving me panting, aroused and fucking pissed off.

"What the fuck, assholes?" I was not beyond begging at this point. Hot and bothered, that was my current state, and these two asshats just smirked at me. "Seriously?"

"Patience, little one," Cillian answered as he started unbuckling his belt. Kieran removed his shirt, taking something from the pocket of his pants before he discarded them as well. His length was straining against his boxer briefs.

My mouth fucking watered at the sight.

Cillian took Kieran's shirt and his discarded one, spreading them on the floor. The hoodie I took off earlier joined them.

Kieran walked to me, his steps slow. He looked like a panther and I was the prey.

"Touch me, baby. I want you to touch me now."

I dropped to my knees, the gravel beneath biting into the skin, but I didn't feel it. Tomorrow I would think about my scraped knees but tonight, this was the important thing.

I moved his briefs down his legs, freeing his dick. I forgot how beautiful he truly was.

The bulbous head was calling to me, the precum already gathering at the tip. I enveloped him with one hand and a groan erupted from his chest.

I loved this.

Even on my knees, I knew that I had full control over him.

I started stroking his length and brought my lips to the mushroom tip, licking the precum.

"Fuck," he groaned and placed both of his hands on the wall behind me. I swirled my tongue around, all the while stroking him up and down and taking his balls into my other hand.

I opened my mouth wide, taking him in.

"Oh God," he groaned. "Faster."

Yes, sir.

On it, sir.

I focused on his face as I moved my head back and forth, enjoying the sounds that were coming from his mouth. I didn't notice when Cillian walked to us, but when the finger entered me from the back, I almost dropped to my hands.

I moaned around Kieran's length, gripping him harder.

Cillian kept collecting the wetness that was still leaking from me, moving it to my backside, dripping his finger in.

He started circling my clit with his other hand and kept going back and forth. I sucked my cheeks in, earning another set of sounds from Kieran.

"Jesus," I mumbled against his dick, as his twin started pushing his finger deeper, curling it, and moving in and out.

His strokes increased as well, and the ragged breathing wasn't only coming from Kieran and me. Cillian was breathing hard as he prepared me for what was to come.

My legs started shaking, but before I could fall forward, Kieran stepped back, removing himself from me.

"Are you ready, birdy?" Cillian asked, plastering his chest to my back. He entered a second finger, then the third one, spreading me wide.

Pain and pleasure, I felt it all, and I wanted it.

"Yes." I fell on my hands, arching my back to him. "Please."

I thought he would let me come this time, but

416

instead, he pulled me up, lifting me from the floor and carrying me to the shirts he spread on the floor.

I looked at Kieran who kept stroking his dick, a condom wrapped around him. Cillian lost his pants, and just like the last time, there was no underwear.

Kieran threw a silver packet at him, and he ripped it open, rolling the condom on.

Cillian laid on his back on top of the shirts, and pulled me down, right on top of him. I rubbed myself over his abs, the friction driving me crazy.

"I need —"

"Shhh, birdy." He moved me back until I was positioned right above his hard length. I kneeled on top of him and started sinking slowly on his dick.

He held my hands in his as I started going up and down, adjusting to his length.

"Jesus, fuck."

He pulled me to him, and my chest brushed against his.

"I love your body, birdy. We are going to fuck you so hard."

I buried my face into the crook of his neck, leaving soft bites there. His dick jerked inside of me, and I knew I hit the jackpot. I placed another bite before replacing it with a kiss, and he rewarded me with a grip at my neck and a tight hold of my hip. He started moving his hips in a sync, hitting all the sweet spots inside of me.

I couldn't move. I was his prisoner, and he didn't let me go as he relentlessly pounded inside, driving me crazy.

I screamed, my voice muffled by him, and the grip on my neck increased. He slowed down as I felt Kieran at my back, spreading my ass cheeks.

I could hear him spitting and the cold fluid hit me, sliding to my opening. Kieran entered me

417

roughly, two fingers at once, then three, until I couldn't think anymore.

I felt full. So fucking full and they were only starting.

"Relax, birdy," Cillian whispered as he stroked my hair. "You need to relax."

He moved his hand from my hip to my clit, leaving small strokes.

Fuck.

All my nerve endings were on fire, but before I could gather my wits, Kieran positioned himself behind me, his cock sliding between my ass cheeks, going up and down. Without warning me, he slid inside, spreading me wide.

"Fuck me!"

Kieran started pushing in and pulling out, and the searing pain slowly started dissipating, turning into pleasure.

"Relax, Ophelia," Kieran said. "I don't want to hurt you."

Jesus. I would like to see him relax with two dicks inside him.

Another wave of pleasure traveled through me as Cillian moved slightly, flicking my clit.

I fell on my knees, taking Kieran with me and pulling Cillian deeper inside.

"Fuck me sideways."

"That's what we're trying to do." Cillian chuckled.

Kieran pushed deeper inside, hitting the spots I didn't think were possible to hit and I groaned, trying to breathe through it all.

"Fuck, fuck, fuck."

"Just breathe, birdy. In and out. Breathe," Cillian whispered in my ear and started leaving a trail of kisses over my cheek, turning my face to him and taking my lips.

Kieran started moving out, and before I could protest, he moved back in, while Cillian moved out.

Oh God.

If I die like this, I would be a happy person.

Kill kept a tight hold on my head, swallowing my cries, my moans, as both of them moved back and forth in sync. The build-up from before, the assault on all of my senses now, it was all too much, and I didn't even try to stop the detonation that came from me.

I screamed in Cillian's mouth, gripping his shoulders as the aftershocks of my orgasm traveled all over my body.

Kieran pulled out, but neither one of them were done with me.

With the strength that I didn't know was humanly possible, Cillian stood up, holding me to him, not once removing his dick from me, and came closer to the wall almost leaning on it.

"Now the real fun starts, little one." He smiled at me as Kieran came behind, entering me in one stroke. I was already too sensitive from my orgasm, but as they started their relentless fucking, I could only hang on for dear life.

"I can't," I moaned. "Oh. My. God."

I gripped the back of Cillian's neck, pulling at his hair and the groan that erupted from him was soon quieted with the bite he left on my neck. Kieran bit the other side, both of them taking me to the heavens with the pace they were having.

"Fuck. I need to —"

"I know," Cillian answered.

"Faster," I begged. "I need you to fuck me faster."

Cillian leaned on the wall, squeezing my legs between his back and the wall, and started pounding inside, bringing me to the brink of insanity.

Kieran's hands sneaked in, taking a hold of my breasts, squeezing tightly.

"Fuck!" I drew out.

"That's it, Phee," Kieran muttered from behind.

"Your pussy is squeezing the life out of me, Ophelia," Cillian mumbled against my lips. "That's it, baby girl. Almost there."

"Do you want to come for us again, birdy?" Kieran asked as he bit my shoulder. "Are you close?"

"Yes, yes, yes," I chanted.

His other hand dropped to my pussy, pinching my clit painfully and I was gone.

Falling.

Drowning.

Sinking down.

The ringing in my ears was only penetrated by their groans. Black spots danced around Cillian's head and I couldn't keep myself upright anymore. My head dropped to Kill's shoulder and with a few last strokes, both of them stopped, their bodies shaking against mine, following their orgasms.

My eyes started drooping down, regret dancing on the edge of my consciousness, but I didn't want to think about it now. The only thing I wanted right now was to sleep and disappear for a moment.

THIRTY-TWO

THE SMELL OF antiseptic tickled my nose, reminding me of doctors in white coats, endless bruises and cuts I had survived over the years in that house of horrors. I begged them to take me away. I begged them to help me, to call somebody, but help never came. The only thing that ever came was the whip on my back and cuffs around my wrists.

It was often painful, remembering innocence lost and the depravity I witnessed, but it was necessary. I didn't want to forget, because then I would have nothing left to fuel this simmering rage I had. It built and built and built, and now was the time to unleash it on all of them. I just had to be patient.

I had to start paying better attention to the situation. If I had, we wouldn't be sitting here at two in the morning, watching over Atlas's sleeping form. His shoulder was bandaged, his skin pale and sweaty as he fought against the infections that were threatening to take over his body. I looked at Indigo whose eyes didn't stray from the man in the bed not for one second—and again I cursed myself for putting us in this situation.

I was cocky, full of myself. I had thought we had handled that situation. I assumed Logan would have additional backup and so did we, but our guys were too far to help us when we needed it, and it was all my fault. I gave the orders, I brought them to that Godforsaken church, and we almost lost one of our brothers.

As soon as we walked out of that door, I called Diego, an ally who didn't belong to the club, nor did he belong to any of the other organizations. He liked to call himself Team Switzerland, but I never thought I would need him for a situation like this. The Old Casino was once a place where underground fights happened, all organized by Italians who had an agreement with us. It all fell apart when the Nightingales burned our people alive and ambushed their boss.

Last I heard, they all retreated to Chicago, holding a grudge against the East Coast.

Diego called in a few favors and once we arrived at the place, a doctor was already waiting with a makeshift operating table and one scared-looking nurse. I didn't ask questions. I honestly didn't care where he found them. The only thing that mattered was helping Atlas. I couldn't remember the last time one of us bled like this. It was probably years since we allowed ourselves to be in this kind of situation. No, I allowed us to stumble into this—blind, reckless, uncoordinated.

The terror I felt when Atlas stopped moving, Indigo's yelling from the backseat of the Range Rover we brought with us, my reckless driving and Hunter trying to calm us all down, it was all still fresh in my mind. Felix kept quiet the whole time, but I could feel his eyes on me. I could feel the accusations and he wouldn't be wrong.

This was all my fault.

"I can hear you thinking, and you need to stop," Indigo muttered, still looking at Atlas. His dark hair was disheveled and there were dark circles around his eyes, but no matter how many times I tried to tell him to get some sleep, he wouldn't listen to me. He disregarded my pleas to get something to eat, to change from his bloody clothes. He wouldn't move.

So, I let him be because I knew that look on his face. I just didn't think that he was ready to talk about it, and it probably wasn't my place to ask.

"I'm not thinking about anything." *Liar.* I was consumed by my own thoughts, but Indigo didn't need to know that. I would spend the rest of my life apologizing to all of them for putting them through this. I just needed Atlas to wake up so that I could make this right.

My legs were sore from standing in the same position, my eyes droopy from the lack of sleep and the only thing I wanted to do right now, the only place I wanted to be was our bed, with Ophelia in my arms. How was I going to tell her that not only did I fail to tell her about the deal, but I almost had Atlas killed, and I lost Logan who now knew that she was with me?

Sliding down the wall, I bent my knees, resting my elbows on them. God, I just wanted to sleep.

"You're gonna want to apologize, but this isn't your fault."

"Isn't it?" I chuckled. "If it weren't for my foolish attempt to get Las Vegas back, we wouldn't be here. I wouldn't be lying to Ophelia about my whereabouts, and we wouldn't be having this fucking conversation. So yes, it definitely is my fault."

"You didn't put a bullet in his shoulder," he argued as he looked at me over his shoulder. "Don't try to make yourself look like a villain when the real one is still out there. We need to get to him and make him pay for everything he did."

I looked at the ceiling, unable to see his face. "I wasn't the one holding the gun, but Atlas wouldn't be lying here if it weren't for me. That, there," I pointed toward Atlas, "that should've been me."

"There's no use in killing ourselves over what-ifs." He stood up for the first time in the last couple of hours, cracking his neck and shaking his limbs.

"I'm sorry."

He crossed the room and walked to me, then sat down on his haunches. "There's nothing to be sorry about, but I do need you to get up and start thinking about a new plan. One that hopefully doesn't involve that church anymore, because I am really tired of seeing it. He's going to be okay." He looked at Atlas, a thousand emotions written over his face. "He has to be."

A better man would know how to tell him that Atlas was indeed going to be okay. The doctor himself said so, explaining that the bullet went right through, avoiding all of his vital organs and bones. He would have a lengthy recovery, but Atlas was going to be okay.

Physically at least.

Placing my hand on Indigo's shoulder, I squeezed tight, trying to show everything I couldn't voice, trying to reassure him. Or maybe I was reassuring myself, I didn't know.

"I'm going to kick his ass if he doesn't wake up," Indigo murmured. "I really will. Who else is going to beat my ass in billiards if he doesn't wake up?"

Denial was such a beautiful thing, given to us humans as a shield when we couldn't deal with the reality of the situation, and Indigo was cloaked in it, denying that the worry he felt had anything to do with his feelings for Atlas. I didn't notice it before, but I could see it now.

The way they always bickered, the way Atlas seemed to follow him everywhere, the way Indigo's gaze would linger on Atlas a little bit longer than necessary, it was all there. They just didn't want to admit it to each other, which was a real shame.

Really? They weren't the only ones not admitting their feelings or talking.

Okay, I was avoiding talking with Ophelia about things that truly mattered, because I didn't want to lose her. But life was too short for missed opportunities and hiding things from those we loved, and I did, love her that is. That night when she killed Sam, I didn't see a bloodthirsty assassin who didn't feel anything. That night I saw a woman who felt everything, who was used as a pawn in their sick and twisted games; a woman that was afraid. What I saw in her eyes, it wasn't just anger. She was afraid, terrified even and something told me that a lot of the things she did, she didn't do them because she wanted to, but because she had to.

"Atlas?" Indigo stood up abruptly, pulling me from my reverie. "Holy shit." He all but ran across the room as Atlas started coughing, trying to lift himself up.

"What the fuck?" He groaned as he fell down with a thud, turning his head from side to side.

"Atlas, hey." Indigo placed a hand on his forehead. "It's okay, you're okay. You're gonna be fine." I had a feeling he was trying to reassure both of them, not only Atlas.

"What happened?"

"You got shot, dumbass," I said as I stood up. "What the fuck were you thinking?"

"I was thinking about tacos and surfing." Atlas groaned as Indigo helped him lift himself up. "I was thinking about stopping that asshole from escaping. Dammit." He pressed his left hand to his right shoulder where the bullet went through, his whole face distorted from pain. "This one hurts like a bitch."

"No shit."

"Fuck off, Storm. You would've done the same." Yeah, I would've, but then I wouldn't be feeling guilty about getting shot. This on the other hand...

"Just don't do that shit, like ever again," Indigo grumbled. "We all lost fifteen years of our lives watching you fall down."

As if finally realizing that Indigo was hovering over him like a mother hen, Atlas's eyes shone as he looked at him, seeing the concern on his face. They needed to talk without me in the background, and when my phone started ringing, I slowly excused myself and went outside to the hallway.

Creed's name flashed on the screen and I knew I couldn't keep ignoring his calls anymore. Dozens of them already went unanswered but I didn't want to talk to any of them until Atlas woke up. Whatever it was, it was far less important than the fact that one of us got shot.

"This better be—"

"Fucking, finally! Do you have any idea how many times I've called you? Phones have been invented for a reason, Storm. Use them!"

"Okay, okay, calm down, Creed." I sat on the floor, leaning against the wall. "What do you need?"

"What do I need?" He huffed. "I needed you to answer your fucking phone."

"Well, I answered it now."

The anger in his voice slowly dissipated with his next words. "And now might be too late."

"What are you talking about?" I straightened up, not liking the sound of it. "Did something happen at the club?" God, no. "Is Ophelia okay?"

What if something happened to her? What if Logan got back there and found her, what if...?

"Trust me, Ophelia is absolutely fine. More than fine, actually." I didn't like the sneer in his tone, or the way he pronounced her name. I didn't like that I hadn't talked to her yet, that I hadn't called her as soon as we got out. "My bike on the other hand, that might not be fine."

"Your bike?"

"Yes, Storm, my fucking bike."

"Did you just call me to bitch about your bike, because let me tell you some—"

"Ophelia took my bike, Storm." *What?* "She's gone."

She's gone.

Gone.

No.

"What?" She wouldn't. She fucking promised. "You're lying." I was on my feet now, passing the length of the hallway. "Get her on the phone."

"I wish I were lying, but I'm not. She ran away, Storm. She knocked one of the prospects down, took my bike and ran away."

No, no, no, fucking no. She promised me. She promised she wouldn't run. She promised me she would stay. Everything was going well, and I told her we would talk. Why did she run away?

"I found something else on your bed," he

whispered, as if he was too afraid to speak about it. "There was a letter from her father to her. We have another spy in the club."

Fuck. "I'll be there in the next couple of hours."

"No, you won't, because you need to find her."

"But she—"

"There's a tracker on my bike. I am sending one of the prospects with the device to locate it. I don't like that letter, Storm, and if that is the reason she ran away... Nikolai Aster is a wicked man, and I have a feeling that he won't show her mercy after she ran from the Syndicate. You're either in or you're dead, and Ophelia is dead if he gets his hands on her."

Creed continued talking about all the reasons why she could be in danger, but I wasn't listening anymore. My mind focused on one word—dead, and I couldn't breathe. The walls started closing in on me as all the words we shared went through my head. All the moments, the taste of her skin, the sound of her moans, of her voice, and I knew I couldn't bear life without her in it.

"Storm? Are you still there?"

"Yeah." I dragged a hand over my face. "I'm sending you our location."

"We will get her back, Storm. It seems that she's close to Las Vegas, but look..." He paused. "I am not sure if her father is the reason behind her departure. She was furious, dude. I have never seen her like that. I thought she would kill me for trying to stop her, and that definitely didn't come from that letter."

What the fuck happened to you, Ophelia?

THIRTY-THREE

Ophelia

I COULD HEAR birds chirping outside, cars passing and a cacophony of voices from the construction site next to the warehouse, but I couldn't quiet my mind. I fucked up, plain and simple. I shouldn't have done this, shouldn't have let my insecurities, my anger take over, because now I would never be able to go back to Storm.

But he betrayed you.

Did he? Did he really? It wouldn't be the first time that I came to the conclusions, refusing to listen to reason. Was I wrong to run away? Was I wrong to enact my revenge in this way? I should have stayed and talked to him. I knew better than to act before thinking, and I did exactly that.

I even knew why. Because I was terrified.

It was easier believing that Storm was just like every other man in my life than to build something with him. I panicked, I ran, and I fucked up when I let Kieran and Cillian inside my body last night. I had to fix this, but I couldn't come up with a suitable solution, and I couldn't lie to Storm. I would have to tell him what happened here, but not before asking him about that call I overheard.

God, I hated feeling like this, not knowing what to do. I hated the fact that so many other people in my life betrayed me, that my first reaction was to run and destroy everything. I just threw away everything we started building together in the trash, and I had no one else to blame but myself.

Cillian laid sprawled beneath me, half of my body on top of his, with a blanket thrown on us. I tried turning my head to see if Kieran was anywhere to be seen, but I couldn't see a trace of him.

I knew what I had to do, but dread spread through me, thinking about the betrayal Storm was about to feel. I did exactly the same thing Kieran did—I cheated. With that thought, my stomach recoiled, and I rolled myself off Cillian before I started heaving on all fours. Jesus-fucking-Christ, was I getting sick? This was the second time this had happened.

Before I could start overthinking and coming up with terminal diseases that could be destroying my body, Cillian rolled over on his side and pulled himself closer to me.

"Good morning, birdy," he whispered against my hair. The fucker was awake the whole time.

"Get off of me, Cillian."

"Hmmm." He started grinding himself against my thigh. "That wasn't what you said last night."

"I said," I gritted through my teeth, still trying to control the heaving, "get off of me."

I pushed his chest and he rolled over, revealing a tight six-pack and the hard length between his legs. However, what pulled at my attention wasn't his body, but the track marks that could be seen on his right arm.

Oh God. He didn't.

He wouldn't do that to himself.

I grabbed his arm and sat on my knees, closer to him. "What the fuck is this, Kill?"

His easy-going demeanor instantly changed and he tried pulling his arm away, but I wasn't having it. The skin at his elbow pit was purple and the tiny mark from where the needle penetrated the skin stood against it.

"Tell me you didn't."

He pulled himself up, avoiding my eyes, but I couldn't not say anything.

"Why do you even care?" he snarled at me. "Three months ago, you would've killed me without a second thought."

"Goddammit, Kill! You would have done the same so cut the crap and tell me that it was a onetime thing."

"It was a onetime thing." He smirked.

"Kill." I came closer. "If I wanted to, I would've killed you a long time ago, but I don't. I like to think that we were friends before this, and I don't want to see you killing yourself with this crap."

"Just because you fucked both of us last night, doesn't make you our friend."

"Fuck you, Cillian."

"You already did that, birdy. Quite loudly if I might add. And—"

I slapped him across the face before he could finish the sentence. I always knew that Kill had demons rivaling even mine, but I never thought that he would do this to himself. He used drugs here and there, but never this.

He never touched heroin, and seeing him like this, seeing those marks on him... This was breaking what was left of my heart.

"Kill," I started, trying to kick some sense into him. "Your brothers already lost a sister. Don't make them lose you too."

His face scrunched because we both knew that what I was saying was the truth. Whatever it was he was battling with inside had to go away, and I wasn't going to stand on the side and watch him destroy himself.

"Don't do this to yourself, please."

He kept quiet for a moment before those bright eyes met with mine.

"You have no idea, Phee." He took a deep breath. "No idea how hard it is dealing with what is in here." He tapped his temple. "I can hear them screaming at me. I can also see them. When I'm high, I just don't feel anything. There's no pain, no anger, no urge to kill myself and just leave this world."

"But I do know. I do know how it is because I live with those same screams on a daily basis." Goddammit, I wanted to hug him, to show him he wasn't alone, but the way he held himself, his body language screamed to back off.

"I am not strong enough, Ophelia. I am just... I am not as strong as you or Kieran, or even Tristan. The original family disappointment, right?"

"Hey, no." I placed my hands on his cheeks. "That's not true. You are actually kind when you want to be, and patient. Please don't let those demons win. I am begging you not to let them win. Find help. Find someone who can help you to overcome this."

I pushed myself up and kissed his forehead. No matter what happened in the past between us, between me and his whole family, he didn't deserve this.

433

Cillian was just another version of me. Used by his father, thrown to the wolves and when he was breaking apart, nobody was there to catch him, to help him and to tell him that it would all be okay.

"Does Kieran know?" I asked him, because if he did know and he didn't offer help, I was going to have to smack him on his head.

"No." He frantically shook his head. "He doesn't and he can't know. Promise me you won't tell him."

"Cillian—"

"No, you can't. He will blame himself and this isn't his burden to carry. You know how he is. He always tries to help, but in the whole process, he starts blaming himself for the things that have happened and this one... This one isn't his fault."

"I won't say anything, okay?" I agreed. "But you have to. I don't know how deep you are, but you need to find help, Cillian. You're killing yourself and you're going to destroy your family as well."

"I know. I—"

"What's going on here?" Kieran's voice penetrated through the air and I removed myself from Cillian, wrapping the blanket around my body.

I wanted to tell him what was going on. I wanted to, but I promised. Cillian's eyes were pleading with me, and I knew that this wasn't something I had to reveal. Kill was an adult and just like I had to, he had to deal with his demons. I just hoped that he wouldn't be too late to realize that he didn't deserve to die.

"Usual." I shrugged. "Kill was hogging the blanket and well, I am a bitch that doesn't like that."

He kept looking between the two of us and it was obvious he wasn't buying my story.

434

"Where did you go?" I tried redirecting his attention to something else. I wasn't going to be the one that would reveal Cillian's secret, but I hoped for his sake and his brother's sake that he would come clean sooner rather than later.

"I brought us some food." He lifted the bag he was holding in his hand. "I thought that you two might be hungry, so I just did a quick run for it."

"Sweet. I'm actually starving." I really wasn't. The mere thought of food made my stomach churn again, but snitches get stitches and all that crap, and I didn't want to be anywhere near these two when they finally had that conversation.

I stood up, leaving a naked Cillian on the ground. I managed to locate my pants, thrown haphazardly on the floor, all the while ignoring the mocking pain from my left thigh, and the mark Storm left there. We never said words, we never placed any labels on what was happening between us, but we didn't have to. What was happening between us was more than just meaningless sex.

"We need to talk, Ophelia," Kieran said, keeping his distance from me.

If I had any worries about how he would react to what happened last night, this was my reassurance. He knew that this was it. This was our last goodbye before we both went our separate ways. I was worried he might start with the whole I-want-you-back speech and I was glad we were both on the same page.

"Right." I answered, turning my back to him. "Let me just get dressed."

I lifted the pants from the ground and pulled them on, gritting my teeth as the fabric dragged over the sensitive skin. I scanned the room for the tank top I had on yesterday, locating it next to the desk. I walked to it and took it off the floor, shaking off the dust and put it on.

Cillian scurried out of the room taking his clothes with him, and I wanted to follow him. I wanted to talk to him about what was going on. I wanted him to ask for help. There was no shame in asking for help, although the world we lived in often made us think that asking for help made us weak. In reality, it made us strong, but he didn't know that right now. I wanted to make sure he wasn't going to kill himself by trying to run away from the demons in his head.

"Are you okay?"

"Yeah. Just generally tired, I guess." *And feeling like I am about to puke, and your brother has a terrible, terrible secret, but I am all good.*

I sat on the ground and Kieran followed after me, dropping the bag between us.

"Phee—"

"What do you have there?" I didn't want to talk about last night, and I could see it in his eyes. He did. So much for us understanding each other

"There's a ham and cheese sandwich for you and a banana. They didn't have any croissants at the gas station so I hope that this would be okay." I expected my stomach to recoil again, but as the smell of fresh bread wafted to me, my mouth watered, my stomach growled, and I prayed I wasn't going to start puking halfway through this meal.

"It's more than okay." I dug into the bag, taking a hold of the sandwich. "Thank you."

Silence descended around us, and without Cillian here, we didn't have a buffer. I didn't have any kind of shield. He studied me for a moment before he too took a sandwich from the bag, leaving another one inside for Cillian.

"You wanted to talk?" I asked him in between bites. "Last night you mentioned something about Storm. What was it?"

He seemed to contemplate answering for a moment. I knew that Storm wasn't his favorite person, but if Kieran had answers that could clarify some of the things that had been happening around me, I had to know.

"Yeah, ah." He looked around as if he expected someone to be listening. "Do you know anything about Project X?"

It was the name on that folder and the same name that he asked me about back in their mansion.

"I already told you back in the mansion, I have never heard about it."

"Shit." He uncapped the bottle of water and chugged half of it in one take. "This is going to be uncomfortable."

"Why?" I didn't like the look on his face. Kieran was never one to worry about the things he had to tell me, so why now?

"Project X is a sex trafficking ring, Ophelia." I'm sorry, what? "When we kidnapped you, our father wanted to know if you knew anything about it. Of course, we wanted to kill you at the time, so we didn't exactly question it. Turns out that both of our fathers are involved in that shit."

"Holy fuck."

"Yeah, holy fuck indeed. He thought that if you knew about it, you could somehow jeopardize their whole operation, what with you being rogue and all that."

"But I didn't know. I swear to you."

"I know, birdy. I trust you."

Our families dealt with some serious shit—drugs, guns, strip clubs—but a sex trafficking ring was something I never expected to see.

"There's more."

"I'm almost expecting you to tell me that they have found a way to revive dinosaurs or something."

"Or something." He chuckled before his face became serious again. "I wish it were dinosaurs, but I need you to know about this because I think they are planning to kill you. This sex trafficking ring is active all around the globe. They have people in Europe, Asia, Africa, Australia, South and North America, they're everywhere, and…" he paused. "There are children involved."

His expression was haunted. "I saw pictures, I saw their names. Most of them didn't survive for longer than a few years, but one of them did."

"Then that person has to go to the police. They need to uncover this shit."

"Phee—"

"No. I've done some terrible things. I killed children, K. I tortured people for my father, but at least it was fast. This shit. This is awful."

"Ophelia. Listen—"

"Can we find him or her? Would they cooperate?"

"Ophelia, goddammit!" He slammed the bottle on the ground, water splashing everywhere. "That person is Storm."

"What?"

No. My father… He… Storm was a victim of sex trafficking as a kid? No. Oh my God.

I dropped the sandwich to the ground and pressed a hand against my mouth, suppressing the reflux and trying to hold in what I already swallowed.

"Storm was sold by his parents to your father when he was only four years old." Jesus. "He actually lived with your father for some time, and a few years before you were born, he was sent to what they like to call The Mansion."

"I am going to be sick."

"I found out something else as well."

"What else could there be?"

"I believe they sold Maya to the sex trafficking ring."

"Oh. My. God."

"I am sorry, Phee." He pulled me into his lap. "I really am, especially because if I wasn't such a fuckup, I would've been able to help her years ago."

"Do you know where she is?" I asked him, my whole body going numb from the news he kept spewing at me.

"I think I do."

"Tell me." I looked at him. "You need to tell me. I have to get her out."

"No, Ophelia. Not this time."

"What do you mean, not this time? She's my sister, dammit. I have to know."

"No, because it would be a suicide mission for you."

"Then what?" I yelled at him. "Should I just leave her wherever she is to rot and die?"

"No, you shouldn't, but you won't be the one going. I will."

"What?" Did he just say what I think he said?

"I need to fix what I've done. Let me do this, please."

Could I let him? Should I? Storm was already looking for Maya, and sending Kieran might be completely futile. But as he held my hands, as he pleaded with me, I realized that maybe this would be his road to redemption. I couldn't forgive him for what he had done to her, but he needed to apologize to her.

439

"Okay." I nodded.

The smile that took over his face was once upon a time a smile that could melt my world. Now, it just brought me a small sense of satisfaction and the notion that when all of this was over, we could put the past where it belonged — in the past.

Unfortunately, as soon as that smile came it disappeared just as fast. "Listen to me. You are not safe on the streets. My father has eyes everywhere, especially in Las Vegas. I need you to go back to Storm and stay there. I will get Maya back, but you have to stay safe."

"No! Hell no. I am not going to hide."

"Dammit, Ophelia. Just stop being reckless for once in your life and listen to me. They will kill you on the spot. There are orders, other assassins that will try to hunt you and kill you. I need you to be safe, okay?"

"Kieran—"

"No, promise me. Please."

The last time I saw fear in his eyes was when I caught him with Cynthia because he knew that I wouldn't be able to forgive that. Now I could see it again, only this time it was ten times worse. He really thought that I was in danger. I was terrified of facing Storm, but if I didn't want to run anymore, I had to go back. I had to face him and admit to everything I had done.

I had to talk to him about all of this, all these secrets.

"Okay. I promise." If I had to, I would grovel and beg for him to take me back.

"Good." Kieran kissed my forehead, and for the first time in years, I felt relieved.

"I did love you, you know?" I looked at him, moving my head back. "I thought that you were the one, but that wasn't the truth, was it?"

He smiled at me. "No, it wasn't. I think I will always love you, though. I think that even after years have passed, you will always have a special place in my heart. Everything we went through. Every single tear, every drop of blood, it wasn't for nothing. We were just kids, you know? We thought we could have it all, but we lost ourselves."

"Yeah, I know. Somewhere between all the pain and sorrow, we lost the love we had."

"I really am sorry for everything I did."

"I know, K. I know because I am sorry too. I don't know where life will take us, but I do hope that you find your happiness."

"My happiness is sitting in front of me right now."

"Kieran—"

"No, listen. I know that what we had would never be the same again. I know that look in your eyes. You were thinking about him, weren't you?"

I couldn't lie to him. "Yes." I moved the hair that fell on his forehead. "I know you don't want to hear it, but he understands me better than you did. And that isn't a bad thing, you know? You and I were too young to understand everything that was going on, and I think that if we grew up differently, we wouldn't be having this conversation. I keep thinking that if there is a parallel universe, you and I are happy there. Together." I squeezed his hand.

"Yeah, maybe." There was sadness etched into the planes of his face. The sadness I knew wouldn't go away that easily, but this had to be done.

"I want to kiss you. Just one last time. I want to feel your lips against mine and then I will let you go."

"Kieran—"

"Please. Just give me this. I don't want anything else, but just this."

441

Yet I couldn't do it. I couldn't let him get that last kiss, because it would be just another nail in the coffin, and I wouldn't be able to live with myself if I kissed him now.

"Kieran." I placed a hand on his cheek. "I-I can't. I really can't."

"Well, isn't this a lovely sight?" A voice boomed around us before Kieran could argue with me. A voice that didn't belong to Cillian.

The one I knew very well. Shit.

I pulled away, feeling the fear slithering over my spine, all the way to my heart, because as I turned toward Storm, who stood at the window entrance, I could see the anger, the betrayal, the sadness, and I knew this wasn't going to go how I wanted it to.

The black shirt he wore hugged his chest and his stomach; every plane of those hard abs visible. The dark pants and the boots I loved on him completed the look. Yeah, maybe he looked more like the devil than an angel. His hair was disheveled as if he'd run his fingers through it a million times, but those eyes held mine captive and what I saw there almost kicked the breath out of me.

There was pain. So much pain hidden by the anger he was showing, and I knew that he knew.

Storm looked around the room, his eyes narrowing at the discarded condoms in the corner of the room. You didn't have to be a genius to realize what had happened here.

"Storm." I spoke first, too frozen to completely move from Kieran.

He didn't look at me. Fuck, fuck, fuck.

When he pulled a gun from behind his back, I knew that this would end up in bloodshed if I didn't do something. I pushed Kieran behind me and stepped in front, facing Storm.

"You know, it's quite funny actually," he started, a sinister smile spreading on his face. "I thought that I would give you time. Time to mourn, time to come to terms with what was happening. I wanted you to come to me willingly, to realize that what I felt for you wasn't a joke. And what did you do, Ophelia? The first opportunity you had, you ran away. And you ran to him."

"I didn't run to him." Goddammit Storm. "I just needed to get away from you. Kieran found me—"

"Oh, he found you. How charming. The next thing you're gonna tell me is that those condoms don't belong to him."

"No, I won't tell you that. I might be a bitch but I'm not a liar."

"So thoughtful."

I took a step toward him, and he aimed the gun at me.

"Do not come any closer, *birdy*," he mocked.

"Storm, listen to me."

"Na-ah. I would've listened to you. Hell, while we've been tracing the bike, the only thought I had in my head was that something could've happened to you already. That maybe somebody got to you. But no. You were perfectly safe, enjoying his dick!" he yelled.

"Storm, please." I took three more steps until I was face-to-face with his gun. "We can talk about this. Just... Put the gun down."

He wasn't going to listen to me. This was the part where he either killed us both or he listened to reason.

If I was going to die today, it might as well be by the hand of the man I loved.

I took hold of his hand and placed the barrel of the gun on my forehead. The shock registered on his face and his hand started shaking with mine on top of his.

"Do you want to kill me, Storm?" I asked him, holding him tight. "Go on. Do it. If you want to kill him, you would first have to kill me."

The emotions in his eyes were too much for me to bear. He was breaking right in front of me, and it was my fault. But it was his as well.

I didn't want us to end this way, but maybe it had to.

"But before you kill me, you need to know you fucked up as well."

"Stop."

"No. Come on, baby. Pull that trigger and blow my brains out. If that is what you want to do, then do it." I grinned at him. "Do it!"

"Stop!" He closed his eyes. "Fuck."

The next moment, his chest was in front of my eyes, and the other hand that wasn't holding the gun wrapped around my neck pulling me to him. His gun clattered to the ground and he enveloped me in his embrace, holding me tightly.

The shuffling of feet behind me told me that Kieran managed to leave the room, and I prayed that he and Cillian would be able to get out of here alive.

"Why did you leave, Ophelia?" His voice was muffled against my hair. "Why the fuck did you have to leave?"

"Why did you lie?" I asked him. It was apparently the wrong thing to ask because in the next moment, my back was against the wall, with his arms caging me.

"I never lied." His forehead was against mine, his breathing labored.

"No? What about Logan?"

"Fuck." He slammed his hand next to my head, making me wince from the sheer force of that hit. I wasn't sure if he would be able to hurt me in this state, but I wanted him to try.

"Storm?"

"Just get out of here, Ophelia. There's a car outside. Indigo is there."

"No." I stood my ground. "You need to talk to me."

He turned toward me, and I hated seeing this expression on his face — this crazed, panicked, hurt expression. I took a step closer, thinking he would let me touch him. I thought he would let me explain, but that didn't happen. Instead, he pushed me away.

He. Pushed. Me. Away.

That shit hurt more than getting stabbed.

"Just get out, Ophelia. I don't have enough strength to deal with your ass right now."

"No, Storm—"

"Get the fuck out!" His voice boomed around us and the realization that I might have lost him dug deep into my bones. His gaze was fixed to the wall behind my head as my ribcage became too tight, too small, because I couldn't breathe.

I couldn't fucking breathe properly as it all slammed into me. As I realized what I'd done.

I lost him. I fucking lost him.

THIRTY-FOUR

Storm

MUSIC PLAYED IN the background, breaking the painful silence we were captured in, yet I couldn't register the words. Not one. My mind was a thousand miles away from here, replaying the memories of the last month like a movie, like an unattainable dream because that's all it would ever be—a dream. This hurt more than chains around my hands and whips on my back. If she had shot me, it would hurt less because this burning sensation spreading through my body, this rage simmering over my skin, this was too much to bear.

She did the one thing I couldn't forgive. I didn't know how. The picture of her wrapped in Kieran's arms was burned in my mind, and it hurt. God, it hurt more than anything I had experienced. Logan's words came back, reminding me that I didn't really know her. She could appear as a little lamb, like the sweetest dream, but she was a nightmare wrapped in a shiny package and I was a fool for believing that she could be mine.

Ophelia didn't belong to anyone but herself. She didn't care about anything but her goals and desires and I was just a pit stop on the road, just a distraction.

We sat inches away from each other, but we were separated by secrets and pain much larger than the two of us. The girl I met four years ago was just a product of my imagination, because I didn't know this version of her. I thought that what we had was real, that she was the one I could tell all my secrets to… But she wasn't.

I rubbed at the spot on my chest, where my heart hid beneath my ribcage, feeling as if it was going to burst out. It didn't belong to me anymore, it belonged to her even though she didn't deserve it.

I caught Indigo's eyes in the rearview mirror, thankful he came with me to find her because I was in no state to drive. While my insides were being eaten by worry that something had happened to her, she was enjoying herself in the arms of one of the men I wanted to kill. And why the fuck wasn't he dead? She destroyed what little sanity I was holding onto when she stepped in front of me and placed the barrel of my gun to her forehead. She was protecting him.

She was protecting the son of a bitch that caused her more harm than good, and that's when I knew. I would never have her. I might have her body, but her mind and her soul belonged to somebody else, and no matter what I did, it would never be enough. I could feel her anger, I could feel the violent energy rolling off her in waves, but I couldn't find it in myself to care about her feelings right now.

I couldn't because she just broke my fucking heart, and I wasn't sure if she even cared.

She pulled her legs up, hugging her knees to her chest, and God, I still wanted to feel her touch. I just didn't want to hurt her, not right now, not like this. She didn't deserve to see what she did to me, how much she destroyed me.

"You know," she started with her head still turned toward the window. "I wanted to stay. I wanted to be your forever, but you are just like all of them. Aren't you, Storm?" She turned, knocking the wind from me with the expression on her face. "You can stop pretending, baby," she mocked on a smile as tears continued streaming down her cheeks. "You can drop the act, because I know you were working with Logan."

"What are you talking about?" Fuck. Was that why she ran? Did she somehow find out about the deal?

"Did it amuse you guys, pulling the strings and making me believe in a lie?" She looked at me then Indigo, who kept his eyes on the road. "What was the expiration date, Storm?" She laughed. "Tell me!" Her eyes were filled with tears, her cheeks red, lips trembling. "I know I fucked up, trust me, I do. But how could I fuck up when what we had wasn't even real?"

Her words felt like knife stabs, burning through my skin, making me bleed all over again. I wanted to pull her closer, but I also wanted to push her away. I wanted to do a million things, yet I couldn't because she had it all wrong. She came to the conclusions without waiting for a proper explanation.

"Is this what you wanted, Storm? For me to fall apart, for me to love you when you couldn't love me back? Is this amusing you? Am I enough now?"

She loved me? No, no, she couldn't. Ophelia didn't know what love was, because if she did, she would've never done what she had.

"You have no idea what you're talking about."

"Don't I?" I looked to the side, unable to take her face in anymore, because every time I did, the smug looking Kieran flashed before my eyes. "Look at me, you fucking bastard!"

"I can't!" I roared, punching the seat in front of me. "I can't even look at you, right now."

"You can't look at me?" Her question was a mere whisper, laced with pain and sorrow, and it killed me that we did this to us.

"No, because every time I look at you, I see him. I see you in his arms. I see our future and yours is entwined with his."

"Storm—"

"You fucking tore me apart!" I bellowed as I looked at her. "You tore me apart and I will never forgive you for this. Not ever."

"No," she cried. "Don't say that. Don't fucking say that!"

I was too far gone in my own misery to let the panic on her face change my mind. I couldn't allow her to pull me back into her web of lies.

"When we get back to the club, I want you to pick up your shit and get out." Even if it killed me. "I don't want to see you, Ophelia. I don't ever want to see you, again."

I thought she would fight me on this. I thought she would yell and plead, that she would try to show me how much she loved me, but she didn't. The corners of her lips pulled into a sad smile before fury blazed in her eyes. She wiped the tears, dropped her legs from the seat to the ground and straightened in her seat. I heard stories about the Ice Queen, about the chilling cold she exuded, but I had never seen it; until now.

She looked straight ahead at Indigo's seat, shutting down in front of my eyes. This wasn't what I wanted, dammit. Her head slowly turned toward me, a robotic movement, and she placed her hands on her knees.

"I understand." She nodded. "But the next time you try to start a relationship with another idiot, try to be a little more upfront about it all. Or did the years with my father fuck you up so much that you don't even know what a real conversation feels like?" Malice dripped from her every word, and it hit me like a freight train. She knew about it. She knew about Project X. "Oh, don't be surprised, Stormy." She chuckled. "Is this the Ophelia you wanted to see? Is this the Ophelia they all talked to you about?"

"Stop it."

"What's the matter, baby boy." She came closer, placing her hand on my cheek. "Afraid of little old me, or everything I know? Did you expect me to beg you to stay with me?" I moved myself away from her, but when my back hit the door, a sinister smile took over her face, coming closer and closer. "You lied to me, Storm. You wanted to use me, and trust me, I could never forgive you for that. I didn't cheat on you, because that would insinuate that you were more than a fuckboy with whom I was buying my time." Her tongue darted out, licking my cheek, and she pressed a kiss next to my mouth, igniting the fire inside. "I guess that my father trained you well."

No, no, fuck no.

I threw her away from me and wrapped a hand around her throat, squeezing until she started coughing from the lack of air.

"Shut up!"

"C-Come on, Stormy," she wheezed. "Tighter. You can't kill a person like that." She wanted me to… She wanted me to kill her?

"Storm!" Indigo yelled from the front seat.

"Don't do it, man, don't fucking do it. You're gonna hate yourself for the rest of your life. Get away from her."

An icy sensation spread over my skin as I realized what I almost did. I almost killed her.

"Oh, God." I lifted my hands, seeing the red imprint on her pale skin. "Oh, God. Oh, God." She started coughing, her eyelashes fluttering against her cheek as her whole body shook. "Hey, hey, Sunshine." I pulled her up and moved the hair from her face. "Breathe, Ophelia. Slowly, that's right."

Hey eyes opened, and it was like staring at a void. There was no trace of my Ophelia in them. There was nothing there.

"Is that all you've got?" She pressed a hand against her throat and pushed me away with the other one. "No wonder you weren't man enough to tell me the truth. At least Kieran was able to torture me when he thought I fucked up."

"That's enough!" Indigo thundered, but she just tilted her head still looking at me. "You guys can talk about this when we get back to the club."

"But didn't you hear, Indigo?" She grinned. "I am leaving. Stormy here doesn't want me anymore. No, wait." She looked at him. "You also knew about Logan and my father, didn't you? Tell me, was it good? Did you guys film me making a fool out of myself, wrapping myself around him, believing that he could be the one?"

"Stop this, Phee," I begged. "This isn't you."

"You don't know me. Revenge against my father was more important than me, so don't fucking sit there and pretend that you do, because you will never get to know me. You want me gone? Fine, baby. I'll be gone. I'll be just a memory after today, and if I ever see you again, I will kill you, Storm. Mark my fucking words."

I wanted her gone, but every word she spoke, every look directed at me felt like lava and I realized that she wasn't the only person who'd fucked up here. The problem was, now was too late to try to fix it. It was too late to try and salvage this thing between us.

"Storm," Indigo called from the front seat, the volume of the music lowered down. "I think we have a problem."

God, could anything go okay today? Ophelia stiffened and looked at him.

"What's wrong?" she asked instead of me.

"Nobody is answering back at the club. I've tried reaching all the guys and none of them answered. Something's happened, I am sure of it."

"Oh my God." She covered her mouth with her hand. "It's Nikolai." She looked at me. "It's my father."

"What are you talking about?"

"He left me a letter, threatening all of you. That's how I overheard that conversation with Creed. I was trying to find him to figure out a way to protect you guys."

She was trying to protect us?

"How much longer 'til we reach there?" she asked.

"Twenty minutes, give or take." Indigo looked at me through the rearview mirror, but I was too busy staring at Ophelia.

"Do you have any weapons in the car?" she asked.

"No, you aren't fighting."

"Like hell I'm not," she argued. "Do you have weapons or not? Knives, guns—"

"I know what weapons are, smartass. And yes, we do have them, but you aren't going to fight."

"Storm," she inched closer to me, "I am and

you can't stop me. He came because of me, and I won't stand on the side and do nothing. Now, do you have some fucking weapons here or not?"

God, I wanted to kiss her and knock her out just so that she wouldn't be in danger. I was so fucking angry at her, but I was also terrified, because if Nikolai Aster really did come to the club, none of us were safe, least of all her.

THIRTY-FIVE

Ophelia

THERE WERE SO many things I wanted to say, so many reasons I wanted to give, explanations to provide, but I didn't. No matter what I said, no matter what I did, I had lost him. His words played on repeat in my head, slowly breaking the mask I put on. And what did I expect? That he would pat me on the shoulder and open his arms to me after I fucked Kieran? Storm didn't operate that way.

Didn't I do the same thing when Kieran cheated on me? I could never erase that picture from my head. I lived with that pain in my heart, with sorrow, and I caused the same to Storm. After today, he was going to be just another demon haunting my soul, yet he was the only one I wanted to stay.

I wanted to stay with him, dammit. I wanted to beg for forgiveness, to ask him about Logan, to apologize for what I said in the car, but I couldn't. My fucking ego wouldn't let me talk even though I was the one that fucked up.

Don't forget that he betrayed you.

I fucking knew that! But I kept going on and on about the same thing, and I wasn't sure that what I heard was the full story. Hell, I heard only one side of that conversation. Did he try to sell me to the highest bidder, or was I just using it as an excuse to run away? You didn't have to be a genius to realize that I had issues with intimacy, with letting other people come too close. I always waited for the other shoe to drop so that I could run.

I sneaked a glance at him, memorizing his profile—every curve, the sharp jaw, tattoos running along his neck, because I knew I would never get to touch him, again. I would never get to kiss him, hold him, love him... I would never... God, this hurt. My eyes misted as the bitter truth slowly settled into the pit of my stomach. I would never hear his voice.

The silence between us was louder than words, but this is what I did. I pushed the people I cared about away. I pushed until they had nothing left to give, until they became too tired to care. Loneliness was a heady feeling, and I never knew when to stop.

When was it going to be enough?

His fist was pressed against his mouth, and true to his word, he never once looked at me. And I just wanted him to look, I wanted him to see how scared I was. I wanted him to see how much love I had to give. How sorry I was. I didn't want to lose him or these feelings that came with him.

"Is anyone responding?" he asked Indigo, slicing my chest open. Couldn't he see I was bleeding in front of him? I was wide open, he just had to ask the questions.

Did you really think he would want to do anything with you?

Yes, I fucking did because I wasn't the only one who fucked up. Maybe I was a disaster, maybe I didn't deserve to be happy, but I wasn't the only one who messed up here. I ran away, I betrayed him, but he also betrayed me.

"No," Indigo responded before he looked at me through the rearview mirror. "Not yet."

I could see the accusation in his eyes. I could feel the blame that was going to be put on me, because if they weren't responding because my father was there, I would be the only one to be blamed. He probably wouldn't be wrong either.

He turned onto a familiar street as fear started digging its claws into my heart. I didn't want to face my father, but what scared me the most was the state of the club and what he was going to do to them.

Maybe it isn't your father. Maybe they're just not responding because they're busy.

God, I hoped so. I wasn't a believer, but if it helped, I would become one. I would promise the eternity of solitude if it meant that he wasn't there, but something told me that prayers wouldn't help this time. I clutched the gun I took from the trunk tighter, bracing myself for what we were about to walk into.

As we parked at the beginning of the street, far enough from the club, I could see three cars parked in front of the gates—cars that definitely didn't belong to us. Dread settled in my stomach as I recognized the symbol on the side of one of them, and I knew that The Dragon was here.

"I know those men," I said as Indigo killed the engine. "Those are the Syndicate's soldiers."

"How do you know?" Storm grumbled, as if it pained him to even talk to me.

It's okay, Stormy. You won't have to see me ever again after we deal with this shit.

"Because that one," I pointed to the blond guy, "almost lost his finger in the ring with me. Any other questions, Storm?" I looked at him, daring him to ask more. Anger was better than indifference because it meant that he still cared. There was still hope.

"So, what's the plan?" Indigo asked when the idiot next to me kept quiet, staring at the three men. "We can't just barge in."

"No, we can't." Storm seemed to think for a moment before he started talking again. "I know what we gotta do. That house," Storm pointed to the house right next to the clubhouse, "has a backyard that's connected with ours. If we go from that side—"

"They will see us," I argued. "Trust me, I know him. He trained me, and the first thing he would've done is to put guards all around."

"So, what do you suggest?"

I started to think, pondering over the ideas, and then it came to me.

"I'm going to the front."

"Abso-fucking-lutely not."

"Storm. They know me. Trust me, both of you would get shot before you could get close enough to see their faces. He wants me, not you. He wouldn't even be here if it weren't for me." He kept quiet, uncertain, but he had no say in this. He wanted me gone? Fine. His wish was about to get fulfilled. "Give me the silencer." I extended my hand, waiting for him to drop the extension. "Storm?"

So, he wasn't indifferent after all, or he at least didn't want to see me die. That was something, right?

"Every minute we spend here arguing about who is going to go in, is a minute lost for the members of the club. If you don't want to give it to me, that's okay, I can just shoot them and get it over

457

with, but I don't want to alert them if I don't have to. And stop with—"

"Here." He dropped the silencer in my hand, refusing to meet my eyes.

I rolled it onto the barrel of my gun and started exiting the car when he pulled me back in.

"Please don't be reckless," he pleaded. "Be safe."

My throat closed and unable to respond to him, to do anything really, I just nodded before I pushed the door open and hid the gun at the waist of my back. I kept calm as I approached them. As their eyes widened at the sight of me, I knew that they recognized me.

"Hello, boys."

"Shit," one of them said.

"*Baba Yaga!*" the blond one exclaimed. Damn, I really missed that nickname.

The third one started reaching for his gun, but I pulled mine, aiming it at him and shooting him between his eyes. The other two started running toward the entrance, but I couldn't have them alerting the rest of the gang that I was here. Not yet.

Daddy Dearest wanted to play games? Well, I could play.

I shot two more shots, hitting both of them in their backs. As their bodies crumbled to the floor, I walked back, signaling to Storm and Indigo to come forward.

"We need to get inside. I've no idea how many of them are here." The words barely left my mouth as Indigo sprinted past us, running toward the side of the house.

"There's a side entrance," Storm answered, seeing the confused look on my face. "It's mostly hidden so I'm hoping they haven't found it."

Without wasting a moment, the two of us

joined Indigo, entering the basement area. I could hear voices from above, but I couldn't make out what they were saying.

Storm pressed a finger to his mouth, indicating for us to be quiet. The three of us moved slowly, going to the area I now knew had the office and was closer to the stairs. A nervous energy resonated around us, all three of us on high alert.

A gunshot echoed from the floor above, stopping us in our tracks. Oh my God. Did they just kill someone?

Indigo tried going up the stairs, but Storm pulled him back, a stern look on his face.

"Zoe is there," Indigo whispered, the vein on his forehead popping. "If I lose her—"

"You won't lose her, but I need you to stay here."

"No, Storm—"

"Indigo, stay here. When the other guys arrive, you will need to let them in. Take everything you need from the armory and hide. We will handle this."

Shit, if they shot Zoe... No, I didn't want to think about it. She was okay, she had to be okay. I couldn't lose another friend. I just couldn't.

"Ophelia." Storm took my hand in his, sending shock waves over my skin. I didn't think that he realized what he did, but I wasn't going to remind him. "I need to go up. I am not ready to let innocent people die while I am hiding here. I want you to go with Ind—"

"No, absolutely not. I am not hiding while he tortures and kills people I care about."

I pulled my hand back, taking a step closer to the stairs. "He wants me. He's here because of me, Storm, and he's not going to stop until he sees me. Until I go with him."

In the blink of an eye, he was in front of me, holding my chin in his hand. "You're not going with him, Sunshine."

"And you have no right to tell me what to do, Storm." I shook him off. "This is a win-win situation. He will get out of here and leave you guys alone, and you will finally be free of me."

"That's not what I meant."

"But that is what you said. Don't worry, it'll only hurt a little bit. You know the feeling of his whip's lashes." He flinched at that, but I was done tiptoeing around the topic. He didn't want to tell me about it and wanted to continue denying everything? Fine, that was fine, but I wasn't going to pretend that I didn't know.

"Do you really think that I don't care about you? That what was happening between us this last month was nothing but a lie?"

"I don't know what to think," I whispered. "All I know now are the things you said, in the car, and it's obvious you want me gone. So here we are, Storm, I am about to be gone."

"No, that's not—"

"We're wasting time, Storm. To be very honest, I don't wanna hear it anymore. You want me to be the only villain in this story? Fine, I'll be your villain. I'll be the girl that broke your poor, little heart. You want us to end? That's also absolutely okay. You don't want to talk to me? You are not the first person that didn't want to talk to me. You said that you couldn't look at me, right?" He flinched at that question. "Well, don't look, baby. Just don't look when he takes me home."

I took two stairs at a time, hating the tremble in my hands and the way my heart hurt at everything I just said to him. It was so easy falling back into the old habits, where pretending was better than showing what I truly felt. If only I could show him everything, maybe he would understand. A hand enveloped around my arm, and when I looked down, I could see the torment on his face.

I was suddenly pressed against the wall, with his body holding mine hostage. My legs were trapped between his and his nose pressed against the pulse on my neck. "I don't know what to do, Sunshine. I don't know what to do."

I knew what I wanted him to do, but I couldn't tell him to choose me, to forgive me, to tell me what was going on. He had to make the decision because I had already made mine.

"You know what to do, Storm. You already did it." I chuckled. "You already told me to leave."

"No."

"We don't have time for this. We really, really don't have time."

"I don't want you to leave."

"And I don't want you to hate me," I countered. "But we don't always get what we want."

I pushed him off me and walked the rest of the way toward the billiard room. I could hear my father's voice now as clear as day.

"So, you're trying to tell me that you don't know where my daughter went?" Not a second later, another gunshot echoed around us and I stiffened, actually afraid for the people there. He wasn't going to stop.

He wasn't going to stop until he saw me. Nikolai Aster either wanted to kill me, or he wanted me to come back with him. I wasn't okay with either one of those options. I wasn't going to go back to the world that destroyed my sanity. I wasn't going to help the family that abandoned me,

461

not anymore.

But I also wasn't going to let innocent people die. Too many of them already did, by my hand no less, and these ones... These people were Storm's family. If what Kieran had told me was true, Storm suffered at the hands of my father more than any other person.

I looked at him, and whatever he saw on my face put panic onto his. Before he could reach me, I rounded the corner, coming face-to-face with the man I never wanted to see.

My father.

My nightmare.

The dragon that shaped me.

"Papa," I called out as the two guards standing near the door advanced toward me. Each of them took a hold of one of my arms, and the gun I held in my other hand clattered to the ground as they knocked it from me.

I would like to say that time wasn't too kind on my father, but I would be lying. Those same eyes I kept seeing in the mirror, day after day, year after year, they connected with mine and a smile spread across his face.

His hair wasn't dark anymore, but rather silver, with dark strands peeking through. He got old.

"*Doch*?" he asked. "Is that really you?"

"Yeah, it's me, Papa." I almost choked on those words. "I am here."

He slowly approached me, and that sweet smile got replaced by a sinister one. "But you aren't alone, are you?"

No.

"Let go of me!" Storm yelled behind me, and I turned around to see three guys leading him to the room. Fuck.

"Did you know, *doch*," my father started. "That I knew Storm for most of his life?"

Shit. Not this.

"No?" He looked at me than at him. Storm looked furious, exactly how I felt. "*Moya malen'kaya igrushka* was such a good boy until he escaped of course. He could've been amazing." He approached Storm, taking his face into his hand. "But he ran away."

"Let go of him, Papa."

"Oh, you're defending him?" This seemed to amuse him, and I didn't like it. I would rather have him furious than amused, because an amused Nikolai Aster equaled terror, and I didn't want that on any of these people. "Put him to his knees," he instructed his men.

Storm tried fighting, but it wasn't enough to shake off the three men surrounding him, pushing him down. Creed was on the floor, his hands tied to the front and a barrel of a gun pressed to his temple. I recognized the man standing behind him, but I didn't know his name. I couldn't see Atlas nor his brother, Felix, and I just hoped that they had managed to escape when this madness took place.

I was frantically looking for the one person I wanted to see standing up, but when her hair sprawled on the floor caught my attention, I almost fell to the ground.

Zoe, my sunshine, ZoZo, laid on the floor right next to the bar with her eyes closed and bruises over her face.

"No!" I wailed, trying to break free from the guards holding my hands.

I didn't know if she was dead or alive and I couldn't let her lie there, unconscious. What if she was seriously hurt? What if I couldn't see the other injuries and she could be dying right in front of my eyes? Her chest rose and fell with every new breath, but for how long?

We didn't have enough time. I was a bitch toward her, and she didn't deserve it. I didn't even get to say goodbye. And Indigo. How would Indigo react when he saw this?

"A friend of yours?" my father asked, snickering at me. "She was pretty." *She still is pretty, you sick fuck.*

"I am going to kill you!" I screamed at him.

"Tsk tsk." He approached me, leaving Storm behind. "Is that any way to talk to your father?"

I couldn't believe that once upon a time I wanted his approval. That I prayed for the day when he would look at me proudly. But that's what you do when they tear everything else from you. You seek approval from those that wronged you, because in the sea of darkness, you can't differentiate who is a friend and who is a true enemy.

And this man in front of me, he was the enemy all along.

"You deserve hell, old man."

The grin he had on his face disappeared as he gripped my face, bringing me closer to him. This punishing grip was nothing compared to everything else he did to me, and I wanted to laugh, knowing that he didn't have another heir to his shitty empire. I killed Theo, Maya wasn't an option, and no matter what, he wasn't here just to kill me.

He wanted me with him, because he knew that I was the only one who could get the job done.

Of course, I could, I just didn't want to anymore. The time of pliant Ophelia was long gone, and if this piece of shit thought that he could manipulate me again to do his bidding, he had another think coming.

"I made you, *dorogoy*," he spat the words out. "I can also unmake you. Don't test my patience because you would end up worse than your friend there."

He had. He made me, but I was the one controlling my destiny now. Not him, not the Syndicate, and not some stupid game of power he loved so much. I controlled what was going to happen.

"Then unmake me. Come on, old man. Kill me. Kill me and we'll see who would reign in your place when your bones are too fragile to even move from the bed. I already killed your son, your other daughter is lost, so that only leaves me. You know that I am the only one with enough bloodlust to do everything you want me to do, but guess what?"

"What?" A vein popped in his forehead because he knew where I was going with this.

"You can burn in hell because I am not going back. So kill me, do it. I won't do everything you want me to do. You can take your empire and shove it up your ass. I. Don't. Want. It."

"Is that so?" he asked, grinning. I didn't like the sinister look on his face.

"That's so."

"Remember what I taught you, Ekaterina. Emotions are your biggest enemy, and you, my dear," he leaned into my ear, "you reek of them. You don't want to come willingly? Suit yourself, but I know what makes you tick now. Your biggest mistake was falling for somebody else, for allowing yourself to come here, to this club. They will burn along with your love for them and whether you want it or not, you're coming back with me."

"No." I started shaking my head. He wouldn't.

But that was just another lie I was trying to make myself believe in. I knew that this monster in front of me would do anything in his power just to get his way. He wouldn't give a fuck how many lives he had to destroy just to get what he wanted.

"I think I will start with my first disappointment." He turned to Storm. "The boy that could've been so much more, yet he decided to throw it all in the fire."

"Fuck you, Nikolai," Storm spewed.

"Now, now, *mal'chik*." God, I hated him. "You almost did that. Did you tell my daughter what you used to do during the first half of your life?"

He placed a hand on Storm's head, petting his hair. The visual almost made me sick, because I knew, I just fucking knew that he was one of Storm's tormentors. I was trying to goad him earlier, using the information Kieran shared with me in the fit of rage, and I shouldn't have. I was as sick as the bastard in front of me, and instead of trying more, I turned into a vicious person using his past against him.

"Did you tell her how you loved to jerk yourself off while I watched?"

Sick, he was completely sick. Where was the end to his depravity?

"Did you tell her how you used to beg to come? How you couldn't come without the pain?"

Storm was shaking, but his eyes were cast downward, looking at the floor. He was ashamed of everything he had to do; I could see it in him. My sick father wanted to humiliate him in front of his people. He loved dominating people and I know that no matter how many years passed, your bully always stayed the person you feared. Storm was strong, but I couldn't even imagine the terror he had to live through in that house.

They broke me when I was a teenager, but they broke him when he was just a mere child.

"Tell me, *mal'chik*." My father placed a hand on his shoulder. "Did you miss me?"

As Storm winced at the pressure my father was applying, that little sparkle of joy shone in Nikolai's eyes, and I had no doubt that he would do anything to hurt Storm and me.

Storm was my weak point and my father always excelled at reading people. My feelings for the man on his knees were written all over my face. I wasn't hiding it anymore. I didn't want to.

But maybe I should've.

Fuck. I couldn't let him die. I didn't want him to suffer.

"Papa," I called out to him. "I'll do it. I'll go with you." I tried making my voice steady, when the mere thought of going with him put every single nerve ending on alert. "Just let them be. They didn't do anything wrong."

"No, Ophelia!" Storm yelled; panic written all over his face. "You can't do that."

"Ah, love. Such a sickening feeling." He didn't look at me as he spoke again. "But you see, Ekaterina, now it's too late. I already decided that I want to see him dead. After all, that is how we treat traitors."

No, no, fuck no.

He nodded at one of the men holding Storm and when the knife shone from the afternoon light coming through the windows, I had a feeling that I wouldn't like what was about to come.

Papa pulled the shirt away from Storm's body, slicing through the fabric, cutting it in half on his chest. The skull tattoo was revealed as the material opened, and he pulled both sides, dropping them to Storm's wrists.

"My, my, my." He started examining the gauze on his shoulder. I hadn't known that he was hurt. "What do we have here?" He ripped the gauze off as Storm's scream echoed around the room, sending chills over my spine.

He took a knife from the guard, placing the tip right above the wound that was still bleeding. The wound seemed shallow, only on the surface, but that just gave more ammunition to the sadist in front of us to start.

"Let's see if you still like pain, boy." He pushed the tip of the knife into Storm's shoulder and a blood-chilling scream tore from him, followed by mine.

"No! Stop it, please!"

"But I am only getting started, Ekaterina." The sick bastard laughed. "I will enjoy this so much. Maybe after this, you will remember where you belong, *Doch*. Maybe you will finally remember your place. Maybe I will even be forgiving."

"I swear to God, Papa—"

"What?" He turned to me, amusement shining through his eyes. "You're going to kill me? Look around you. There are guards everywhere. You can't even free yourself, let alone kill me."

My blood boiled, my eyes narrowing at him, but he didn't give a shit about any of it. He turned around, crouching in front of Storm.

"Ah, *mal'chik*." He patted his cheek leaving a bloody trail behind. "This is really unfortunate, but I have to kill you."

"Noooo!" I wailed as Storm's eyes connected with mine.

"It's fine, baby—" My father dug the knife deeper into his shoulder and the sickening sound of skin breaking reverberated around us. Storm started falling forward. My heart broke, seeing this strong, fierce man brought to his knees.

I wasn't going to give up. I wasn't going to

give up on the one person that understood me. Fuck everything. If he wasn't here with me, my life wouldn't make sense anymore. He might not want me anymore, but he wasn't going to die on me.

Storm's chest was filled with blood now, his tattoos almost hidden by the red hue spreading from the wound. The monster pulled the knife out, wiping it on Storm's pants.

I tried pulling my arms out, tried moving out of the grip of the guards that held me hostage, but it was futile. We were not going to make it. God, I was going to lose him.

My father craned his neck, looking at me, and I hoped that he could feel every ounce of hatred I felt for him in that moment. He gripped the knife and started tracing patterns on Storm's chest.

I could hear the cries of women and children held here with us, but my sole focus was on two of them.

"If you kill him," I gritted out, "I will never forgive you."

"I wasn't asking for your forgiveness." He moved the knife away and in the next moment, buried it into Storm's stomach, turning it around, digging deeper.

"Noooo!" A scream tore from me.

Storm started falling forward, but my father held his head as he pulled the knife out and stabbed him in his chest.

The buzzing in my ears, the pain, the rage, it was all mixed together. My eyesight blurred and the first tears fell out, coating my cheeks.

"No, no, no," I kept chanting, but my father didn't stop.

Another stab into Storm's stomach, and then another, and another, and I stopped counting after the fifth one.

After the first grunt, Storm quieted down, blood seeping from his mouth.

I was shaking. I was fucking powerless to stop him.

Nikolai pushed him back and as Storm's body hit the ground, the two guards moving away from him, I couldn't see anything else but the body of a man I loved.

I loved him and I just lost him. I thought what I felt earlier was devastating, but this... this powerlessness, this inability to move, not being able to do anything, it fucking destroyed me.

I was going to kill him. I was going to kill them all and destroy the empire they built. I was going to erase our last name from existence.

He slowly walked toward me, still holding the knife. I couldn't fucking look at him. I couldn't look at any of them.

Please Storm. Just get up. Just fucking get up.

But he wasn't going to get up. The blood started spreading around him, the dark red substance the same color as my vision.

My father stood in front of me, dropping the knife at his feet. He enveloped my cheeks, and I could smell the blood on his hands—Storm's blood.

"There, there, Ekaterina," he cooed. "There will be other ones. I will give you another toy to play with." He smeared Storm's blood over my lips, over my cheek and started playing with my hair, pulling me forward. "Taste it." He lifted the knife in front of me, grinning from ear to ear. "It tastes wonderful. The fresh kill, the fulfillment... Just taste it."

He thought this was funny? He thought Storm was only a toy I was playing with?

No, oh no. I was going to play, but I was going to play with him.

Movement on the top of the staircase caught my attention, and when I saw Hunter and Felix with a couple of other guys, rifles in their hands, I knew that this was the end of the road for us.

This was where I would finally end this story.

"Ah, Papa." I smiled, licking the blood he smeared on my lips. "You know how much I always loved to play."

As the first shot echoed through the room, I jumped up, hitting him in his chest and pulling the guards backward. I could see shock and confusion on my father's face, but as I fell to the ground, taking the guards with me, I quickly pulled the knife out of my boot, stabbing the first one in his stomach.

Before the other one could recover, I pulled myself up and dragged the knife over his throat.

My father pulled himself up and started heading toward the billiard room, but I wasn't going to let him go. No, this time he was going to pay for everything he ever did.

My father's soldiers were slowly falling and I could see Felix with several other guys taking them down one by one.

I pushed myself up, and just before he could exit from the room, I ran after my father and pulled him back in, holding him by the neck.

I pressed my chest to his back, placing the knife at his throat.

"Not so fast, Papa." I mocked him, "Did you really think I would let you escape?"

"Don't be hasty now, Ekaterina." A nervous chuckle escaped him.

"That's not my fucking name, you piece of shit." I pressed the knife harder, and the first rivulets of blood seeped from his throat. I held his hair with one hand and started turning him around

471

to where Storm laid.

"Do you see that man?" I kicked his knees, pushing him to the ground. "He is a bigger man than you will ever be, and you tried to take him away from me. I don't want a toy, I want him."

"Let's talk about this, O—"

"There's nothing to talk about." I stopped him. "This is where you'll die, old man." I moved to his front. "I will destroy the Syndicate. No one will ever know that you even existed." I sneered at him. "The name Aster will be forever lost."

His eyes widened and I knew I'd hit a nerve.

"You can't do that," he whispered.

"Oh, I can. And I will. I would say that you can watch me do it from the other side, but we both know that where you're going, you won't be able to."

"I am your father!" he spat out. "You can't do this to me. You would betray your family for him?"

"I would burn this world for him!" I thundered. "And I don't have a family. You made sure of that. Blood is just that, blood. Family is much more than the red substance connecting us. And you," I leaned down, looking into his eyes, "you have no idea what real family means."

"I can tell you where Maya is. I can help you—"

"I already know where Maya is, and I am going to save her." He was grasping at straws. "You have nothing to offer me, old man. Absolutely nothing."

"You are my daughter! You are the daughter of a dragon."

"No." I pulled the knife away, placing the tip under his chin. "I am not the daughter of a dragon. I am the dragon."

"Oph—"

I pushed the knife in before he could say anything else, his eyes still on me. His blood ran over my hand, and I pushed deeper, enjoying the sight.

Nikolai Aster.

Gone.

Dead.

I could finally be free.

The moment I let go of his body, he fell to the ground, and with him, my anger. It scattered around me in pieces, along with the need for revenge and I turned toward the man that still needed me. A man that held my heart.

I fell to my knees right into the puddle of Storm's blood and pulled him into my lap.

"No, no, no. Storm." I started shaking him. "Storm, you can't leave me." Goddammit, my chest was splitting in half. "You can't fucking leave me. I just found you. I want to have a future with you. You can't leave me."

The tears erupted from my eyes, falling on his face. I pressed my fingers against his pulse, feeling a weak response. He was still alive. Oh my God. He was alive.

"Help!" I yelled to the room. "Somebody call a fucking ambulance."

He couldn't die. He couldn't. I wasn't going to allow it.

I pressed against the wound on his stomach, the one that was bleeding the most.

"You can't leave me, Storm." I sobbed against him. "I love you, goddammit. You can't. I need you with me. I won't be able to survive this without you."

I lowered my head to his, pressing our lips together.

"Just stay with me, baby. Stay with me."

His blood was coating my hands. It was all over my clothes, over my face... He couldn't fucking go.

"Felix!" I called out, looking frantically around the room. When he dropped in front of me, his eyes running over Storm's body, I could see the panic written all over him.

"He's still alive," I told him. "Call the ambulance."

"Ophelia—"

"Call the fucking ambulance! Don't give me that look. He will survive."

"Okay." He nodded but I knew that he didn't believe me. "We already called them. They're on the way."

"Alright." I tried calming myself down. "Press on his chest wound. I don't want him to bleed too much."

I could see the hesitation on his face, but he did what I asked and pressed his hands against Storm's chest.

"It's gonna be fine, Storm." I moved the hair from his forehead. "You're gonna be fine, you'll see."

Atlas's stare was heavy on me, but I didn't look away from Storm's face.

"I love you, Storm," I whispered in his ear. "I fucking love you and you're gonna stay with me, right? You're going to be fine." Everything was going to be fine. We were going to be fine, him and me.

We were going to grow old together, we were going to have kids together. He couldn't leave me alone in this world, he just couldn't.

I grabbed Storm's hand, feeling Felix's eyes on me, and squeezed tight. A cacophony of voices exploded around us—crying, screaming, Indigo barking orders—but I couldn't move my eyes away from him. I had a feeling if I did, he would just disappear. He would be forever gone.

Just stay with me.
Just fucking stay with me.

Ophelia's story is far from over.

Pre-order the third book in **The Rapture Series: OBLIVION**

Pre-order now

ALSO BY L.K. REID

Sign up **for the Newsletter to get exclusive news, giveaways and teasers!**

THE RAPTURE SERIES
Ricochet

SECRETS OF WINWORTH
Apathy
(October 1st, 2021)

TWISTED TALES COLLECTION
Elysium: Hades and Persephone Dark Romance
Retelling
(January 21st, 2022)

ACKNOWLEDGMENTS

I WROTE EQUILIBRIUM back in October, just after I finished writing Ricochet, and at the time I thought it was amazing. That feeling definitely didn't last, and it took me a long time to realize what wasn't working and what had to be changed. Fast forward to February of this year, and I decided to rewrite the entire book. I contemplated even publishing it, because I know that this story and these characters aren't for everybody. Ophelia definitely isn't everyone's cup of tea.

But I did it, and there's one person I need to be extremely thankful for—Stephanie. My Momager, my beacon of light, and the first person that believed in me, outside of my family. Thank you for being you, for the late night talks, and the love you have for these characters. Storm and Ophelia wouldn't be who they are today if it weren't for you.

To my friends—thank you for understanding my need to disappear from the real world when characters talk a bit too loud.

My mom and my brother, thank you so much for all the love and endless support.

To one very important person, Zoe. Thank you for loving the story even though you're hardcore #TeamKieran. I couldn't have done this without you.

Neli, my favorite Aquarius, your support means the world to me.

To all of my author friends, and you know who you are, I cannot express how thankful I am to have you in my life. Thank you for all the advice, for words of encouragement, and just for being you.

My absolutely fabulous editor, Maggie. I am so glad to have you in my life. Thank you for prettying up my words and helping me deliver this book in the best way possible.

My amazing Street Team, my Queens of Carnage. You guys keep surprising me with your support, and I wouldn't be here if it weren't for you.

Needless to say, my ARC readers, you guys are absolutely amazing. Thank you!

To every blogger, bookstagramer, thank you for taking a chance on me and reading my books. Never in a million years would I have expected this level of support.

To all of the readers, thank you so, so, so much for loving Ophelia and her crazy little world.

And last but not least, to music. For always being there, keeping me afloat and helping me shape this book, this whole world into what it is today.

ABOUT THE AUTHOR

L.K. REID IS a dark romance author, who hates slow walkers and mean people. She's still figuring out this whole "adult" thing, and in her opinion, Halloween should be a Public Holiday. She has a small obsession with Greek Mythology and all things supernatural. Music has to be turned on from the moment she wakes up, all the way throughout the day and night.

If she isn't writing, she can be found reading, plotting upcoming books and watching horror movies.

Stay in Touch

.instagram.com/authorlkreid
pinterest.com/authorlkreid
facebook.com/authorlkreid
.goodreads.com/authorlkreid
The Reid Cult